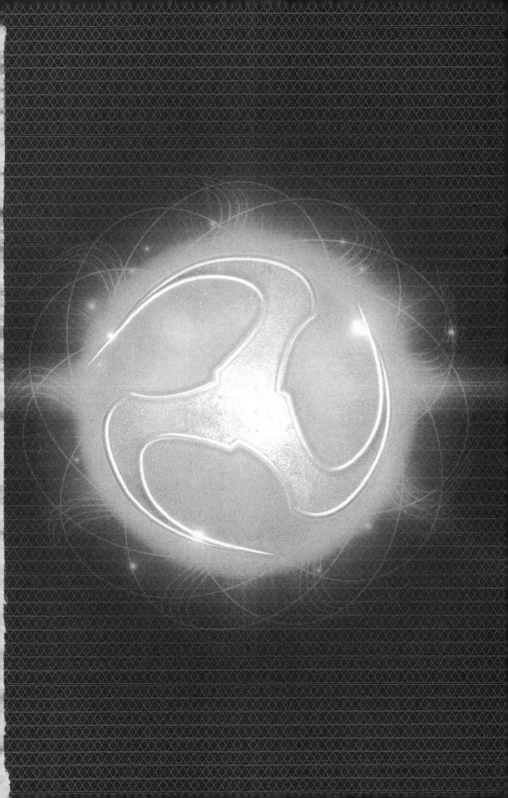

# THE
# WIDTH
## OF THE
# WORLD

VEGA JANE BOOK THREE
A NOVEL BY

# DAVID BALDACCI

 SCHOLASTIC PRESS | NEW YORK

Library of Congress Cataloging-in-Publication Data available

ISBN 978-0-545-83196-3

10 9 8 7 6 5 4 3 2 1      17 18 19 20 21

Printed in the U.S.A. 23
First edition, March 2017

Book design by Elizabeth B. Parisi

*To Sandy Violette and Caspian Dennis,*
*For being so awesome from day one*

"There is some good in this world, and it's worth fighting for."

— J. R. R. Tolkien

"In a time of universal deceit, telling the truth is a revolutionary act."

— George Orwell

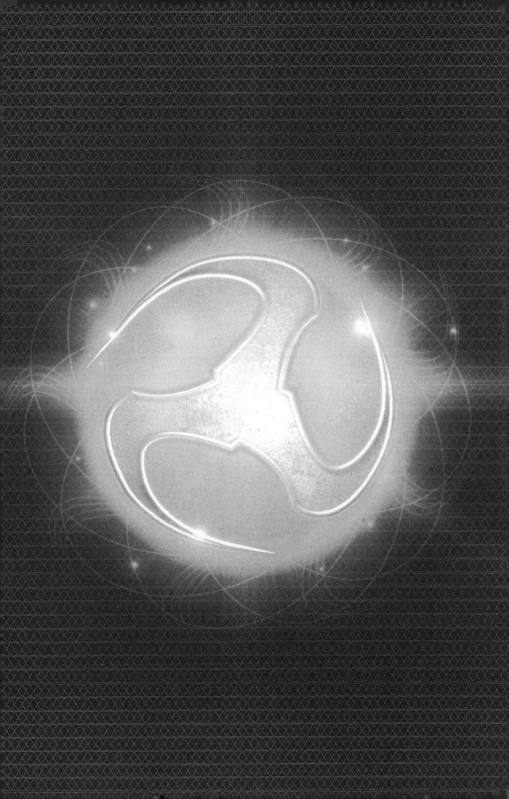

# A Place Called True

W E LANDED, INVISIBLE, on the cobbles and were nearly killed.

Petra Sonnet cried out, Delph Delphia grunted in surprise, my canine, Harry Two, yipped and I, Vega Jane, jerked back on the magical tether holding us all together, as the deafening contraption charging down on us flashed past.

It was boxy and made of metal and wood with windowed doors on either side. It also had four what looked to be wagon wheels, only there were no sleps pulling it.

The infernal thing was moving of its own accord! It was puffing and wheezing, with what sounded like metal clanking on metal. Bright lights like powerful candles housed in lanterns were perched on the front of the thing, providing illumination. The front piece was shiny metal with ridges. Etched on it was a name: RILEY.

Riley? Was that the bloke who owned it? Or maybe the bloke who built it? We'd had a wagonmaker back in Wormwood named O'Dougall who put his name on the side of each one.

In a few moments the Riley, swaying from side to side and with a belch of smoke coming out its hindquarters, turned the corner and vanished from our view.

A pale Delph looked at me. "What the ruddy Hel was that?"

I shook my head because I had no idea what the ruddy Hel it was. Rattled, I scratched Harry Two's remaining ear.

We all had scars from our journey across the Quag.

Delph's arm had been burned and blackened.

Harry Two had lost an ear.

Petra had injured her hand.

And I had the mark of the three hooks upon the back of my hand. It had been burned into my skin by some unknown means.

I drew a breath and was about to return us to visibility by spinning my ring around when the pair of males appeared.

We froze, each holding our breath, lest they hear even that slight sound.

"You sure it was from here?" the taller of them asked the other.

The male nodded.

My mind was whirling. These were the blokes we had seen earlier, after escaping the Quag. How could they have followed us?

I glanced at Delph and Petra. They looked as terrified as I felt.

I pointed to the right and we shuffled off around the corner.

We set our tucks down and I breathlessly whispered, "They followed us. How?"

Petra shook her head. But Delph said, "You reckon they can detect magic? Because you done that to get us here." He pointed to the magical tethers that kept us all invisible.

2

I looked down at my wand like it had just bitten me. *Could that be true?*

Delph said, "Look." He was pointing to the right. Down the cobbles at the very end of the street was a tall building made of stone and brick and timbers. I stared up at the highest point of the edifice.

"Steeples," I said in wonder.

"It's got a bell too," said Delph. "Me dad said Steeples had a bell once, before it broke."

"Steeples?" said Petra, looking confused.

"The place back in Wormwood where Wugmorts would go to listen to Ezekiel the Sermonizer deliver his very long soliloquies," I explained. "Telling us to be good while scaring us half to death with tales of how badly our lives would turn out regardless of what we did."

But Delph had a point. At night Steeples had always been empty. I wagered this building might be the same.

We shouldered our tucks and crept along the cobbles until we came to the double wooden doors that constituted the entrance to the place.

There was a sign next to it.

"Saint Necro's," I read. I glanced at Delph. "What do you reckon that means?"

"Dunno, do I?" he replied. "Never heard-a no Saint Necro. Alls I know is Steeples."

I tried the doors but they were locked. I pointed my wand at the heavy wrought-iron lock and was about to whisper *"Ingressio"* when Delph grabbed my arm.

"Magic," he said warningly.

I nodded and slowly lowered my wand.

Delph tried to open the door but it was clearly bolted shut. Then Petra noticed a window on the side. "It's not locked."

Delph boosted her up first and she slid through. I followed. Delph lifted Harry Two through the opening and into my arms, and then he brought up the rear.

We looked around at a vast chamber that was far larger than Steeples, though it was configured quite similarly, with brightly colored windows, rows of seats and a raised area up front where sermons were no doubt given. I wondered whether the sermonizer who spoke here was as depressing as Ezekiel. Petra said in a hushed tone, "Where do we go now?"

I pointed to a set of stone stairs that led upward. "Let's see what's up that way."

"Why not down?" said Petra, pointing to another set of stairs that apparently led to a lower floor of this saint's place.

"No," I said. "Up is better."

She gave me a skeptical look, but I didn't wait for her approval of my plans. They expected me to lead; well, that's what I was going to do! I bustled over to the stairs with Harry Two gliding along next to me. Delph and Petra hurried after us.

That's when we heard the footsteps at the entry.

We ducked down between two sets of pews as I heard someone say, "*Ingressio.*"

The doors flew open.

We heard footsteps approach. I lifted my head a bit so I could see over the backs of the pews. It was the same two cloaked figures.

But this was impossible. I hadn't used magic before they got here. How could they be —

I looked down at the mark on my hand and gaped. Was it that?

As the footsteps drew closer, I heard one of the males say, "Are you sure?"

I peered over the edge again in time to see the other bloke hold up his wand. "See for yourself," he said.

The wand was glowing.

The other one nodded. "Right."

He crept along until he got to where we were hidden.

"There!" he snapped. He pointed his wand and said, *"Infernus!"*

*"Embattlemento!"* I instantly cried out.

His blast of fire ricocheted off my shield spell and he had to duck to avoid being incinerated.

The second bloke rushed forward, casting spell after spell our way, each more powerful than the last.

Petra cast a shield spell as well, and his magic rebounded off it and smashed into the pews, destroying them.

Spells were now being cast so fast I could barely follow them. The inside of the building was being pummeled.

Glass shattered. Wooden pews disintegrated, and a small statue of a female exploded when hit by a glancing blow from a rebounding spell. I had never been in such a battle as this one. The sheer ferocity and speed nearly paralyzed me. And though we were still invisible we were in terrible danger of being killed simply by being in this confined space.

I was hurling spells so fast I could barely remember thinking of the incantation before sending it off. When I glanced at Petra, I saw both terror and fury in her eyes. Somehow, this filled me with resolve.

I slid on my belly, squeezed under a pew, came up behind the bloke and said, *"Impacto."* He was blasted off his feet and flung against a wall.

But the bloke rebounded off it, turned and fired multiple spells in my general direction. I ducked, then threw myself over a pew. I turned in time to see Delph get slammed against another pew by the force of one of the spells.

I heard someone cry out and looked to see Petra fly over another pew and crash into the floor.

I whirled around on the same bloke and fired every spell I could think of. The problem was he was deflecting them left and right. My arm was growing weary, and Petra had not recovered enough to help me. When a spell hit so close to my head that it made me wonky, I ducked under a pew for a moment to catch my breath and clear my senses.

When I looked back up I almost cheered as I saw Delph slam into the male, lift him up, turn him upside down and pile drive him into the floor. I had seen Delph use that same move in the Duelum back in Wormwood. The bloke went limp.

The next instant a light shot right past my face, hit the wall behind me and knocked a hole in it. The concussive force of the spell knocked me heels over arse and broke the magical tether keeping the others invisible.

"Got you!" roared the other bloke who had shot at me as he pointed his wand right at Delph's exposed chest.

Before I could regain my feet and aim my wand, a voice called out, *"Subservio."*

Petra's spell hit the bloke square on, and he instantly went rigid and his wand hand dropped. He then simply stood there looking blankly ahead.

We rose on shaky legs and approached him.

"Thanks, Pet, you saved me," said Delph weakly.

"Yes, you did, Petra," I said. "That was quick thinking."

She let out a long breath. "I'm . . . I'm just glad it worked. I couldn't let him hurt you, Delph."

They locked gazes for a moment, and I felt my face begin to burn. I was glad that she had saved Delph, but did she have to give him *that* look? And did he have to give it right back?

"Look at this, Vega Jane."

While I had been thinking all this Delph had gone over to check on the other fellow. Petra and I rushed over with Harry Two next to us.

Delph pointed at the wand still held in the bloke's hand.

I stared down at it, stunned.

Etched on his brightly glowing wand was the mark of the three hooks! The same mark that had been burned onto my hand. The mark on the wand was pulsing as though alive.

Delph said, "*That's* how they managed it. Your mark, it must give off a signal."

I nodded, for he was assuredly right about that. But then what was I to do? I couldn't very well cut off my hand.

"Vega Jane, your glove!" said Delph.

"My what?" I said distractedly.

"Your glove. It has powerful magic. See if it can block the signal."

I plunged my hand into my cloak pocket and pulled out the glove Alice Adronis had given me in order to handle the Elemental, which was now also my wand. I had once thought I needed the glove to hold the Elemental, but Astrea Prine back in the Quag had shown me that this was not the case.

I hastily pulled on the glove, covering the mark. I hoped whatever magic the glove had was enough.

I looked at the fellow's wand and breathed a sigh of relief. The mark of the three hooks was gone from it and the wand was no longer glowing.

"That was brilliant!" said Petra to Delph.

She gave him a hug and a peck on the cheek. I saw him smile. Yet when he glanced at me and saw my expression was one of granite, he coughed, turned red and said, "'Twas nothing really."

"It was actually very smart of you, Delph." I turned to Petra. "But if we give out hugs and kisses every time someone does something smart, I reckon we might not have slivers for anything else."

Petra gave me a haughty look and rubbed Delph's arm.

Gritting my teeth, I turned, pointed my wand at the unconscious bloke, performed the *Subservio* spell and removed any memory he might have had of this. I did the same with his mate. Next, Petra and I repaired the damage to the building.

Finally, I turned the ring back around, attached the magical tethers, and we became invisible once more. It was only then that I released the blokes who had attacked us from the spell.

They both looked around.

One said, "What the blazes are we doing here?"

His mate looked down at his wand. "I don't know. Was it something to do with my wand?"

The other fellow shook his head. "Last thing I remember

I was in me bed. And that's where I'm going back to," he added angrily.

He turned and left. His mate gave the place one more searching look and joined him, shutting the doors behind him.

I let out a long breath. "Now let's go find a place to hide."

The long winding staircase carried us upward. It would, I was sure, lead all the way to the bell tower. But I stopped short of that. There was a door to the right. I tried it. Locked. I pulled out my wand, and a moment later the door opened.

I had grown accustomed to being able to do things like this, but I never wanted to take it for granted. I had come to completely adore being a sorceress!

Inside the room were old trunks. There was also a window. Which I had hoped there would be.

I closed the door behind us and locked it. I pointed to the window. "And when the light comes, we can watch the goings-on down there. Get the lay of the land."

"Right good plan," opined Delph, though Petra merely shrugged.

"We should get some sleep," I said. "But like back in the Quag, we'll take turns keeping watch, just in case."

I offered to take the first watch, and the others settled down on the floor, with their tucks as their pillows. We had retrieved some blankets that were stacked neatly in a corner, for the floor was hard and the room was cool.

I took up watch by the window for a bit with Harry Two lying next to me. I didn't see any movement down below. I was hoping that I would see another of those metal-and-wood things with wheels, but I didn't. In the distance I thought I heard a long, high whistle of sorts, but I couldn't be too sure of that, for the sound carried strangely up here.

I finally turned to some of the trunks and, trying to remain as quiet as possible so I wouldn't wake the others, I started searching them, hoping they would give us some idea as to the place we were now in.

The first trunk was filled with clothes. Trousers, coats, shirts, shoes and frocks. Even some hats. They were of a style, cut and material I had never seen. I looked down at my own clothes under my long cloak. Then I had an idea. I pulled out a number of the clothes and matched them up as best I could. If we were going to fit into this place, whatever it was, we had to dress like the others who were here.

I put these aside and opened the next trunk. When I saw what was in there I felt like I had happened upon a treasure trove.

Books! I pulled a goodly number of them out, sat on my haunches and, using the conjured light from my wand, began to look through them.

The first few books were filled with what looked to me to be sermons that someone like Ezekiel would deliver in ponderous tones meant to intimidate rather than uplift. However, the next book was far more interesting and potentially useful.

It was entitled *A Book of True*.

True, I quickly came to learn, was the name of the place we were in. Astonishingly, there were words in the book that I had never seen before: *years, horse, man, woman, church* and *motor* being among them. Fortunately, at least for most of the words, there were accompanying pictures. Thus I learned that man and woman were like our male and female and both were referred to as people, not Wugmorts.

My education continued. A horse was our slep. A canine was a dog. Sessions translated to years, which were divided up into twelve *months* and the twelve months were divided up into something called *days*. And slivers were minutes. And sixty of those minutes represented something called an hour. The church was the place we were currently in. And a motor was the contraption we had seen rumbling along. Oh, and there was something called the morning, which apparently was when the sun was coming up, and the rest of the light was called the day. And the Noc was called the moon.

I leaned back against the coolness of the stone and repeated these terms over and over, hitching them to the pictures in the book. I didn't know that learning a new language would be required here, but why not? Everything about this journey had been totally unpredictable. Just because we had escaped the Quag, that simple rule needn't change.

And if we wanted to fit in here, we couldn't very well go around this place calling horses sleps and the moon the Noc.

As I continued to read, I learned that True had experienced several centuries — a word I had learned previously — of peace following some difficult periods of war and uncertainty. There were pictures of Wugs — or I guess "people," since they never lived in Wormwood — engaged in fun activities with their youngs, who were called children. I looked at the illustrations of the smiling children and wondered how that fit with what I had been told about the ruthlessness and savagery of the Maladons, the magical race that Astrea Prine had told us had beaten her kind in a great war. Presumably the Maladons now ruled this place.

But hang on! Had perhaps these people fought and overthrown the Maladons? That would explain the reference to past wars followed by peace. But how had the people done this? Were they magical? How else could they have beaten the powerful sorcery the Maladons supposedly possessed? After all, they had thrashed my kind, who were powerfully magical in their own right.

And most telling of all, I believed we had run into a pair of Maladons twice already. So they *were* here. It was truly puzzling.

I continued to read and learn as much as I could.

I gazed at the picture of the motor and marveled how it could move without sleps, or horses rather, pulling it. Had this been created by magic?

Before I knew it, the sun was coming up outside. I had forgotten to awaken Delph or Petra to take over my watch. But I was not tired in the least. My head filled with all this new information; my mind was swirling with questions and possibilities. But mostly questions, I had to admit.

I moved back over to the window and looked out. With the sun up, I could see things quite clearly now. True was larger than it had appeared last night. I could now see spires of many buildings in the distance. Wugmorts — I caught myself — *people* were emerging from buildings. I waved my wand and muttered, "*Crystilado magnifica.*" Instantly, I was seeing all of this as though it were inches from my face.

I noticed, gratefully, that the people looked like us at least; otherwise it would be awfully hard for us to fit in. And their clothes looked like the ones I had pilfered from the trunk. Again, a good thing. But, then again, we might stand out anyway. We were three strangers with a canine. How would we explain our presence here? A clattering sound caught my attention, and in my magnified line of sight came another motor speeding down the cobbles. It was followed by a second motor. The second motor looked different — it was bigger than the other and had more people riding in it. They rode in one lower and one upper level that constituted the thing. At one corner the bigger motor stopped and some people got off and others got on. On the side was a sign that read TRUE TRANSPORT. This must be how they moved from one place to another, I thought.

"Blimey!"

I whirled around to find Delph and Petra staring over my shoulder.

"You didn't wake us to take a watch," said Petra disapprovingly.

"I thought I'd just let you sleep," I replied a bit lamely.

Delph said, "Vega Jane, you can't do this alone. I know I can't do magic, but I didn't fight my way across the Quag to be useless!"

His words cut into me with the force of a hurled blade. Delph never talked to me that way. I glanced at Petra. I could tell she was pleased by Delph's comments, which made my blood boil.

I composed myself and said, "You're right, Delph. But I've learned quite a lot actually."

I took some time showing them the clothes and the books and telling them of the new terms I had learned, like *people* and *dogs* and *morning* and *horses* and *motors*. They took this all in, though I could tell they were even more overwhelmed by it than I had been.

Then I heard Delph's belly rumbling.

It was then that I realized I was starving. I looked in my tuck to find that my larder was basically empty. Delph and Petra did the same, with similar results.

Even Harry Two's expression was one of abject hunger.

I decided on a course of action and parceled out the clothes I had found in one of the trunks. We swiftly dressed and put our old clothes and boots along with the spare new items in our tucks. I slipped the book on True into my coat pocket.

Petra said, "But what now? We can't go outside, can we?"

I replied, "I've seen lots and lots of Wu —" I stopped. "I mean I've seen lots of *people* coming and going. And almost never did I see one of them hail another. I think this place is far larger than we initially thought. We only saw it coming in during the darkness. If there are lots of blokes around, then maybe, in our new clothes, we can blend in with them."

"But what about Harry Two?" asked Delph.

"You saw the pictures of canines — I mean dogs — in the book. And I've seen four people walking ca —" I stopped again, frustrated with having to learn a new language so quickly. "DOGS!"

Delph said, probably equally frustrated, "Can we speak Wugish for now?"

I nodded. "Yes, but we can't when we're dealing with blokes from here. We have to start thinking in their language,

Delph. And since only those from Wormwood are Wugs, we have to call the blokes here 'people.'"

"That makes sense," he replied.

"Maybe best we say nothing a'tall, till we hear some of them blokes talk," suggested Petra.

"That's a good idea, actually," I replied, giving her a smile. I wanted to like and trust Petra, I really did. And if she turned out to be a Maladon, I hoped I could kill her before she killed me.

Delph nodded. "All right, then, but that doesn't explain how we'll get food to eat. We got nothing to pay with."

I hadn't thought about this.

"We'll face that bridge when we get to it," I said gamely.

I returned us to visibility and we headed downstairs.

We had reached the front doors of the place, and I had just opened them with my wand when a voice cried out.

"Oi! What in blazes are you lot doing here?"

I didn't even look for the source.

As we had so often done in the Quag, we just ran for it.

# The Absence of Evil

WE SPRINTED AS hard as we could, turning corner after corner until we stopped, hunched over, breathless.

"W-what-wh-who was that?" Delph finally got out.

I shook my head. "D-dunno. But he saw us for s-sure."

Petra drew in one long replenishing breath and said, "He was some fat bloke in a long black cloak with a white collar around his neck. Older, gray hair. He had some papers in his hand. Maybe he works there. Doubt he was there last night or else he would have heard all the fighting."

I looked at her admiringly but also felt disappointed in myself. She had had the good sense to at least peek at who had yelled at us. I had just run.

"We best budge along," said Delph nervously.

I followed his gaze to see folks on the cobbles staring at us as they walked by. Some were on two-wheeled things that were propelled along — at least it seemed — by their feet going around and around on short pieces of rubber attached to what looked like a gear. Strapped to the front of the contraption, where the rider placed his hands, was a wire basket to carry things. I had seen a picture of this in the book too. It was called a bicycle.

We darted across the cobbles only to almost be hit by a motor coming through. The male behind the funny wheel raised a fist at us, and a great honking sound like from an enraged goose blasted from somewhere out of the metal-and-wood creation. We scooted to the other side of the cobbles and reached firmer footing where folks were walking.

My heart beating painfully fast, I turned left and we trooped single file to another corner, where I turned right. And stopped.

Wugs — I mean *people* — were queued up outside a shop. And I knew why. The most wonderful smells were coming from within. I could hear my belly rumbling. I thought I could hear Delph's too, though that could have been my imagination.

"Blimey," said Delph, staring up at the sign over the shop. "Caspian's Creations." He looked at me. "What you reckon that is?"

I said, "I reckon it's a place to eat. Look."

There was a window in the front of the shop and we could see people seated around neatly spaced wooden tables. They had plates and cups and saucers in front of them and were chomping away using shiny metal knives and forks and spoons.

"Reminds me of the Starving Tove back in Wormwood," said Delph.

"Reminds me'a nothing," declared Petra. "I've never seen anything like it."

Her tone and look were of absolute wonder. And it made me think, not for the first time, that as bad as I had had it in Wormwood, it was but nothing compared to what Petra had endured living in the Quag.

Delph's and Harry Two's face and snout, respectively, were pressed against the glass as they peered longingly inside. Behind a wooden counter there were males and females in aprons filling — I supposed — orders of customers. Behind them I could glimpse other folks dressed in white shirts and aprons laboring over stoves and pots and pans. Piled high in wire baskets on the counter were loaves of bread and stacks of pastries and chocolates. And on racks next to them were cakes and pies and . . . the most delectable puddings. I felt my head spinning.

As I pulled my attention away from this splendid cornucopia, I could see paper and coin exchanging hands between those behind the counter and the customers. With sinking spirits, I could see that it looked very different from Wormwood coin. As hungry as I was, I dared not even try to use our coin, since it would give us away as not belonging here.

Delph had evidently seen what I had because he said, "You reckon we can find something to do to earn some proper coin so we can buy food?"

I looked around when I heard the noise.

A large motor had pulled to a stop in front of the shop. The metal grille had a name etched on it: ZEPHYER.

There was a bloke in front steering the thing with the big wheel. And there was a bloke way in the back. He was dressed in very fine clothes indeed. And he wore a hat that was very tall and very black. His nose was red and bulbous. He was yelling at the fellow in front, who jumped out and came swiftly around to the glass in the back of the motor where the other bloke was.

The glass came down and the bloke with the high hat could be heard clearly.

"I'm late. I'm late because of you, Wainwright. I don't have time to eat a proper breakfast. You will go in there and get what I want. I can eat along the way."

The male called Wainwright, who was dressed in knee-high brown boots, a jacket with lots of shiny buttons and a hard-sided cap with goggles wrapped around it, said pleadingly, "But, sir, there is a very long queue."

"That is not my problem, is it? Deal with the queue as you see fit, but you will get what I want immediately. I will require the usual. Here is the money."

I watched as he opened a brown leather pouch he'd taken from his coat pocket. He withdrew a piece of paper and a few coins. Apparently this was called money. From here I could see that he had more paper and more coins in the large pouch.

These were the moments in my life where clear choices could be made. Do it or don't do it. Often, the decision was difficult. This time the choice was easy.

The git obviously had far too much money. I was just going to relieve him of a bit, and he'd be none the wiser.

I looked around and slowly withdrew my wand. I slid it inside my coat sleeve and held it by the end. I raised my arm and pointed my wand at the pouch.

"Delph," I said out of the side of my mouth, "I need another one of your little distractions."

"What?" He had observed what I had done with my wand. Now realization spread over his features. "Oh, right."

He looked around for a moment and then cried out, "Oi, what's that, I wonder?"

He pointed into the air and across the cobbles.

"Look at that!"

His deep voice was so loud and carried so far that everyone within earshot glanced sharply that way, including the two blokes at the long motor.

"*Rejoinda* some of the, uh, money stuff in that bloke's pouch," I muttered under my breath, moving my arm toward myself.

Some paper and coins shot from the pouch, zipped past the chin of the fellow in uniform, who was looking across the cobbles like everyone else, and landed neatly in my other hand.

I slipped the paper and coin into my pocket and we joined the queue.

"But that's stealing, ain't it, Vega Jane?" admonished Delph.

Petra said, "So what? It's how me and Lack survived in the Quag all that time."

"But we're not in the Quag now, are we?" countered Delph sternly.

"Do you want to eat or not?" I asked Delph.

Well, *that* shut him up good and proper.

We finally made it inside the shop and a bit later stepped up to the counter.

A female in a long white apron with a matching cap faced us. Her skin was paler than mine and her eyes were large and round. Her long black hair was pulled back into a knot at the nape of her neck.

"What would you like, dearie?"

"Um, what do you have?" I said timidly.

She pointed to a board on the wall that listed lots of things. "All that there, plus what you see on the counter. All good; we make it right here in True."

Petra stepped up and said boldly, "What do *you* like the best?"

The female smiled, looked at her and said in a low voice, "Well, I must admit, number four is my absolute favorite."

I looked up at the number four on the board. To my surprise, it was all things I recognized. "Sounds good. For the three of us."

She looked down and saw Harry Two. "Dogs outside, please."

"Oh, right," I said.

She said, "He's a cute one, he is. What do you call him?"

"Um, Harry; just Harry." I figured telling her his real name would only prompt questions I didn't want to answer.

"Why, the poor thing's gone and lost most of an ear," she noted, clucking sympathetically.

"I know. He, uh, got into a fight with another cani — dog."

From the corner of my eye I saw Delph tug down the sleeve that covered his blackened arm. And then I noticed Petra slipping her injured hand into her pocket.

I quickly led Harry Two outside and told him to wait by the window. Then I went back inside and paid for our food. I handled the paper a bit funny but she didn't seem to notice. She gave me back some other paper and a few coins and I put them away in my coat pocket.

"Just the one glove, dearie, and an odd one at that?" she observed.

21

My throat constricted a bit. "My mum gave it to me. I lost the other. But I keep it on for her."

"Well, ain't that nice of you. I've got three daughters of me own. So I well understand, luv."

I smiled weakly and hurried off.

We took a table near the window when another group of blokes was finished with it.

When our food came, I took a portion out to Harry Two.

When I rejoined Delph and Petra, my gaze caught and held on her.

She was staring down at her meal like it was the most beautiful sight she had ever laid eyes on: scrambled eggs and bacon and fat sausages and warm buttered bread and hot tea and porridge topped off with a pile of kippers.

She caught me looking and her face reddened and her features took on a look of shame. I reached out my hand and gripped hers with it.

"I know what it's like to be hungry. But I was never hungry like you and Lack were. So I say eat up and enjoy a very fine meal."

She thanked me with a smile.

For the next ten slivers all we did was eat, swallow and drink.

Delph mumbled between mouthfuls, "Looks like the food ain't so different here."

Petra looked at him askance. "Maybe for you. I've never had such a feast in all my life."

I saw that she had no idea how to wield the fork, knife and spoon. So I used mine in a slow, exaggerated fashion, so

22

that she could mimic me, without my telling her. I knew she would resent that.

When our bellies were full, we rose and made our way out. Harry Two had long since finished his meal and was relieving himself against a corner of a building.

"What now?" asked Petra, looking refreshed and ready to have a go at exploring True.

Well, she had slept all night, but I hadn't, and I was full-out knackered.

"We find a place to stay," I said.

"But shouldn't we look around?" she replied.

"We can do that while we find a place to stay. And then afterward as well."

Delph edged over to me as we walked along. "Where do you reckon the Maladons are, Vega Jane? You think they live here?"

"Dunno," I said. "Maybe. I mean, they *do* look like the other blokes."

"Are we sure there are Maladons here?" asked Petra.

"Who in the blazes do you think those two blokes were last night?" I snapped. In my mind I thought the Maladons would be easy to spot because they would be hideous in figure and murderous of temper. The blokes last night were certainly murderous, but they looked like everyone else in True. That was a scary thought — not knowing who the Maladons were until they pulled their wands.

Delph looked at all the bustling activity.

"It don't look like what I thought it would," he remarked.

Delph was exactly right about that. We had been told

that the Maladons were evil and killers and, most important, victorious over our kind. That meant they were out here, ruling everyone.

So why did everyone look happy and . . . free?

We walked around True for a while. On every corner we turned down there was something new and different to see. The large double-decked motors I had seen from the church window now clearly appeared to carry folks where they wanted to go. They got off at certain places where there was a sign on a post with a picture of the motor carrying them. They paid coin, or money rather, for the ride.

We watched folks walk in and out of buildings. Many carried packages and bags, and some had youngs in tow or in their arms. Some pushed around baskets on wheels that had very youngs inside of them swathed in blankets.

I inwardly sighed. *Children. They were were called children, not youngs.*

These observations made me think of my family. My parents, my brother, John, and I would often take rambling walks together. I remembered my father's strong grip, my mother's loving smile and my brother's curiosity about all things. Tears clutched at the corners of my eyes. I caught Petra looking at me curiously. I quickly wiped my eyes.

"Let's budge along," I said.

There were blokes on some corners holding stacks of papers and calling out, "Warehouse fire blamed on lax hygiene" and "The mayor calls for more pencils in school." Then other blokes would take one of the papers in exchange for some money. I had no idea what any of it meant.

Some hurried along and others moved more slowly.

There were males in shiny uniforms with lots of brass buttons standing in the middle of the cobbles and pointing the motors where to go and whether to stop and start.

There were some carts on the walkways where males wearing aprons sat and sold food and drink to passersby. And in the middle of it all, children were rushing around and exhausting their mothers and fathers. *That* clearly hadn't changed.

Some folks had stopped and were chatting as Wugs did back in Wormwood. But there was an air of prosperity here that my old village could never claim. And I saw no Council members roaming around in black tunics looking intimidating.

But the thing I really *wasn't* seeing disturbed me most of all.

Where was the MAGIC?

Aside from the pair last night, I had seen nary a wand nor a spell cast; no one was soaring along on a conjured airstream. There were no evil creatures to battle.

But those blokes from last night *could* do magic. They had attacked us and very nearly killed us. I was convinced they were Maladons. How else would they have been able to track the mark on my hand? So how did that murderous presence, which we had expected, match up with the serene world we were seeing now?

I scratched my head. The whole thing was sixes and sevens as far as I was concerned.

"Uh, Vega Jane," muttered Delph.

We were walking along the cobbles.

"What?"

"I think a bloke back there is following us."

I immediately started to look behind us, but then caught myself.

"Why do you think that?" I asked nervously.

Petra answered, "Because he's been back there ever since we left the place where we ate, that's why. Don't you use your bloody eyes?"

I shot her an angry glance, but I felt more upset with myself. If Delph and Petra had noticed this, why hadn't I?

I crossed the cobbles and came up on the other side. I did it quickly enough that Delph and Petra had to hustle to catch up. I turned to look back at them, but what I was really doing was looking for the fellow following us.

It wasn't hard. He was making it fairly obvious. He was short and plump and I had caught him hustling across the street, his gaze locked on us. He wore a matching jacket and pants with a white shirt, a long strand of red material around his collar and an oddly shaped hat that I had seen other males here wearing.

"What do we do now?" asked Petra in a petulant tone as we hurried along at a good clip.

I looked up ahead and said, "We passed that little alley on the way here. Let's turn down there."

We reached it, made the turn and as soon as we did, I pulled out my wand, conjured the lasso, attached it to the others and then turned my ring backward. Invisible, we moved back against the brick wall of the alley and waited.

We didn't have to wait long.

The bloke came hurtling into the narrow space and then

stopped dead. I could only imagine what he was thinking as he looked up and down the long space that was quite empty.

His eyes boggling, he hustled down the alley until he reached the end. He gave a searching glance left and right, then he hustled back to where we all stood watching him.

He took out what looked to be smoke weed, lit it with a match and blew smoke out his nostrils as he tapped his shiny shoe against the cobbles and rubbed his chin.

I was waiting for the bloke to pull out his wand and start blasting spells down the alley. If he did, I would blast them right back. My fingers loosely gripped my wand. Around my waist, Destin, a chain that, among other things, allowed me to fly, hugged me a bit tighter, as though sensing the mixture of fear and anticipation that I was feeling.

I hoped that Petra had her wand at the ready too. As I looked over, I saw that this was so. The expression on her face was one of intense concentration without, I had to admit, a smidgen of fear.

I turned back to our pursuer. If this bloke *was* a Maladon, my confidence level would soar. He didn't look remotely dangerous. Hel, I thought, even pathetic Cletus Loon from Wormwood could take the little git if need be.

He finished his smoke weed, crushed it underfoot with the heel of his shoe and, giving the alley one more penetrating look, turned and left. We waited a bit to make sure he was gone good and proper, and then I reversed the ring and lifted the spell of the conjured lasso.

"Who you reckon that bloke was?" asked Delph.

"A spy for the Maladons, maybe," I said. "If he were magical, you'd think he would have used his wand to find us in here. It's what I would have done."

"Aye, that's a right good point," said Delph, looking impressed by my logic.

"But that means that the Maladons may control this place and use some of the folks here to help them. Even if they can't do magic, they're our enemies."

Delph looked unnerved by this. "So everybody here might be against us?"

"It's possible, Delph," I said.

As I continued to gaze around, something struck me. Everyone here looked very different from one another. I know that blokes look different from other blokes. But back in Wormwood, Wugs all looked pretty much the same. Same general facial features, hair color and pale skin. Morrigone with her bloodred hair was really the sole outlier. But here I was seeing features and skin color I'd never seen before. Black and brown and skin far paler than mine, and all sorts of combinations thereof. I liked it. I wished we'd had more of that in Wormwood. Fortunately, there were also a great many pale skins in True too, so we didn't stand out.

"Well, we're strangers here," said Petra, interrupting my thoughts. "And that prat who chased us from the church might have told others about us. So if these Maladons are smart, they'll put more blokes like that one out here till they find us. We can't stay invisible forever."

"Aye, that's a right good point too," said Delph, gazing at Petra with admiration.

I inwardly sighed. I felt like I was in a competition with

Petra Sonnet that had no bloody end. It made me exhausted just thinking of the countless possibilities.

"So what do we do now?" Petra asked.

They both looked at me — or all three of them did if you counted Harry Two, which I always would.

I thought quickly. "We need to find another place to hide. Until dark. And then maybe we leave here and head on somewhere else."

"Okay, but *what* place?" persisted Petra.

It was then that we heard a great roaring sound.

"Come on," I said.

We rushed off in the direction of the racket.

We scampered over the cobbles, using the noise as our guide, and finally came out into an enormous square filled with folks rushing hither and thither.

And that's when we saw it, a long metal thing all strung together. It had windows and there were people inside it. At the head of the thing was a huge black contraption that made the motors we'd seen look positively puny by comparison.

Smoke belched out of what looked to be a metal chimney at the front of the thing as it roared along, then slowed and disappeared behind a large building.

I looked at the others and then raced toward this same building. As I drew close to the front doors, they opened for a crowd of people leaving the place.

From inside I could hear a very pleasant voice boom out, "The 9:10 express train to Greater True, boarding now. The 9:10 express train to Greater True. All authorized persons, please make your way. And ladies and gentlemen, and the

29

kiddies too, mind the divide between the train and the station platform."

Delph said, *"Express train?"*

"Seems to be a way that people get about," I said slowly.

Petra said, "Greater True? What the Hel is that?"

I said, "Obviously a place other than, well, just plain True. And greater means bigger, so it probably is."

But something else the pleasant voice had said was bothering me.

Who were these *authorized persons?*

I stared up at the brick building that this express train had apparently pulled into. The sign on it read TRUE TRAIN STATION.

My gaze ran over the large facade.

"I think we just found our hiding place," I said.

"What, with all these blokes?" said Petra skeptically.

"That's kind of the point," I shot back. "Let's go."

# Abandoned

THE TRAIN STATION was a cavernous place, bigger inside even than it had appeared from the outer side. And it was filled with people carrying bags rushing about. There weren't this many Wugs in all of Wormwood.

I looked around and spotted something. On one wall was a large sign. On it were the names of I supposed places, and next to them were numbers. People would stop and stare up at it, glance at timekeepers wrapped around their wrists and then scurry on.

"I reckon it's the schedule of the train things," opined Delph. "Kind of like a plan of when they come and go." He elaborated. "Those must be times and train numbers. They tell people where the trains are going and when."

"How do you figure that?" I asked.

"We had something like that back at the Mill," he replied. "We had to load up the flour sacks and we had a board hung on the wall that told us when we had to make deliveries and who they were going to."

I nodded, thinking he was exactly right. But it was still so shocking that a place like this could exist right next to the Quag. And that Wormwood could be on the other side of

that Quag, a village stuck well back in another time as compared to here, which had motors and trains and just . . . stuff
that I had to admit was far nicer.

As I looked around, I could see a sign blinking over an
entrance leading to a long sleek train that had pulled into the
station.

GREATER TRUE.

I saw males — er, men — standing in front of the glass
doors that led to the train. A line of folks had queued up in
front of the doors. They were all very well dressed and properly clean and looked, well, sort of like the angry bloke in the
big motor — like they were better than everybody else. They
held out their tickets and then something else to the two
men. I drew my wand, hiding it up my sleeve, and muttered,
*"Crystilado magnifica."*

I could see clearly now what was on the "something else."
It was their picture and name and other information in a small
notebook. And I noticed they were all holding up their hands
to the fellows at the entrance. There was something on their
palms, but I couldn't see what it was.

I noticed that many of the people in the station were carrying the paper things I had seen the blokes on the cobbles
selling. Some had them folded under arms. Others were sitting on benches and reading them. One of them left his on
the bench. I ventured over and picked it up. I looked down at
it. It was filled with writing and some pictures too, of a kind I
had never seen.

"Blokes here do seem *so* happy, don't they?" said Petra,
with mild disgust in her voice.

She had come over to stand next to me and was watching a woman on her knees scrub the stone floor with a large sponge and a bucket of soapy water. The woman was smiling and humming away as though she had all the coin in the world, but still didn't mind working on her knees scrubbing off dirt left by others.

As I looked around, I noted the pleasant countenances on just about everyone I saw. It had been the same back at the café, and on the cobbles outside. All except for the angry bloke in the long motor. And the bloke who had chased us from the church. And the male who was following us hadn't looked all that pleased. But Petra was correct; just about everyone else looked very content.

But we couldn't stand around here. For all I knew, the bloke who had been following us would turn back up. And then maybe all these "happy" citizens of True would pull out their wands and start blasting us. As back in the church, my natural inclination was to go up. I spotted a set of stairs and we hustled over to them and started climbing. We kept going, passing blokes along the way until we stopped passing anyone and were all by ourselves. We turned right and left and then up another set of steps. We passed down a corridor with a series of doors lining it. I used my wand to see behind the doors. They were rooms filled with odds and ends. But then one appeared that was not.

I opened the door and we stepped through.

It was empty, but set against one wall was the backside of the sign we had seen holding the schedule for the trains. When I drew close to it, I could see that there were slits in it.

Through them I could see the interior of the train station we had just left. I leapt back when the sign started to vibrate. Things were spinning around faster than the eye could follow.

"What the Hel!" I exclaimed.

But Delph was not at a loss. "New train times," he said. "Lots of trains, I guess, so's you have to change things up, eh? Let folks know."

"Right," I said, still a bit unnerved. But we wouldn't get much rest if that thing was going to do that all the time.

I had anticipated seeing death and destruction and the bloody Maladons ruling over all of it. But there was none of that here. There was peace and prosperity and apparent freedom.

I was so disappointed. And then I immediately felt guilty. Who wouldn't prefer peace to war?

But then I thought about it some more. We had originally left Wormwood to find the truth. The truth of our past, and then the truth of our future. In the Quag we had run into Astrea Prine, the Keeper of the Quag, who had trained me up as a sorceress. She had told us of our past: the lost war against the Maladons. Then the creation of Wormwood as a hiding place to keep the survivors of that war safe, and the Quag conjured around it, both to keep Maladons out and us in. I had convinced her to allow Delph and me to try our luck at crossing the Quag and taking up the fight with the Maladons once more. Now, the blokes who had tracked and attacked us were magical, sure enough, but were they Maladons? Did the

Maladons even exist anymore? It had been eight centuries since the war, after all. A lot could happen in that time, I reckoned.

I looked up at Delph and could tell from his expression that he was thinking the exact same thing.

"Maybe the Maladons got beat," he said. "Beat by the blokes what live in this place."

I looked at him in disbelief. "But how? They can't do magic."

Petra said, "We don't know that."

I shook my head. "Other than the two that followed us, we haven't seen anyone perform any. What about that bloke that chased us from Saint Necro's? And the one who was following us? If he could do magic, we wouldn't be here, would we?" I paused. "And there's something else." I held up my gloved hand. "Their wands could detect the mark of the three hooks. That's our symbol: peace, hope, freedom, everything the Maladons apparently hated. So the two we fought in Saint Necro's *had* to be Maladons, otherwise how would they know to track the three hooks?"

Petra started to say something but then stopped and looked bewildered. Delph looked equally out of his depth.

My mind was so tired I couldn't really think anymore. I turned to the sign when it started to whir. And in those spinning pieces of metal I saw my own mind whirling wildly out of control. What if I was wrong? What if the Maladons didn't control this place?

What if Astrea Prine and her lot had made a colossal

mistake that had doomed all Wugmorts to the bleakest existence possible?

I looked down at my wand. *Magic might be useless to me if there is no battle to fight. If there is no war to win. If there is no grand enemy to vanquish.* So I was here and my brother, John, was back in Wormwood enduring the tutelage of Morrigone that had already transformed him into something unrecognizable to me. Had I left him for no good reason?

And then a sudden thought struck me, although in truth it had always been very near the surface of my thinking.

My parents! And my grandfather!

Were they here, in True?

I sat up straighter, cheered by this possibility. If we searched this place thoroughly, I might just find them. I found Delph staring at me.

"Don't make much sense, does it?" he said.

"What doesn't?"

"Well, your grandfather Virgil's this Excalibur, right?"

"Right."

"An Excalibur?" interjected Petra curiously.

"Right powerful sorcerer from birth," explained Delph. "And he left Wormwood in a ball of flames a long time ago when me and Vega were just wee things."

Petra looked stunned, but said nothing.

"I know that, Delph," I said sharply, wanting him to get to the point.

"So maybe he came here."

"Maybe he did. I was just thinking we might find him here. And my parents."

He continued as though he hadn't even heard me. "So maybe he came here and saw what we have."

"You mean a peaceful place where everyone is so very happy and well fed?" I said snidely.

"Right. But then he did what he did."

My brow furrowed in puzzlement. "What did he do?"

"He summoned your parents, like Astrea said he done. And that wasn't all that long ago."

"Okay, but so what?"

"Well, why would he'a done that if something weren't outta sorts? I mean Virgil was always one smart bloke. Don't think he woulda done that for no bloody reason, eh?"

I mulled this over. What Delph said *did* make sense.

But then my mind veered to another possibility. One that perhaps even Delph had not considered.

My grandfather had not summoned *me*. He had not rescued me or my brother from Wormwood.

In fact, he had done nothing for me . . . except leave me behind. And my parents had never tried to contact me after they had left Wormwood. So I supposed they didn't care about me either. For all I knew, they were just fine with me spending the rest of my life in Wormwood.

Without them.

"What are you thinking, Vega Jane?" asked Delph, who was watching me closely.

I felt tears rising to my eyes, but I looked away and brushed them off. I didn't want Delph to see me like that. And I definitely didn't want to display any such weakness in front of Petra.

I composed myself and said, "I'm thinking that we're

going to have to figure this out on our own. Because I don't think there's anybody here that can or will want to help us."

I looked at each of them in turn before settling my gaze back on the floor.

"We're alone."

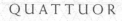

QUATTUOR

# The Late Train

WELL, HERE WE were ensconced in another little room, like mice in a hidey-hole. And I didn't like it one little bit.

Delph and Petra were asleep on the floor with their heads on their tucks. Harry Two had his head on my lap and was snoring softly. As usual I could not sleep. Whether here, in the Quag, or back in Wormwood, sleep had never come easily for me. My mind was whirling far too fast. I looked enviously over at Delph and Petra, perched as they were close together, perhaps too close. I recalled her touching his arm and giving me that *smile*. This was going to come to a head at some point, I knew. I just didn't know what the result would be.

Restless, I turned to look out through the back of the sign. It must be very late outside, I thought. In fact, the train station was quite empty now, with nary a bloke toting a bag in sight. I couldn't see the front of the sign so I didn't know if any more trains were coming in.

I had slumped down and closed my eyes when I heard it. A low, faraway whistle. Then another. Then I heard a rumbling. It was growing closer.

I opened my eyes and looked around.

"It's like last night, eh?"

I turned to stare at Delph, who was awake and looking at me.

He said, "When we were coming to True for the first time after leaving the Quag. It was about this time of night, I reckon. When we heard the whistle. And the rumble."

He was right. We *had* heard these sounds when flying toward True last night.

"But, Delph, why would a train be coming in this late?"

"Dunno, but it's definitely coming here," he said. "The rumbling is picking up."

We waited a few more minutes, during which time Petra woke.

The rumblings became louder and louder, and our gazes were fixed through the slits in the sign on that part of the station. We could see through glass doors the location where the trains would come into the station. I had early on guessed why, because I had seen the steam and smoke pouring out of the lead contraption in the train that I knew now was called the engine. I knew this because there was a little version of a train on display on the main floor of the train station. Next to each car of the train was another sign telling what it was called. Thus I also learned that the last car was known as the brake van.

Though it was now dark, I knew we would have no trouble seeing the train come into view because they had little lights on inside. I had seen that on other trains.

I looked at the others and saw they were as curious as I was. The rumbling became very loud, and I tensed since I knew the train would be appearing in our line of sight momentarily.

But it didn't. In fact, the sound went away and there was never a glimpse of the actual train at all.

"What happened?" said a surprised-looking Delph.

"Well, there's only one way to find out." I got up and headed to the door. The others followed me.

We reached the main floor of the station and peered around.

In a low voice Delph said, "Vega Jane, maybe being invisible would come in handy now."

I nodded and ensnared everyone with my magical tether and then turned my ring the wrong way around. We instantly vanished from sight. As we moved along, I kept gazing around and listening. I thought I could hear something, but it wasn't clear where it was coming from.

We passed through the glass doors and stopped at the edge of the train platform, where shiny metal rails ran in parallel with stout wood laid perpendicularly in between. This was what the train ran on, and it was clever indeed. In fact, I thought wistfully, it might be something my brother, John, would have invented given the opportunity.

I whispered, "Well, the train didn't stop here."·

"But the thing is," said Petra, "we didn't see it go through the station a'tall. I mean, doesn't it have to run on those metal things?"

Delph said, "She's right. Why would it come close to True and not come into the station? It had to be ruddy close or else we wouldn't have heard it from where we did."

"Maybe there's another place for the train to stop." I looked down. "*Under* the station?"

They both looked at me quizzically. "But why would it do that?" asked Petra.

I felt my skin start to tingle all of a sudden. I didn't know what made it do that. But then again, maybe I did. I had always relied on my instincts. And maybe they were sending me a message.

"Why would a train be coming in this late at all?" I asked.

Delph said, "To keep it secret-like from everybody, 'cause most folks are sleeping now."

"Exactly."

Petra looked around and pointed. "Those stairs head down."

We scurried over to them and peered down. It was so dark we could see nothing. I said my incantation, pointed my wand and the area was magically magnified.

"Big doors," said Delph. "With a bunch'a signs that say DO NOT ENTER."

"And I bet they're locked," added Petra.

I had no doubt they were. I led the way downward and when we reached the doors, I pointed my wand and said, "Ingressio."

I heard locks click, and one of the doors moved an inch or so. I gripped the knob and pushed it open just far enough for me to peer through.

There was a short corridor and yet another set of doors. We passed through these, and then the stairs headed steeply downward.

I had to get us through two more sets of doors, and it felt like we were about a mile underground.

We stepped through the last set of doors and looked around.

It was dark and musty and huge. I wasn't sure the space down here wasn't as big as what was up top.

Delph said in a hushed voice, "Do you hear that?"

It was a rumbling sound, but not like the noise before. It was lower and seemed to be made of many little noises accumulated somehow.

We raced over to a door set in the wall and put our ears to it.

"I hear something," said Petra.

I pointed my wand and said, *"Crystilado magnifica."*

Revealed on the other side of the door was a long hall. And it was full of people: males, females and youngs walking along. I was so nervous, I momentarily couldn't recall the other terms used here so I had reverted to my native Wugish.

And next to them the darkened train was sitting on the tracks, the engine belching smoke.

Everyone had obviously just gotten off the train. They carried small tucks with them.

They marched along in silence, staring straight ahead as though in a trance.

"The hall is too full of people for all of us to go out," I said. "You hide behind those crates over there because I have to break the magical tether."

"But, Vega Jane," Delph began in protest.

"I'll be back in a jiffy," I said. "Petra, keep your wand ready."

I released the tether once they were safely hidden. Invisible, I used my wand to open the door just enough to allow me to slip through. Luckily, no one was watching the door. When the last of them had passed by, I fell in behind the group.

At certain points along the way were more cloaked blokes holding wands, who I assumed were Maladons. When the line wasn't moving fast enough, they roughly pushed people along. As I watched, a small girl with dark skin was knocked down by one of them. When a female I supposed was her mother went to help her, she was struck by the same Maladon and fell next to her daughter.

The others marched on, not once looking back at their fallen comrades. As soon as the column had disappeared down the long hallway, the mother and daughter were jerked up, taken over to a far wall, lined up against it and the men stepped back and raised their wands.

"'Tis a heavy price to be paid for dawdling, vermin," he hissed.

The horror I was witnessing was even greater than what I had experienced in the Quag. At least in there the blood-thirsty predators had the excuse that they were *beasts*.

Without even thinking, I raised my wand and said, *"Impacto."*

The spell shot out from the tip of my wand and blasted both men off their feet. They sailed through the air and landed hard against the floor of the platform, their wands flying from them.

I rushed forward to help the girl and her mother, but they just stood there impassively. It was then I realized that they were under the *Subservio* spell. I released them from it and they slowly focused and looked around in confusion.

"Are you okay?" I said.

But I had forgotten that I was still invisible. When I spoke, the mother screamed, clutched her child and they ran off in the direction opposite from where the column had marched.

"Wait," I said. I was about to make myself visible when I heard feet running toward me. I turned and leapt out of the way as a group of cloaked Maladons with raised wands rushed past me. I lifted my wand to attack them from behind, but then I heard spells being cast and people screaming and more sounds of running.

Overwhelmed by all of this, I turned and ran in the other direction, toward where the column of downtrodden had headed. I reached a door through which they must have passed. I eased it open and slipped through.

On the other side of the door was a long, dark hall. I heard noises coming from the other end. People were talking in raised voices. Obviously everyone was on alert now.

Not waiting for anyone to come to me, I rushed headlong down the hall, protected by my being invisible, though someone could certainly collide with me — invisibility did not mean that I was no longer a solid being.

There were no doors along the hall, but I knew there had to be some place they had taken all those people.

"*Crystilado magnifica*," I said, pointing my wand ahead.

Instantly in front of my face was the most bizarre sight.

The room was enormous, cavernous really; easily the largest room I had ever seen.

And in the middle of it was a huge crowd of people. Some I recognized as having just gotten off the train. In front of them, on a large white wall, were images moving back and forth. There was nothing really recognizable on the wall. It was just a sense of something there and movement, that was all.

But everyone in the room was staring at it, transfixed.

As I looked away from them and glanced back at the wall, I heard something. Again, as with the images on the wall, I couldn't make out actual words; it was simply murmuring, something less than a whisper and a bit more than silence.

When I looked at the mass of people, I froze. They were now rocking from side to side, in unison it looked like, though it seemed unfathomable that such a large crowd could do anything so perfectly in time with one another. Then each reached out and gripped their neighbor's hand.

When I looked back up at the wall and listened to the murmurings, something happened to me. I too started to sway back and forth. I felt my mind start to, well, dissolve. It wasn't frightening. In fact, it felt right; it felt safe. I wanted it to happen. Memories that I had were starting to fall away from me. I felt good. My eyes began to close.

"Vega Jane! Are you here somewhere?"

My eyes snapped open and I looked wildly around.

"Delph?" I whispered. "I'm over here, by the wall."

From the darkened shadows stepped Delph, Petra and Harry Two.

I revealed myself to them by turning my ring back around. "How did you get down here?"

"Weren't easy," said Delph. "Some angry blokes with wands come through, and we decided where we were hiding wasn't all that safe. They went through a door and we slipped in behind them before it closed. Finally worked our way down here."

"What'd you find out?" Petra asked.

"There were lots of people on the train. And they went to that big room right over there where they were doing something to their minds. If you hadn't called out, I think I would have lost *my* bloody mind."

"Messing with their minds?" said Petra, looking stricken.

I nodded. I was actually thinking about the *Omniall* spell I had used back in the Quag to banish the mind of a creature called a wendigo. Was that what was happening here, a banishment of all those people's minds?

"Then what happens to 'em?" said Delph.

"Maybe they come to live here, all docile-like," I replied, the puzzle blocks tumbling into place in my head. "Maybe that's why it's so peaceful here. Why blokes get along and all. And why even people scrubbing stones are smiling like they have the life of leisure."

After I made us all invisible again, we headed back the way we had come until we could see the train once more. Then some cloaked figures holding wands appeared and we darted into the shadows.

Behind us I could hear the train gathering more and more steam. I looked out from our hiding place and flinched. The group of cloaked and wanded figures was heading our way. They *had* to be Maladons. They were dressed like the blokes at Saint Necro's.

In as low a voice as I could manage and still be heard I said, "They know someone who shouldn't be is down here."

The Maladons were walking side by side, spanning the entire passage and waving their wands in front of them. Light was coming out of the end of each. Their plan, evidently, was to find whoever was down here by magic!

I ducked back down and eyed the open train carriage door directly behind us. It was our only possible escape. "This way, quick!" I hissed.

We moved backward and onto the train carriage and then flitted inside. Thankfully, it was empty.

And then I looked out the window and saw the Maladons heading our way.

"Blimey, it's like they know where we are," I blurted out.

"Where do we hide?" exclaimed Petra.

We hurried to the rear of the train and shrunk back against the wall.

The Maladons entered the train and looked around.

After looking around, it seemed that they were satisfied that the train was empty. All had turned to leave save one. Inexplicably, he took a long whiff of the air, and his features turned puzzled. And then they turned suspicious. I looked desperately around and then gazed down at Harry Two.

Invisibility did not shield our *smell*. Perhaps the accursed bloke was sniffing out my canine.

Before the Maladon could do anything I pointed my wand and whispered, "*Confusio.*"

The spell hit him and he immediately went funny in the face.

One of his mates turned, saw him, gripped him by the arm and pulled him off the train, cuffing him on the head for good measure.

With a lurch and a long rasping noise, the train pulled out of the station.

I let out a long breath that very nearly turned to a shriek, so happy was I. And then my thoughts ventured to all those people in that room having their minds emptied and filled up with nothing but tosh, and my smile vanished.

It was like my life in Wormwood — filled only with lies.

"Vega Jane, who do you suppose is driving this here train?" asked Delph.

"Dunno, do I?"

"And where do you suppose we're heading?" asked Petra.

"Same answer," I said irritably.

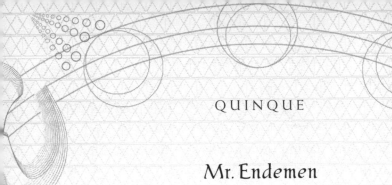

# Mr. Endemen

WHEN WE WERE clear of the station, the train gathered speed and we were soon roaring through the dark countryside. I gazed out the window and was stunned at how fast a train could go.

I was also wondering why we were the only ones on it. Yet maybe there were people in the other carriages?

As a group, covered by the invisibility shield, we searched the rest of the train, but every carriage was empty.

But one of the carriages was different from the others. There were no windows, and, ominously, there were chains attached to each seat.

We looked at them silently for several long moments and then glanced anxiously at one another before hurrying back to our carriage.

As we settled down in our seats, Delph said, "I wonder who they put in chains?"

I shook my head. "Not the ones that they're taking their minds from. I think they stay in True. And you don't need to chain people who can't think for themselves."

Petra added, "Well, they apparently all stayed in True tonight, since there's no one on this bloody train."

Delph looked up ahead and said, "But some bloke's got to be steering this thing, don't he?"

I took out my wand, pointed it toward the front of the train and said, *"Crystilado magnifica."*

There were two males sitting in comfortable seats. They weren't wearing cloaks but blue uniforms with caps, like the blokes I had seen directing the motors on the cobbles. In front of them, set into a large wooden board, was a vast array of shiny buttons and levers. And behind little bits of glass built into the wood were small arrows wavering between sets of numbers. One of the blokes lit up a pipe and smoke started seeping from it. He and the other man were chatting aimlessly, it seemed to me. In front of them was a large window showing what was in front of the train as it sped along.

I relinquished the magnification spell and looked at the others, who had seen what I had.

Delph seemed relieved. "Well, at least someone is steering."

"But I wonder where we're going?" asked Petra.

"Well, we're not going in the direction the train came in from," I pointed out. "It would have had to turn around to do that, and it didn't. So that means we're heading somewhere new."

"To pick up more folks, do you reckon?" asked Petra.

"And bring them back here in the middle of the night and do things to their minds?" added Delph nervously.

I looked out the window again and wondered how long the train would keep moving. And what we would do when it arrived at its next destination. I touched my temple and shook my head slightly. The effects of whatever was happening in that room back in the bowels of the train station were gone, for the most part. But something lingered in my mind. Something so pleasing and wonderful and, well, perfect, that it instinctively horrified me more than anything I had seen or fought in the Quag possibly could.

I looked back from where we had just come.

A place called True.

Ironic, I thought, since I now doubted there was even a smidgen of *truth* in the whole bleeding place. Simply more lies, like back in Wormwood.

*Lies.*

Ironic that my kind — who were supposed to be the good ones — and the evil Maladons would use similar methods to keep people in line.

I rubbed my temple some more, as though trying to massage what I had seen into proper focus. I had been feeling wonderful, it was true, but there had been images associated with that feeling. I wanted to try to remember what they were.

A hand was reaching down from what looked to be the sky. In it was something truly bedazzling. I focused even more. In the palm of the hand was . . . me! I was smiling and felt as light as air. I had never felt so perfect and happy and just beautiful. The possibilities were truly limitless. I could accomplish anything. And what I wanted to accomplish was . . . Here the images darkened a bit, but that didn't detract from my happiness in the slightest. I was just sure that whatever my desires turned out to be, I would be perfectly satisfied. I had a very brief vision of myself baking bread. And then I was on my hands and knees washing the cobbles. The next instant I was sweeping the floor.

And then my features relaxed.

They weren't *my* desires.

They were the desires that someone else was telling me were my own.

It was so astonishingly awful that I visibly shook. What was being taken from those people was simply their lives. And the only thing the poor blokes had to do was keep on living the life that someone *else* had chosen for them.

The train roared on.

Delph took the first watch. I would relieve him for the second.

For once I slept soundly. The gentle swaying of the train carriage was rather hypnotic. I awoke refreshed, my mind once more eager to take on what lay ahead of us.

As Delph sat back in his seat and dozed off, I glanced out the window and noted the passing countryside. I glimpsed clusters of small homes, cows and sheep dozing or grazing, the bulge of a knoll, a stand of trees, open fields.

"Delph, Petra!" I exclaimed.

They immediately awoke. I looked down at Harry Two. He had never fallen asleep. Now his hackles were up and his fangs were bared. That's what had drawn my attention. And now I knew why my dog was on high alert.

"What is it?" whispered Delph nervously.

"The train is slowing down."

It was indeed now rapidly decreasing its speed.

I looked out the window, but there was only darkened countryside. There couldn't be a station hereabouts, could there?

Next instant my features froze.

Things were whirling across the sky so fast I could barely see them. They were like shooting stars, only far closer to the ground. I knew instinctively what they were doing here.

They were coming for us!

"Get up," I said hurriedly. "We have to get out of here."

"What!" said Petra. "Why? Where are we going?"

"Out of here," I snapped back.

The flying shapes were now paralleling the path of the train. One pulled up close to our window.

It was a male dressed in a suit and a vest. A brown bowler hat, like the one Duf Delphia used to wear, somehow managed to remain on his head despite the speed at which he was traveling.

A wand was clutched in his hand.

He peered inside the train carriage, his gaze sweeping all points of it. I could imagine his companions were doing the same to the other carriages. They had realized that we had somehow gotten onto the empty train. And they had caught up with us.

"Vega," said Petra. "Look!"

She was pointing to the other side of the train. There were two more figures there, flying along and peering inside. They had their wands out too. I suddenly knew what was about to happen.

I grabbed the others and pushed them flat to the floor. A moment later the windows on the train exploded inward, showering us with glass, as spell after spell blasted across the width of the carriage.

We crawled on our bellies toward the rear of the carriage. A piece of glass hit me in the face, scratching me. I heard Delph moan as a piece of a destroyed seat smacked him in the leg.

I thought about putting up a shield spell, but I knew that would certainly give us away as things magically rebounded off it.

So the torrent of debris continued to rain down on us.

I looked up in time to see one of the men shoot through the open window and land on the floor.

He held his wand up, moving it back and forth, as though he was using it to ferret us out. I turned on my back, my wand pointed directly at his chest. If he gave any indication that he saw us, I would blast him off the train.

We scuttled backward, reached the door to the train carriage in the small vestibule and stood.

Suddenly the carriage door was ripped open and another man hovered there. He was, like his companion, dressed neatly in a suit and bowler hat. He alighted on the floor and looked around as we shrunk back.

I glanced over and saw that Petra had her wand out and it was pointed at his chest. I held up a finger, signaling her to wait.

The man moved past us and joined the other in the carriage.

"Now," I said quietly.

We stepped to the doorway through which the man had entered. Right before we made our leap, the train slammed to a halt, throwing us against the inside of the vestibule. Luckily, our yelps of surprise and pain were covered by the groans of the train coming to a stop so violently.

We picked ourselves up and jumped, hitting the ground and rolling for a few feet, but fortunately our magical tether held and we remained invisible. We settled down in the tall grass and peered about.

The train sat motionless while blurred figures soared around it. We could see that all the windows in all of the carriages had been blown out in the search for us. That was actually a positive thing, as it showed they had no idea where on the train we had been.

However, my good feeling lasted only a few moments.

The two blokes in the blue uniforms who had been steering the train were hauled out by two men in suits and hats and dragged over to stand in front of the carriage we had been on.

The two men who had been in our carriage stepped outside and walked over to stand in front of the others.

The taller of the two twirled his wand in his hand as he surveyed the other chaps, who looked terrified. This was the bloke I had seen flying next to the carriage. When he took off his bowler hat I could see that he had straight dark hair, combed neatly around his head. His nose was long with not an imperfection on it. His mouth was but a slash of lips, cruel and remorseless. His eyes were so dark it was like looking at twin morta barrels.

He ran a hand through his hair and replaced his hat. When he spoke, his voice was calm and quietly menacing. "You saw no one?"

"No one, Mr. Endemen, sir," said one of the train drivers, his voice quivering.

*Mr. Endemen?* I thought. They called him sir, so he must be important.

Endemen replied, "Yet they *were* seen."

*What did he mean that we were seen? We were invisible.*

Endemen continued smoothly. "A very tall young man with long dark hair? And a pretty young woman with long blond hair? A dog with one ear partially missing?"

My heart sank. They must've seen the others while I had been down below with the late train. But his next words froze me.

"And there was another. A woman. Even taller than the blond. Darker hair. She's gangly and dirty."

I felt my face flush with anger.

But then my knees went weak. How had anyone seen me?

"We . . . we saw no one, sir," stammered the same man.

Endemen scrutinized him. "And, as per your duties, you did a *thorough* search of the train before you left the station? We've had stowaways before, as you well know."

The men in uniform gazed at each other. Though I couldn't see their faces fully, I could only imagine the terror that was going through them.

Endemen snapped his fingers.

Instantly, six more blokes wearing suits and bowler hats appeared out of thin air and encircled the pair, wands out.

"Well, we did a look-see in all the carriages," said one of the men, his voice quite faint.

Endemen smiled. "A look-see? Do you mean you walked through each carriage examining them thoroughly, or did you merely peek through the windows to see that everything was all right?"

"Well, we hadn't any reason to believe that —"

He would never finish what he was saying.

"*Rigamorte*," said Endemen. The blast of black light hit the man full in the chest. He toppled forward and . . . just . . . died. Right there.

I drew in a quick breath of air.

His companion instantly dropped to his knees, his hands clasped together.

"Please, sir, Mr. Endemen, we meant no harm. We was only —"

"*Rigamorte.*"

A moment later he joined his colleague on the ground, quite dead.

Endemen looked down at the pair that he had just murdered. He had done so as though he were merely addressing a bothersome insect. There had been no hesitation, no buildup of anger, no . . . nothing. He just did it, like it was the most normal thing ever. As though the emotion needed to do so — which I found nearly impossible to conjure unless I, or someone I loved, was in mortal peril — was at the ready all the time. I couldn't fathom how anyone could be that . . . cruel.

He stroked his wand as though the twin acts of killing had pleased him and then slid it back into his inner coat pocket.

Endemen looked around, which caused all of us to duck down farther in the grass.

"We will search this entire area," said Endemen. "From the air and the ground. We will find them."

He looked down at the two dead bodies. "Dispose of these, Creel," he said to the shorter man standing next to him. "And as for the families, provide the standard evil Campions explanation. Appropriate compensation for their loss, any help we can convey, et cetera, et cetera. Be off with you."

"Yes, Mr. Endemen."

I felt my head whirling with new thoughts. *The evil Campions?*

Creel pointed his wand downward at the bodies and mumbled something I didn't catch. The two corpses were instantly bound in heavy blankets, with rope cinched tightly around them. Creel rose into the air and used his wand to direct the covered bodies to do the same. Then he was off in a flash of light.

Endemen looked at the others, who were all dressed as he was: pin-striped suit, vest, tie, brown bowler hat, shiny shoes. And deadly wands.

He said, "We will spread out. Half to the air, half down here. Keep the spell work to a minimum. Signal if you see anything. Wait for me before you kill. I want to ask some questions. Right, let's get to it."

Since I knew this was coming, I had started leading the others away while the bodies were still being bound up by Creel.

We silently lifted into the air and flew away as fast as I could manage. Petra was on the end, her wand pointed behind her at the group of evil sorcerers, who could fly fast and kill even faster. I knew if they spotted us, the fight would be a short one. We were no match at all for them.

The image of the two frightened men tumbling to the

dirt dead was still seemingly imprinted on my eyeballs. I doubted I would ever be free from it.

As the partially destroyed train faded from view, I could hardly keep my mind from running away faster than the train had been going.

Then suddenly I felt my wand point directly down, and a moment later that's the direction we were headed too.

Try as I might, there was nothing I could do.

We were plummeting from the sky.

And we were going to die.

## A Guiding Wand

RIGHT BEFORE WE would have slammed into the ground, my wand pointed slightly upward and we landed hard, but safely. I looked up in time to see a half dozen forms heading our way. It was Endemen and his cohorts.

My wand jerked toward the left and I felt myself being pulled to my feet by the power within it.

With my wand pointing the way, we raced toward the thick woods.

We reached the tree line and plunged into the welcome cover of the trunks and canopies. We ran until we could run no more. Then we stood, bent over, gasping for air. Even Harry Two was panting heavily.

Slowly, we all straightened.

I looked at Delph. He stared back at me. His features wore the same expression as mine:

Terror.

Petra broke the silence and said breathlessly, "Well, I think we truly found the bloody Maladons."

"What now, Vega Jane?" said Delph.

I made us visible and said, "We need to find a place to hide out and regroup."

I was about to say something else when my wand jerked so violently to the left that I was nearly pulled off my feet. I had no way to stop it.

I was jerked through more thick forest, over a knoll, down to a narrow stream and, once I forded it, the wand pulled me back into the thicket of trees.

The others were hustling behind me, doing their best to keep up while my wand forced me along like a slep on a rope.

I raced through still more trees, dodging thick trunks and bending low to avoid branches and tearing through bushes, which left me scratched and bloody. But still my wand pulled me on. I was exhausted and growing more and more scared with each lunge of my legs and heave of my chest.

And then I cleared one last stand of trees and stopped dead.

Because my wand was no longer pulling me along.

It was simply pointing straight ahead.

I was standing in front of an old, rambling house. It was a higgledy-piggledy mix of lichen-coated stone, aged brick and blackened wood. Its roof was made of mossy slate shingles of the kind that I had seen back in Wormwood. The windows were old and mullioned and the front door was stout oak with rusted iron bands across it. Half a dozen chimneys sprouted from its roof, but not a single one belched smoke. The place looked abandoned. The grounds around it were all grown over, neglected and full of weeds. A meandering stone path led from the edge of the grounds up to the front door.

I was deciding whether to approach the house when, with a rush, Delph, Petra and Harry Two hurtled into the clearing to stand next to me.

"What the bloody Hel, Vega Jane," gasped Delph as he doubled over, sucking in air, his huge chest rising and falling erratically.

Petra looked at me suspiciously. "Are you mental or what?" she snapped. "We thought you'd gone off your bleeding rocker taking off like that without a word."

Harry Two was staring at the house I'd just discovered. It seemed like his eyes were actually sparkling at the sight of it.

"It was my wand. It . . . it had a mind of its own." I pointed at the house. "It was leading me here," I added.

Delph straightened, saw the place and gaped.

Petra gasped. "What is that thing?"

"I don't know."

"What do we do?" asked Delph.

"I reckon we should go see what's inside," I said.

"What if it's full of the kinds of blokes that were back there by the train?" he said.

"I don't think it is, Delph," I said. "This place looks like it's been abandoned a long time."

"Well, that's true enough," he said, giving it a long look.

"But what if those blokes happen upon it?" pointed out Petra. "They'll find us. It's bloody enormous. You can't exactly miss it."

She had a point there.

The next moment we heard behind us what we had all feared we would. Voices and footsteps.

"Quick," I snapped. I raced up the meandering stone path and to the front door.

The others sprinted behind me.

I saw with a quick glance that there was a brass

plate bolted to the wall next to the door. On the plate was a word.

EMPYREAN.

I had no idea what that meant.

"Vega Jane," said Delph. "Let's become invisible again before we go in."

"Good idea." I turned the ring round and attached the magical tethers. We vanished from sight.

I breathed a sigh of relief when the portal opened at my push. We all slipped through the door and I closed it quietly behind us.

We eased over to one of the windows and anxiously peered out.

Petra saw them first.

"There," she said in a low voice.

From the left a man emerged from the woods. I caught a breath, for it was Endemen.

He was immediately followed by two of his men. They all three had their wands out. Dressed in their immaculate suits with their bowler hats perched on their heads, they looked completely out of place strolling through the woods.

But they weren't strolling, I reminded myself. They were *hunting* us.

And they would kill us if they found us.

Although we were invisible, we automatically ducked down lower in the window as Endemen's gaze passed over us.

Endemen and his men were now within ten feet of the house.

I turned to Petra. "When they come into the house, if

they appear to know where we are, use the *Impacto* spell on the other two. But leave Endemen to me."

She nodded, her eyes full of fear, as I'm sure mine were.

I had tried to sound confident, but I wasn't. I had the sinking feeling that whatever spell I used against him, Endemen would easily parry it before finishing me and then the others off.

The men started toward the house. I glanced quickly at Delph. He had taken Lackland's old, rusted sword out of his tuck and was holding it ready.

Yet even as I found his gaze, I knew what he was thinking.

A sword against a wand was not really a fair fight.

Harry Two nudged my arm. At first I thought he was telling me he was ready to fight to the death, though I already knew this.

Only he wasn't.

He was nudging me to look back outside.

I did so, and received quite a shock.

Endemen and his blokes were standing around and talking in low tones.

"They must have gone another way," said one of the men to Endemen.

Endemen just kept looking around. Occasionally his gaze hit the house squarely, but he gave no reaction.

The wonderful truth hit me.

I said, "He can't see the bloody house."

"Aye, he can't," agreed Delph.

"Is it because of your invisibility spell?" asked Petra in a very low voice.

I shook my head. "I can't think how it would be able to hide a place this big."

"Look, they're heading off," exclaimed Delph.

I gaped at this, but whatever the reason, I was very glad to see the back of them.

As Endemen reached the tree line, he turned around for a moment and gazed thoughtfully in our direction.

As though attached at the hip, the four of us immediately ducked down below the windowsill.

When we looked back out a few seconds later, he was gone.

We collectively breathed a sigh of relief.

I turned to look over my shoulder at the interior of the house.

"Who lived here, I wonder?" asked Delph.

"Dunno. But I'm awfully glad it *is* here."

"What do we do now?" Petra wanted to know.

I stood erect.

"Find out what this place is, of course," I said firmly.

# Empyrean

VIRTUALLY EVERY BUILDING I'd ventured into since leaving Wormwood had held elements of incredible danger. And this place might not be any different. Yet I took solace in the fact that we were still invisible, though if anyone lived here, they would probably wonder how their front door had opened and closed apparently on its own.

"Be alert," I said to the others as we moved forward.

The first obvious thing was the size of the place. Though from the outside it didn't appear nearly that large, it seemed to me that both Stacks *and* Steeples would fit comfortably inside this place.

A suit of armor stood guard in the large entrance hallway. It was spotless, though it had several large dings in it. In a holder by its side was a long, deadly-looking sword.

Every room we entered seemed larger than the last. The walls were wood, or stone, or tile, or even metal. The furnishings were large and comfortable. There was weaponry on the walls, battle-axes and lances and knives and other things I didn't recognize, but which looked deadly enough.

The place was lighted by things we couldn't see, but it seemed to me that captured in the ceiling were little swirls of illumination, almost like the cucos we had seen back in the Quag.

There were fireplaces aplenty, and washrooms like the one I had seen at Morrigone's ages ago.

We entered a book-lined library and found a large desk and comfortable chairs. Next, there was a kitchen so enormous it was hard to see the other end. It had a huge blackened metal stove and a fireplace with a large metal pot hanging from an iron hook. There was a long wooden table for eating and a cupboard full of plates, cloth napkins, cups and utensils, all neatly stacked.

I poked my head into another cupboard that was full of food of all types, again all neatly organized and obviously fresh. This was odd since the place seemed abandoned. Though the style was old, from the worm-eaten beams on the ceiling to the venerable and colorful rugs on the knotty walnut floors, it all looked well kept, which, again, was strange.

Yet what fascinated me the most were the portraits on the walls. They were numerous, and each was of a different male or female. And they all had the names of the subject on a little brass plate attached to the frame.

Thus, I knew that it was Bastion Cadmus's painting hung over the enormous fireplace in a room that was the largest we had seen thus far. He was a tall, strongly built, fierce-looking fellow with a short black beard, startling green eyes and thick brows that nearly touched in the center of his forehead. I could understand why our lot had made him their leader. His masterful, tough, confident appearance seemed to fit the type.

So was this his old home? If so, that gave me some hope.

At least I knew he was a good bloke. And yet I wondered what had happened to this place after he had died. Had it passed into the hands of his descendants? But if our lot had fled to Wormwood, they couldn't have stayed here. Had the Maladons taken it over? But Endemen and his cronies couldn't see the place, which argued against it having fallen into Maladon hands.

Not knowing really what to think, I turned away from the portrait and kept exploring.

Astrea Prine occupied a prominent place in the library between two sets of bookcases. She looked like she had when we'd stayed at her cottage in the Quag. Young, intense, a bit foreboding really. A portrait of my ancestor Jasper Jane hung in a dark corner of a short hallway. I didn't know if this was because he liked to dabble in *dark* sorcery or not. But he had helped me in the Quag, or at least his soul had, so I had nothing but good feelings about him. Although the Fifth Circle of the Quag, which he had designed, had very nearly killed us all!

And then there were many other portraits of people I had never heard of, but who apparently held some important place in the magical world.

I found Delph in one corner of a room off the main hall staring at something.

I went over to him. "Delph, what is it?"

In answer he pointed to a painting on the wall. It was a male astride a winged slep, or *horse* I guess these blokes would call it. And on his shoulder was a large, menacing-looking hawk.

"Who is it?"

He pointed to the nameplate at the bottom of the painting.

"Samuel Delphia?" I read. "Delph, he's an ancestor of yours," I added excitedly.

Delph nodded. "And it looks like he gets along with beasts. Same as Dad. Bet they woulda got on right well."

I put my hand on his shoulder. "I bet they would have."

He rubbed his eyes and wiped at his nose. "I miss him, y'know, me dad. Hope he's okay."

"I miss him too, Delph. But remember, he wanted you to leave Wormwood."

"I know, Vega Jane, I know."

He rubbed his eyes again, and then his expression changed.

"Hang on, though."

"What?"

"Well, there was that bloke Barnabas Delphia back at Wolvercote Cemetery. And now Samuel. They were both magical, I 'spect."

"I guess so," I said slowly.

"But I'm not. No mark on my hand or nothing."

He said this lightly, but I could tell by his features that he so desperately wanted it not to be true. Delph wanted to be magical. But it wasn't in my power to make him so.

"I know I never would have gotten this far without you, wand or not."

He thanked me with a smile and then looked around. "You think this is a friendly place, eh, Vega Jane? I mean, it seems to only have our kind in the paintings. No Maladons, right?"

"R-right," I said cautiously. "But remember how things started with Astrea Prine. And she's our kind."

At my words, Delph instantly gripped his sword more tightly even as Petra and I kept our wands at the ready.

I *wanted* to believe that this was a friendly place, but I had been fooled before.

Finally, starving as we were, I led us back to the kitchen — with enormous enthusiasm from Delph — and we set about making a meal, although I cautioned that we should keep our guard up. There was no telling what was in this place, or whether Endemen and his fiendish cronies might come back and suddenly see this pile of stone and brick good and proper. So I decided to keep us invisible.

I got the stove hot and put cured ham and sausages and a great slab of beef that was perfectly fresh into a big skillet. Petra started cutting vegetables she'd found in bins in the pantry. And Delph got the kettle in the fireplace filled with water from a pump in the sink and started a fire under it. He announced that he would be making soup.

There was a chamber off the kitchen behind a thick door. It was freezing inside and for good reason. In addition to the meat I had already gotten out, there was milk and cheeses and other perishables, including dough for bread. I took as much as I could carry.

Very soon the aromas of all the cooking food commingled into a mass of flavorful scents that made my mouth water. Poor Harry Two was actually panting in anticipation.

But this was not making me feel more comfortable. It was making me feel more on edge.

Petra sidled over to me and whispered, "Vega, all this food here is good and fresh."

I nodded, knowing exactly where she was going with this.

"Someone lives here," I whispered back. "And they might be here right now."

"So I wonder when they're going to show themselves?"

"Well, *we* haven't shown ourselves yet."

"Right, but they must know someone is here. We're moving things around."

"They might be scared. Things floating through the air and all."

"They might," she said, clearly not believing this.

Petra and I had laid out the plates, bowls, cups, utensils and napkins on the long wooden table.

I put food down for Harry Two, and when everything was ready we commenced eating, and didn't stop until our bellies were near to bursting. I had never had enough food to eat growing up. So I savored every mouthful, every bite and every swallow of the deliciously cool milk. I did so because I had no idea what the next day would hold for us.

We finished our meal and walked up to the second floor of the house, reached by a broad, balustraded stairway that reminded me of the one at Stacks.

I looked at the others. "Okay, with all the food and such here it seems that this place is *not* abandoned, yet we haven't seen anyone. But they could be hiding. Now, we could all stay together and invisible for the night. That might be best."

"Are you nutters?" Petra snapped. "That'll make us one bleeding easy target, all together like that. We searched this floor. There's no one up here and there are three bedrooms in a row. We can each take one and we'll be close enough to cry out if something happens." She paused and gazed appraisingly at Delph. "Or Delph can stay with me and Harry Two with you."

"Why not Delph with me and Harry Two with you?" I retorted.

"Because your canine is loyal to you, that's why. He'll be pining all night for you. So Delph with me. And we each have a wand. So that works."

I glanced at Delph, whose face was turning redder by the second. "Each going to our own bedrooms works just fine," I said tersely. "Delph's room can be in the middle and I can put a *shield* spell on his door so *nobody* can disturb him."

Petra looked at me, and I thought I saw a condescending smile begin to tug at her mouth.

I took a deep breath and convinced myself not to attack her.

I released the tethers, and we said our good nights and trudged off.

I turned my ring around so I became visible. If anything were going to attack us, I didn't want them to only go after Delph and Petra.

My bedchamber was large and well-furnished. I hung up my few pieces of clothing in an ornately carved wardrobe, undressed and climbed into bed.

The house had inexplicably grown dark as soon as we finished our meal, so we had found and lit some candles, which we had carried upstairs.

Harry Two jumped up onto the bed and settled down at the foot of it.

I blew out my candle and lay my head back against the pillow.

That's when I saw it.

Or rather *her*.

I very nearly screamed.

She was staring down at me from the ceiling.

Then I realized it was simply a painting of a young woman. She had long, flowing blond hair and large blue eyes. Her cheeks were pink and healthy, but the expression on her face wiped all of that glowing beauty away.

I don't believe I'd ever seen a sadder look in all my life.

I felt my own mouth curving downward into a frown as I stared at her.

I wondered who she was. And why was her portrait on the ceiling and not framed on the wall like the others?

I sat up, and then something else struck me. How could I see her in the darkness? There was no light coming from the window. When I had blown out my candle, I could barely see Harry Two lying a few feet from me. And yet the ceiling was a good twenty feet high.

It made no sense.

I lit my candle to get a better look.

And received my second shock.

She'd disappeared. The ceiling was now merely blank plaster.

I thrust off my bedcovers and stood on the bed and then on my tiptoes to get a better look. I held my candle as high as I could.

Yet there was nothing to see.

I sat back down and blew out the candle.

And waited.

Sure enough, there she appeared.

Then I blinked and rubbed my eyes. A stroke of fear slashed through me.

Her hair was still long and still blond.

But now it was moving.

I instinctively grabbed my wand off the nightstand and held it ready.

I had experienced so many surprises going through the Quag and now in this new place that I well knew that anything, no matter how innocent it might first appear, could be planning to murder me.

But she made no sudden movements. Her eyes now blinked and her mouth moved slightly. I had the distinct impression that she was watching me, perhaps wondering what I was doing here.

What happened next proved me right.

"Who are you?"

The words floated down to me, soft, lovely sounding, but inked in them was, well, despair, I guessed, coupled with an enormous feeling of loss.

"I-I'm . . ." *Steeples help me, I'd forgotten my own name!*

"Vega . . . I'm Vega Jane," I finally managed to blurt out.

I grabbed a quick breath when the woman, body and all, floated down from the ceiling to sit next to me.

I couldn't take my eyes off her, but I did see, in my peripheral vision, Harry Two turn to stare at her. But he made no sound. This buoyed my spirits because my canine always sensed danger before I did.

"Vega Jane?" she said.

The large eyes took me in, from head to foot.

I nodded. "Who are you?"

"I am called Uma."

*Uma? Uma?* I had seen that name somewhere; I just couldn't remember where.

"Is this your home?" I asked.

The thing was, I could see pretty much right through her. And her clothes were not of this time. She was clearly from the past.

"No. But I came here often. I like it here."

"Are you . . . ?"

She nodded. "I *am* dead. And have been for a very long time."

Then it struck me where I'd seen the name before. On a gravestone at Wolvercote Cemetery, right before we'd entered the First Circle of the Quag.

"You're Uma Cadmus?"

She nodded.

"Your father was Bastion Cadmus?"

She nodded again.

"Are you a ghost?"

She shook her head. "Not a ghost, no."

"I'm not seeing your soul then, am I? I saw my ancestor Jasper Jane's soul once."

"No, I am not a soul."

Well, I had exhausted all my possible choices. "What are you, then?"

"Regret."

"Regret? What exactly does that mean? We all have regrets."

"Indeed we do. But some are far greater than others. And if they are powerful enough, they can consume you completely. That is my fate. For eternity."

And with that ominous answer, she vanished. I lay back in bed after giving Harry Two a reassuring pat.

So this wasn't her home, even though there was a large painting of her father downstairs. So this place must have belonged to someone else. And regret? I wondered what she regretted so much.

I pulled the bedcovers up closer around me, as though the bit of fabric would protect me from all evil.

And that's when I heard the scream.

# This House of Mine

A S I PASSED Delph's bedroom, I heard him pounding on the door. I released my shield spell and the door flew open, revealing Delph in his nightshirt.

He gasped, "Who's screaming?"

"It's Petra!" I exclaimed.

We ran to her door, Harry Two growling and barking with concern.

I had my wand out and ready.

Delph reached the door first and tried to open it. He bounced off.

Petra screamed again.

Delph charged the door once more, slamming his full weight against it.

He was flung back off like he weighed nothing.

I pointed my wand and said, "*Ingressio.*"

My spell rebounded, but I saw the door buckle a bit.

"*Impacto,*" I cried out, and the door exploded into fragments.

We rushed inside to see Petra hanging upside down from the ceiling, a maelstrom of light, flashing figures and fire all around her struggling body. Things were striking her from all angles, and each collision caused another cut or slash to her skin.

I was so stunned by what I was seeing that for a moment I didn't know what to do.

"Vega! Help me!"

I broke out of my muddle to see Petra looking at me with panicked eyes.

I raised my wand and cast a shield spell around her.

The lightning-fast objects bounced off it and whizzed around the room.

Delph, Harry Two and I had to duck down as a wall of out-of-control flying objects shot over our heads.

I raised my wand once more. *"Paralycto."*

The explosion of whizzing things froze in midair.

We all slowly rose. I pointed my wand at Petra at the same time as I said to Delph, "Get ready."

I shouted, *"Unlassado."*

A light shot out from the point of my wand and hit the ceiling next to Petra's feet.

She was freed, and plummeted to the floor.

Or she would have if Delph had not been there to catch her.

I watched, a bit unhappily, as she wrapped her arms around Delph's thick neck and buried her weeping face in his massive chest.

"'Tis okay," he murmured to her. "'Tis all right now, Pet."

Delph looked over at me. Then his gaze drifted behind me and I saw his eyes widen in terror.

I whirled around, my wand at the ready.

The breath caught in my throat.

In the doorway stood the suit of armor that had been in the entrance hallway. Even as I watched, a gloved hand rose and opened the metal visor.

I staggered back because there was no face behind the visor, only darkness.

A voice boomed out as the gloved hand pointed straight at Petra.

"*She* is a Maladon! *She* must die the death of a thousand wounds."

I kept my wand raised even as I thought how best to respond to this accusation, which I knew to be, in part, true.

I turned to look at Petra. Her face was no longer buried in Delph's chest.

She was staring at the suit of armor.

"I'm . . . I'm not a Maladon," she said weakly.

"Liar," roared the armor. "We know. We always know when one is in our midst. And we are never wrong. We waited until she was alone, lest she try to hurt the two of you." Now the helmeted head turned in my direction. "You are obviously a sorceress and not a Maladon. Thus, you must kill her. She is your sworn enemy."

"No," I said. "She's not my enemy. She's my friend."

"*Kill her!*" The suit of armor screamed so loudly that I thought for a moment my eardrums had shattered.

"No," I yelled back.

"Then you leave me no choice."

He drew out his long sword and raised it up high in preparation for the killing stroke.

I backed away until I was standing between the armor and Petra.

"To kill her, you have to kill me. And I'm, well, I'm a bloody handful, I am," I finished awkwardly.

The armor stared at me, if a faceless thing can stare, that is.

For a moment I thought he *was* going to attack me.

"You turn against your own people?" said the armor accusingly.

"I turn against no one, uh, what is your name?" I asked, trying to calm matters. I had no idea whether my wand would be enough to defeat this thing. And since it appeared that he really was on my side, I didn't want to hurt the metal bloke if I didn't have to.

"Lord Unctuous of Pillsbury," he announced in a dignified voice.

"Okay, Lord, um, is it Lord Unctuous, or Lord Pillsbury, or do I have to say all the words when addressing you?"

He took a moment to consider this. "Lord Pillsbury will suffice," he said, his metal chest puffing out a bit.

"Right. Okay, Lord Pillsbury. Petra here has helped me fight and defeat a number of Maladons already. And we managed to escape a bloke calling himself Mr. Endemen, right beyond the trees that surround this place."

When I said the name Endemen, I saw Lord Pillsbury flinch. Or at least his metal body did.

He said gruffly, "Endemen? Endemen, did you say?"

"Yes, I do say. Who is he?"

"A Maladon," barked Pillsbury. "A horrible, mad, evil, ruthless, disgusting —"

"Right," I said, interrupting. "Well, that one I'd figured out on my own."

"He is very dangerous," Lord Pillsbury said more soberly.

"I saw him kill two blokes and smile about it."

Lord Pillsbury shivered in his armored hide. "Most distasteful."

I had a sudden idea. "But he couldn't see this place, could he?"

"Obviously not. Else he would be inside now attempting to murder us all. The enchantments around this structure are designed to make it totally invisible to Maladons."

"So true Maladons can't see this place at all?"

"Precisely."

I pointed at Petra. "But *she* can see this place, obviously. She's inside it. So logically speaking she can't be a Maladon."

Again, Pillsbury seemed to flinch. His visor swiveled around to Petra. He looked her up and down. A moment later he swiveled back to stare at me.

"I think you might have a point," he conceded.

"I think I might," I said smoothly.

He lowered his sword. "'Tis a bit delicate, though. Our anti-Maladon warning enchantments are normally quite accurate."

"Your best one being that this place is hidden from them?" I said.

All the combativeness seemed to drain from him. "Quite right. Well, absolutely no sense in allies fighting among themselves."

I relaxed and lowered my wand. Now something he'd said made me curious.

"Lord Pillsbury, you said you had never been wrong about Maladons being in your midst."

"Absolutely."

"But if they can't see this place, how could a true Maladon ever come to be here?"

"Ah, well, that was *before*, wasn't it?"

"Before what?"

"Before the war. Before they started calling themselves the *Maladons* actually," he added derisively.

I still didn't completely understand, but I was curious about something else. "And you're . . . what, exactly?"

"I'm part of the rear guard, left behind to do our best to prevent the Maladons from finding any of our kind or what they left behind. And also to do whatever we can to wreak havoc on the blasted creatures. We've been quite successful with the first part."

"And the wreaking havoc on the Maladons part?" I inquired.

"No luck at all, I'm afraid. But it's early days yet," he added confidently.

"Early days!" Delph blurted out. "It's been about eight hundred bloody years, mate."

Lord Pillsbury stiffened once more. "Has it really? Well, that obviously shines a different light on things, I suppose."

"Uh, Vega Jane?"

This came from Delph, who was still holding Petra in his big arms, much to my annoyance.

"Yes, Delph?"

"She's bleedin' and all," he said, indicating Petra.

"Holy Steeples," I cried out. I ran past Lord Pillsbury,

dashed down the hall, grabbed the Adder Stone from my cloak, ran back and waved it over Petra, thinking good thoughts. Her cuts and gashes instantly vanished, along with the blood.

I looked at Delph. "I think you can let her down now, Delph," I said, trying to sound as casual as possible, though part of me wanted to rip her out of his arms.

"Right."

He nearly dropped poor Petra on the floor.

I tried not so very hard to hide my smile.

I turned back to Lord Pillsbury, who was staring at me closely.

"Did . . . did this young gentleman call you Vega *Jane?*"

"Well, that is my name."

"Do you mean to say that you're a *Jane?*"

"Yes. And this is Delph Delphia and Petra Sonnet and my canine, Harry Two. We were in the town of True; do you know it?"

His helmeted head swiveled back and forth. "No. But then again, we never leave this place."

"Which might be why you haven't managed to wreak havoc on the Maladons," I replied gently.

"Once more, I believe you have a point, milady."

"How many more of you are there?"

"Oh, about four dozen, if you count the outside staff and the lads in the cellar."

"Are you all suits of armor?"

"Oh, no. I'm the only one of those. The majordomo, as it were. The rest are a mishmash of lamps, the odd bit of furniture, various household instruments, that sort of thing. Oh, and some portraits, though they don't get around much, being hung on a wall and all, but they do add a bit of style, I've always thought. And five marble statues, three rakes, two wheelbarrows and a scythe that take care of the grounds. All good blokes."

Petra said in a contemptuous tone, "Well, the grounds are in pretty bad shape. Maybe you should spend more time tending them rather than trying to kill your bloody guests!"

"Petra," admonished Delph. "They didn't know."

"They bloody well didn't ask either. They just stormed in here and commenced attacking me!"

Lord Pillsbury nodded his visor. "I do apologize for our, well, our unseemly behavior. Now, in answer to your observation about the grounds, there's been no real reason to keep them up, having no one staying here who can enjoy them."

"How did you all come to be?" I asked.

"Our masters bewitched us long ago. Long before the war. We served them faithfully." He added somberly, "Right up until the end."

"When I mentioned the Endemen bloke, you seemed to know who he is."

"Yes."

"How can that be if you never leave this place and he can't see that it's here?"

"We've seen him lurking outside. I reckon he knows something is here, he just doesn't know what. And I've heard some of his men refer to him by that name, Mr. Endemen." He paused.

"And what?" I said, sensing there was something else.

"And we've also seen him kill."

"Kill; kill what?"

"Folks he brings around here. And animals. He kills animals for pleasure," he added disgustedly.

I had hated Endemen up to this point. Now I positively loathed the foul man. I automatically put out a hand and scratched Harry Two's one remaining ear.

"What would you do if he finally overcame the enchantment and was able to see this place?"

"We would of course fight to the death. Those were our instructions. We would gladly give our lives — well, whatever it is we actually have, to defend this place."

I looked around. "And this place? What exactly is it?"

"Why, if you're truly a Jane, you should know."

"Know what?"

"Empyrean is your ancestral home, Mistress Vega."

## A Heart Revealed

M-MY AN . . . cestral h-home?" I spluttered.

Lord Pillsbury nodded. "Absolutely."

"Wait a mo'. I saw a brass plate by the front door with the name you just mentioned. *Empyrean*."

"Yes. That is the name of our home. And now yours."

"Do you know which Janes lived here?" I said excitedly.

"Well, at the very end of course it was Mistress Alice Adronis."

"But her last name wasn't Jane," I countered.

"Her *maiden* name was Jane. She married Gunther Adronis and he came to live here with her. You might have seen his portrait. He was quite bighearted, was Master Gunther." He added sadly, "Perhaps too bighearted."

I was dazed by these revelations.

"So you knew them?" I asked.

If a suit of armor could show emotion, Lord Pillsbury had just accomplished it. The metal seemed to shimmer with some strong feeling.

"I had the honor of *serving* them, yes."

"What were they like?" I asked. I well remembered the dying Alice Adronis. She had seemed noble and brave and all those good things. But I also knew that Alice was one of the fiercest warriors our side had, killing Maladons left and right.

"They were very kind, Mistress Vega. Very kind indeed. They wanted no part of a war. But they fought because, well, they had to."

It was as though the metal bloke had read my mind.

"That's good to know, Lord Pillsbury."

"Please, make it merely Pillsbury. Since you are a Jane, I am but your humble servant. The lord part is just for, uh, *show* to certain . . . persons." He cleared his throat in an embarrassed fashion.

I felt myself blush a bit. "You don't have to serve me. I'm used to doing things on my own."

"Please," he said in a pained voice. "We've really had nothing to do for the longest time. It would bring all of us much joy to be able to once more serve the House of Jane. The outside staff is champing at the bit to get the grounds up to snuff, I can tell you that. And now they have proper reason."

I glanced at Delph and Petra. They were standing there openmouthed, no doubt as gobsmacked as I was by this development.

I turned back to Pillsbury. "Well, all right, Lo — um, I mean, Pillsbury. If you're sure?"

He clicked his metallic heels. "Quite sure, milady. Quite, quite sure. Now, as it is rather late, I would suggest that you all return to your bedchambers. That will give us time to spruce up the place. Bit of dust everywhere. We were not expecting company, you see. Would you like to convey your breakfast orders now, or shall I receive them after you've awoken?"

"You'll prepare our meals?" I said, rather stunned by this.

"Of course. That is one of the chief roles of a household staff. And you will find that Mrs. Jolly is a very fine cook."

"Mrs. Jolly?" I said. "We made ourselves dinner, but we didn't see anyone in the kitchen."

"Well, the fact is, Mistress Vega, we couldn't see you! Gave us quite a turn when doors started opening and pans, knives and plates started floating through the air. Thus, Mrs. Jolly was quite naturally hiding in the broom closet half frightened out of her twigs. And then when we *could* see you, we of course showed ourselves."

"You mean you attacked me!" blurted out Petra.

"Well, that's all water under the bridge now," said Pillsbury cheerfully.

I said, "You said she was half frightened out of *her twigs*. What exactly is Mrs. Jolly?"

"She *exactly* is a broom, hence the broom cupboard. But she does a steak and kidney pudding that is, well, if I required food, I'm sure I would enjoy it very much. Now, your orders? Or shall you prefer to wait?"

Delph spoke up at once. "I'll have, well, pretty much everything."

Pillsbury swept a long quill from the inside of his visor and wrote this down on the metal palm of his hand. "Full-on breakfast, outstanding." He looked up at the enormous Delph. "Yes," he said appraisingly. "I would imagine it takes quite a lot of wood to keep your chimney hot, young sir."

His visor came to rest on Petra. She scowled back at him.

Petra said tightly, "So when we separated into our bedrooms and then you could see us, you decided *I* was the dangerous Maladon?"

89

Pillsbury, perhaps noting this — it was quite hard to tell without a face — said in an apologetic voice, "That is just what happened, miss, yes. Ever so sorry that we got off on the wrong foot. Now, what can we arrange for your breakfast?"

She suddenly looked uncertain. "Well, um, I guess a spot of tea and some biscuits would be nice."

I added quietly, "I'm sure Petra is just being polite so as not to overtax Mrs. Jolly, Pillsbury. None of us have had much to eat lately, and I know that Petra has a wonderful appetite, so perhaps you might suggest some things for her, and for me too. I'm not sure what to ask for either."

Petra shot me a glance, her features full of surprise at my words.

Pillsbury said delightedly, "Oh, absolutely, milady. Some eggs, perhaps? Mrs. Jolly does a wonderful omelette with bacon and tomato with just a touch of the freshest basil. I do love a good pesto fragrance in the morning," he added enthusiastically.

"Yes, thanks," said Petra, bravely attempting a grin.

"And of course Mrs. Jolly prides herself on her croissants; perhaps a couple of those. And then there's the porridge, piping hot and so filling. And what would breakfast be without some plump sausages, eh?"

"That . . . that sounds wonderful," said Petra.

"Smashing," said Pillsbury, before turning to me. "And you, Mistress Vega?"

"I'll have what Petra's having," I replied, glancing surreptitiously at Delph. "We like the same things, apparently."

Pillsbury wrote all this on his palm. "Excellent. Well." He looked at the pulverized door and then at me. "Mistress Vega, would you care to do the honors with your wand? Or would you rather I summoned one of the lads to clean this up?"

"What? Oh, right, I'll fix it."

I pointed my wand at the shards of wood, recalled the proper incantation Astrea had taught me and said, "*Assemblage.*"

The pieces of wood flew back together into a door that hung itself neatly back on the hinges.

"And may I say very nicely done, Mistress Vega," said Pillsbury.

"You don't have to call me that, you know."

"Oh, but we do. As a Jane, you are now the mistress of this house. And we are here to serve you."

"Okay. But how do you know I really am a Jane? I just said I was. I could be lying."

He pointed a metal hand at my wand. "That is Mistress Alice's wand. I will never forget it. It was also her —"

"Elemental," I said, cutting in.

"Precisely so. Only a true Jane could wield magic with it."

I glanced at the re-formed door. "So that was a test, then?"

"I do apologize. But one can never be too careful in such troubled times, milady. Now I'm off. I hope you sleep well. If at any time you need anything, you only need to say my name and I shall appear."

And with that remark he turned and lumbered out of the room.

We all looked at one another.

Delph gasped, "Pretty bloody unbelievable."

Petra was looking around in awe. "Of all the bleeding luck. You walk in here and you're the 'milady' of the place."

"I had no idea it was my family's house when I got here," I reminded her.

"I know. It's just . . ." Her voice trailed off, and she looked away.

I glanced at Delph. "You should head off to bed," I said.

He glanced at Petra, then back at me.

"You sure?"

"Quite sure," I replied firmly. "I'd like a quiet word with Petra before I turn in."

"Well, if you're su —"

"Delph!"

He nearly ran out of the room.

I turned to face Petra, who sat back on the bed looking defiantly at me.

"I'm not one of those Maladons," she said sharply. "I don't care what their blasted enchanted whatsit says."

"No, I don't believe you are."

"Yes, you do!" she shot back. "I see the way you and Delph look at me. And even Harry Two there watches me closely, like I'll attack you or something given the chance."

"I think you're being a bit silly about this."

"Silly! I was very nearly killed by your *servants*!"

"And I stopped them, didn't I?" I snapped. She was about to say something else, but I suppose my harsh words gave her pause.

She said grudgingly, "Yes, you did. And I thank you for that."

"You're welcome. But my point is, why would I have done that if I thought you were a Maladon?"

"Well, I've got Maladon blood in me, haven't I?"

"But you can *see* this place, can't you? So even if you have a bit of Maladon blood in you, it's obviously been outweighed by, well, good stuff."

"So what? Someone in my family was your enemy. I don't know who it was, but it's tainted me. I'm not like you. I'm . . . I'm unclean or something. Leastways I feel like I am."

I sat on the bed next to her. I could actually understand how she was feeling. I felt that way back in Wormwood when I discovered I had powers that no one else there did. And I also wanted to know things about my past. I wanted to know what was beyond the Quag. Other than Delph, no one in Wormwood was interested in any of that. It made me feel like an outsider, like I didn't belong. Like I was different in a bad way.

"Petra, you have no way of controlling who your ancestors were, or what they did. Same as me."

"But at least your ancestors were good. They fought to protect themselves from the Maladons. And if this Endemen bloke is what all Maladons are like, well, they're just evil. Which . . . which means that I . . . that I . . ." Her lips trembled and she couldn't finish. She looked away so I wouldn't see the tears in her eyes.

I put a hand on her shoulder. "You've had plenty of chances to be evil, Petra. You could have hurt us easily enough when we were going through the Quag, but instead you helped us get through. Without you we wouldn't have made it. You were brave and strong and you fought *against* the evil. Not for it."

"But what if . . . what if down the road I change. What if . . ."

"You become evil because Maladon blood runs in your veins?"

She was looking at me now, her features twitching. I knew what she wanted me to say: that she could never become evil. That she could never truly become a Maladon. But I couldn't say that because I wasn't sure if she could or not. I could only say what I was feeling.

"I trust you, Petra. I've trusted you with my life before. And I will trust you with my life again."

"You really mean that?"

"I really mean that," I answered, squeezing her shoulder.

She wouldn't meet my gaze, and under the pressure of my fingers, I could feel her trembling. She slowly turned to look at me, her face so rigid that I thought someone had cast the *Subservio* spell on her.

Finally, after a few moments, her features relaxed, and she touched my hand with hers and said, "I trust you too, Vega. You, well, you saved my life, more times than I can count."

"We have to be there for each other. We're both magical. Delph isn't. We can't let anything happen to him."

"I'd die before I let him come to any harm," she said immediately.

This both pleased and bothered me.

Petra had very clearly lost her heart to Delph.

And love was a funny thing. It could be wonderful and positive and simply good.

Or it could be the power behind things truly ugly. And right now I had no way of knowing how her feelings for Delph would turn out.

"Get some sleep," I said.

She nodded and climbed under the covers.

As I reached the door, I turned to see her watching me.

Her look was searching but also somehow inscrutable.

I closed the door behind me and walked slowly back to my room with Harry Two beside me.

I shut and locked my door and climbed under the covers.

I took out my wand and stared at it. I hadn't had it all that long, and yet now it seemed like I had never been without it. Even had I not known that Empyrean was Alice Adronis's home, I should have. Because the wand had sensed the proximity of the place and had led me right here.

Alice and her husband, Gunther. Uma Cadmus. Her father, Bastion. All the rest of the men and women in those portraits all over this place. They were my past. Some were my family. My future too would be borne out by what happened here in the days ahead.

But after so much danger and nearly losing our lives, it was so very wonderful to have a safe haven such as this. Food in our bellies, a house full of loyal servants, warm beds and rooms to explore. I stretched out like a feline, so good did I feel about all of it. Part of me thought I could spend the rest of my life here, and quite pleasantly indeed.

I fell asleep with this sole thought in mind.

## Uma and Jason

THE RAPPING ON the door brought me awake. I rubbed my eyes and sat up in bed.

"Hello?" I said groggily.

"'Tis Pillsbury with your breakfast, Mistress Vega."

"Oh, okay. Come in, then."

Harry Two popped up when the door opened, and there was Pillsbury, his metal gleaming so brightly that I suspected he might have polished himself up during the night. He was carrying a short-legged wooden table, upon which sat several dishes covered with pewter lids.

"If you would care to sit up just a bit more, milady," he said graciously as he approached the bed.

Confused, I sat up straight against my pillow.

Pillsbury placed the little table over my lap while I further adjusted my position to accommodate this rather strange way of having one's meal.

He uncovered the dish lids, and my eyes lit up when I saw the foods underneath. And then I took a deep breath and the most wonderful smells invaded my nose.

I looked up at him and said in a near moan, "This is fantastic, Pillsbury."

"Mrs. Jolly will be so pleased." He uncovered one more bowl, which had a divider. One half was filled with food and the other with water.

"I took the liberty of preparing Harry Two's meal as well."

He set this on the floor, and Harry Two jumped down, gave a bark of thanks and dug in.

Pillsbury unrolled my cloth napkin and handed it to me, and then poured out a steaming cup of tea.

"I hope everything will be to your liking, Mistress Vega."

"I'm sure it will. And I'll be sure to pop down to the kitchen and tell Mrs. Jolly myself."

"She would be extremely pleased and honored if you did," he said, his metal visor seeming to beam with pleasure at my words. "Now, tuck in and I shall leave you to it. When you're done, you need only say 'Pillsbury' and I will return straightaway to collect the dishes."

As he turned to leave I said, "Uh, Pillsbury?"

He immediately pivoted. "Yes, milady?"

"I had a visitor in my room last night. Her name was Uma?"

The metallic Pillsbury seemed to wilt under my words.

"Oh, dear. I had no idea. I thought she might have left us. It has been a very long time since I've seen her."

"I know she's Bastion Cadmus's daughter. And I saw her grave in the Quag at Wolvercote Cemetery. But that's really all I know."

He seemed to leap back at my words.

"You . . . you saw her grave?" he sputtered.

"Yes, I did. The tombstone said —" I paused, thinking back.

Pillsbury said somberly, "The Strength of Love, the Fallacy of Youth."

I looked at him in amazement. "Yes. How did you know?"

"We knew the Cadmuses well," he said. "They visited here often when Mistress Alice was alive. Such happy times. But it was so very sad what happened. Her father was so cut up over it, I can tell you that."

"What *did* happen?"

He said imploringly, "Please, miss, your food will grow cold."

I looked down at the tray, my stomach overcoming my brain.

"Okay, but when I'm done, will you tell me?"

"You need only utter my name," he said a bit grimly.

He left, and I instantly started to eat. The food was wonderful. I thought I could hear myself purring.

Twenty minutes later I was done. I pondered what to do next. I moved the tray aside and opened the door next to my bed. This was a washroom, like at Morrigone's back in Wormwood.

I did my business, cleaned up, changed into fresh clothes, left my room and knocked on Delph's door.

"Delph? Are you decent?"

The door opened, and Delph stood there fully dressed in some of the clothes we had nicked from Saint Necro's back in True. A white shirt with a collar, a vest, a tweed jacket and pants, and sturdy shoes. He had cleaned up and washed his hair, which was long, thick and smelled wonderful.

"Have you finished eating?" I said, a bit wonky from how he looked and smelled.

I glanced over my shoulder to see that Pillsbury had had to bring in an entire rolling table to accommodate Delph's "full-on breakfast." I could also see that every plate and bowl was so empty, they looked clean.

"Yep," he said. "That Mrs. Jolly knows her way round the dishes, she does."

"Can you come back to my room? Pillsbury will be joining us. He's going to talk about some stuff I want you to hear."

"Okay. Er, what about Petra?"

I glanced down the hall toward Petra's door. "After last night, let's just let her have a lie-in," I said.

Delph looked at me uncertainly. But he fell in behind me as we walked back to my room.

We arrived and I said the name "Pillsbury."

He instantly appeared at the door, as though he could perform the *Pass-pusay* incantation.

"Yes, Mistress Vega? All done, are we?"

"Yes, Pillsbury, and it was absolutely amazing. Now, I want you to tell Delph and me about Uma Cadmus."

Delph glanced sharply at me but said nothing. I didn't know if he recalled Uma's name on the gravestone back at Wolvercote Cemetery.

Pillsbury marched forward slowly. "Yes, miss, of course." He hesitated, his metal feet shuffling a bit, his visor pointed to the floor. "Where to begin, where to begin. I wonder."

"Perhaps at the very beginning?" I suggested in what I hoped was a helpful tone.

"Yes, yes, of course." He cleared his throat as Delph and I settled down in two comfortable chairs to listen.

99

"Bastion Cadmus was the leader of our people, and he and his wife, Victoria, had only one child, Uma. She was everything to them."

"Then it's doubly sad that she died so young," I said.

"Yes," said Pillsbury, not meeting my gaze. "Very sad indeed. Well, anyway, Uma was a lovely girl. Beautiful on the outside, and so full of goodness on the inside. And as she grew up, it naturally became a topic of discussion and speculation as to whom she might marry one day."

"I'm sure there were many young men who would have been right happy to marry her," I said.

"Oh, indeed there were. Yes. But you have to understand that this was before the war with the Maladons. However, things were already happening that would lead to that terrible clash. The Maladons' leader, the accursed Necro —"

"Necro?" I exclaimed. "There's a Saint Necro in the town of True. It's a place where people go to worship."

"Indeed?" he said curiously. "Well, Necro's followers *did* worship him, though he was a foul man."

"You knew him?"

"He came here, several times. You see, there were efforts to forestall a war. Talks, discussions, negotiations. The Janes and the Adronises and Bastion Cadmus were at the head of this effort. I well remember the bloke. His face, oh so pale and smooth, and his voice, so silky. But there was pure evil in him. I knew from the moment I laid eyes on him that these efforts to avoid an all-out war were doomed from the start. Necro wanted to be the ruler not simply of the Maladons, but of *everyone.*"

"And Uma?"

"Well, Uma *did* find a young man whom she dearly loved. His name was Jason."

I glanced over at Delph but just for a moment.

"That's, um, nice," I said.

"He was the son of Necro."

"What?" I nearly shrieked.

"Blimey," said Delph. "That was a bit awkward, eh?"

"More than a bit," conceded Pillsbury. "Anyway, they kept their relationship a secret for a long time. But it was eventually discovered."

"And what happened?" I asked.

"At first folks thought it was a positive development, because with the way things were deteriorating between the two camps, it was believed that a truce might be possible. And there were those who felt that perhaps Jason, who was very unlike his devilish father, might come to power one day and ensure peace, aided by his wife, Uma. But alas, that was not to be."

"Why not?"

"Jason died," Pillsbury said simply.

I exclaimed, "He died? But he must have been very young."

"Oh, he was. Not more than twenty."

Delph said, "How did he die?"

With this question, Pillsbury seemed to collapse. His metal just drooped like a flower in the hot sun.

"He was stabbed. His killer was never caught, but there were suspicions."

"Like what?" I asked.

"That his father had had him killed because Jason was in

love with Uma. You see, Necro did not want a truce. He wanted war."

"But to kill his own son?" I said.

"As I told you, Necro was evil. He would kill anyone if it meant his rise to power would continue."

"And Uma?" I asked.

"So very sad. When she discovered that Jason had been killed, she put stones into her pockets, walked into deep water and drowned herself."

"Holy Steeples!" I exclaimed.

Delph shook his head sadly. "'Tain't right," he said. "Just ain't right."

"Then what happened?" I asked breathlessly.

"Well, Necro of course claimed that our side had murdered his son. He swore revenge. He rallied his followers. All talk of peace crumbled. And . . . and the war commenced." He paused, tried to say something but couldn't.

"And our lot lost," I finished for him.

His visor nodded up and down. "Yes, quite so. Our lot lost."

As he finished speaking, I had only one thought:

*Don't let us lose again.*

After a few moments of silence, Pillsbury said brightly, "Would you care to see Jasper Jane's workshop? It's quite interesting. And located in the highest turret here."

"Yes, please," I said.

And so we set off.

# A Painting Comes Calling

IT WAS A bit unnerving, really, seeing my ancestor Jasper Jane's chambers. This was because they reminded me a great deal of Thorne's laboratory back in the Quag. As Pillsbury had noted, it was on the very highest turret at Empyrean. He had brought me, Delph and Harry Two up here straight away.

There were tables and benches overflowing with odd devices, and reams of parchments covered in spidery handwriting. Shelves and cabinets against the walls were crammed with bottles containing different colored liquids and jars with bits of things I didn't recognize. Big bottles with tubing connecting them were perched on one long table in the center of the room. Little canisters I recognized as the flame boxes we used at Stacks were under some of the bottles. There were also boxes of powders, and huge books that would take me a long time to read, provided I could even understand them.

Animal hides were nailed to the wall and also lay on the floor. Heads of creatures completely unfamiliar to me were either hanging from the walls or seated on tall pedestals.

Delph just stared in silence.

Harry Two let out a protesting howl when he saw the myriad animal heads.

I looked around, feeling quite nervous.

Pillsbury said proudly, "Master Jasper had quite the active mind, he did. Was always into something or other. Would be up here all hours, days on end. I'd have to bring him his meals in here. And the smells." His metal body shivered. "Well, they were memorable, I'll leave it at that."

I didn't know where to start. I really didn't even know why I was here. Well, I *did* know actually. This was my family. My long-ago family I never knew even existed. I had to find out as much as I could. Not just because it might help me survive. I mean, weren't you *supposed* to know about your own family?

Pillsbury, perhaps sensing my indecision, said, "May I leave you to it, Mistress Vega? I have a few things to attend to in furtherance of my household duties."

"Oh, right, yes, go ahead, Pillsbury. We'll be fine."

He gave me a comically deep bow — I actually thought he might get stuck in the down position — and then he was off.

Delph came to stand next to me.

"Blimey, Vega Jane. What do we do with all this?"

"We just start looking."

We had begun to search the chamber when a disheveled-looking Petra suddenly appeared in the doorway.

She said crossly, "I've been looking all over for you two. I saw Pillsbury on the stairs. He said you were up here. Why didn't you come and get me?"

Delph automatically looked at me.

*Males!*

I said, almost truthfully, "We thought we'd let you sleep in, Petra, after last night. You'd suffered so much."

She drew a deep breath and nodded. "Right, well, thanks. It *was* nice to have some extra rest." She looked around. "What is this place?"

I explained about my ancestor Jasper, then debated for a moment before deciding to tell her about Uma and Jason. And also that I had seen Uma's, well, whatever it was, in my room. And how terribly unhappy she had been.

After I was done, Petra looked very unsettled.

"That's very sad," she said at last. "So very sad."

That was definitely not what I was expecting her reaction to be. From her face, I thought she might start weeping.

"Yes, it is," I agreed, watching her nervously.

"So you're searching this place to find, what, answers?"

I nodded. "Any bit of information might prove useful."

"Well, I'll help, then."

So we set about it. We found many things; many obscure, inexplicable things. Some showed that Jasper, as Astrea Prine had already told me, was indeed intrigued by dark sorcery. But none of what we found held many clues that might help us figure out what to do about the Maladons lurking outside our door.

I found an old diary in a desk drawer. There was no writing inside it, so I thrust it into my pocket with the thought that I would make use of it with my own notes and thoughts.

A few minutes later I picked up a mirror encased in silver that was lying on Jasper's desk and held it up to my face. I rubbed at a spot on my cheek and then looked at my teeth. Not overly clean, and my hair was a bit of a mess. I quickly turned to see if either Delph or Petra was watching, but they were busy in far corners of the room.

When I looked back, I thought my heart had stopped.

Uma was inside the glass.

I nearly dropped it.

Her mouth was moving, but I couldn't hear what she was saying. Then I realized she wasn't talking to me.

Another figure came into view to stand beside her.

He was, well, he was spiffing gorgeous. Tall and broad shouldered with long dark hair and the most amazingly beautiful blue eyes.

I glanced across the room. He actually looked a bit like Delph, come to think.

When I looked back, he had his arm around Uma's waist. And when they looked at each other, so obviously in love, I knew who he was.

Jason, Necro's son.

The two tragically doomed lovers were right here in front of me.

As I continued to watch, they leaned toward each other and kissed, deeply. So deeply that I felt my cheeks growing red.

I have to admit, it was quite a snog.

Embarrassed that I was intruding on such a private moment, I looked away. When I glanced back, the glass was empty.

They were gone.

"Vega Jane?"

I screamed and dropped the mirror. It hit the desk and shattered.

I looked at Delph, who was next to me.

"What?" I said crossly. "And look what you made me do!"

"S-sorry, Vega Jane. But I'd been calling you and you didn't answer. I thought something was wrong. Like you'd" — he glanced down at the shattered mirror — "had magic done on you or something."

I picked up the pieces of the mirror and without looking at him said, "I'm sorry, Delph."

By this time Petra had joined us.

"What's going on?" she asked. "Find anything?"

I held up the pieces of the mirror. "I just saw Uma and Jason in this mirror snogging."

Delph gasped and took a step back.

Petra looked skeptical.

She said, "In that glass. You're sure?"

I nearly crossed my eyes in frustration. "Oh, no. I might have imagined a dead bloke snogging a dead woman who was on my bedroom ceiling last night. Quite forgettable."

After another hour, we closed the door behind us without knowing that much more than when we'd entered.

I returned to my room to wash up while Petra and Delph went to theirs to do the same. We arranged to meet for lunch shortly, which Pillsbury had come and told us would be served in the conservatory, whatever that was.

When I came out of the washroom, I noticed it.

There was a painting hanging on the wall across from my bed that hadn't been there before. As I drew closer, I could see who it depicted.

Alice Adronis.

Alice *Jane* Adronis, more precisely.

I wondered why I had not seen a portrait of her until now; it was her home, after all.

I remembered the painting I had seen of her back in Astrea's cottage in the Quag. She had been dressed fetchingly in a dazzling gown with a plunging neckline, her hair piled on top of her head, her features so sharply defined, her eyes so . . . masterful. She was very beautiful, but I had been more captivated by the sense of strength and barely restrained power in her whole being.

By contrast, in this portrait, Alice was in full battle gear, chain mail, helmet in one hand, the full-size Elemental in the other. This was Alice Adronis as perhaps she was meant to be, where she was the most comfortable, the most natural. The most formidable. Not at a party about to drink and eat, but as a warrior about to enter a battlefield and fight to the death with every bit of strength, courage and cunning she had.

I had seen her do this very thing.

And I had also seen her die.

I looked into her eyes, which seemed to hold flames in their center, and shivered. I knew that Alice would be unafraid of even Mr. Endemen. She would battle him as an equal.

And she would have won. I was sure of it!

I dearly wished she could be here with me right now.

But I wondered again how the portrait had come to be in my room.

I said, "Pillsbury?"

An instant later he was standing at my doorway.

"Yes, Mistress Vega?"

I pointed to the portrait. "Did you put that in here?"

He came forward and stared at the painting. "No, I didn't. I've no idea how it came to be here."

He seemed genuinely bewildered.

"Well, there is one thing," he ventured.

"What's that?" I said sharply.

"This home has its, well, its peculiarities."

"Such as?" I said.

"Things come and things go. And some things turn up where they *naturally* should be. That's the best way I can explain things. And now I must see to the finishing up of lunch."

In another instant he was gone.

I slowly turned back to the painting and received another jolt.

I rubbed my eyes. It couldn't be. It was impossible.

When I looked at the portrait once more, it was all as it should be. Alice stared back at me from the depths of the oils and canvas.

But for one moment, one chilling, electrifying, terrifying moment, I thought . . .

Well, I thought that it was *me* in the portrait.

## A Choice to Be Made

WE TROOPED INTO the conservatory for our luncheon. Actually, we had no idea where it was until Pillsbury came and led us there.

It was huge and the walls were glass, supported by a metal framework. There was a door leading outside to the rear grounds, which now looked spectacular, with everything in bloom.

I mentioned this to Pillsbury, who, again if it was possible for metal to do so, beamed at my words.

"Well, the lads worked all night to get things up to scratch for you. It does look splendid."

"They did that for me?"

"Of course. The outdoor staff takes great pride in keeping things just so for the family they serve."

"Where is the outdoor staff?"

He pointed to another part of the garden. Through the window I could see marble statuary toiling away in the grounds with trusty gardening tools. In another part of the garden, a rake was collecting grass clippings. Farther back a scythe was mowing down weeds. Then a wheelbarrow came into view. It was full of twigs and dead leaves and was rolling itself down a flagstone path.

"The outdoor staff," said Pillsbury proudly. "All fine lads."

"Please give them my thanks."

"I will indeed."

Another door leading into the conservatory opened and in whirled, well, I supposed it was Mrs. Jolly. Pillsbury hadn't mentioned any other broom in the house that could move about. There were long wooden appendages that she used as arms to push a small cart loaded with covered plates and pewter cups alongside a large pitcher filled with water. At the end of these appendages were wooden fingers.

Unlike Pillsbury, however, on the top of the broomstick, which fanned out to a good six inches, was set a pair of eyes, a nose and a mouth, which were not made of wood and seemed very similar in appearance to mine. As she looked at me Mrs. Jolly broke into a lovely smile that warmed my heart like a cozy fire.

"Hello, luvs," she said brightly, her voice as uplifting as the sound of music.

"Hello," we all said back.

"I'm sure he's told you I'm Mrs. Jolly," she said, indicating Pillsbury.

I smiled and nodded. "Yes," I said. "Your cooking is the best I've ever had."

She beamed as Delph ravenously eyed the cart she had pushed in. Even with the little lids on, the most wonderful aromas were escaping into the room and from there into our nostrils.

"Right you are," exclaimed Delph. "And I'm bloody famished."

"Well, we shall take care of that."

111

With a sweep of her hand the lids came off and the plates rose into the air and then settled neatly on a table where napkins and cutlery suddenly appeared at three place settings.

I peered over at Petra. As I thought it would be, her face was a whirl of wonderment. After the life she'd led in the Quag, she must believe she had fallen into the most wonderful world imaginable: a beautiful home, food prepared for us, servants galore and a safe warm bed in which to sleep without the worry of snarling beasts desiring nothing more than to end her life.

It would be very easy to live here forever, I concluded, taking up my thread of thought from the previous night.

On the floor, a bowl of food and a bowl of water appeared in front of Harry Two.

"Now, tuck in while it's still hot," Mrs. Jolly advised.

While Delph and Petra began to eat, I looked outside and then slowly lowered my fork. My happy thoughts had suddenly turned to something far darker.

"What's up?" asked Delph in between bites. "Not hungry?"

"No, it's not that."

He lowered his fork too. So did Petra.

"What is it, Vega?" she asked.

"I was thinking about everybody back in Wormwood. And those living in the Quag. I mean, they don't have food like this to eat, except perhaps for Morrigone and Astrea Prine. And they're not living in such comfort either. Or safety."

Delph looked stricken at my words, and stared down at his plate like it was a serpent about to bite him.

Petra said, "So what? I don't know what you have to be sad about. Everyone has a different lot in life. This is yours. What they have is theirs."

I looked at her in surprise. When I had told her about Uma and Jason she had become so sad. But now her words were cruel and uncaring.

"Well, we *can* do something about that," I said firmly.

"But, Vega Jane," said Delph. "For the longest time we had nothing. And we crossed the Quag, where we were in danger every sliver. I think we might've earned a bit of comfort, eh?"

Though his words were eminently reasonable, they made me more upset than Petra's had.

"Well, Delph, if you want to forget where you came from," I said sternly, and then immediately felt bad for saying it, because he got the most hurt look on his face. But I couldn't take it back. So I got up and went outside and into the garden, leaving them behind to no doubt talk about "crazy Vega."

I found a bench in a secluded spot, out of sight of the house and also away from all the hustle and bustle of the "outside staff." I just wanted to be alone and to think.

I had to admit, I loved this place. I mean I truly loved everything about it. I had never owned anything in my whole life. I'd rarely had a sausage to my name. And then to be told that this magnificent place was mine? Well, I just could hardly believe it. And yet a big part of me also didn't think that I deserved it. After all, I hadn't built it. I hadn't fought in a war in an attempt to save the world in which Empyrean had been created. It wasn't really mine at all.

As I sat there, Harry Two bounded around the corner. He had no doubt sniffed me out. He sat next to me by the bench and I idly stroked his fluffy ear while I continued to ponder what it was I had to do.

Last night I had dreamed of perhaps staying here forever, safe and well fed, admiring the lovely grounds and exploring the home of my ancestors. It was such an appealing thought. And now, I felt so conflicted, as though my previous yearnings were somehow a betrayal of . . . of what?

I nearly leapt from my seat when it happened.

Something was moving in my pocket. For one panicked moment I thought it might be a serpent that had slipped in there.

But then it came flying free and came to rest suspended in the air in front of me.

It was the blank diary that I had found in Jasper Jane's room.

As I watched, spellbound, the pages started to flip open.

They were all still blank, and I was wondering what the Hel was going on when I received another jolt.

A voice seemed to rise from the pages, like fog from the ground, and said, "At midnight, the fourth staircase, the third hall, the last door on the right."

Then the book fell to the ground.

I just sat there and stared at it, making no move to retrieve it. I was waiting for it to start talking again.

Harry Two sniffed at it and then gingerly nudged it with his paw. Then he looked up at me, as though awaiting instructions.

I slowly bent down and picked it up. I flipped through the pages but they were still all empty.

I could feel myself breathing fast; my chest felt tight and constricted.

*Midnight? Fourth staircase, third hall, last door on the right?*

As I looked up at Empyrean, I calculated that this spot would be right near the top of the house, near Jasper's old chamber.

And at midnight that was exactly where I was going to be.

I COULD BARELY keep my nerves together as the time drew near for me to go on my nighttime journey.

I listened for the large case clock down the hall to gong the time.

When it hit the first stroke of midnight, I made a beeline from my room with Harry Two on my heels. I could have had him stay behind, but frankly I wanted some company.

We raced quietly up the massive staircase until we reached the very top landing. Then we snuck down the third hall and reached the last door on the right.

I took the diary out of my pocket. I had brought it just in case it would be useful somehow.

I stared at the wood of the door, suddenly unsure of what to do. Finally, I reached out and turned the knob. It was locked.

I held up the diary, waiting for the voice to tell me how to proceed.

But it remained absolutely silent.

I thrust it back into my pocket and pulled out my wand.

I pointed it at the door. But as soon as I did, it swung open noiselessly.

I crept into the room, loyal Harry Two right next to me. His hackles were up and a low growl was emitting from his throat. It was like he was trying to warn whatever was in here that we were not to be trifled with.

As we stepped fully into the room, the door shut and locked behind us. That made us both jump, but I didn't know why I was surprised. Pretty much every creepy room I'd ever gone into had a door that shut and locked behind me.

The room, dim before, now became fully lighted. As my eyes adjusted I gasped.

The walls were filled with objects that left me weak-kneed.

Bloody clothing hung on one wall. On another was a whole line of weapons that were also bloodstained and severely damaged. One ax had a big chunk of metal taken out of it. A sword blade was broken in half. A dented shield hung next to a chain-mail helmet with a hole drilled in a spot that would align with someone's forehead. A breastplate had four large gashes in it. Everywhere I looked was the evidence of a battle hard fought.

And ultimately, as I now knew, a war lost.

I wandered the space for a very long time, hours it seemed, though in every corner I turned there was something new to see. The room seemed to go on forever.

Finally, I saw a dim light come on in the farthest reaches of the space.

I hurried toward it.

And stopped dead when I saw what it was.

A coffin.

Its top was open.

As I approached it, two tall bronze torches resting in holders on either side of the coffin burst into flame, allowing me to see that the coffin was made entirely of shiny metal.

In Wormwood, we only used simple wooden coffins to bury our dead.

Harry Two and I drew nearer and, though I didn't want to, I crept close enough to look down into it.

A body of a man lay inside, surrounded by soft white cushioning.

He was obviously pale, his eyes closed, his skin tight, his hands folded over his chest. At the base of his neck was a long darkened mark. As I drew closer, I saw more clearly what it was.

His death wound.

Someone had slit his neck from one side to the other. It was a wonder his head had remained attached.

I recoiled from this gruesome sight and looked down at the rest of him.

He was dressed in very fine clothes that reminded me of the garments I had seen in the paintings back at Astrea Prine's cottage in the Quag. He looked familiar but I couldn't place him.

And clutched in his hands was a wand. It was one of the finest wands I had ever seen, though I really hadn't seen that many. It was made not of wood or crystal, but of silver.

I skirted around the edges of the coffin until I came to the shiny brass plate at the foot of it.

I read off it, my lips moving over the words but no sound coming out.

HERE LIES GUNTHER ADRONIS, HUSBAND OF ALICE, AT THE PLACE HE LOVED MOST, EMPYREAN.

I looked back down at the body.

Gunther Adronis. Alice's husband. Empyrean had been their home. She was buried at Wolvercote Cemetery, yet he was here.

I moved back away from the coffin, suddenly trembling all over. This room was so terribly sad. There was death and defeat and despair in every part of it.

I had no idea why the diary would have had me come here. I mean, what was the point of it?

As if in answer to my unspoken thought, the diary began to tremble in my pocket once more. With shaky hands I took it out and held it up.

The pages swirled, but again no writing appeared.

Instead the same voice said, "You must know the price that will have to be paid. You must look upon these walls and upon that body and fully understand what it is that is demanded of you. It is awful but it is necessary. If you are unwilling to pay this price, then you may stay here, at Empyrean, in comfort and safety, until your last days. But if you are willing to pay the price, aid will be there for you."

When I glanced down at the body in the coffin, I nearly fainted. Gunther was no longer there, and the coffin had swelled to three times its original width.

And lying inside the coffin were Petra, Delph . . . and me. With our necks slashed and our lives gone.

I rushed pell-mell from the room, down all the stairs and back to my room. I flung myself on my bed and lay there, paralyzed. A moment later Harry Two, panting, jumped up and lay next to me.

He nudged my hand, but I didn't respond.

So many had fought and lost their lives. They had done so in the war. The *lost* war. It seemed to make their ultimate sacrifice not worth anything.

And beyond just me, would I want to sacrifice Delph and Petra to this same failed fight?

I had no answers to any of these questions. And suddenly I was unsure of what I would do.

Time marched on.

Then Harry Two nudged my hand again.

I pushed him off, but he wouldn't stop.

Finally, I looked down at him.

"Harry Two," I began.

And then I stopped.

Dead.

It was not Harry Two looking back at me. I mean it was his face, but the eyes, his eyes were different.

I swallowed a large lump in my throat and sat up.

There was only one pair of eyes I had ever seen that looked like those.

I was here in this room right now —

With my grandfather. I didn't know if this was simply my imagination , but I so wanted to believe that he was here with me now. I needed my family. I needed them so much.

And though Harry Two could not speak, one sentence formed in my head:

*Be not afraid, Vega, for you are never truly alone.*

# The Peril of Petra

I RUSHED FROM MY room, down the hall and, not bothering to even knock, I pushed open Delph's door and called out his name.

He sat up in bed and stared over at me.

I was breathing so hard and my stomach was churning so badly I thought I might be sick.

"Vega Jane?" he said warily. "Are you okay?"

I stumbled forward, took a moment to calm myself and then perched on the edge of his bed.

"Vega Jane?" he said again. I could tell that Delph was fearful. I had come bursting in, looking like a madwoman, and I hadn't uttered a word.

I told Delph about the diary's message, my visiting the room, what I had seen, particularly the body of Gunther Adronis. And, finally, the image of our three bodies lying there in the coffin.

As I spoke, he sat up straighter and straighter and his eyes grew wider and wider until I thought they might simply plunge off his face.

When I got to the part about Harry Two's eyes and hearing my grandfather's voice in my head, I truly believed that Delph might fall off the bed in a dead faint.

"Y-your grandfather? In your head? H-Harry Two? His eyes? B-but h-how?"

I said, "Am I going mad, Delph?"

I was suddenly so tired I lay down on the bed and curled into a small ball.

Delph reached over and clutched my shoulder. "'Tis okay now, Vega Jane. You're safe."

I abruptly sat up, making him lurch back.

"But that's the thing, Delph. We *are* safe here. If we stay here we won't be harmed. But we can't do that. It's not why we came all this way, is it?"

He took a long breath and studied me. I had always known there was far more to Delph than most folks believed. Big, strong, simple Delph. Only he wasn't simple. Not close to being simple. He had proved that time and again.

There was a lot of thinking going on inside his head. In many ways he was ruddy brilliant.

"That's what you meant at lunch," he said.

I nodded.

He looked around the room. "'Tis a nice place. A very nice place. A bloke could get used to being here, all right. Especially after the Quag."

"In the Quag, everything can kill you," I noted.

He nodded and gave me a weak smile. "But you're right. We didn't come here to live in a place like this. We came here for answers." He paused and didn't speak for such a long time that I thought someting was wrong. "But we need to do it in a smart way."

"How?" I said eagerly.

"Well, to start with, we need to go on little scouting trips. Like me and my dad would do when we would go hunting in the forest. You find out where what you're hunting likes to be, and that way you don't have to keep searching for them every time you go out."

"So we go out but then come back here?" I said doubtfully.

"It makes sense, Vega Jane. That way we learn things and then come back here and sort through them. Then go out and get more knowledge and return here and do the same. Way I see it, we nearly died in True because we had no safe place to return to while rummaging through this new bleeding world we're in. This can be like our camp. It won't help no one if we go and get ourselves killed because we tried to do too much too soon." He paused and blurted out, "It's all so . . . new, Vega Jane!"

I slowly nodded, his words striking me as both thoughtful and accurate.

"I agree," I said.

"So when do you want to leave?" he asked.

I looked out the window.

"I want to leave now, while it's still dark."

He looked at me funny, the reasoning for my use of the word *I* sinking slowly into him, like an illness taking you.

"You're not going to go alone, Vega Jane," he said forcefully.

"I am, at first, Delph, just to get the lay of the land. It'll be easier and safer with just one. Then you can come."

"But —" he began to protest.

123

"It's just the way it has to be, Delph."

Before he could say anything else, I rose from the bed.

"I need to get ready. I'll see you when I get back, Delph."

I added, to myself, *I hope.*

I QUICKLY DRESSED, wearing clothes that we had taken from the trunk in True, and slipping my cloak on, I retrieved my wand from the nightstand, put the Adder Stone in my pocket and took the diary as well. The thing hadn't spoken to me again, but one never knew when it might do so once more.

When I was done with that, I looked at Harry Two, who sat still as a statue on my bed.

"You stay here, Harry Two. I'll be back soon," I said, giving his solitary ear a rub.

I left the room and hurried down the hall.

I passed by Delph's door. I knew he wasn't sleeping. He would be up until I got back, I was sure.

I next passed by Petra's door and then stopped.

I took out my wand, pointed it at the door and said quietly, *"Crystilado magnifica."*

A split second later I could see inside her room. I had expected her to be asleep. Only she wasn't.

Petra was squatting down on the floor, her wand twirling in a practiced fashion between her fingers.

She pointed it at a chair next to her bed and muttered an incantation.

*"Mutatio hydrus."*

As I watched in horror, the chair transformed into a writhing mass of deadly vipers.

I nearly fell over as I watched.

The next instant she calmly said, *"Rescindo."*

Where in the world had she — and then the truth hit me. That spell had been in a book in Jasper Jane's room.

A book of *dark* spells.

Even as I looked, I saw her take some pages from her pocket and glance down at them. As I looked more closely, I could see that they had been torn from a book, or books.

She had stolen dark spells from my ancestor's room and was now practicing them.

I was horrified. I had told Petra that I trusted her. And I had. But now?

I looked down at my wand, unsure of what to do. Should I place her in some sort of prison? Should I paralyze her and deal with it when I got back? I shuddered. Should I . . . attack her, or even . . . ?

Fortunately, as I was pondering all of these awful possible solutions, Petra rose, put her wand and pages away, got into bed and blew out her candle. I waited long enough to hear her breaths lengthen into gentle snores.

I retreated and continued on down the hall.

I had other things to command my attention, and if I wanted to survive to return here and deal with Petra, I needed to keep my focus.

I reached the front door, luckily without running into Pillsbury.

But even as his name entered my head, there he was, appearing out of nowhere.

"Mistress Vega?" he said. His visor seemed screwed up in confusion. "Are you leaving us?"

"Just going for a stroll, Pillsbury. I won't be long."

Before he could say anything else, I opened the front door and then closed it quietly behind me.

I looked out into the darkness and then turned and eyed the facade of Empyrean. So solid, so peaceful, so just *there.*

Remaining here for life would have been so . . . easy.

I looked down at my ring, turned it round and vanished instantly.

I had no idea how the enchantments round the house and grounds worked or how far they extended, but I would take no chances of being seen by the forces that I knew were aligned against us.

I touched my waist, around which lay Destin. Should I fly? Should I walk?

Then an absolutely brilliant idea occurred to me.

I reached down, tapped my right leg twice and muttered, *"Pass-pusay."*

I had one destination in mind.

Greater True.

I just prayed it would work.

It didn't.

I tried it again. Nothing.

I thought about it for a bit.

*Okay,* I thought, *let's give this another go.*

*"Pass-pusay,"* I said, and in my mind this time my destination was not Greater True, but the town of True.

An instant later I was standing in the middle of a street.

I looked around. This was True all right. And then it hit me. The *Pass-pusay* incantation apparently only worked if the place you wanted to go to was one you had already *been* to. *It would have been nice if Astrea Prine had told me that,* I thought irritably.

So now my dilemma was how to get to Greater True. Under cover of invisibility, I headed to the train station.

I wasn't going to take a train. I was just going to follow one heading to Greater True.

An hour after I arrived at the station, the big marquee board announced the boarding of the early morning train with a final destination of Greater True.

With Destin around my waist, I took to the air and waited, hovering there.

A few minutes later, the train pulled out of the station and headed onward.

I followed from the air. The trip included a few other stops at stations along the way. These places were far smaller than either True or Greater True. Two people got off at one stop, and another climbed aboard at a second stop. The countryside in between was dotted with small homesteads and, where the winks of lights were more numerous, perhaps tiny villages that appeared even smaller than Wormwood.

Finally, I could see tall buildings rising up in the distance. I passed the train, reached town and landed. Unfortunately, confused a bit by the lingering darkness, I landed in the middle of a roadway.

The next second I leapt out of the way or else — just as had occurred in True — I would have been crushed to death by a huge motor flashing past.

It was gone so fast I couldn't even see who was inside.

I pressed myself against the stone wall of a building and took a long look around.

The streets were empty of people, which made sense, it being so early. The buildings were larger and grander than what I had seen in True. Some were made of stone, others of fine brick. They rose higher than anything I had observed in True. As a former Finisher, I marveled at the intricate carvings, moldings and cornice pieces. I knew that it had taken great skill to craft all these things.

I slowly walked to my left. I didn't have a plan really, but I did want to see as much as I possibly could. I tugged my glove tighter over my hand to make sure the mark there was covered.

The next second I flattened myself against the wall again as I heard footsteps racing toward me.

Around the corner came a small, old fellow dressed in a suit, huffing and puffing, his chunky legs moving in a jerky fashion, as though they were rarely used for running.

My breath caught in my throat as pounding footsteps drew closer, and around the same corner came three men in suits and brown bowler hats.

It was not much of a chase. They caught up with the fellow, and one of the Bowler Hats raised his wand and the spell hit the little fellow in the back. He slumped to the pavement in great pain. He looked up at those gathered around him, his eyes filled with the most intense fear. They all pointed their wands at him.

I pulled out my own wand, pointed it at the blokes and said three times rapidly, *"Anesthe."*

All three instantly crumpled to the pavement.

I waited anxiously to see if any other Bowler Hats showed up, alerted by my incantation. But none did.

The old fellow cowered for a few more moments, his hands over his head, until he noticed that his attackers were lying unconscious on the street.

Since he didn't seem inclined to flee, I said softly, "Run."

That did the trick. He took to his heels and was soon out of sight.

I turned and quietly backed away until I was around another corner. Then I ran for it too. Ten minutes later I slumped breathless against a building, nursing the pain in my side from running so hard.

So Greater True was not as peaceful as its counterpart True. Not when Endemen's blokes went about attacking defenseless people. I wondered what the old fellow had done to command such attention. Yet after what I had seen Endemen do to those poor men on the train, I concluded it wouldn't take much for him and his blokes to kill you.

THE STREETS WERE empty wherever I walked, and I realized that I had actually picked an unfortunate time to explore this place. Most people would still be in their beds for several more hours at least.

Well, I would have to find a place to hide until the sun came up.

And hope that I survived.

# Greater True

I MOVED TO MY right and turned down another street. I kept going until I reached a bridge. I started to cross, always wary of anyone lurking in the shadows, but I saw no one.

I wrapped my coat more tightly around me because it was cold and raw and the skies threatened rain.

As soon as I thought this, the clouds opened up and it started to bucket down.

My first impulse was to use my wand to provide cover against the elements, as I had back in the Quag. But then I realized I couldn't. How would it look for a shield spell to be blocking the rain from hitting . . . nothing? It would be a dead giveaway. And that's what I would be: dead.

I rushed across the bridge and then hooked a sharp left and slunk down under the structure. I hurried toward a stone support column near the bank. At least here I was shielded from the rain.

I huddled down, cold, wet and miserable, leaned back against the stone piling of the bridge, closed my eyes and gratefully fell asleep.

My eyes snapped open when I heard the noise. It was directly above me.

The sound of marching.

Still invisible, I crept out from under the bridge. It had stopped raining, thankfully, but it was still cloudy and there was no sign of the sun, though I could tell that the night had fully passed.

I scrambled to a spot where I could see the top of the bridge.

A stream of black-helmeted and booted men was striding across the bridge in a double column. As they reached the end where I was, I saw to my horror that they weren't full-grown men.

They were . . . boys.

They all carried what looked to be very sophisticated mortas supported by straps over their shoulders. They all wore scowls. And they all looked . . . so proudly angry as they whipped their arms and legs in perfect synchronization.

The one leading them brandished a gleaming sword and was calling out orders. Another in the front carried a flag. On it I saw a symbol.

It was a five-pointed star, but it had two black dots in the center of it. As the columns drew closer, I could see that the black dots were actually eyes. I shuddered because they were the most frightening pair of eyes I had ever seen.

They seemed capable of piercing my skin and burning right into my soul.

I had to look away.

The column marched on.

Shaken, I looked around to get my bearings as Greater True awoke from its slumber. The pavement was slick with the rain, but the windows glistened as shafts of light broke through the shallow storm clouds and reflected upon them. Noises were starting to percolate out of various spots.

The streets were in excellent shape and well laid out. I couldn't see a bit of rubbish anywhere. Even the air seemed more pure than what I was used to.

As I watched, the wind drove the clouds away and sunlight swept down and embraced me.

Motors were starting up, and several of them began to appear on streets near the bridge.

I could see the people inside the motors. They looked like the ones boarding the train to Greater True I'd seen previously — their features coldly arrogant. I had taken an instant dislike to them back in True and my opinion had not changed in Greater True. I was surprised that they even condescended to travel to True. I also wondered again what was on the palms of the hands they had shown the guards at the train station. I vowed to solve that mystery on this trip if I could.

As I continued to watch, a man and woman dressed in quite handsome clothes came down the cobbles. They were tall and good-looking, but the pompous looks on their faces made my blood boil.

Walking behind them was a smaller man dressed in a stiff suit and wearing a shiny hat. His shoes gleamed and his skin was pink from where it had been scrubbed clean. As I looked more closely, I suddenly recoiled in horror.

The smaller man's eyes were blank. No pupils, just all white. I didn't know how he could even see.

I also didn't know whether he was with the couple or simply following closely along behind them.

However, I soon found out. The woman carried a bag. As she opened it, something fell out and plummeted toward the cobbles. The smaller man darted forward just in time to catch whatever had fallen.

So he *could* see! And his reflexes were quite good as well.

He doffed his hat in a show of politeness, and handed the object — a small bottle — back to her. Instead of thanking him, she snatched it from his hand.

"You almost let it shatter, you fool," she admonished as he replaced the hat on his head.

Well, I thought, *she'd* been the one to drop the thing. And he had caught it before it had hit the cobbles. She was acting like it was his fault.

Her companion reached down and struck the other man across the face so hard that his hat flew off.

I saw the welt rise on the other man's cheek.

He didn't try to defend himself but merely raced to retrieve his hat while the couple continued down the street, laughing. The other man hurried to catch up while rubbing at his swollen cheek.

I was furious at what I'd seen. And my anger overcame my common sense.

*"Engulfiado."*

The geyser of water hit the man and woman directly in the chest and washed them away down the cobbles. By the time they stopped, they were soaked and filthy, their condescending attitudes struck clean from them.

I couldn't stop myself from smiling.

The other man hurried after them to help. My smile

vanished when they started berating him, as though what I had done was his fault.

As more people emerged from the grand buildings, I noted that several were followed by either a man or woman dressed in the same fancy clothing and walking behind them like some sort of pet — and not a well-loved pet either.

And all of their eye sockets were filled only with white.

It was somehow the saddest thing I had seen here.

My anger began to rise once more, but the next moment I forgot all about that and focused on the crisis that had just presented itself.

Endemen had turned the corner barely a hundred yards in front of me. A split second later three other Bowler Hats appeared behind him.

As I shrunk back, Endemen surveyed the streets, his gaze flitting over where I stood, invisible. Then it came back the other way, seemed to hesitate at a spot uncomfortably close to me and then continued on to observe the legion of morta-toting boys still marching away.

Endemen strode over to stand next to a man in uniform who was surveying the columns of marchers.

Endemen said, "Their training is going well, I fancy?"

"Very well," said the man. "It's a nice crop of recruits. Perhaps one of the best yet."

"Good. Very good indeed."

"They are our pride and future, after all."

*Pride and future?* What exactly did that mean? These boys were no doubt being trained up as warriors. But the thing was, they were using mortas as their weapons. Did that mean they had no magical abilities?

I knew that Endemen and the Bowler Hats were sorcerers. They had wands and they could fly. I scratched my head, my poor brain unable to make head or tail of it.

Then I thought of something else.

I wanted to see what was on the palms of the people who lived here.

Invisible, I skittered forward until I was very near a group of them watching the boys march along. One of the men raised his hand to shield his eyes from the sun.

Burned onto the palm of his hand was the same symbol I had seen on the flag: the five-pointed star with the pair of hideous eyes.

I drew back, shuddering. I suddenly realized that all of these people must have that terrible symbol burned into their skin.

My attention was drawn back to Endemen, who had left the man in uniform and joined the other Bowler Hats. I sidled up to where I could hear him if he spoke.

He pointed to the couple I'd doused and said quietly, "The *Engulfiado* spell, undoubtedly."

"Clearly," said one of the Bowler Hats. "We will explain it as a water main break and will demonstrate concrete evidence of that to the citizens. But there was no sign of the person performing the spell."

"What can you tell me about the other matter?"

I was certain I knew what the "other matter" was.

*Me knocking out three men last night.*

The man said, "We sent a response immediately, but nothing was to be seen. The men were rendered unconscious. We believe it was not by ordinary means."

I nearly laughed at his choice of words. But what he said next froze me to the bone.

"And the quarry?" asked Endemen.

"He was captured two streets over. And dealt with summarily."

My heart sank. I had saved the man for the length of two bloody streets only.

Endemen said, "I do not like what I am seeing. The breakdown of law and order. Of respect. We must come down hard on any who show similar signs of independence."

"What could be causing it, sir?"

Endemen shrugged. "I will recommend that we commence to increase the intensity level of the Mesmerizer. That may very well do it. And then have periodic updates on it for our, um, 'friends.'"

"Of course, Mr. Endemen. Right away, sir."

*Mesmerizer?*

I wondered if that was the thing back in True on the wall. Where people's minds were taken away and replaced with rubbish.

Endemen said, "And no additional sightings?"

"None, I'm afraid."

"The matter cannot be allowed to remain in such a state," Endemen said firmly.

"No, sir," the man replied quickly, and I noted a hint of fear in his features.

Endemen suddenly strode off and his men followed.

Curious, I scurried after them, reaching a darkened alley in time to see Endemen take off his hat and look inside it.

There seemed to be a light shining inexplicably from the interior of the hat.

He put the hat back on. "I have been summoned," he said.

"Yes, Mr. Endemen," said one of the Bowler Hats. "Shall we accompany you?"

"No. You remain here and keep watch." He added, "I assume no one is looking."

"It's quite clear," said another of the men who was keeping a lookout.

Ironically, he was standing within ten feet of me, the git.

"Keep me apprised."

Endemen rose six feet into the air, tipped his hat and shot off so fast that in a few seconds he was visible only as a distant blur.

And before I could really think about it, I sprang into the air and soared after him.

# Maladon Castle

I HADN'T FLOWN THIS fast in my life. Yet Destin appeared up to the task. I'd had to put on my goggles or my eyes would have been watering so badly I wouldn't have been able to see a thing.

I managed to keep Endemen in sight as we flew higher and higher. Finally, we reached such an altitude that we plunged into a bank of low-level clouds.

My stomach seemed to lurch into my throat. I couldn't see one foot in front of my face. I was flying blind, and I was terrified that I would plow right into Endemen if he halted for some reason.

Thankfully, cold and drenched with moisture from the clouds, I finally flew free of the mists and took up the chase once more. Endemen was wearing no goggles but seemed to have no problem seeing. He was flying in a prone position, his arms at his sides. His bowler hat was still perched neatly on his head, unaffected by our speed and the buffeting winds.

Finally, he started to slow down. I matched his reduction in velocity. I could feel Destin around my waist. Its chain links were like ice. I didn't take that as a good sign.

As Endemen slowed, he also began to descend.

I looked down and gasped.

Spread out far below us was a rugged mountain shrouded in blackness, though it was fully light out. And on the very topmost part of that mountain was a truly enormous building.

I pointed downward and continued to follow Endemen as he hurtled toward the dirt.

He landed smoothly with not even a stumble — I had to admit, the lout was a remarkable flyer, far better than me.

I hesitated in touching down, hovering ten feet off the ground.

The building I had seen from above was now revealed to me.

It was a castle with high, blackened stone walls, battlements and turrets. It looked a bit like Stacks in Wormwood, only larger.

Endemen was marching resolutely toward the largest pair of gates I had ever seen. They made the massive doors back at Stacks look puny by comparison.

A flag waved from the topmost battlement. As I gazed upward, I could see the symbol clearly. It was the same image that the black-booted and helmeted lads back in Greater True had carried on their flag: the star with two terrifying eyes at its center.

When he reached the portal, Endemen took out his wand and waved it from left to right in front of the massive entrance. The mighty gates silently swung inward.

He passed through the opening. And then the doors began to close.

I drew a tortured breath, put my head down and shot through the narrowing gap, clearing it seconds before the wood thudded shut behind me.

I landed softly and peered cautiously around. My heart was beating so fast that I was terrified Endemen would be able to hear it.

He was about fifty feet ahead of me. As I watched, an incredible transformation took place. His suit, shoes and bowler hat vanished and he was suddenly clothed in a luxuriously long robe the color of blood, with a black hood that was down around his shoulders. And that wasn't all. As he turned to the side, I could see that his face had changed too. All parts of it had elongated and become hideously demonic. His complexion had turned so pale it looked silver. A thin, sharply angled bloodred beard now covered the lower part of his chin. He looked like a vulture with a man's body.

As I followed him, I gazed around, taking in as much as I could.

The walls and floors were stone, cold to the touch, and indeed an icy chill seemed to radiate out from them. The corridor was ill lit, perhaps intentionally so, casting flickering shadows here and there. Dozens of corridors snaked off the main one I was on, and blackened and bolted doors lined the hall. My mind conjured images of prisoners behind each of them, awaiting their doom.

Next instant I heard a low moan followed by a scream emanating from deep within the bowels of the place, which gave credence to my thoughts. The terrifying sound sent cold ribbons of fear coursing over me. I involuntarily shivered and drew my cloak closer around me.

I hurried on, as Endemen had picked up his pace, striding purposefully down the center of the wide, darkened corridor. I wondered why no one had come to greet him. And why there had been no guards posted at the front entrance. It was as though the place was uninhabited, but that made absolutely no sense. More likely, they had no fear that anyone uninvited would dare try to get into this fearsome place.

I heard it before I saw it. The sound was unmistakable, and one I knew well. It was actually two sounds: slithering, followed by screeching.

A second later, the creature turned the corner and came into full, towering, terrifying view as it confronted Endemen.

It was a jabbit, an enormous serpent with at least two hundred and fifty heads (no one faced with one had ever lived long enough to properly count them). One bite from a single venomous head was enough to drop a two-ton creta.

Part of me was actually happy to see the dreaded beast heading right for Endemen.

*Bite him*, I thought. *Kill him! Please.*

Yet I should have known better. Endemen lazily held up his wand, and the jabbit stopped dead in its tracks. Next he casually walked up to it, and even patted one of its venomous heads!

My spirits plummeted to new depths.

Endemen walked on, leaving the jabbit behind in the middle of the corridor. Before I could even move, the huge beast came slithering toward me. I shrunk back against the wall, wishing I could climb inside the dark stone. All Wugs had been taught to fear the jabbit above every other beast, and I was no exception. The trunk of the serpent passed right next to me. I could have sworn that one of its poisonous heads actually brushed my cloak.

Then the thing froze. And so did I.

Each of its heads twitched back and forth.

It hit me like a lightning spear what was happening.

They were *smelling* me!

I didn't know what to do. I was afraid to move, terrified to even breathe, so I held my breath.

I stared at the awful creature as it swayed back and forth next to me. I willed it to move on, away from me. For one agonizing moment, my gaze locked with one of the pairs of eyes. I could swear that thing could *see* me.

*Go away. Please.*

And then the most amazing thing happened.

The jabbit slithered away and disappeared down the corridor.

With a gush of relief, I let out my breath. I was definitely feeling light-headed and uncomfortably nauseous. But I forgot about that as I looked wildly around.

Endemen was gone!

# People of the Glass

I HURRIED DOWN THE stone passageway until I reached a large chamber that had multiple corridors fanning off it. I had no idea which one, if any, Endemen had passed down.

I quickly picked one option and shot down it as I heard footsteps approaching in the distance.

There were a number of doors along this way, also all shut. I was about to turn the knob on one of them when a door across the passage opened and a short, brutish man with a trim beard and only a single eye (the other socket being empty) walked out. Like Endemen he was dressed in a long black cloak with a red hood.

Without thinking I shot my invisible self past him and into the room before the door closed.

I huddled back against the wall and tried to catch my breath. My poor heart felt like it might leave my chest and go off skipping down the cobbles.

I managed to calm myself, but a moment later my heart was in my throat again as I heard the voice.

"Please," it wailed. "Please, don't. Spare me. Please. I c-can't take any more. No more. P-please!"

The pure horror in the voice cut through me like a sword into skin.

It was coming from just around the corner. As I steeled myself to look, another voice, equally terrified, burst forth.

"Mummy, no, Mummy. Help me. Don't let them! Mummy, please, help me!"

This was the voice of a child, someone perhaps younger even than my brother, John.

Still invisible, I sprang noiselessly around the corner, my fingers curled around my wand.

What I saw staggered me.

There was a line of looking glasses hanging on one wall. Inside each glass was a person. They were clothed in filthy rags. They were all bent over, apparently gripped in the throes of terrible pain.

I could now see the source of the voices I had heard.

A mother and daughter were trapped in looking glasses hung side by side. Their skin was very dark. I had never seen skin like that in Wormwood. And their hair was black and hung down around their shoulders. They were screaming in pain, the child futilely reaching out to her helpless mother in the next looking glass, even as the mother was desperately clawing at the edges of her glass prison, trying to get to her child.

I had never seen such anguish.

I turned my attention to the other side of the room.

A man stood there holding a wand. He was leisurely pointing it at the people in the glass.

Unlike the bloke I'd seen leaving earlier, this man was tall and broad-shouldered, with a massive, veined neck. His face looked burned and his eyes were set too close together, giving him a permanently overfocused but also menacing expression. His beard was large and bushy. His clothing was the same black-and-red cloak.

And the mouth revealed amid the mass of beard was twisted into a starkly malicious smile.

He fired another spell at one of the looking glasses, and the person trapped there doubled over and screamed.

As I looked on in horror, I saw what appeared to be sparkling dust falling from inside the glass and gathering in a bottle that had been placed on the floor directly under the glass. Indeed, there were bottles lined up under each glass. All of them held some measure of the sparkling dust.

"Please, don't," screamed a woman.

"Mercy," pleaded a man behind the glass.

"Have p-pity," moaned another man, who was on his knees hunched over in agony.

These pitiable outbursts only made the bearded man's cruel smile deepen.

As I looked behind him, I gasped.

Lined up in deep niches on the walls were glass bottles, and they were all filled with the sparkling dust. And each bottle was stoutly corked.

The evil git called out to a moaning man in the looking glass. "Here now, guv, you're gonna love being an Ordinary, eh."

An *Ordinary*? What exactly did that mean?

When he raised his wand again, I matched this movement, readying an incantation of attack.

But then I hesitated. If I performed magic, would I reveal myself?

However, I couldn't simply let this monster continue hurting these poor people.

An idea occurred to me.

I willed my wand to become what it had been when I had first acquired it.

The Elemental.

It grew into a spear taller than me that was the color of gold.

I hurled it at the man as he prepared another spell to cast.

The Elemental struck him full in the chest, lifting him off his feet and sending him sailing against the far wall.

He hit the stone with a heavy thud, and I thought I heard his skull crack. Two of the glass bottles were dislodged and fell on top of him, but the glass didn't break.

The Elemental automatically returned to my hand as the man slid to the floor, blood flowing from the back of his head.

His wand had fallen from his hand and rolled across the floor.

I stooped and picked it up.

It was made of wood that was so blackened it looked as though it had at some point been set afire.

I slipped it into my pocket and turned my attention to the poor people in the looking glasses.

"Hello?" I said quietly. "Can you tell me who you are?"

To my surprise, none of them looked at me.

"Hello, I want to help you. How did you get here?"

I edged closer to the glasses. "Hello, can you hear me?"

Then I realized I was invisible.

I turned my ring the right way round and my invisibility vanished. I edged closer still.

As I did so, one man slammed himself against the glass, scratching and clawing at the surface in an attempt to escape.

I watched in horror as he slumped down and curled into a ball, his body shaking.

I backed away and looked down at the glass bottle under him. It was over half full with the dust.

I glanced at the looking glass that held the young girl.

She turned her face to me, and with a stab of horror I saw that her eyes were nearly blank. She groped blindly around, and then suddenly struck the glass with her fist before slumping to the floor.

I looked at the woman in the glass beside her. Her mother. And her eyes were completely blank.

I looked down at the bottle underneath her looking glass. It was very nearly full.

And I realized with a shudder that she was very nearly gone.

I gripped my Elemental, wondering whether I should throw it at the looking glasses in an attempt to free these people. But then how would we get out of here? Would my invisibility cover work for them all? Could I take them back with me to Empyrean? Did I dare put everyone at my ancestral home in danger that way?

But how could I leave these people? My heart was breaking right in two. If I left them, they would end up as slaves to those gits back in Greater True, for now I realized that was what they were. And it was here that they were *made* slaves.

I hoisted the Elemental and took a deep breath.

"Oi! Who the blazes are you?"

I looked around to see the short, brutish man I'd slipped past earlier, now standing there staring dead at me with his one eye.

He raised his wand and fired a spell at me.

I instinctively deflected it with my Elemental. The spell sailed toward one wall and blasted a hole two feet deep in the stone.

Without wasting a moment, I hurled the Elemental right at him, willing the spear to do my bidding.

It hit him with such force that he simply vanished into nothing, which was what I intended.

The Elemental banked to the left and returned to me.

I looked at the burned hole in the floor where the man had been. I had just killed a Maladon.

I panicked. What did I do now? Where could I go?

I looked at the people in the glass and my heart sank. I couldn't save them. I . . . I would have to leave them.

I didn't know why I did it, but I raced over and picked up the bottle of dust underneath the mother's looking glass. There were lines of empty glass bottles and a basket of corks on a table set against one wall. I grabbed a cork and stoppered the bottle. Then I placed it in my pocket. I reversed my ring and turned invisible once more.

I ran to the door, eased it open and saw that the hall was clear.

I slipped out and ran down the passageway in the opposite direction from which I'd come.

I turned the corner and had to slam myself against the wall as a half dozen cloaked Maladons raced past me, wands raised and ready.

I waited for them to be well out of sight before I hurried off.

I had to get out of here, but I still wanted to locate Endemen. I desperately wanted to know who had "summoned" him here.

I ran headlong down the corridor, turned the corner and stopped dead.

The garm was only twenty feet from me. But I had never seen a garm like this before. Like the others of its breed, it had four huge legs, armored skin, a mouth that breathed fire, and blood that ran perpetually down its massive chest.

Yet there was one significant difference.

*This* garm was tethered to a huge leash made of chain links and was being led down the corridor by an enormous man.

The garm's snout was close to the cobbles and it was sniffing.

This was not good. Garms could pick up a scent from miles away. I suspected they had figured out I was invisible and were taking no chances in tracking me down.

I turned and hurtled the other way.

But rushing footsteps were coming from that direction too.

I passed many doors as I raced down this corridor and that corridor. Then, just up ahead, I heard a roar of a garm. I looked back to where I could see the other garm coming on fast.

I was trapped!

I pushed open the door closest to me, leapt inside and bolted it behind me.

I put my back against the wall and caught my breath. I

knew I was in serious jeopardy of being captured. And I had no doubt what they would do to me if they did catch me: They would place the *Subservio* spell on me to make me tell them all I knew. And then they would force me to show them where Empyrean was and then they would kill everyone there before finishing me off.

I moved away from the door, hoping that somehow the garm would not be able to smell me in here.

Too late. Something smashed into the door. And I heard the growls and insanely terrifying screams of the garm on my scent.

It would be in here in an instant, and invisible or not, the garm would find me. And that would be the end of Vega Jane.

Then I had a brilliant idea. I tapped my right leg with my wand and said, *"Pass-pusay."*

Absolutely nothing happened. I was still rooted to the spot. There had to be something here that blocked one from leaving that way. So now what the Hel did I do?

I looked at the Elemental, still fully formed in my hand. Then I looked at the opposite wall.

I had never attempted what I was about to try. I had never even thought of attempting it. But I really didn't have any other option.

I gripped the Elemental tightly, willing it to do what I wanted it to. I thought back to what Alice had told me on that battlefield long ago when she had given me the Elemental.

*When you have no other friends, it will be there for you.*

The garm hit the door with another blow and this time it toppled inward. The beast and the man leading it burst into the room.

It was now or never.

I threw the Elemental directly at the far wall.

But this time I didn't let go!

I was lifted off my feet and the tip of the Elemental slammed into the wall, dissolved the stone and, together, we hurtled through the fresh opening.

We were in another room and we smashed through another wall, and passed into another chamber. Things were happening in each of these places, and I had glimpses of hideous goings-on, lunacy, insanity, the most despicable, disgusting events one could imagine.

We hit and exploded through one more wall and I felt my heels hit the floor.

The room we had just landed in was truly enormous. I couldn't see how there could be a larger one even in a building as gargantuan as this.

I could barely see the ceiling, which was made of glass. There were colorful banners covering the walls. They all held the symbol I had seen earlier. The five-pointed star with the terrifying pair of eyes.

And then my gaze alighted on what looked very much like a throne. It was huge and made of what appeared to be solid gold with a curved armrest that I could see featured the actual heads of foul creatures. It had a high back emblazoned with the same awful star symbol.

Then I focused on the man sitting on it.

He was shrouded all in red, including the hood covering his head. His hands poked out from the sleeves and they were unnaturally elongated, curved and so burned-looking I wondered how he could be alive.

And standing in front of him, in his own long robes, was Endemen.

My entrance had not been quiet.

Both of them turned to look in my direction. And though I was still invisible, they well knew, by the destruction that had unfolded, that someone was there.

Endemen had his wand out and pointed it toward me.

But the creature on the throne simply waved his hand, and I felt the very air around me begin to harden.

I couldn't move.

And something else happened.

In my head came a voice.

*Go now. Go now or you are lost.*

I pointed the Elemental up and, like a fired morta, I soared up, up until I smashed right through the ceiling, sending huge chunks of glass plummeting.

Next instant, I was out into the open air.

I was free!

But then, as I looked back, I realized I was very much mistaken.

# Home Again

T HE CHASE WAS ON.

I kept the Elemental at full size and clutched in my hand. I lay prone in the air, willing Destin to fly faster than it ever had before.

As I looked back, I saw no fewer than six Maladons soaring after me, led by the lethal Endemen.

I knew they couldn't see me. But I wondered if they could somehow still follow me.

I pointed my head down and zoomed toward the ground.

They instantly followed.

How were they doing this?

Now spells were blasting my way.

I rolled and dove and then shot upward, dodging them all.

I straightened out as a new volley of spells hurtled my way.

I couldn't keep this up, I knew. One of their spells was going to find its mark.

*Okay*, I thought, *two can play at this game.*

My wand was my Elemental and vice versa. Well, why couldn't it be *both* at the same time?

I attached a magical tether to the Elemental, using the Elemental as a wand. That would ensure it would remain invisible once it left my hand.

I flipped onto my back, avoiding a series of spells, drew back my arm and told the Elemental what to do.

I hurled it directly at the Maladons. It blasted forward like a runaway train. They were heading right for it though they couldn't see it.

When it was ten feet from them, I muttered, "*Impacto.*"

A white light blasted from the Elemental and smashed into the Maladons.

Four of them were knocked heels over arse and were flung out of the sky. I saw them fall for a long time until they hit the dirt with enormous thuds.

The Elemental turned and flew back to my hand.

Endemen and two of the Maladons had managed to somehow avoid my spell. They were still chasing me, but I saw Endemen whip his wand in front of him.

I instantly knew that he had cast a shield spell to protect from another such attack.

I turned and flew as fast as I could. But still they were coming after me.

What the bloody Hel? How were they doing this? I was invisible!

Then it struck me. *The wand!*

I groped in my pocket and pulled out the wand I'd taken from the man I'd blasted to nothing. I broke it in half and dropped it.

The pieces fell to the ground even as I swooped upward.

I looked back.

Sure enough, Endemen and his group were still heading downward.

They touched down, and I saw Endemen pick up the broken pieces of the wand and look around.

Then he looked up and screamed the bloodiest scream I'd ever heard. Even the shriek of the jabbits had never inspired such terror in me. I shuddered and very nearly fell out of the air.

But I recovered and urged Destin onward.

When Endemen and his men were out of sight, I took out my wand, tapped my leg and said, *"Pass-pusay."*

I had one destination in mind.

A moment later my feet hit something solid. I staggered a bit and then stood upright.

I was on the doorstep of Empyrean.

I turned my ring around and waved my wand; the door opened and I passed quickly through.

With another wave of my wand, the door shut and bolted.

The next instant something lifted me into the air. So on edge was I that I was prepared to blast it with my wand. Fortunately, before I did so, I saw that, to my relief, it was Delph.

"Vega Jane!" he shouted in my ear, nearly deafening me. "You're alive."

"Blimey," I said. "I'm right next to you, Delph. And I could hear fine until you screamed in my ear."

But I smiled and hugged him back.

Around his feet danced Harry Two, barking his head off.

Over Delph's shoulder I was stunned to see what looked like most of the staff of Empyrean lined up watching me,

Pillsbury and Mrs. Jolly standing at the head of them. There was an assortment of floor lamps, coatracks, the rake, the wheelbarrow and two marble statues, one of a man in chain mail and the other of a sinewy horse.

On the wall I saw the portrait of a queenly looking woman, and in another painting a cow pictured in a field staring anxiously at us and then whispering to each other.

Pillsbury, his armor squeaking slightly, lurched forward and patted me gently on the shoulder as Delph finally set me down on the floor. Harry Two rubbed against my leg and I automatically scratched at his lone ear.

"'Tis good to see you, Mistress Vega," Pillsbury said. "Master Delph told us that you were off to . . . We thought, well, we thought perhaps . . ." He was unable to continue, so I finished for him.

"Me too, Pillsbury. But I'm back, safe and sound."

I looked around but didn't see Petra. I asked Delph where she was.

"In her room," he said quickly. He wouldn't meet my eye.

"I have lots to tell you," I said, letting the issue of Petra pass for now.

"And I want to hear all of it," he replied. "Every little detail."

Mrs. Jolly stepped forward. "I'm sure you're famished. Shall I prepare a meal?"

"That would be wonderful, Mrs. Jolly, thanks."

I went to my room, took off my dirty garments, cleaned up, put on fresh clothes and headed back downstairs.

Delph was already waiting for me in the kitchen. While we ate, I told him all that had happened to me.

"You done all that?" he said incredulously as I finished. "In just the time you've been gone?"

I nodded, for the first time realizing just how much I had been through.

"This bloke under the cloak. The one Endemen was summoned by? Did you get a look at him?"

I shook my head. "But he was very powerful, Delph. I felt the entire air around me hardening. Another moment and I don't think I could have escaped."

Delph rubbed his jaw and thought about this. I could almost see the gears in his head whirring as I sipped my tea.

"Show me the bottle."

I had placed the bottle of sparkling dust in my pocket when I'd changed clothes. I pulled it out for Delph to see.

He took the bottle from me and held it up to the light.

"So maybe what's in there, Vega Jane, is *them*. Them on the inside, I mean."

I stared at the bottle in horror. *This was them?*

"Delph, the man taking it from them told one of them he was going to become an Ordinary."

"That must be what they call nonmagical folks. Ordinary. How very *kind* of them." His look was one of unbridled disgust. "The Maladons are vile, Vega Jane. I'd take an army of jabbits after me over one of them blokes."

"But how would the Maladons know these people were magical to begin with?" I asked.

"I dunno exactly. The ones off the train in True, they just messed with their minds, making 'em happy with their lot in life. But these poor blokes at the castle were having a lot more done to 'em. A lot more!"

He rose and said, "Be back in a mo'."

A minute later he returned carrying a large book. He set it down in front of me.

"While you were gone, I found this in the library, behind a panel."

"How'd you find the panel?"

"It was an accident. Hit it with my elbow."

I looked down at the book. It had no title.

"Turn to page two twenty-four," said Delph a bit ominously.

I flipped to the page. It was a chapter heading.

*"Incada Masacarro?"*

"It's a spell. A wicked one, and it looks mighty tricky to manage. It tells how you can remove the magical powers of another. It's done through a series of torture incantations. It leaves the person with nothing inside."

I turned the pages of the chapter and saw the drawings there. Disgusting drawings. But I knew Delph was right, because what I saw there matched what I had seen back at that room in the castle.

"This is horrible, Delph. So what happens to the person after this is done to them?"

"That's the other awful part. Since there's nothing there, they can be filled up with anything you want. Make 'em slaves for life. That part's at the end."

I read this section and drew a quick breath. "Delph, when I was in Greater True, I saw a man following behind other people. He was dressed very formally, but he was clearly there only to do his master's bidding. He was treated foully but never complained. And his eyes were blank, like the people in the looking glasses back at the castle."

He nodded, his gaze on the page I was reading.

"I think you saw the result of a full bottle taken, then, Vega Jane," he said grimly. "A sorcerer or sorceress turned into an Ordinary and then enslaved."

I was so upset I could barely process this. I blinked away tears as I thought back to the eyeless man in the top hat who had saved the woman's precious bottle but been yelled at and struck for his trouble. Was that to be the fate of all those back at the castle?

*All those you left behind, Vega?*

And then I thought of the full bottles in the niches along that wall. Each bottle represented a person who used to be magical but was now a slave.

Then I glanced at the spine of the book, where there was something printed in faded letters. My eyes widened in disbelief.

"Delph, look who wrote it!" I exclaimed. I showed him the name. "Colin *Sonnet!* Now, how much coin would you wager that he's related to Petra?" I added triumphantly.

To my surprise, he shook his head. "I already saw that. So what? We've got our ancestors on the walls here, so why can't Pet have something too?"

My face collapsed. "Why can't *Pet* have something too? Delph, do you hear yourself? Colin Sonnet had to be a Maladon!"

"We don't know that. And remember, the book belonged to Jasper Jane. You saying he's a Maladon too?"

"Of course he wasn't a bloody Maladon. He needed to know about the dark forces so he could better fight them." I tapped the name on the spine of the book. "Like this evil bloke."

"Vega Jane," he began in a weary tone.

"Wait, there's more!" I couldn't believe I had forgotten.

I told Delph about my seeing Petra casting dark spells in her bedroom.

Instead of the shock I was expecting him to show, Delph looked completely unmoved. "Well, like Jasper Jane was doing, maybe Petra was studying those spells so she could better fight the Maladons, eh?"

"Why do you keep defending her?" I said suspiciously.

"Because she's proved time and again that she's on our side."

I studied his features and thought, *Or is it because you want to snog her, Daniel Delphia?*

I could not let it go. "But what if her Maladon blood *is* coming out in her? Maybe from reading these dark sorcery books. Or from being close to that Endemen git?"

"I don't believe that she would ever hurt either of us, Vega Jane."

"You didn't see how happy she was to be casting these dark spells, Delph," I shot back. "She had a chair full of serpents. She . . . she was giddy about it all."

"You just can't get past this, can you?" he asked.

"I'm being practical. If she turns against us, we need to be ready."

"Well, I think we just need to have this out now."

He rose.

"Where are you going?" I said, looking up at him in consternation.

"I think it's time to talk to Petra."

I gaped. "Delph, no, we shouldn't do that."

"Vega Jane, I believe in Petra, but you obviously don't. So we need to put this to rest once and for all. Otherwise, you're going to be looking over your shoulder all the time, and what will that help?"

"If she is our enemy, she won't admit it."

"We won't give her that opportunity, will we?"

"But how will you do that?"

"Just leave it to me, Vega Jane. But we can't take Harry Two with us."

"Why not?"

"You'll see."

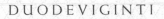

# A Blood Oath

W E KNOCKED ON Petra's door and at first received no answer. We knocked again, harder; Delph actually pounded with his fist against the stout wood.

"Who is it?"

Petra's voice sounded tight and unnatural.

Delph said, "Me and Vega Jane. She's back. We need to fill you in on what she found out. About the accursed *Maladons*! You might find it interesting, them being your kind and all."

I stared at him, wondering why he was being intentionally antagonistic toward her when just moments before he had been so fiercely defending her.

We heard hesitant footsteps coming toward the door.

It opened and there she was.

She was dressed in her nightshirt though it was well into the day. Her long, bare legs were clearly visible. Her hair was damp and tousled and fell down over her shoulders in, I had to admit, a very fetching manner. I breathed in, and the scent of vanilla and roses filled my nostrils. She must have just taken a bath.

In her right hand was her wand.

I slipped my hand into my pocket and gripped mine. Just in case.

"So you're back," she said, looking at me in a disquieting manner. "You've been gone long enough."

"I heard you haven't come out of your room?" I paused. "Practicing your spell casting? How's it going for you?"

"What are you talking about?" she said defiantly.

I took a step closer. "The pages you took from Jasper's room. They were from the book on dark incantations."

She instinctively shot a glance at the nightstand next to her bed. "How did you — have you been spying on me?" she finished accusingly.

Delph pushed past her and into the room. I followed and closed the door behind us.

He whirled round to face her. "So, Vega Jane found out quite a bit 'bout them Maladon blokes." He turned to me. "You want to start filling her in?"

"Okay," I said hesitantly. I still had no idea what Delph was up to.

I started telling Petra what had happened. I had just gotten to the part about entering the castle when, with a scream, Delph ripped a broadax off the wall and swung it toward me.

I was so stunned that I had no chance to protect myself. I just stood there waiting for the blow to fall. I could only imagine that Delph had simply gone mad.

"*Embattlemento*," Petra cried out.

The force of her spell was so strong that Delph and his ax were tossed ten feet backward and he crashed against the wall.

"What the bloody Hel!" shouted Petra, her wand aimed at Delph's chest.

"Wait," I said. "Delph, are you okay?"

I rushed over and helped him up.

As Petra watched, mystified, Delph dusted himself off, put the ax back on the wall and shook his head free of the collywobbles that the impact with the wall had no doubt caused.

"Well, I figure she's okay, eh?" he said, rubbing the back of his head.

"That . . . that was your ruddy *plan*?" I shouted. "Almost getting yourself killed?!"

"What plan?" demanded Petra.

Exasperated, I turned to her. "Show her the book, Delph."

He pulled it from his pocket and passed it across. At first she didn't know what she was to do with it. But then she saw the author's name and her face paled.

She looked up at both of us. "I don't know who this is."

"I'm sure you don't. But he's probably an ancestor."

She shot a glance at Delph. "So you were pretending to attack Vega to see what I would do?"

"Well, yeah," he conceded. "And it worked."

She swung her wand so fast I barely saw it move. A moment later she'd blasted Delph across the room again and he landed in a heap against the wall.

I snatched out my wand and raised it, but Petra had already let hers drop. She stood there, her lips quivering.

"You still don't trust me," she said. "After all this, you still don't bloody trust me. What do I have to do? Tell me, what?"

My thoughts, all garbled until this point, seemed to crystallize. "You can stop practicing dark spells behind closed doors without telling either of us. And you can stop being so bloody sensitive about everything!" I added, my voice rising shrilly.

I helped Delph up once more. He looked so battered that I pulled out the Adder Stone and waved it over him, thinking good thoughts. He perked up right away, the bruises on his face vanishing.

"It was a trick," wailed Petra with a devastated expression on her face. "It was a bloody trick. I thought you cared about me. I thought we were friends. I'll never forgive you for this, Delph. Never."

I didn't think she'd heard a single word I'd just said.

He stared down at her, not looking the least bit sorry. "And you wouldn't have done the same if things had been the other way round?"

She started to answer but then stopped. Her hesitation was response enough. Her face reddening, she looked away.

"Petra," I began.

She held up a hand. "Just don't. I don't want to hear it. Not now."

"We *want* to trust you. But the Maladons are so very evil."

"And because their blood runs in me I must be evil too, eh?" she snapped.

"I've seen what they can do," I replied quietly. "I've seen what they do to people. How they turn them to . . . well, nothing. Take their powers away and collect them in bottles. And then enslave what's left, little though it is."

I thought Petra was going to shout at me again, but her jaw dropped and she simply gaped at me.

"They . . . t-they d-do that?" she said, her voice cracking.

I held up the bottle of dust. "This is what they take from them. Their magic, their souls, everything that makes them who they really are." I added bitterly, "And it leaves nothing behind except a blank-eyed slave."

Petra stared at the bottle, and fresh tears filled her eyes.

Delph held up the book. "The spell that does it is in here. Written by your ancestor."

"But I'm not my bloody ancestor, am I?" she positively shrieked.

I was about to say something but Delph beat me to it. "There is something, something that each of you can do, to put this matter to rest once and for all."

We looked at him expectantly.

"What?" I asked.

He held open another page in the book. We stared at the writing there.

*"The Oath of Oblivion?"* I read out.

Delph nodded. "What it basically does is, you each take a bit of your blood and give it to the other."

"Give each other some of our blood, are you mental?" asked Petra.

Ignoring this, Delph continued. "You swear allegiance to each other, touch your wands together, say the spell at the same time and a bit of your blood is magically transferred to the other."

"And if we don't keep our promise?" I asked.

"Then you go into oblivion," said Delph. "And from the pictures in the book, you *don't* want to go there."

Petra and I stared at each other.

I said, "I . . . I don't know."

"Me either," said Petra.

"Well, then that's a bit of a problem," said Delph, his features unusually dark. "Because, Vega Jane, I'm getting bloody well tired of having to come back to this question of Petra being loyal or not."

I flinched because it felt like Delph had just slapped me.

I glanced at Petra and saw the trace of a smile on her face. I felt my blood start to heat up, but Delph's next words reversed this.

"And you, Petra, I'm sick of you always complaining that everyone is against you. You're not the only one who's had it rough."

The smile on her face vanished. We both just stood there staring up at Delph as the force of his words continued to swell.

He barked, "There's a whole world out there we have to confront, and it's got plenty enough evil in it, I reckon. Too much for us to have to worry about whether we trust each other. So it has to end. Now!"

He abruptly stopped and glared at each of us.

"Well?" he prompted.

"Shall we have a go at it, then?" I finally said to Petra in a small voice.

Petra seemed to roll this around in her head, too long to suit me, but she said at last, "Okay. I guess."

Delph showed us the exact language we had to use, and also showed us the diagram on how to hold our wands. We couldn't touch them at first. We had to say the oath and then touch the wands, then incant the spell. Then our blood would be transferred.

Somehow.

We said the oath first, together, and then we ever so carefully touched wands. I think both of us were afraid that doing so might result in some sort of explosion, or perhaps in us being killed or, even worse, somehow joined at the hip forever! But that didn't happen.

Yet something else did.

As soon as the wood of our wands touched, they held fast to each other, like they had been sealed together. This sudden move of the sticks caught both of us off guard. Petra gasped, and I heard myself do the same. The astonished look on her face, I'm sure, simply mirrored the one on mine.

"And now the spell," said Delph.

We read off the words, saying them at the same time, our voices surprisingly similar as we did so, as though important parts of us had already been conjoined. When the last word rolled off our lips, we both yelped in pain.

Gashes had opened on our foreheads. As I watched, horrified, the blood poured down Petra's face, leapt from her skin to her wand, then onto my wand, and from there it catapulted directly to the wound on my face. The blood seemed to disappear inside me. I felt a sudden chill and then a comforting surge of warmth. Next I could sense the skin closing up and the wound healing. The exact same thing had just happened to Petra.

Our wands parted and we instinctively stepped back.

For some reason we were both breathing heavily, as though we had just fought some duel or run a long distance.

We simply stared at each other. I couldn't find words, and apparently neither could Petra.

Delph stepped between us and said, "The oath is done. You two, I reckon, are in this together, for as long as it takes. So no more fighting between you."

I slowly lowered my wand and gazed at it. When I looked closely enough, I saw a new indentation there. It was crimson. Apparently not all of Petra's blood had entered my body. A bit was still on my wand.

When I looked at her, she was gazing at her wand and seeing the very same thing.

She slowly lowered her wand and put it away in her pocket.

Petra said, "I found the incantation book. I was curious. I knew the spells were dark, but I still wanted to attempt them. It just seemed like a good idea. To know how the other side fights."

I said, "My ancestor Jasper Jane thought the very same thing. So it probably is a good thing. I'm sorry if I thought otherwise."

"But that's not the only reason," confessed Petra, her face reddening and her voice wobbling a bit. "There was something in those spells that . . ." She faltered for a moment. "That seemed natural to me. They were compelling me to try to perform them." She drew a deep, tortured breath and looked directly at me. "So I'm glad we took the oath, Vega. I would never want to do anything to hurt you. I would never do anything to help these blokes who put people in bottles."

"I know," I said, overcome with the clear truth in her words.

A moment later I could feel Delph's arm around my shoulder. His other one went around Petra, and he drew the three of us together into an embrace that lasted for a long moment.

When we parted, I was smiling, and so were Delph and Petra.

I looked at Delph and said, "Thanks."

"Yes, thanks, Delph," echoed Petra, her look one of grudging admiration. "And I'm sorry if I hurt you."

"Tosh, I'm fine," he said.

"Wait a mo', why didn't you want Harry Two to come along?" I asked him.

"Are you mad? When I 'attacked' you he would've torn me apart."

I laughed. "I think you're right about that."

Delph said, "Are we all good now?"

We both nodded.

"And now we need to figure out where we go from here," he said.

I shivered at his words. I well knew where we would need to go.

Directly into the black heart of the Maladons.

And we might never get back out.

## Bimbleton Station

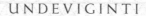

LATER THAT LIGHT, Mrs. Jolly put together a wonderful meal and brought it into the library for all of us.

Through bites of meat, cheese and potatoes, Delph listed the more pertinent items of discussion about our future actions.

Something occurred to me and I felt my stomach lurch sideways.

"Delph, I don't how to get back to the castle. I followed Endemen there, but I wasn't paying attention to directions. And then when I fled the place it was the same. They were after me and I had to distract them with that bloke's broken wand. Then I used the *Pass-pusay* spell to get back here."

"Why not use that spell to go back there?" suggested Petra.

"I don't think I can. When I tried to leave by incanting, it didn't work. I had to use the Elemental to break out. And I would imagine that it would prevent me from using the incantation to get *in* there. Besides, even if I could, I'm not sure I want to just *appear* in that place. I might land right in a mess of garms and jabbits. And Maladons!"

"That's all right, Vega Jane," Delph replied. "I don't think we need to go to the castle, at least not yet."

"What are you talking about?" I snapped. "Not go to the castle?"

"I think *first*, we need to go back to the beginning," he said, his voice calm despite my near hysterics.

"To the beginning?" I retorted. "What, the beginning of the Quag?!"

"Not that," he said. "I meant we should go back to True."

Well, this brought me up short. "What is there in True?" I asked.

"The people on the train."

"But we've seen them. We know they do this brainwashing what-you-call-it to them."

Petra added, "And some of them, the ones with magical ability, are taken on to the castle and tortured, and their magic stolen from them by the Maladons."

"And," I said, "they're forced to be slaves for the high and mighty in Greater True."

"Right," said Delph. "But what we *don't* know is *where* the blokes on the train into True come from."

I thought about this. "Well, that's right enough," I said. "But why will that help us?"

"I was thinking that maybe by going to the source, we could help all of *them*."

I let out a long sigh. Leave it to Delph to come up with a noble plan to help others, while my thinking, though practical, was far more limited to its positive effect on *my* goals and our survival. I felt quite ashamed. I really did.

We set off next night. I wasn't exactly sure how long it would take to travel to where we were going, but I didn't want to get there while it was light.

Pillsbury and Mrs. Jolly saw us off.

We stepped outside the front door, which Pillsbury firmly closed behind us.

"Are you ready?" I asked Delph and Petra.

They both nodded, and Harry Two, who dangled in his harness, licked my hand.

I tethered all of us together with my *Lassado* incantation and then reversed my grandfather's ring, making us invisible.

"Are you going to use the *Pass-pusay* spell?" Delph asked.

I shook my head. "I've never done it other than by myself. And Astrea never said it was meant for more than one to use. I'm afraid something might go wrong."

We kicked off and soared upward, Delph on my right and Petra on my left, like a pair of wings.

We all kept our gazes swiveling, looking for any sign of Endemen or his cohorts.

We flew over the trees, and I tacked back in the direction of where he had been traveling on the train.

I kept my gaze pointed down searching for it, but Petra saw it first.

"There," she said.

I looked where she was pointing and saw the train tracks.

I nodded and took a moment to get my bearings.

I peered around for a landmark that might be helpful to orient me better, and I found it in a bluish hill to my left. We had passed that coming from True. That meant True was to the left and Greater True was located off in the distance to my right.

I turned to the left, changing our flight path to match the route of the tracks.

There was no train, so sometimes it was difficult to follow the tracks, particularly when they entered trees or went through tunnels carved in to the hills.

Finally, after nearly losing the bloody thing a couple of times, I pulled out my wand. I was about to employ the *Crystilado magnifica* incantation, but then something occurred to me.

"Petra," I said. "Use your wand to do the magnification spell."

She looked at me strangely but pulled out her wand, pointed it downward and spoke the pair of words.

Instantly the tracks were right in front of us and we followed them easily.

Delph looked at me curiously for a moment, but I shook my head. My reasoning was clear enough.

Endemen had been able to track the wand I had taken from the bloke back at the castle. I wanted to see whether they could detect Petra's wand too. It might have Maladon elements in it for all I knew.

When no suited gents with bowler hats showed up, I let out a relieved breath.

With the magnification spell to lead us, we had no trouble following the train route all the way back to True.

Although we had traveled quite a ways, it was still nighttime when we arrived in True. However, with the aid of the spell, I could see a couple of people walking and one motor passing down an otherwise quiet street.

Then True was behind us as we continued to follow the train tracks.

We passed a number of towns and smaller villages, none near the size of True or Greater True. We kept going until Delph said, "There!"

Below was a structure where the train tracks ended.

I descended slowly, scanning the area to see if anyone was around, but the place looked deserted.

We alighted at a spot about a hundred yards distant from the structure. I could see that it was small and wooden with a metal roof and was open to the elements on all four sides.

"It's just a shelter really," whispered Delph. "For folks to gather under and wait for the train."

Still invisible, we drew closer. There was a sign hanging from one of the support posts.

"Bimbleton Station?" I said. "I wonder what that is?"

"Must be the name of this here place, I reckon," said Delph.

"But I don't see a *place*," I protested. "It's just this thing in the middle of nowhere."

Petra said, "I never saw that name on the schedule sign at True Station."

Neither had I.

A moment later, a young boy dressed shabbily with dirt smudges on his face and no shoes on his feet came out of a nearby copse of trees. He was carrying a wooden basket.

As we watched from the shadows, he started picking berries off a bush and putting them in his basket. When the basket was fairly full, he walked around the shelter and stopped and gazed up at the sign.

He reached up on tiptoe and ran his finger along the letters spelling out the station name.

I looked at the others; they were all staring at this curious spectacle.

He walked on and soon disappeared from our sight.

"Let's go," I said.

"Where?" asked Delph.

"Wherever he's going," I replied.

We made up the ground quickly and soon gained sight of the boy. The walk through the woods took about twenty minutes, and I wondered at the boy's family allowing him to wander alone at night. Was this place safe?

Delph noticed it first.

"The light," he whispered.

I looked up ahead, to where the boy was heading. Light was filling the sky there only we didn't know what the source was.

I instinctively reached into my pocket and gripped my wand with my gloved hand. I noted from the corner of my eye that Petra did the same.

We continued to follow the boy and I felt my heart start to beat faster and my breaths quicken as we went.

He disappeared around a bend in the path and we hurriedly followed.

When we cleared the curve, I stopped so fast that Delph bumped into me.

The lights we had glimpsed before were coming from wooden shacks clustered around a small center patch of grass. Smoke was rising from stone chimneys. Maybe a hundred people or more were gathered around porches or walking along paths dimly lit by the shack lights.

They were of all different ages. Most were dressed poorly, like the boy, who had disappeared into one of the wooden houses with his basket of berries.

We eased forward and cautiously gazed around.

Delph put his mouth next to my ear and said, "What now?"

I whispered back, "Let's watch and listen a bit."

He nodded, and we drew closer to one group clustered on a crumbling porch.

"But when will it come again?" asked one young woman a little older than me. She wore corduroy pants, a ripped and dirty coat and falling-apart shoes on her feet. An old tuck was slung over her shoulder. Her dirty face was lined well beyond her years.

An old man in a slouch hat with a droopy mustache was seated on the top step busily whittling down a piece of wood with a small pocketknife.

"The *train*, you mean?" said the man.

The woman and the others nodded. "Well, 'tis hard to say." He scratched his forehead with a gnarled finger. This pushed his hat back a bit, revealing tangled white hair. "I hear tell that other trains show up in other places, not that I've been to those places, but I hear things from folks ambling down the road from time to time."

"So there are other trains, then?" asked another man.

"Guess so," said the first man. "Lots of people, lots of trains."

"Do they all go to the same place?" asked the man.

The man shook his head. "Dunno. Now, *I can* tell you

that it does show up at odd times. Nothing scheduled about it, you see. But you hear the whistle. Always hear the whistle, you do. And right after that, it appears."

"And do they take everyone?" the disheveled young woman asked. "I heard they might."

The old man shook his head, as did several others gathered there.

"No. Look at me. Been here a long time now. And I'm *still* here. And lots of you folks will still be here when the train leaves next; just the way it is."

"How do they decide, then?" asked a young man who was standing next to the young woman. He held an old battered canvas bag in one hand.

It then occurred to me that they were traveling together.

"We just got here and know nothing about it," he added.

The old man pointed his whittled stick at the fellow. "No rhyme or reason that I can see. They just pick."

"How many?" asked the man.

"Now, that varies too, don't it? Sometimes a lot. Sometimes not too many."

"And 'tis a good thing?" asked the young woman. "I mean, where they go?"

Another man said, "No one's ever come back to complain, I can tell you that." He added bitterly, "Course I'm still here, just like 'im." He pointed at the old man.

"Course it's better," bellowed the old man. He looked around. "I mean what wouldn't be better than what I got? And none of you would be here if your village had enough food and could take care of its folks. Roofs over your heads, medicine when you need it, education for the young ones. Work your fingers to the bone and for what?" He spat on the ground. "Where I'm from it's dirt poor, it is. And I'm tired of it." He pointed at various people in the crowd with his knifepoint. "Any different for any of you, eh?"

I saw folks shaking their heads, their gazes downcast.

Apparently life for all of them was as hard as it had been for us in Wormwood. When I thought about what I'd seen in True and Greater True it was like two different worlds coexisting somehow. The "have-alls" and the "have-nothings."

The old man said, "I thought as much. So I mean to stay here until I gets on that damn train."

"Why does the train even come here?" said a young woman.

"This is the *train* station," replied the old man. "'Tis where it stops."

"What does a train look like?" asked the same young man.

"Bloody something," said the old man. "Long and metal and it runs on those little tracks you see at the station. Folks climb on, and off it goes. Fast it is. Gone in a blur."

Many people looked around in wonderment, as though they couldn't believe what they were hearing. But then again, I had never known that a train existed until I got to True.

Then I wondered why these people didn't simply walk to True. Why bother with the train? I knew with Greater True you needed to be authorized, but that wasn't so for True. At least I didn't think it was.

The young man slowly nodded, and then he and the young woman withdrew from the group and walked off.

I said instantly to the others, "I'm going to become visible and follow those two. I want to talk to them."

"But should we be giving ourselves away like that?" asked Delph nervously.

"I'll only be giving myself away. If something happens we can get away quickly enough. But by their own words they just arrived here and don't really know anything."

"But if they don't know anything, what can you learn from them?" asked Petra.

"I can learn *where* they came from," I replied.

"But, Vega Jane," Delph began to protest.

"Delph, I'm going to do this, okay?"

He frowned. And Petra glared at me. But I didn't care. I was too focused on what I was going to do.

We moved to a darkened corner of the place and I slipped off the ring and passed it to Petra. She slid it on, making sure to keep the ring turned inward. Petra used her wand to maintain the magical link among the three of us. I looked around and then headed off after the pair while the others, still invisible, followed.

It didn't take me long to catch up to them.

"Hello," I said.

They both whirled around to stare at me.

"I'm sorry," I said. "I didn't mean to startle you."

"Where did you come from?" asked the man.

"A long way away. I just arrived here."

"For the train?" asked the woman.

I nodded. "I'm Vega."

The man said, "I'm Russell; this is Daphne."

"Have you been here long?" I asked.

Russell shook his head. "Like you, we just arrived."

"And where did you come in from?" I asked, trying to keep my voice casual.

He was about to answer when Daphne said, "Why do you want to know?"

I glanced at her, saw suspicion on her features and realized that I'd overplayed my hand.

I quickly regrouped. "No reason. I was just wondering if you had come from the same direction I had."

Daphne folded her arms across her chest and just scowled.

Russell said, "Daph, she's just curious."

Daphne said, "Okay, so am I. So what direction did you come in from?"

Without really thinking, I immediately pointed to the left. "About five li — days' journey," I said.

"And the name of the place?" she asked, still glaring.

Now I folded my arms and glared back. "Wormwood. And you?"

"I'm not telling," she replied with a smirk.

"Daph," said Russell.

"Shut it, Russ. She just wants to get on the bleedin' train and doesn't care how she does it. I bet she's looking to bump us right off our seats."

I gaped. "How would knowing where you came from help me get on the train instead of you?"

She said stubbornly, "I don't know, do I? Best reason not to spill the beans. For all I know, they may not let folks where we're from get on the train."

"Well, don't you think they might ask where you're from before they let you board, then?" I asked, with more spite than was probably called for.

"Oh, I'm ready for that, I am," she shot back. "I'll convince 'em to take us."

"Fine," I said. "Good luck." I spun on my heel and walked swiftly away.

"Oi, wait," called out Russell.

But I heard Daphne exclaim, "Oh, let her go. She's no bleedin' use to us. And I'm not going back to our village. I'm not, Russ."

I walked purposefully back to the group gathered around the porch, knowing full well that Delph, Petra and Harry Two were right behind me under the invisibility shield.

The people were all standing there, hands in pockets, talking among themselves. The old man whittling before had set down his work and was drinking from a pewter flask.

They all looked at me for a moment before returning to their conversations. I supposed strangers routinely showed up around here.

I sat down next to the old gent. He lowered the flask from his lips, and I could smell sweet wine on them.

"Who be you?" he asked.

"I be Vega. And you?"

"Geoff. You just in?"

I nodded. "And you?"

He capped the flask and chuckled. "Oh, I've been here a while, missy. May be here a while still."

"Where does this train thing go?" I asked.

He shrugged. "Nobody knows that 'cept the ones on it. They don't never come back here, I can tell you that. So wherever they go must be better than what they left behind."

*Yeah, freedom for slavery.*

He had on woolen gloves with the fingers cut off, revealing strong, thick and dirty fingers. He blew on his hands and stuck them in his pockets along with the flask.

"But, Geoff, how do you really know the place they're going to is a good one?"

He looked at me strangely. "What?"

"Well, if you don't know the place they go to and they never come back here, the place might be a bad place, and that's why they never come back."

He laughed, took up his knife and began whittling again. "Whistling in the wind, you are. What rubbish."

I could tell that he so very badly wanted to believe that a better life was just a train ride away that no logic I might employ would persuade him otherwise.

"How long have you been here?" I asked.

"Two years."

"Why did you come here?"

He shrugged. "Where I come from there ain't much there. Been hard times for as long as I can remember."

"Why is that?" I asked.

He shrugged again. "Just has been. Heard tell there was some war or such. Not that I saw or fought in it. I'm old, but t'were long before my time. But it still lingers, you know. People never did get back on their feet. My little village, you can't rub two coins together. No work, people just getting by. No . . . hope. If you want to get somewhere you walk. So most folks don't get nowheres. 'Tis sad, it is."

"Well, why do you have to wait for a train?"

"Eh?" he replied.

"You said you walked here. Why not just follow the train tracks to wherever the train goes?" I almost said "to True" but caught myself.

"Oh, right. Well, I'm not stupid, so I tried doing that once after the train left me behind the first time."

"What happened?"

"I was following the tracks like you said, and . . ." He stopped, and his face took on a confused expression.

"And what?" I prompted.

"Well, I got lost. Couldn't find the bloody tracks. Got turned around and ended up back here. Tried it another time and same thing happened."

I looked around at some other people who were listening to this. They were nodding. One man said, "Aye, me too."

I didn't take me long to figure it out. The Maladons had used a spell, maybe something like *Transdesa hypnotica*. We had encountered that in the Third Circle of the Quag. That meant they would never be able to find their way to True. The train was their only option.

The destinations we had seen on the schedule board at True Station must be towns that the Maladons let people freely travel back and forth to. But those travelers had already had their minds manipulated and weren't a threat. So True apparently was the great clearinghouse for all of this.

"Okay, but that doesn't explain why you came to this particular place."

"Oh, that? Well, word gets around. Want a better life, get yourself to Bimbleton Station. Least what I hears in my village."

I nodded but didn't say anything.

After a few moments of silence he looked sharply at me. "Well, why'd you come here, then?"

"Word got round where I'm from too."

He smiled and chuckled. "That it would. I knew it. Yes, I knew it."

I looked at the shacks. "There's the train station and these shacks. Who built them?"

"Dunno. They've always been here, least I think so. Nice place. Plenty of wood for the fires. Food in the woods. Fresh water from the river."

"Why haven't you been picked to go on the train?"

He stopped whittling and considered this. "Fact is, missy, I don't know why. It's not like they give you a reason."

I pounced on this. "Who is 'they'?"

"Blokes."

"What blokes?"

"Them blokes in suits and hats."

I stiffened and thought, *Blokes in pin-striped suits and bowler hats?*

He continued. "Right fancy clothing. They must be rich. Now, I wouldn't mind being rich neither. Don't know where they come from. Odd chaps. But nice enough."

*Nice enough,* I thought, *for barbaric murderers.*

He started whittling again.

"Yeah, right funny chaps. Like to know how they pick who goes and who stays. Don't know how much time I've got left. Might keel over before I gets my turn on the bloody train."

"What do the blokes in the suits and hats do?"

He pointed around with the tip of his knife. "Well, when we hears the whistle, we all rushes down to the station like. Now, them blokes in the funny hats, they get off the train and they looks round and they talks to folks. And they lines up those what's going on the train. They boards and then off they goes."

"And the others just stay behind and come back here?"

"Some does. Others get fed up and just go back to wherever they came from. Not me; I ain't moving from here 'less it's on the bloody train."

"You said they talk to people? Have you ever heard what they say?"

He shook his head. "I tried to ask somebody once, but they told me it weren't allowed."

"Allowed?" I exclaimed. "Why wouldn't it be allowed to answer a simple question?"

"Well, aren't you the curious one?"

I glanced to my right and saw a strange man standing there staring at me. Behind him was . . . Daphne.

I inwardly groaned.

"She was asking us questions too," said Daphne huffily. "And now she's pestering him the same."

I said nothing.

My gaze remained on the stranger, who also never took his gaze off me.

He had on a long coat, but I could see the lapel of the pin-striped suit where the coat held a gap. I wondered where his bowler hat was. Perhaps magically shrunk and in his pocket.

"You want to come with me, luv?" he said smoothly.

My gloved hand slid inside my pocket and curled around my wand.

"Not really, no."

"Just over there," he said, pointing to his left. "I can answer all your questions."

My gaze drifted to the left, and I rose and said, "All right, let's go." I motioned for him to lead the way.

He did so. I followed him for a few minutes. As soon as we were far enough away he whirled, his wand out.

But I had been expecting this, and if my time in the Quag had taught me anything, it was to be prepared with an action plan.

As he tried to cast his spell, I flew above him, lashed out and delivered a thundering kick to his head with my booted feet. He toppled over and hit the dirt, his wand flying away.

A moment later I heard Petra's voice. "Vega, what do you want us to do?"

"Give me a mo'."

While the man was struggling to his feet, I said, "*Subservio.*"

A white light shot out from my wand and hit the bloke directly in the head. He slumped back down.

I knelt next to him and spoke in low tones. I was basically erasing everything that he had heard or experienced to do with me. I then dragged him deeper into the woods and placed him in a sitting position against a tree and put his wand back in his hand.

I searched his pockets and came away with one item that staggered me.

I couldn't believe it. I really couldn't.

It was a picture.

Of my parents.

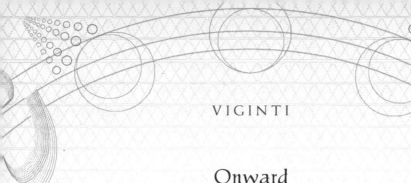

# Onward

I COULDN'T TAKE MY eyes off the image of my mother
and father on the paper.

"Vega Jane?" whispered Delph.

I broke out of my trance and refocused. I hadn't realized
I was holding my breath and it came out in a rush.

"Just give me a sliver," I said desperately, my mind
whirling.

I vacillated on what to do with the picture. It wasn't a
drawing; the images seemed real, burned into the paper. For
a terrifying moment I thought that, like the poor people in
the looking glasses back at the Maladons' castle, my parents
had also been trapped in this thing somehow.

I turned it over and received another shock.

The writing there was crystal clear.

*Be on the lookout for these campions.*

I turned the paper back over and stared at the images of
my mother and father. I thought back to that awful night at
the Care in Wormwood when my parents had been engulfed
in flames and then had disappeared. I felt my lips tremble as I
traced their features with my shaky finger.

*Mom? Dad? Where are you? How can I find you?*

I felt something touch my arm.

"Vega Jane?" hissed Delph. "Are you all right?"

I slowly put the picture away in my pocket. "I'm fine."

"What was that thing you were holding? We couldn't see."

"It was a picture of my parents," I said slowly.

"Blimey!" Petra exclaimed.

"Your parents?" said Delph in disbelief. "But how can that be? The Maladons? I . . . I . . . Are your parents okay?"

"I don't know. But it was them."

I took the picture out and held it up to them.

"You look like your mum," said Petra, studying the image. "She was very beautiful."

I looked at her in surprise. This was the last thing I had expected to hear from her.

"Thank you, my mum *was* very beautiful. I mean, she *is* very beautiful."

"So what now, Vega Jane?" asked Delph.

"I need to talk to that man again."

"What, the old bloke?" said Petra.

"He might have seen them come through here."

"But what if more suits and hats show up?" said Delph.

"It won't take long," I said.

And that's when we heard it.

The whistle!

I said, "The train. It's here! Come on."

I joined the invisibility shield and we ran as fast as we could back to the shacks. Then we stopped.

Geoff was no longer on the porch.

There was no one around at all.

"They've all gone to the bleedin' station," exclaimed Petra. "To try to get on the train."

And that meant that the Bowler Hats would be there. Perhaps Endemen as well.

But we had no choice. We had to go to the train station too.

We reversed our course along the path and soon found ourselves at Bimbleton Station.

There could not have been a greater difference from when we had been there previously.

First, a shiny black train was parked next to the humble station.

And where before there had been only one small boy, now the place was jammed with what I estimated to be hundreds of people jostling one another to get closer to the train.

Then one of the carriage doors opened and he appeared.

And the four of us took a collective step backward.

It was Endemen.

He smiled and doffed his hat, and the crowds around the train instantly quieted.

"Hello," he said. "I welcome all of you to Bimbleton Station. My associates will be going through the lot of you to have little discussions and ask certain questions and then we'll be off. Does that sound all right to you?"

He was being ever so polite, and I wondered how this would go over with such an energetic crowd, many of whom I'm sure had gone through this before, only to be rejected and left behind.

To my mild surprise, they all instantly stepped away from the train and allowed space in between them and their neighbors so as to give some privacy for the little discussions.

When I looked up near the head of the train and saw a Bowler Hat surreptitiously putting his wand away, I knew magic had been the reason for the sudden mass acquiescence.

Endemen, still smiling, stepped off the train. He was followed by over a dozen of his men. They spread out among the crowd and started interacting one by one with the folks congregated there, while Endemen watched with great interest.

"Come on," I whispered to the others.

We drew as close as we dared and, ironically enough, found ourselves within a few feet of Russell and Daphne, the couple from before. I was still irked that she had ratted me out to one of the Bowler Hats, but my anger was quelled some by the nervous expression on her face.

It took a while, but one of the Bowler Hats finally made his way over to them.

He was about my height, thin, with a shiny black mustache and flinty cheekbones.

When he smiled at them, it came out more as a leer.

Russell looked nervous but Daphne stood her ground and stared back.

"So you're the one what decides if we get on the train or not?" she said firmly.

He said nothing at first, appraising her and then Russell.

"From where do you come?" he asked, his voice low and throaty.

"Clarendon on Hillshire," replied Daphne. "Just got in a bit ago. It's a long hike."

"I imagine it is," said the man. "But you're in good hands now. And your surnames?"

"He's Everett and I'm Lloyd. But we're going to get married. Our given names are Daphne for me and Russell for him."

"Nice, very nice."

The bloke pulled a book from his pocket, opened it and riffled through the pages.

"Lloyd, you say?"

"Yes, Daphne Lloyd."

"Have you had others in your family take the train?"

"No. Least not that I'm aware of."

The man swiveled his gaze to Russell. "And you, Mr. Everett?"

He nodded. "My grandfather George — that was long ago of course, before I was born. We never heard from him again."

"Because he went on to a better life," noted Daphne.

"Right you are," said the man. "A *much* better life. Might I see the backs of your right hands, please?"

Daphne and Russell looked at each other. Russell was about to raise his when Daphne, with proper spirit, said, "What does that have to do with anything?"

"It has to do with a great deal. Just let me see the back of your right hand."

Russell said, "Daph, just do it."

She muttered, "Bloody Hel," and raised her hand.

Russell's hand was blank. But with a thrill of horror I saw a faint outline of a shape on the back of Daphne's. The mark of the three hooks! I wondered why I hadn't noticed it before.

"Very nice, thank you," said the man. "That will do. You can lower them."

They did so and waited expectantly.

"That mark on your hand?" he said, looking expectantly at Daphne.

"What of it? It don't come off, case you're wondering. It's . . . it's like a birthmark, I guess. Had it always, I have. Ain't nothing wrong with it. Or me."

She self-consciously covered it with her other hand.

"Well, I wouldn't exactly agree with that."

The man did it so smoothly I almost missed it.

"*Subservio,*" he muttered. And then I saw the tip of his wand poking out of a hole in one of his pockets.

Daphne and Russell instantly went rigid and their eyelids fluttered.

"Now, Ms. Daphne Lloyd, let's go to the train, shall we?" said the man. "We have a very special carriage for you. Your friend will be riding on another one. My mate will be along presently to toddle him off."

She immediately followed him, while Russell simply stood there like a stone.

I glanced at Russell, and my plan came together in an instant. I pointed my wand at him and said softly, "You will go back to Clarendon on Hillshire and tell them that the train is a trap, an evil trap. It carries folks to their doom. Anyone with a mark on the back of their right hand is at particular risk. You must all go into hiding after spreading the word to never to come to this place, do you understand me?"

Russell nodded dumbly.

I looked around. Others were either under the *Subservio* spell or else being led away toward the train because they had "passed" the bloody test, whatever that was.

The Maladons were all preoccupied with escorting people onto the train. "Go now," I said. "As fast as you can."

Russell turned and raced off. He was soon out of sight.

"Now what?" asked Petra.

"Now we get on the train and do what we can."

There was something else of course. I knew that Daphne
Lloyd and others like her were headed to one place and one
place only.

Maladon Castle.

Where their magic would be drained, and the only future
they would know would be that of a slave.

And so that's where we were headed too.

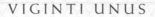

## Clarendon on Hillshire

W E SNUCK ON at the last instant and shrunk back
against the wall of the vestibule connecting one car
to its neighbor. I watched, my anger building as Daphne
Lloyd and the others were led to their seats and shackled.
Under the *Subservio* spell they could offer no resistance.

This car had no windows, so no one out there could see
what was happening. And the passengers who were in other
cars and not shackled were also under spells and could not
fight back. The ones who had not been chosen had either
walked back to the shacks or else started their journeys
home. I had to admit it was all very well planned. And yet
the Maladons had had centuries to perfect what they
were doing: unobtrusively enslaving an entire people while
at the same time destroying all those who could rise up
against them.

I did wonder why some had been left behind. I could
understand ferreting out all the ones with brands on their
hands, but why not take all who came to Bimbleton?

I took out my wand and muttered the magnification spell.
Instantly, I could see up and down the train carriages.

And now I knew how they chose whom they did.

The ones on the carriage without brands were all young, most under thirty. There was not one old person on the train. And I had seen some folks back there, though young, who were on wooden crutches, or had some other type of disability.

Delph, who was privy to what I was seeing, whispered, "They just take the young and healthy. They mess with their minds and put them to work. They leave the old and sick and damaged behind."

"To die off," said Petra, also looking at the images. "It's the young and strong that will challenge them. They're nipping that right in the bud. Pretty soon there won't be any of 'em left."

I had never heard of anything so devious. And yet I knew in my heart that they were exactly right.

The carriage we were in had two guards, one at each end. One was the bloke who had taken charge of Daphne. He was at the far end. His mate was at our end, just inside the carriage, barely five feet from where we stood in the vestibule.

Then I wondered why the Maladons could not simply track all those who had the mark across the land like they had me. Why invent this Bimbleton Station falsehood? Was the mark perhaps too faint to be traced?

But then another possible answer occurred to me.

If they started swooping into places and forcibly removing people, they would be inviting reprisal from others. I knew it was magic versus no magic, but for all I knew there were far more "Ordinaries" than there were Maladons. Just at

Bimbleton Station on one night there had been hundreds of them. And magic or not, a war might not be won by the Maladons, or if they did prevail it would be at a high and perhaps unacceptable cost to them, especially if some with the mark figured out they could do magic as well. Far better to induce those with the mark to come to them. Then they could be quickly and quietly gotten out of the way. And their families would just believe they had gone on to a better life and would never think of attacking those who took them.

It really was quite brilliant.

But more diabolically evil than brilliant.

Our dilemma was quite apparent now.

Did we attack the guards and free the branded folks in the car?

Or did we stay on the train until we reached Maladon Castle? That would be useful since I didn't know how to get back there.

As the train pulled off, the guard nearest us moved down the car and toward his companion. They began to chat far enough away that I felt comfortable whispering to Delph and Petra.

I voiced my concerns about what we should do.

Petra hissed, "How can we be sure they'll take all these blokes to Maladon Castle?"

"Because they need to steal their magic. And for that they need to go there."

"That's right," said Delph.

"Okay," she said in a hushed voice. She glanced at the shackled passengers. "We can't let that happen to them."

198

I understood exactly what she was saying, but if we tried to free them now, we could all be killed and no one would be saved. I didn't know how many Bowler Hats were on this train but we had seen at least thirteen. We had a sum total of two wands, and Petra was relatively inexperienced and had not been trained up as I had.

I said, "We need to just stay invisible and see what happens. We can't fight them all yet, Petra. We'll lose. And then so will everyone."

She scowled at me, obviously disagreeing with my assessment.

Delph said, "She's right, Petra. We just have to see what happens."

Petra nodded at Delph. Not me. It was clear she respected *his* opinion, not mine, despite my words to her at Empyrean. I didn't know what to do with her, I really didn't. We had shared our blood with each other, made an oath that if broken could kill us, and here she was, seemingly as opposed to me as ever.

"All right, Delph," she said, refusing to look at me.

Delph glanced at me. "Now what?"

"The train will stop at True first, and those without brands will be let off to undergo this mind-erasing thing."

"And we can't stop that?" said Petra.

I looked at her. I mean I really looked at her. "Do you want to win a single battle, or do you want to win the bloody war? Because I don't reckon we can do both."

Now she looked back at me. At first there was anger on her features. And then, surprisingly, understanding. "I can see that, Vega," she said. "You're right."

*Bloody Hel,* I thought. I never knew which Petra I was going to get. Crazy Petra or Rational Petra.

I said, "So after True will come Greater True, or perhaps the train will take us directly to Maladon Castle."

Delph asked, "When you were at the castle, did you see a train or tracks running up to it?"

I shook my head. "But I was keeping my eyes on Endemen. I wasn't looking at the ground all that much."

I stiffened and motioned to the others to flatten themselves against the wall as I saw the very man enter the carriage from the other end.

Endemen was dressed in his usual attire, a pin-striped suit with a vest, a bowler hat and shiny shoes. This was in stark contrast to his appearance at the castle. I wondered if all Maladons had a hideous self under their outer layer.

I felt myself glance surreptitiously at Petra. Was a foul interior being hidden by her outer beauty? I wondered how Delph would feel about her if she suddenly turned into a hideous hag. And I was a bit ashamed to admit that a tiny smile dwelled upon my lips at this thought.

Endemen greeted each of the passengers in the carriage. Still under the spell, they mumbled their replies.

He looked them over and then knelt down next to Daphne, who was seated at the rear of the carriage only a few paces from where we were standing.

He pulled out his wand and gave it a little flick. Daphne slowly shook her head and focused on him.

Endemen said, "Your village is Clarendon on Hillshire, correct?"

Daphne nodded. "Yes."

Endemen gripped her hand and held it up. "Are there others who live there with this mark?"

Daphne looked at her hand as though seeing it for the first time.

"Yes."

"How many?"

She shook her head slightly. "A few at least. I don't know the exact number."

"Any in your family?"

"No. I'm the only one. What does it mean, this thing?"

Endemen looked at the mark, then at her, and smiled in a way that seized me with terror. It was like a jabbit about to eat its dinner.

"Well, at the very least it means the end of you." He let her hand drop and said, "Now you will tell me exactly how to get to the village of Clarendon on Hillshire."

She spoke the directions as Endemen used his wand to write her words visible in the air. Then he flicked his wand again and the images went directly into his head.

Without another word, he turned and walked over to one of the Bowler Hats.

The man said, "Do you want to leave immediately for this village, Mr. Endemen?"

"There's no particular rush. I have some things to accomplish here. And it's not like those louts are going anywhere."

"Right you are, sir."

"Bloody Hel," said Delph. "The Maladons are going to that village and they're going to kill everyone there!"

"We have to stop them," I said.

They both looked at me.

"But how?" asked Petra. "We're headed to the castle."

"We *were* headed to the castle. Now we're headed to Clarendon on Hillshire."

Petra said, "You already sent that bloke Russell to warn them."

"I have no idea if the folks in the village will listen to him, or if they do, how fast they'll flee."

"But what about that winning the battle but losing the war stuff you were spouting off about?" she said icily. "Was that just a load of tosh, then?"

I gazed at her. "No, Petra, it wasn't. But I have my reasons."

"What are they?" she demanded.

"I have my reasons," I said. And my expression was so ferocious, I suppose, that Petra flinched and turned away.

"But we don't know how to get there," said Petra.

"Yes, we do," said Delph.

We both looked at him and in unison said, "We do?"

He nodded. "She told that bloke Endemen. Didn't you hear?"

"Well, yes," Petra said. "But they were directions. Even he had to write them in the air."

Delph tapped his head. "I have them all up here."

Petra looked at me. I said, "Delph has always been good with directions."

"Okay, so how do we get off the train?" asked Petra.

I had no choice but to try the spell with all of us together. It would either work, or we'd be lost in oblivion. I didn't really have time to think about it.

I tapped my wand against my leg and said, *"Pass-pusay."*

In an instant we were back at the train station in Bimbleton, which had been the destination in my head.

We crouched behind one of the shacks and looked around. There were few people about. Most, I imagined, were inside the shacks or else had struck off back to wherever they had come from, disappointed that they had not been selected, when, in fact, they should be thanking their good fortune.

From there we rose into the air and headed west, following Delph's instructions.

It took us a while because we were four bodies flying together. I was desperate to get there as quickly as possible and feared at the rate we were going that Endemen would have already been and gone by the time we arrived.

I finally looked down and saw it. A tiny hamlet set on the side of a grassy hill.

I pointed us down as I searched for any sign of Endemen and his behatted cronies.

We alighted silently a bit to the east of the town proper.

We crouched down and looked around.

"Do you see anything?" I asked, my wand at the ready.

Petra had her wand pointed ahead of her but shook her head. "Nothing."

"I don't see no bodies lying around, or houses blown up," added Delph.

Petra hissed, "There's that bloke Russell."

It was indeed Russell. As we watched, Daphne's mate sprinted into the center of the village and started pounding on doors. When they opened, I heard him telling the people there what I had told him to say. The fear in their eyes told me that his warnings had been believed.

He was at the fourth house and word was spreading quickly. People were outside. Some were already holding packed bags in preparation for fleeing.

"I wonder where they'll go that will be safe?" asked Petra.

I was wondering this too. At least for a moment.

And then it happened.

"They're here," exclaimed Delph.

Endemen and five Bowler Hats had appeared on the edge of the small village square.

The villagers looked back in terror.

Endemen smiled and raised his wand. In unison, so did the other Maladons.

The villagers were so stunned they were rooted to the spot.

"*Embattlemento,*" I said, my wand pointed between the Maladons and the villagers.

Their spells hit my shield and the explosion was so fierce that all the villagers were nearly knocked off their feet.

"Run!" I shouted from my invisible perch.

Russell echoed this command. "Run. Run!"

The villagers turned and raced off.

Endemen was not focused on them. He was looking wildly around for the source of the spell that had blocked his.

I lifted off the ground, pulling the others with me as Endemen and his men spread out and charged ahead.

They passed directly underneath us.

I descended and we touched dirt near the spot where Endemen and his cronies had initially appeared.

I looked back at Endemen. He seemed to have forgotten all about the villagers. He was focused on finding us.

204

I rose again, and the others levitated with me. We followed the path of the villagers down below as they raced toward the dense forest that we had passed on our way here.

I looked back in time to see Endemen and his men take to the air and give chase.

They were so bunched together that an idea occurred to me.

I whispered it to Petra and we both raised our wands.

"*Impacto*," we cried out at the exact same time.

Our combined spells hit the blokes with a thunderous blow, and they were all blasted out of the air and landed unconscious in a massive heap.

I led the others down to the fallen Maladons.

"Help me search them," I said to Delph and Petra.

Delph said warily, "But what if they wake up?"

I raised my wand and made whirling motions with it around the fallen Maladons. "*Ensnario*."

Thick golden cords spilled from my wand tip, and soon all of them were bound tightly. Then I used my wand to drive the ends of the cords deeply into the ground.

"Right," said Delph, and he started searching the pockets of one of the Maladons.

I searched Endemen. In his hat I saw a bit of looking glass attached to the very top of the interior. Was this what he had been looking at back in Greater True when he said he'd been *summoned*? By the awful creature on the hideous throne back at the castle? I was pretty sure it was. It somehow allowed communication from a great distance. I pondered whether to take it, but then thought better of it. They would know it was gone and then might use it to track us somehow.

As I stared into the glass it became smoky and an image started to appear. I dropped the hat.

It had shown the foulest face I had ever seen.

Endemen had looked grotesque when he had changed into whatever he was upon entering the castle. But I would take that image any day over what I had just seen in the glass. I actually felt sick to my stomach.

It wasn't a person. It wasn't even a corpse. It was worse than dead, if that was possible.

Then I became worried. If Endemen didn't answer what might have been a command from this bloke, legions of Maladons might start popping up all over Clarendon on Hillshire.

"I'll be right back."

I soared into the air and found the villagers shaking and whimpering in the woods. I landed in their midst.

"You!" exclaimed Russell.

One man raised a knife and started toward me. "You're one of them lot."

"Kill her!" screamed several others together.

Russell got between us. "No. She was the one who warned me. You saw what happened back there. She protected us."

The man with the knife stopped in his tracks and looked at me apologetically.

"S-sorry, missy."

"You need to keep going," I said. "Those blokes back there are the Maladons. The Mal-a-dons," I added for empha-sis. "They use Bimbleton Station and others like it to entrap and then enslave all who board the trains. They take mostly young people because that way your kind will die out faster."

I looked around. "Who here has a mark on the back of their hands? Of the three hooks?" When none stepped forward, I urged, "Please. Nothing will happen to you, I promise."

Two men and a young woman stepped forward. "We three do," she said. "But we don't know what it means."

"It means you are magical, like I am. And it also means you could possibly be tracked by it. Come here."

They stepped over next to me. "Hold out your hands."

They did, and sure enough, there was the faint mark.

I raised my wand, pointed it in turn at their hands and said, "*Embattlemento.*"

A glow covered the mark and then sank into their skins.

I had just thought of that. I hoped it would work on their marks, because they were not very strong to begin with. But for all I knew the marks would grow stronger, and thus more traceable, as they became older.

I looked at all of them. "You must warn everyone you come across of the Maladons' plan. They want to rule all of you. And they will kill anyone who tries to stop them."

Russell looked at me. "They . . . they took Daphne. She had that mark on her."

I nodded. "I know. She's on the train right now. And I promise I will try to save her, Russell. I give you my word."

He nodded, tears in his eyes. "I knew this whole train thing was dodgy. But Daph said we should try. Is . . . is that why you were asking all those questions, Vega?"

"Yes."

The man who had held the knife said, "Are you going to try to stop them?"

"Yes, I am."

"If it's just the one of you, what chance have you got?"

"I have a chance to win. That's all I ask." I hesitated. Another idea had occurred to me. "But one day I might come and find you and ask for your help in defeating them."

Russell glanced at his mates and then back at me. "And we'll be willing and ready when you do."

I thanked him with a smile. "Now go. Quickly!"

They all turned and raced away.

I returned to the others.

"We need to get going," I said sharply.

"Right," said Petra. "So we kill 'em, right?" She held her wand at the ready, and her features screwed up as though she were marshaling all of her energy for the death spell.

I shot Delph a glance. He looked as surprised as I felt.

I turned and gazed at Petra.

She read my expression easily enough.

"Like they wouldn't kill us given the chance," she snapped.

I had no doubt she was correct. But I wasn't like these blokes, which, after all, was the whole point. Yet maybe Petra was far closer to the Maladons than I had thought. But, I had to concede, what she said did hold truth. We might never get another chance like this. I looked down at my wand. I had no doubt I could summon the requisite emotion to do the deed. I pointed my wand at Endemen's chest. It would be over in a sliver, and with one of our strongest enemies vanquished, we would not have to worry about him anymore, the evil, despicable git!

But as I stood there I realized I could not kill someone in cold blood. If he were trying to kill me, yes. But not this way. I lowered my wand.

I glanced up in time to see Delph look relieved.

When I gazed at Petra, she simply looked disappointed.

"So what, then?" she demanded in disgust. "Just leave them here so they can wake up and keep killing?"

"I have another idea."

I snatched up all their wands, flew into the air with them, raced a hundred yards away, blasted a deep hole in the ground, dropped the wands in it and then used another incantation to cover the hole back up such that the ground looked completely undisturbed.

I returned to the others, tethered us together, and we lifted off.

I tapped my leg with my wand, said, *"Pass-pusay,"* and we were instantly transported back to the train roaring on its way to True.

Well, I thought, we had done a right good job back there.

I didn't yet understand how far out of my league I truly was.

But I would, soon enough.

And then I would very much regret not taking Petra's advice and killing Endemen while I had the chance.

## The Battle Begins

THE TRAIN PULLED into True as it had before, in the middle of the darkness with a belch of smoke and a rasp of brake. We were all alert as the train came to a full stop.

We heard the sound of doors opening but not in the car we were on. This did not much surprise me. I didn't expect any of the "branded" ones to get off here.

Petra and Delph looked at me questioningly.

They obviously wanted to know what we should do.

I was torn. I knew that the people taken off here would have their minds altered by the bloody "mesmerizer." But I also knew that whatever happened to the people getting off in True, it would pale in comparison to what would happen to the poor devils who would *not* be getting off here.

There were no windows on this train car so I couldn't tell if it was still night or if the sun had come up. I was tense and on high alert because I was wondering when my spell on Endemen and the others would wear off. Would they be able to easily retrieve their wands? Were they right this minute on their way to intercept us somehow?

*You should have listened to Petra, you git. You should have just . . .*

I shook my head, trying to clear it. Obviously I could do

nothing about Endemen now, so I counted for the tenth time the number of other passengers in the car.

There were five of them, including Daphne. They all sat rigid in their seats, staring at nothing, oblivious to the awful fate that awaited them.

I looked behind us. "Come on. I want to go into the next car and see what's happening. Then we'll come back here."

We rose quietly, and I led the way toward the car attached to this one.

We passed by the guard at that end. He made no sign of having seen or heard us. I looked over my shoulder to make sure the other guard wasn't looking and then I quietly opened the door into the next car. We passed through and Petra closed it behind us.

The car was quiet, as I knew it would be. The people there were not restrained, but they were all under the *Subservio* spell and could do nothing to escape. As we watched hopelessly, the doors to the car opened and a Maladon entered. He waved his wand and all the passengers rose as one and started to file out. When the train car was empty, the doors closed and we started moving again. We would be heading on to Greater True now, I thought. I had just turned to go back into the other car, when the train came to a jolting halt.

"What the Hel?" exclaimed Petra.

We next heard a gnashing of metal on metal, and then came another jolt.

Delph saw what was happening first.

"They're disconnecting the train cars," he said.

"Oh my holy Steeples," I snapped. "Quick!"

I rushed back toward the windowless train car. I opened the door in time to see it start to rise into the air. I leapt and gripped a handrail on the exterior of the train car. The others leapt after me and attached themselves to the train car however they could. I grabbed Harry Two and secured him in his harness. We did all this not a moment too soon, for the car soared into the air and then shot forward with such velocity that had we not been holding on tight and tethered together, we would have assuredly plummeted.

As we raced along, I wondered if we should simply let go and fly along behind the car. But we were moving so fast that I doubted, with all of us along for the ride, whether Destin could have matched the car's speed. Thus I just held on as tightly as I could.

It was freezing up here, and my teeth involuntarily clacked together. I looked at the others and saw they were experiencing the very same thing.

After what seemed like forever, we began to slow and then descend. It was still dark, but I perceived the lights down below.

I said over my shoulder, "I . . . I think it's Maladon Castle."

As we flew lower and lower, my fears rose higher and higher.

We were directly over the castle now, and as we hovered in midair, a huge dome that I had not noticed on my previous visit started to open. Once it was done, the train car lowered down into the now uncovered space.

When the train car landed with a hard jolt on the floor of the castle, I immediately looked around. The space we were in was large and open and lighted by torches lining the stone walls.

A large door set against one of the walls opened.

And there he was.

I inwardly groaned.

It was Endemen.

And he was leading a tethered garm.

As he drew more fully into the torchlight, I saw with some satisfaction that his suit was dirty, his sleeve torn and his hair disheveled. And he had a large lump over one eye, no doubt due to my *Impacto* spell.

He looked murderous.

And in his other hand he held his wand.

Why hadn't I destroyed them when I had the chance? I shot Petra a glance. She was glaring at me in a way that said, *I bloody well told you so, you git.*

He was followed into the room by the same group of Bowler Hats, who looked as rumpled and angry as he did.

I let go of the train and beckoned the others to follow me. We paused at the door and looked back.

The train car door opened, and in went Endemen and the garm. No doubt they were going to use the garm to sniff us out before blasting us to smithereens.

We stepped through the door Endemen had come through and then peeked back around the corner, watching.

Minutes passed as the garm no doubt went from one end of the train car to the other. Nothing happened. There were no spell blasts.

Next thing the branded folks were being led off the train car.

"Quick," I said. "I know where they're going. And we can't let the garm close enough to smell us."

We retreated down the passageway. Finally, we reached a part of the castle that I recognized, and, gaining my bearings, I led the others toward the room where the branded ones would be taken to rob them of their magic.

The door to this room was open, no doubt because they knew the fresh batch of victims were on their way. We slipped inside and then over to a far corner so we could look around.

Surprisingly, there was no one here.

I showed the others the looking glasses on the wall. They were now all empty, and my heart ached at what this represented. I especially remembered the little girl who had pleaded with her mother to save her. I wondered where she was right now. Was she already a slave in Greater True?

Then I pointed out the bottles with the fine dust in them that were stacked in the niches as before.

I saw Delph and Petra pale as they looked at them. Even poor Harry Two gave a little whine of sadness.

"Vega Jane, look; the bottles are *labeled*," said Delph.

I looked more closely and saw what I had not seen before. Each bottle was engraved with the name of the person, I assumed, from whom the dust had been taken. I recoiled, but only for a moment, because an idea had occurred to me.

I pointed my wand at the bottles and said, *"Minamite."*

All the glass bottles instantly shrunk down to where I could have held them collectively in the palm of my hand. I scooped them up and thrust them into my cloak pocket.

"But, Vega Jane," said Delph. "They'll certainly notice they're gone."

Petra had opened a trunk that sat against one wall.

"Look here."

It was full of empty bottles. That made sense, as they would always need more bottles.

I looked wildly around. We needed something to fill them with.

Then I saw it. The large hole in the wall from my previous battle was still there.

"Delph, grab that bucket over there."

He did so.

"Hold it under that hole in the wall."

I pointed my wand at the hole and said, *"Springato erupticus."*

This spell wasn't simply for water. It would take out of something whatever was inside of it. A moment later, fine grains of sand started pouring out of the wall and into the bucket.

When it was full up, I used my wand to quickly fill all the bottles with the sand and then corked them.

"The names," said Delph. "The bleeding names."

Petra and I used our wands to magically engrave some names we had seen on the bottles, but only on the ones in the front of the niche because we hadn't time to do them all. We had just finished this when Delph said warningly, "They're coming."

The door opened all the way, and in marched the branded ones along with their captors, including Endemen. Thankfully, he had left the garm behind.

Still, we shrunk back into the farthest corner and watched, our breaths held tightly as we tried to stay perfectly still.

Daphne and the others dutifully lined up against one of the walls and stared at nothing as Endemen paced back and forth in front of them.

I clutched my wand, and I observed that Petra was doing the same.

Delph had balled his hands into fists.

Endemen finally turned to face the group.

He lifted his wand and pointed it at Daphne. Without him saying any words, a light shot out and plunged directly into Daphne's chest.

She stiffened even more, and her rigid gaze focused on Endemen.

"Did you meet a stranger at Bimbleton Station?" he asked.

Daphne nodded. "It was a young woman."

"Her name?"

"Vega."

Endemen shot one of the Bowler Hats a glance and then returned his gaze to Daphne.

"What else can you tell me about her?"

"She was asking questions. Who we were and where we were from. Very nosy, she was."

I frowned as I watched Endemen ponder this.

"Did she say where she was from?"

"A place called Wormwood."

Endemen froze for an instant. "Well, well," he said, smiling.

I felt my panic rising. I never should have told Daphne where I was really from. I should have just lied. I inwardly groaned at my stupidity.

"What else?" queried Endemen.

"That's all."

"You lie!"

He snapped his wand at her and she fell to the floor screaming in agony.

Petra raised her wand but I grabbed her hand. I looked at her in fury and mouthed the word *no*.

I turned back to see Endemen standing over Daphne, who was still twitching on the floor.

"Tell me the truth," he said.

"I am, I swear," she sobbed. "I was afraid she was trying to get on the train ahead of us so I left her."

"But you told her how to get to Clarendon on Hillshire."

My heart sank, even as my guilt rose. He didn't know we had overheard her telling him!

"No, I didn't. I swear it."

"You lie." He looked at the others. "You all lie."

Then suddenly, with no warning, he shouted, *"Rigamorte,"* at the same time he gave a backward slash of his wand. A black light shot out of it and slammed into all of them.

They toppled to the floor as though roped together. We all stood there, stunned. I looked down at Daphne.

Her eyes were open and fixed.

He had just killed her.

He had just *murdered* her.

I looked at the others. He had just murdered them all. Waves of molten anger poured over me.

But before I could do anything, Endemen and his cronies had vanished through the doorway.

I just stood there, my chest heaving, my eyes filling with

tears as I stared over at dead Daphne, and then at the others. They were all young, barely older than me. And their lives were already over, because of a mark on their hands, and a madman who liked nothing better than to kill.

I fingered the Adder Stone in my pocket. I knew it could not regrow limbs. And I believed it could not bring back the dead. But it had brought Harry Two back from very near death twice. So there was the possibility . . .

I took it out, waved it over Daphne's body and thought the best thoughts I could.

And she remained as still and lifeless as ever.

I finally felt something tug on my sleeve. It was Delph. He looked at me questioningly. I slowly put the Stone away.

I had lied to Russell. I had done nothing to save Daphne. I had done nothing to save any of them.

The shame I felt was beyond belief. It felt like I had no control over my limbs.

But I took several long breaths, steeled myself and marched out the door with the others behind me.

I told myself that if I ever had another chance to kill Endemen I would not hesitate.

# The Thing in the Tower

W E SKITTERED DOWN a hall and turned a corner. And there good fortune finally found us.

There was a Maladon in a cloak. And behind him, attired in elegant clothes but with blank eyes, was a tall man with skin the color of a walnut. He was one of the enslaved. They had them here too!

There was no one else around, and I whispered to Petra what I needed her to do. She nodded and we raised our wands together.

"*Impacto*," I said. My spell struck the Maladon full in the chest and he slumped to the stone floor.

"*Subservio*," said Petra, and her spell hit the tall eyeless man.

He instantly became rigid.

I performed the magnification spell and saw that a room across the corridor was empty.

Delph lifted up the stunned Maladon and carried him into that room. I used my wand to bind the Maladon tightly.

Then we turned our attention to the eyeless man.

His clothes were shiny and neatly pressed and looked to be of the best quality. I wondered, and not for the first time, why they would dress slaves in such finery.

We gathered around him in the small space and I released the invisibility shield by turning my ring around.

"Can you see us?" I asked.

He nodded.

So despite the blank eyes he still retained his sight.

I said, "What is your name?"

"I have no name. I am a Victus."

We looked at one another. "A Victus," I said. "What does that mean?"

The others shook their heads.

I thought back to the labels on the bottles. I hadn't seen a Victus, but then I hadn't had time to look at them all.

I looked back at Victus. "How came you to be here?"

"I just am here. I do not know how I came to be here."

I sighed. This bloke wasn't being much help.

Delph whispered, "Vega Jane, they've probably removed his memories. So ask him about now. What he's learned about being here."

I nodded. That was a cracking good idea.

"Okay, Victus, what can you tell us about Mr. Endemen?"

"He is one of my masters. A great sorcerer."

"And does *he* have a master here?" I asked sharply. "The man in the cloak who sits on the throne in the big room?"

"That is our king. Necro. The ruler of everything there is."

I looked at Delph. "Bloody Necro. The bloke's still alive."

My greatest fear had just been realized. The evil bloke who'd defeated my ancestors was still *alive*.

"Victus," I said, "have you heard of anyone named Virgil here?"

He shook his head.

"How about a man and a woman named Hector and Helen?"

"No. No one with those names."

"How many Maladons are in the castle?"

"Hundreds. This is where most of my masters live."

"Have you been to True or Greater True?"

"I served my masters in Greater True before coming here."

"They keep garms and jabbits here. Any other creatures?"

"No." He paused. "But I have not been to all parts of the castle. There is the Tower Room."

"Do you know what's in the Tower Room?" Petra asked.

He shook his head. "I do know it's heavily guarded."

"By what?" I asked.

"Two jabbits, for one thing."

"So not just jabbits?" I said, my spirits plummeting.

"Well, there's magic o'course."

"O'course," I parroted back, and then my expression changed. "Would you like to ever leave this place, Victus?" I asked.

He shook his head. "Never. This is my home. 'Tis an honor to serve my masters."

"Even though they don't treat you well? They hit you and curse you, don't they?"

"'Tis my fault when they do. For I have displeased them somehow. They are fair and just."

I sighed. This was not going well. The bloke's mind was simply too damaged for him to see the truth any longer. Now my thoughts turned to what could possibly be in the Tower.

I looked at Victus. "Do you know how to get to the Tower?"

He nodded dumbly.

"Then tell me."

"But why do you want to go there?"

"Please, Victus, just tell me. I'd really appreciate it."

To my surprise, his lips quivered.

"Yes, miss; of course, miss."

And he told us.

I looked down at the bound Maladon before glancing up at Petra. I know what she wanted to do: kill him. And a large part of me wanted to strike as well. But my practical side took over.

"If they find him dead, it will alert the whole castle."

She slowly nodded, but didn't look pleased.

I removed the bindings from the Maladon and cast a *Confusio* spell over him to muddle his mind enough to where he would not know what had happened. And, most important, would not blame Victus for anything.

I turned once more to Victus and explained what I had done and why.

"I don't want you getting into any trouble for helping us," I said.

His lips quivered once more.

I put out my hand. "And I want to thank you so much for helping us, Victus."

He slowly reached out and shook my hand. For a brief moment I thought I saw something else in his blank eyes, something that perhaps had always been there until it was buried so deep Victus had been unable to find it.

I performed the incantation to release him from the *Subservio* spell. However, his look didn't really change. But I thought there was an expression I recognized somewhere deep in his features: gratitude.

We left them behind and, safely under the invisibility shield, we made our way cautiously toward the Tower.

We rose higher and higher, following Victus's directions, climbing stone stairs and wooden ladders and winding steel steps.

Then we reached a corridor and I knew we had arrived.

I knew that by the sounds.

A pair of jabbits was screeching.

We rounded the last corner and there they were.

Each was poised on either side of a large metal door. Inside that door was the Tower Room, along with whatever was so important that it required twin jabbits to guard it.

The serpents were swaying back and forth, their hundreds of eyes surveying the hall in front of them, but luckily not seeing us. But I was pretty sure they could smell us, or soon would.

"How are we going to do this?" whispered Delph.

We had dealt with jabbits before, as he well knew. But this was tricky. We couldn't have a pitched battle in here with the bloody things. The noise from that would summon every Maladon in the castle.

I looked at Petra and told her the spell to cast.

She nodded and took aim at the serpent on the right while I focused my attention on the one on the left.

Delph and Harry Two stepped back and waited.

"*Paralycto*," Petra and I said simultaneously.

The spells shot out and hit the jabbits right in the chest. They froze in midscreech.

We lowered our wands and glanced appreciatively at each other.

"Right good one," said Delph.

Harry Two licked my wand hand.

We cautiously moved forward. Victus had said that magic also guarded the Tower Room, but I had no idea what shape this defense would take.

We reached the door safely, though my heart was beating uncommonly fast. It was unnerving to be so close to the vile jabbits, paralyzed or not.

I looked at the door, studying the lock. Astrea Prine had shown me several spells that would open locked doors. And I was deciding which one would be best to use now. I did not think that the *Ingressio* spell would work. But another might.

I raised my wand and said, *"Securius terminus."*

To my delight, the door swung open.

My delight turned to suspicion, because it suddenly occurred to me that all this was far too easy.

But we were here and we needed to see what was inside the room.

I eased the door open and we stepped through.

Delph said, "We need to hurry, Vega Jane. Someone might come along and see the jabbits all frozen-like."

The room was not large, so at least it would not take us long to see what was here.

The walls were stone. And there were openings in the Tower Room about six inches wide, too narrow for anyone to pass through, but they did provide some light and air. It was chilly in here, and I wrapped my coat more closely around me as we crept forward.

As I glanced at Delph, I saw him take a long knife from where it was tucked inside his belt. He looked grimly at me.

Harry Two's hackles rose, and a low growl emitted from his throat.

I used my wand tip to illuminate the center of the room. I gasped.

Sitting in a wooden armchair was a crumpled pile of a creature dressed in rags. It was tall and painfully thin, its atrophied muscles taut against the bone. The head was overflowing with long white hair and was bowed until it was almost touching a bony knee.

The thing, no doubt seeing my light, turned its head in our direction.

It was all I could do not to scream.

It had no face. No eyes, no nose, no mouth. It was just flat skin so pale that I couldn't believe that it was alive. I was frozen looking at the pitiable thing.

And even though it had no eyes, I felt that the thing could see us.

Petra gasped, "What is that?"

I shook my head. It looked like nothing I had ever seen before! Could the poor thing be one of the branded? But if so, why would it be kept in the Tower Room, and not enslaved like the others?

It turned back around and its head once more bent down. I put out my wand light.

"Why would they keep this thing up here under such heavy guard?" asked Delph. "What's so important about it?"

I moved around the room, keeping an eye on the creature until I reached one of the slits in the wall and looked out over the countryside.

I turned back to the others. "This has been a waste. And now we need to get out of here," I said.

I couldn't explain why, but I had a premonition of something truly awful happening.

I hurried over to the door and tugged on it.

It wouldn't budge.

I cast my spell to unlock it. It didn't work. I tried every spell I could think of to open that bloody door and not a single one worked.

I put my ear to the metal. I was listening for any sound from the jabbits, but I heard nothing.

"The magic," said Delph. "Victus said there was magic guarding this room. I reckon if you get past the jabbits and get in here, they got spells that make sure you don't get *out*."

My spirits sank. It had been so stupid to come up here. We were trapped.

I ran to the slits in the wall and looked out. If I could enlarge one of them, we could fly right off the Tower and head back to Empyrean.

I pointed my wand at the slit and cast my spell. It immediately rebounded on me and knocked me heels over arse across the room.

I slowly rose, rubbing at a painful newly risen knot on my head.

"Bloody Hel," I said.

As I walked back across the room, I passed close by the creature. It shot out a hand and grabbed my wrist. Though terribly emaciated, the creature was ridiculously strong. I dug my fingers into its flesh to make it let go, but it was like I was attempting to shed iron shackles.

Delph came to my aid, but even with his immense strength, he could not break the creature's grip.

Petra pointed her wand at it and said, *"Impacto."*

Her spell ricocheted off the thing and she had to duck to avoid being hit.

"Uh, Vega Jane," said Delph.

"What," I barked.

"Is it my imagination, or is this room getting smaller?"

I looked wildly around.

He was absolutely right.

The walls were moving toward us. Already the room was half as large as it had been.

I tugged with all the strength that Destin provided me and still I could not break the creature's grip. And the walls were barely two feet from us and were closing in with alarming speed now.

My wrist was being crushed by the thing and the walls were within a foot of us. And they would crush more than my wrist.

"Let go!" I screamed.

"Vega," cried out Petra.

I had my feet up on the side of the chair the thing was sitting on and used it for leverage.

"I . . . can't . . . break . . . its . . . bloody . . . grip!"

The walls were barely six inches from us, and in a few more seconds we would be smashed flat. I felt one wall hit me in the back.

Delph was pushing back against another wall with all his strength, but it was useless. It pushed him right into me. Petra was next to me and Harry Two on the other side. The walls would be touching within a few seconds.

I screamed again and jerked madly on the creature's withered hand.

Petra cried out as the wall pushed her hard into me. I looked up and saw the wall on the other side of the chair hit the wooden arm and crush it.

It was over. We were done for.

Harry Two jumped up and licked the creature's arm.

It immediately let me go.

I pointed my wand at the oncoming walls.

*"Embattlemento."*

My shield spell sprang out all around us. When the walls hit it, they ground to a halt.

But only for a moment. Then they started moving forward again, but at a much slower pace. Yet they didn't have far to go. The four of us were literally pushed right against all sides of the chair, with the hideous creature breathing heavily in the middle of us. I could feel his rank exhalations on my cheek, so close was I to his mouth.

The walls pushed us closer. My lungs were constricted as Delph, Petra and Harry Two were shoved more tightly into me. Our faces were now an inch apart. There was no room left to even breathe.

My mind started to shut down with the lack of oxygen. But right before my eyes closed for the final time, I felt my wand hand jerk.

Of course!

I willed my wand to return to its form as the Elemental.

"Everyone hold on!" I shouted.

Then the door to the shrunken Tower Room was vaporized by a spell.

And there he was standing in the opening. The space was now so small that he could reach out and touch me.

It was Endemen.

I knew he couldn't see us, but he bloody well knew we were there.

He pointed his wand at the narrow space that was all that was left of the Tower Room.

As I had before, I tossed the Elemental upward, but held on.

We were all immediately ripped off our feet, bound together as we were by the magical tether.

The Elemental hit the stone ceiling and blasted right through it.

We were out in the open.

I gulped in several large breaths and knew the others were doing the same. I didn't think I'd ever been in a tighter place. I could still feel the stone walls wedging themselves against me.

I leveled out and flew forward in the direction from which we had journeyed here.

When I looked behind me, I became sick to my stomach.

Endemen was behind us, astride one of the jabbits, which, as it turned out, was of the *flying* jabbit variety, as I had seen from my brief journey back in time when I lived in Wormwood.

Behind him were a dozen Bowler Hats.

Well, I had managed to lose them before. Perhaps I could again.

I zigzagged across the sky, but they matched me move for move, as though they could actually see me.

The jabbit put on a burst of speed and came so close to me that one of the heads tried to bite my boot, but I kicked it away in the nick of time.

Then Delph cried out, "It's the jabbit. It can *smell* us."

And I knew if we attempted to fire spells at Endemen and his cohorts, it would truly give away our positions and we'd have a wall of deadly curses hurtling right at us. In fact, that was going to happen regardless. They had to know where we were generally, invisible or not. I put on a burst of speed and pulled away, but I sensed that Destin could not keep up this pace.

Next instant I saw that Endemen and the jabbit had closed the gap by half and were moving up fast.

"We can't outfly them, Vega," cried out Petra.

"Then we'll just do this!"

I turned so sharply that the others were swung out wide on the tether.

Now I was heading right for Endemen and the jabbit, though they couldn't see us.

But the jabbit could smell us, and I could tell from its hundreds of confused expressions that it didn't know quite what to make of its prey coming so willingly to the slaughter. I mean, after all, who would be that bloody stupid?

I readied my wand, but Delph shook his head and said, "Spell cast will give us clear away." He pulled out his long knife and said, "I'll kill it with this, Vega Jane."

Petra exclaimed, "A knife? Against that! Are you barmy or what?"

He said, "My dad told me once that the underbelly of a jabbit is the softest spot on it. And my dad never told an untruth in his life."

He gripped his blade and readied himself as we roared toward the hideous flying serpent.

I looked up ahead and saw Endemen barely ten feet from us. At our combined speeds, we would crash into each other in another few seconds.

I counted one, then two.

The screech of the jabbit was ear-shattering. I could see every mouth open, all the venomous teeth about to tear into us.

"Vega!" screamed Petra.

I felt Harry Two go rigid in his harness.

They were right on us. I could see the darkened pupils of Endemen's eyes.

"Now," I shouted.

I dove.

We soared directly under the jabbit.

"Now, Delph, now!"

He pointed the blade straight up.

It ripped into the serpent's underbelly.

Delph somehow managed to keep the blade in the same position as we roared the full length of the monster, the blade cutting open its belly all along the way. Jabbit blood and guts rained down on us.

We cleared the tail and I dove to avoid crashing into the other Bowler Hats.

All they could see, I knew, was blood pouring from an enormous slash in the jabbit's belly without being able to see what had caused it.

As I looked back, the jabbit was falling away, already dead.

Endemen had just lost his ride.

I expected him to soar upward under his own power, but he didn't. It seemed that he was having trouble reaching his wand and that his legs were pinned inside the wings of the dead jabbit.

He plummeted downward and all of his crew plunged after him.

I hoped the dead jabbit crushed the lot of them.

I turned back around and accelerated to Destin's top speed. I felt the links of the chain against my skin. They were like ice. It was as though my chain instinctively knew that our very survival was at stake. It was giving our escape every bit of power it could provide.

We were far enough away now.

I raised my wand, tapped my leg and cried out, *"Pass-pusay."*

The image of wonderful, safe Empyrean was firmly in my mind.

The next moment we landed at the front door of the place.

I lunged for the huge doorknob, opened the portal and we all fell inside.

Delph leapt up and slammed the door shut before he slumped to the floor alongside us.

We all just lay there panting and shaking and living with our own horrible thoughts of a calamity barely avoided.

As my head cleared, I looked up from the floor to see Pillsbury there.

"Mistress Vega, are you all right?"

I slowly stood with the others. We were all covered in jabbit yuck.

"No, Pillsbury. In fact, I doubt I'll ever be right again."

# Bottles of Ruin

EXHAUSTED AND UNABLE to even think or talk about what had just happened, the three of us simply sat on the floor in the front hall of Empyrean covered in jabbit guts looking at one another.

We had finally convinced Pillsbury that we were okay and needed no help in any way.

He had reluctantly clanked away, leaving us alone.

At last I found my voice.

"We need to clean this vile stuff off. Then let's meet back in the library."

The sun was starting to come up as we headed for our respective rooms. I took off my soiled clothes and poured pitcher after pitcher of clean water over me. It magically replenished each time. I scrubbed every inch of me hard with a bar of soap. Then I did the same with Harry Two. I dried us both and I put on clean clothes that Pillsbury had previously placed in my cabinet.

When I got back downstairs, Petra and Delph were already there, looking somewhat revived in their clean clothes and skins, but the memory of what we had gone through still lingered in their haunted looks. As I'm sure it did in mine.

"What *was* that thing in the Tower Room?" asked Petra. "It . . . it had no face."

"I don't know. I know I couldn't make it let go of me."

"But, Vega Jane, what made that thing so special that it was under such heavy guard?" asked Delph.

I looked at where it had clutched me.

Then I glanced at Harry Two. "If not for Harry Two, we'd be dead. He was the only thing to make that creature let go."

I patted Harry Two's head, and he gave me an appreciative lick.

When I looked back up, Petra was staring directly at me.

"Endemen killed Daphne and the others," said Petra in a hollow tone underlined with dread. "Like it was nothing."

"We've seen him kill before," I said. "Those poor blokes on the train. He doesn't care who he kills, Petra."

If I was expecting her to merely agree with this statement, I was destined to be sorely disappointed.

She bellowed, "And yet you let him live back in Bimbleton! If you'd bloody well taken my advice, Daphne and the others would still be alive."

"That's not fair," Delph said defensively. "Vega Jane had no way of knowing."

"He's murderous, Delph," snapped Petra. "The point is how could she *not* know. Or how *you* couldn't, for that matter!"

I finally found my voice, although it was unlike my normal one.

"To kill in cold blood takes a different sort of Wug," I said quietly. "And as much as it would truly be convenient to be so bloody evil, I'm not that sort of a Wug. Neither is Delph." I paused and then asked the question I was sure she was waiting for me to toss out.

"Are you?"

"Maybe I am," she retorted. "Since I'm not a *Wug*!"

"So why didn't you just kill them yourself? You didn't have to listen to me. You could have done it, if you'd *really* wanted to."

She started to answer but apparently decided to hold her tongue.

"What, Petra? Why don't you say it?"

"If I had killed them, that would have just been proof to you that I'm really and truly a bloody Maladon."

"Is that the only reason?" I asked.

"What if it is?"

"I don't think it is."

"I don't care what you think," she snapped. "They have a bloody army! They have magic beyond us. They've rounded up all sorts of blokes who could have helped us. If we leave Empyrean again, chances are very good we won't come back alive. But if we don't leave Empyrean, then we can't defeat the Maladons and turn things right again. So what was the bloody point of us fighting our way through the damn Quag!" she positively shrieked.

I looked at her, resisting the urge to turn her to stone.

But in truth she had neatly summed up our plight as well as our limited options.

"I have no intention of spending the rest of my life safely within the lap of luxury here at Empyrean. I fought my way across the Quag to find my family. And to find the truth. Since I haven't discovered either yet, I intend to keep looking. You can do whatever the bloody Hel you want, Petra Sonnet. I've no time or patience for cowards."

She looked like I had punched her, and with words I guess I had.

"And I reckon that's enough talk for one night," said Delph, glancing nervously between us.

I ignored him and rolled my wand between my fingers. I watched as Petra did the same.

Delph must have noted our rising anger, because he added, "Well, I'm knackered, so I'm going to get some sleep."

We watched him head up the stairs, and then Petra and I locked gazes once more. She eyed my wand and I hers.

"Do you really want to have a go at me, Petra?" I said coolly.

For just an instant I saw something familiar flicker in her eyes. I strained to think where I had seen it before.

Was it the calm, deadly look I had seen in Endemen's eyes after he'd murdered those two poor train blokes?

I steeled myself for her attack.

But then she turned and stalked off up the stairs.

I let out a long breath.

I waited until she was out of sight, I wasn't sure why, and then I marched up the stairs too.

I didn't know how many more of these confrontations I could endure without actually attacking her!

And poor Delph. If he thought Petra and me taking a blood oath and swearing allegiance to each other would completely solve our differences, well he just didn't understand females.

Though the sun was coming up I fell asleep almost immediately, with Harry Two right next to me. However, I awoke much later somehow feeling just as tired as I had when I'd gone to bed.

As I washed up, I gazed at myself in the looking glass. It seemed that I looked older, more haggard and lost. My limbs were stiff and I had very little energy. I rubbed at a pain in my neck as I walked down the stairs. I was suddenly worried that some of the jabbit venom had gotten into me when its belly had been opened up by Delph's blade.

Pillsbury was in the kitchen, where Mrs. Jolly had laid out a truly sumptuous meal. A few moments later, Petra and Delph staggered in looking as lethargic as I felt. This made me feel even more concerned about the possibility of jabbit venom.

After Pillsbury and Mrs. Jolly left us, we sat down and started to eat. None of us spoke a word or snatched a glance at one another. It was like we were each eating alone.

The meal finished, I started to feel a bit better. I set down my glass and looked over at Delph.

He finally gazed back at me, while Petra looked back and forth at us.

"We were almost goners last night about a dozen times," he said.

I nodded weakly, my spirits turning even bleaker, if that was possible.

"I feel awful," I said. "You don't suppose we got some jabbit venom in us somehow?"

Delph said, "Vega Jane, if we'd done that, we'd be dead."

"That's true," I said thoughtfully.

"It seems to me that the thing was a prisoner there," said Delph. "And if it was, maybe it's an enemy of the Maladons."

I shot him a glance. "Then that might make that thing an ally of ours."

He nodded. "That's what I was thinking."

"It was in the Tower Room guarded by jabbits and magic," said Petra. "That certainly sounds like it was a prisoner."

"Maybe we should have rescued it and brought it back here," said Delph.

I shook my head. "Too risky. Don't forget that the damn thing nearly got us killed. And the Maladons are quite tricky. It might have been a trap. If we brought the thing back here, it could have destroyed the spells that keep Empyrean safe and led the Maladons right to us."

Delph nodded. "'Tis true enough."

I slapped my forehead and leapt up.

Delph jumped out of his chair. "Vega Jane, what is it?" He looked at me like maybe I *had* swallowed some jabbit venom.

I ran upstairs, grabbed the coat I had worn the night before and ran back into the kitchen. I put my hand in the pocket and drew out the miniaturized bottles.

"Bloody Hel," said Delph. "I'd forgotten all about them."

I set the bottles on the floor, drew out my wand and made the reverse incantation.

The bottles immediately returned to their full size.

"They're all slaves now," I said in a hollow tone.

Petra glanced over at me. "But why did the Maladons not just kill them, like they done to Daphne? Why keep them alive at all?"

After the look I had seen in her eyes the previous night, my suspicions of Petra were running high. I said heatedly, "Because to them killing is nothing special. But to rob their enemies of their magic? And then enslave them? Make them do their bidding? Treat them like cow dung? Now, that would be something truly *special* for those monsters."

My unspoken thought was: *Monsters maybe like you!*

We all stared down at the bottles, each representing a shattered life.

"We learned a lot last night," I said. "About how the Maladons operate, how they get their victims right where they want them. And we've been to the castle."

Delph said, "We didn't see that bloke you talked about. The one on the throne that made the air turn solid."

"And I'm glad we didn't. He makes Endemen look positively harmless."

I picked up one of the bottles and looked at it. "I wonder where Clive Pippen is."

"Why?" asked Petra.

I held up the bottle to show the name CLIVE PIPPEN engraved on the side. "Because I'd like to return this to him."

"You can do that?" she asked, her voice full of wonder with a smidge of disbelief.

"I don't know. Maybe."

"Well, that's a big maybe, that is," she retorted.

I said, "I don't disagree, but first thing we need to write down all the names of the people on the bottles. I'll get an ink

240

stick and some parchment from the library. There's some in a —"

I stopped talking when Pillsbury came in carrying an ink stick, a bottle of ink and a small journal.

"I happened to hear what you required, Mistress Vega. Here it is."

"Thank you, Pillsbury."

The next moment he was gone.

"Helpful bloke, that one," noted Petra.

Delph said, "Vega Jane, you got nice handwriting from all your work at Stacks. So Petra and I will read off the names and you write 'em down like."

I settled at the table, filled my ink stick from the bottle and let it hover over the first blank parchment page of the journal.

"I'm ready."

They started reading off the names and I dutifully wrote them down.

*Amicus Arnold, Pauline Paternas, Tobias Holmes, Reginald Magnus, Charlotte Tokken, Alabetus Trumbull, Clive Pippen, Dedo Datt, Aloyisus Danbury, Cecilia Harkes, Sybill Hornbill, Miranda Weeks, Dennis O'Shaughnessy, James Throckmorton, Artemis Dale.*

Then they abruptly stopped reading off the names, although I knew there were many more bottles.

I looked up, my ink stick poised over the parchment, and saw Delph holding an especially large glass bottle. He was staring at it, openmouthed.

Petra was doing the very same thing.

"What is it?" I asked.

They both slowly turned to look at me.

"What is it?" I asked again, a bit more gruffly because they were just sitting there looking incredibly stupid.

Instead of answering, Delph simply handed over the bottle.

I took it, a bit put out that he wouldn't simply read off the name.

I said, "I wonder why it's bigger than the —"

Then I saw the named engraved on the glass and all other thoughts were struck clean from me.

VIRGIL ALFADIR JANE.

# Delph's Idea

I WAS SO SHOCKED that I nearly dropped the bottle. Then I gripped the glass so tightly that I was afraid I was going to crush it in my hand.

Finally, I just set it down on the table and closed my eyes.

When I opened them the bottle was still there. Part of me was hoping we had all just imagined its existence.

"They've . . . they've got your grandfather," said Delph. "They've got Virgil."

I looked down, trying to gather my wits about me.

It was all so overwhelming I could barely breathe, much less actually think.

I glanced at my arm where the creature in the Tower Room had grabbed me.

Then I glanced at the mark of the hooks on the back of my hand.

The mark was burning brightly.

"What is it, Vega Jane?" asked Delph, who was watching me closely.

"I don't know. It just feels really odd. And my mark looks stronger than before, don't you think?"

"Maybe it does."

Petra interjected, "So what do we do? If they can beat your grandfather, a bleedin' Excalibur, what chance do we have?"

"It's not clear that they *have* beaten him," I said defensively.

She looked at me like I had gone barmy. "Really? And what, he just gave up his bloody magic all on his own?"

I fought a serious urge to pull out my wand and empty Petra of all her magic!

"All I'm saying is that we don't know for certain."

"Well, it seems *certain* to me that he don't have no more magic," she retorted. "It's in that bottle."

As much as I didn't want to agree with her, I had to.

Delph said quietly, "Do you think your grandfather is one of them slaves, maybe in Greater True?"

I shook my head. "I don't think he is, Delph."

"You can't know for certain," said Petra, throwing my previous words back in my face. She was so very good at making me absolutely furious.

Blimey, it was like we were sisters!

I picked up the bottle holding my grandfather's magic.

"I'll tell you what I *do* know. This bottle is larger than the others. That's a lot of magic. An Excalibur level of magic, I reckon."

"So?" said Petra.

"So I don't think they would treat him like all the others because he's not like all the others. They would give him extra special treatment, and not in a good way. I mean punishment. Terrible punishment."

244

Delph said, "I'm not sure I know what you mean, Vega Jane."

I took a deep breath. Even I was not totally sure what I meant, or I didn't want to be. "I think my grandfather was the faceless creature in the Tower Room."

I held up my arm.

"He touched me here and it burned like mad. But my mark also became more pronounced. And why else would it have let me go when Harry Two licked his arm?"

Petra of course did not look convinced. "Why would they keep him alive? Why not kill him like they did Daphne?"

"I don't know. Maybe they want to keep him alive for some other reason."

"Like what?"

I slowly lowered my arm. "I don't know!" I felt my face flush. "You always have lots of questions, but never any answers," I added emphatically.

She gazed steadily at me. "I came to this whole thing a lot later than you. I don't know anything about your grandfather, or this place called Wormwood, or the Maladons or even magic really. I . . . don't like not knowing things. Maybe that's why I ask so many questions. But I guess it's not fair to always expect you to have all the answers."

She looked away, and I thought that was as close as I'd ever likely get to an apology from Petra Sonnet.

Yet back in Wormwood I'd asked lots of questions too, because I also liked to know things. So maybe Petra and I were a lot more alike than I cared to admit.

Delph broke the silence. "They could be trying to get information from him."

"What sort of information?" I asked.

"Well, he's from Wormwood. Don't you think these Maladon blokes would just love to get to Wormwood and kill everybody there? I mean, we've all been in hiding there, though most of us didn't know it. They may believe that Virgil can tell them how to get there."

"Through the Quag?" I said. "Good luck with that."

"But Virgil didn't go through the Quag, did he? He was able to bypass it somehow."

I said, "We don't know for sure what he did. We just know that he disappeared from Morrigone's home in a whirl of flames. And I believed that was the case when my parents disappeared from the Care too. I just later assumed that he had summoned them somehow. Maybe they were all captured."

Delph shook his head. "Your grandfather left a long time before your mom and dad vanished. Why would he wait all that time to bring them to him? And remember, the Maladons are on the lookout for your parents. So I don't think they've been caught."

Petra said, "Well, if they were captured your parents could have escaped but Virgil somehow didn't manage it."

Delph shook his head. "I'm not sure how likely that is."

I was sorely confused now. "But, Delph, if my grandfather summoned my parents and they either appeared here or traveled through the Quag, they would have been together. So if the Maladons have Virgil, which appears likely since his name is on this bottle, and the bloke in the Tower Room might well be his shrunken, faceless self, and they're still looking for my parents, then they must have escaped somehow.

Perhaps my grandfather held off the Maladons while they got away."

"Now, that's possible," conceded Delph.

Petra added, "So I wonder where your parents are now? If they are magical, we could certainly use a couple more wands."

I sat there staring at the tabletop. I didn't know where my parents were. I had no idea if they were magical, or if they even had wands.

I took out the picture of them and looked down at it. The Maladons must have at least seen my parents somehow, otherwise how could they have made a picture of them?

But what I was most thinking about was my grandfather. Was that really him up in the Tower Room? That faceless, shrunken, pitiable creature?

Had I been so close to Virgil that he had actually touched me on the arm? The Wugmort I had been searching for all this time might have been right next to me. And I had managed to leave him behind.

I rubbed my eyes. Despite my recent sleep I felt so weary I was afraid I might topple over.

But there was one fact staring me in the face. And it did not bode well for our chances of beating these fiends.

As Petra had said, if they could reduce a mighty Excalibur to that, what hope was there for us to prevail?

I looked up to see Delph staring at me. The way he looked, it was almost as if he could read my thoughts.

"You escaped from them, more'n once, Vega Jane. And you took Endemen's wand from him after blasting him with a spell."

My eyes widened, for it indeed seemed that Delph *had* read my thoughts.

"So don't shortchange yourself in any fight with them blokes. Like I did back at the Duelum, I'd bet on you to win against them."

"Thanks, Delph," I said quietly.

When I looked at him, I saw something in his eyes. Like he wanted to hug and then snog me. I mean really snog me! My skin started tingling as I realized I wanted to snog him too!

"I'd bet on you too, Vega," added Petra, breaking the moment.

Delph coughed and looked away.

I turned and smiled compactly at Petra, nearly convinced that she had done this on purpose to interfere with whatever was going on between Delph and me, rather than meaning what she'd said.

"Thanks," I said coolly.

I glanced at Delph. "I thought the hard part was getting through the Quag. Now that seems the easiest bit of it."

Delph said, "Way I see it, we need help if we're going to beat the Maladons. Lot more of them than there are of us."

"Agreed," I said. "But how do we change that?"

Delph pointed at the bottles sitting on the table.

"I think the answer lies there."

"How do we get the magic back into all those people? We don't even know where they are."

"We have to find them, don't we? And I think a lot of them are in Greater True. From what you said, that seems to be where the hoity-toity live. Sort of like blokes on Council

248

back in Wormwood. And I didn't see no 'slave' types like you described when we were in True."

"Okay, let's say they're in Greater True. How do we go about finding them? Just wait on the street and see them coming?"

"Well, that happened to you, didn't it?"

"Delph, I don't think you get it. Let's say we find one. Then what? We take the person, bring him or her back here and restore their magic? Okay, but they'll know the person is gone. They'll probably figure out the magic dust has been taken. They'll put both things together and deduce what we're doing. And then they'll be on their guard and we'll never be able to get to any more of these enslaved blokes. They might just kill the lot like Endemen did with Daphne and the others."

In answer Delph held up a single finger. "We can start with one, Vega Jane. Just one. And we'll figure out a way so they won't know what we're doing. But we have to make sure that we *can* restore the magic. That's the point of all this."

I shook my head, still confused. "What exactly is the *point*?" I asked.

Delph glanced over at the bottles once more and then back at me.

"Why, they're going to be your army o'course."

# The Path Ahead

THAT NIGHT I couldn't sleep. The thoughts in my head were swirling so fast it was like there was a blizzard in my brain.

Groaning, I rose from bed, put on my cloak, snagged my wand and, leaving a sleeping Harry Two behind, made my way to the library. I shut the door behind me, conjured a fire in the fireplace and sat down in the desk chair facing the flames.

I opened the journal that I had put in a drawer there earlier. We had finished writing down all the names from the bottles, which were lined up on a broad shelf across from me.

I gazed at the bottles. To me they weren't simply glass and dust; they represented flesh-and-blood people whose lives had been savagely ripped from them.

I opened the journal and read down the list of names.

The problem was matching the names and the dust in the bottles to the actual people. How did we find them?

In frustration I slammed the journal shut and slumped back in my chair.

I rose and held the bottle with my grandfather's name on it, peering closely at the letters forming his name.

How had they known he was *Virgil Alfadir Jane?* Had he been forced to tell them? And how had they gotten a picture of my mother and father? Again, was the source my grandfather? I couldn't believe he would give that up voluntarily. Was that why he was in such a horrible state? Because of torture? Why couldn't they simply use the *Subservio* spell on him? Or, being an Excalibur, was he somehow impervious to its effects?

I looked beyond the name to the dust contained in the bottle. Not only was the bottle different by virtue of its size, but the dust was slightly different as well.

I looked more closely. It was a fine texture, when the dust in the other bottles was a bit more granular.

I had a sudden awful thought.

What would *my* magical dust look like if the Maladons were able to do this to me?

Depressed, I stared into the flickering fire.

Suddenly I had an idea. I raced back to my room and opened the drawer of my bedside cabinet where I kept my enchanted piece of parchment and pulled it out.

"Silenus?" I had discovered this bloke in the Quag.

His face instantly appeared on the page.

"Silenus? I have a problem."

He looked expectantly at me.

"Tell me, Vega."

I explained to him what had happened at Greater True and then my two excursions to Maladon Castle. And the possibility that my grandfather might be a prisoner there.

Then I held up the bottle and told Silenus what it contained and how it had gotten there.

He looked as repulsed by my tale as I felt telling it.

251

"The thing is, Silenus, we would like to be able to get this dust and all the other bottles back to their rightful owners. Only we don't know how to do that. Their names are on the bottles but we don't which persons go with which bottles. And we have no way to track them down. And if we do find them, we don't know how to return the magic to the people. I know of no spell to do that. The Maladons might know, but they're not going to tell me."

Silenus nodded. "I can see how that would be a dilemma of significant proportions," he said somberly.

"Right," I said, a bit irritably, for I already knew *that*. "Do you have any ideas on how we could do it?"

Silenus was silent for some time. I waited with increasing anxiety, never taking my gaze off him. If he didn't have an idea, what was I to do?

Finally, he said, "You will recall, Vega, that we once spoke of the true purpose of magic; the probability of improbability, let us call it."

I nodded. "You told me that spell casting came out of necessity."

"Yes, I did. What is magic but the will of the owner of such power to accomplish something which is desired? You say you want to match the bottles to the people? And then return the magic to them?"

"Yes, of course."

Silenus now stared over at the bottle of dust containing my grandfather's magical remains. "If that does indeed contain the magic that once flowed through the spirit of your grandfather, then all that you need is within those grains."

I said dully, "I'm not sure I understand."

"You say the creature in the Tower Room is Virgil Alfadir Jane?"

I nodded and said eagerly, "Yes, exactly. Well, I think it is."

"You are wrong."

"Excuse me?" I said, half in anger, half in disbelief. "I'm wrong about what?"

Silenus said, "The creature in the Tower Room is simply a husk, the remains of an animal carcass, only in this case the carcass still breathes." He eyed the bottle once more. "There, in that vessel, is your grandfather. He is with you now."

I looked at the bottle, my spirits soaring, but then an element of doubt crept into my mind.

"So how do I get him out of the bottle?" I said.

"That is largely up to you. And your wand. But the key element, Vega, is that you must believe. Even a smidgen of doubt and it will not work."

"How do you know that?"

"Because I have seen what doubt can do, Vega. It can wreck the best-laid plans."

"I don't understand. Is it that hard to really believe in something?"

Silenus smiled the weary smile of someone who had seen this very thing over and over.

He said, "It is actually the hardest thing of all."

And with that enigmatic statement, he vanished from the parchment.

I felt my mouth turn downward in disappointment.

*Well, that was clear as dung.*

Why couldn't the bloke give me a piece of uncomplicated advice just ONCE!

I looked at my wand and then at the bottle.

I raised my wand, pointed it at the bottle and said, "Virgil Alfadir Jane, please come to me."

Exactly nothing happened.

I refocused. I willed myself to believe that my grandfather truly was in that blasted bottle.

I waved my wand again, touching the tip of it against the glass of the bottle.

"Come back to me," I said.

My eyes widened slightly when I saw just a little pop of light at the end of my wand, but then it quickly died out.

I tried several more times, but nothing else happened.

I put the bottle in my pocket and slid the journal in the drawer of my cabinet.

I went back to the library, walked over to the fireplace, gripped the edge of the stone mantel and bowed my head.

How was I supposed to have no doubt when doubt was all I'd had ever since leaving Wormwood?

As I stared into the flames, I felt the tears creep to my eyes. I didn't want this to happen, it just did. I had fought so hard. Come so far. And now it appeared that I could go not one inch farther.

I slumped down to the floor and curled up into a little ball.

As the timekeeper on the mantel ticked away, I just lay there, not moving. It felt like no energy would ever come back to me.

*This is not helping, Vega.*

*This is stupid.*

*You're stronger than this.*

I rose and turned away from the fire.

I had to do something. Anything that would make me feel like I was accomplishing something.

To make me feel that I was not a failure.

I picked up the bottle with my grandfather's dust in it. I put my face right next to the glass. I closed my eyes and envisioned my grandfather as I had last seen him.

I opened my eyes and gasped.

My grandfather was in the bottle.

He was hovering above the pile of fine dust. Suspended in air.

When I blinked, he was gone.

I had only imagined it.

There was nothing there.

I knew there had never been anything there.

I set the bottle down and pondered what to do as I sat back down in the chair.

Empyrean was very quiet. I knew Delph and Petra were asleep.

I didn't know if Pillsbury actually slept. I wasn't sure that a suit of armor ever got tired.

As though in answer to my thoughts, Pillsbury appeared next to me.

It happened so fast that I nearly toppled from the chair into the fire.

"Do you require anything, Mistress Vega?" he asked.

"What?" I gasped. "No, I'm . . . I'm fine."

His visor quivered just a bit.

"May I be somewhat impertinent, Mistress Vega?"

I wasn't sure what he meant. I gazed up at him.

"I suppose so," I replied uncertainly.

"You have a great deal of burden on your youthful shoulders. If you don't mind me saying, it would overwhelm someone far older and more experienced."

I blinked. "I guess so," I said calmly, but then retorted, "but I can't use that as an excuse to fail, Pillsbury. I really can't. It's not like I'm going to get another chance to make it right."

"I recall that Mistress Alice was in a similar predicament when she lived here."

I perked up at this. I was beginning to feel a strong connection between Alice and me. I only wished that she were here right now. But Pillsbury *had* known her. That might be the next best thing.

"What sort of predicament?" I asked.

"She knew that war was coming with the Maladons. I remember seeing her sitting in the very chair you're in now, far into the night, thinking and worrying, thinking and worrying."

"Did she tell you what she was thinking about?"

Pillsbury nodded. "I appeared before her, something I did not do lightly. She was a very forceful person, was Mistress Alice." One did not like to intrude on her.

He hesitated and rubbed his metal mitts together.

"Go on, Pillsbury, please."

"Well, I could sense that she might need to talk to

someone, or at least voice her concerns out loud. So I provided a way for her to do that."

"But surely she had her husband, Gunther, to do that with."

To my surprise, Pillsbury slowly shook his head.

"Master Gunther kept very much to himself on such matters." He paused once more and then plunged on in a rush. "He did not want war. But it also got to the point where Master Gunther . . . where he . . ."

He ground to a halt once more.

"Where he what? Please, tell me," I implored.

"Master Gunther, it seemed to me, would have avoided war at all costs. *All* costs."

I slowly revolved this around in my head before saying incredulously, "What, you mean even if it meant the Maladons would take over and rule them?"

Pillsbury nodded.

"I could never imagine doing that!" I said forcefully. "I would much rather die."

"As would Mistress Alice. As she did," he added sadly.

I thought this through, trying to connect the dots that Pillsbury was putting out there, however haphazardly.

"Was she worried that Gunther might do something foolish regarding the Maladons? Something that might hurt Alice and her allies in the war to come?"

I didn't know where this inspiration had come from.

"I think she was worried about a great many things," Pillsbury said diplomatically. "And I daresay that might have been one of them."

"You said that Necro came here before the war."

"Yes."

"How recently before the war started?" I asked, for I thought the timing might be important.

"As recently as the night Master Gunther died," said Pillsbury.

I slowly stood. "Pillsbury, I have seen Gunther's body in the coffin here. His neck was slit. Are you telling me that . . . ?"

Pillsbury nodded, and I saw a solitary tear emerge from under the visor and meander down the metal skin.

"That foul Necro came here late that night. Mistress Alice didn't know. It was on the pretense of preventing the war. That's what he told my master. They met in this very room. Just the two of them. And when I came in later to see if they needed anything, there lay my poor master in a pool of his own blood. And the fiend Necro was nowhere to be seen."

"He *murdered* Gunther?"

"Yes," exclaimed Pillsbury. "As sure as I'd seen him do it."

"And what did Alice do?"

"She would have killed him, I'm sure of it, or tried to. But the Maladons started the war the very next day."

"You said that the war started because Uma Cadmus and Necro's son, Jason, had fallen in love but ended up dead."

"That's only partly true. Necro blamed Jason's death on our side. Said that we'd had him murdered. Even said that Uma had done it after bewitching Jason at the behest of her father. And he said that Master Gunther was a coward who had slit his own throat because he knew his side could never defeat the Maladons."

"What a pack of lies!" I snapped. "Total rubbish."

"Of course it was. But nevertheless, the Maladons wanted a war and they got it."

"And they won it," I reminded him miserably.

"Yes," he said, his gaze on the floor.

We both stood there in silence for a bit.

"Pillsbury, there's going to be another war," I said.

He didn't look at me, but his visor went up and down.

"Yes, Mistress Vega. I daresay there will be."

"I can't guarantee the outcome. I don't know that we won't be beaten a second time, and utterly destroyed. But I can tell you that I will fight to the death. I don't want peace with the bloody Maladons. I've seen what they're like. I'd rather die than have anything to do with that lot."

Now he looked at me. I mean he *really* looked at me.

"I have no doubt of that, Mistress Vega. If you're not the spitting image of Mistress Alice, then I don't know what you are."

He left me on that note.

I sat back down and stared at the fire for a while. I thought about all that he had told me. It wasn't that I needed more reasons to hate the Maladons, but if I had, Pillsbury had supplied me with plenty more.

They had an army of well-trained sorcerers who could fly and fight and kill.

I had Petra, Delph, Harry Two and a bunch of bottles with dust in them.

Some army.

And I didn't know how to lead an army, even if I had one.

I could barely lead myself!

What I needed, I decided then and there, was my grand-father. A mighty sorcerer, an Excalibur.

I knew exactly what I had to do.

I had to travel back to Maladon Castle and rescue him.

Otherwise, all of this was for nothing.

# A Loss of One

MALADON CASTLE WAS directly in front of me.

Harry Two hung in his harness. I had ventured out without Petra and Delph. I felt strongly this was something I needed to do without them. I had brought Harry Two because he seemingly had a connection with the creature in the Tower Room. Inside my pocket was the bottle with my grandfather's magical dust.

The castle rose from the darkness like a hideous mass ready to kill all who ventured close.

Well, I would be doing more than venturing close. I was going to invade the place and rescue the Wug I desperately hoped was my grandfather.

As I drew even nearer, my jaw dropped.

I had assumed the castle would be quiet at night.

Instead I saw a scene of manic activity.

Figures in cloaks were hustling to and fro. The castle was ablaze with light. The front gates were open.

What the Hel was going on?

I suddenly had a truly wondrous thought: Had my grandfather managed to escape?

But how could he have done that? His magic still rested in my pocket.

To be sure, I took out the bottle and checked. The dust was still there.

I put it away and eyed the castle once more.

The chaotic scene I was witnessing did provide certain advantages.

I unbuckled Harry Two and attached him to me with a magical tether from my wand.

*Okay, here we go.*

We set off at a trot toward the castle.

We quickly reached the circle of light thrown off by the entrance. To the left and right of us were Maladons in long red cloaks. I couldn't see their faces because their black hoods were drawn up.

For some strange reason I felt no fear being in the midst of my enemy. I felt, instead, a certain inexplicable calm.

We were ten feet from the open gates when I saw him.

Endemen burst forth from the entrance to Maladon Castle like a raging storm.

His hood was down and I could see his evil features. Then, as I stood there watching, he transformed into what he really was: that hideous, malformed creature I had seen before. It was far more terrifying than the conjured face he normally wore.

He shouted to his fellow Maladons in some language I could not understand. His voice sounded urgent, but also strangely jubilant. I could make neither head nor tail of it.

My feet started moving and I was past Endemen and through the open gate.

Harry Two and I darted off to a side corridor.

I had to find the stairs up to the Tower Room again.

I searched my memory even as we flattened ourselves against the wall as a group of Maladons rushed past us.

The third corridor on the right? The second stairway off that? Up to the left? Or was it the right?

*Oh, to Hel with it.*

I drew my wand and muttered, *"Pass-pusay."*

The Tower Room corridor was firmly in my mind.

An instant later we were outside of it.

Well, that was informative. I could use the spell to travel *within* the castle. I apparently couldn't use it to enter or leave the place.

The first thing I noted: There were no jabbits stationed outside.

The second thing I noted: There was no bloody door.

I looked desperately around. What had happened to the door? Or had my spell somehow gone awry?

But as I calmed, my reason returned.

They knew someone had been in the Tower Room before.

So they had walled it up.

Now the question became: Was the prisoner still in there?

I pondered this for a few moments even as the sounds of whatever was going on down below reached my ears.

I drew close to the wall and put my ear against it. I could hear nothing.

But that wasn't good enough.

I pointed my wand and whispered, *"Crystilado magnifica."*

Now I had my answer. The room was completely empty. Even the slits in the walls were gone.

Okay, the prisoner had been in the highest point in the castle.

So they had obviously moved him somewhere else.

With a spark of logic, I thought: *Perhaps to the* lowest *point?*

I cast my gaze downward. I could only wonder what was in the bottom of this awful place. I well remembered my time under the Obolus River with the charming likes of Orco and his wall of the despairing dead.

I turned around, and Harry Two and I made our way back down.

The activity had diminished quite a bit, and we didn't have to dodge Maladons flying through the corridors.

I spied the stairs heading down into the bowels of the castle. They didn't look the least bit appealing.

*Victus!*

He was walking past me carrying something.

I skittered over to him with Harry Two trailing right next to me.

"Victus," I hissed.

He turned and looked around with his all-white eyes.

"It's me, Vega. I asked you before about the Tower Room, remember?"

He slowly nodded.

"I . . . I can't see you," he said.

"I know. It's just that I don't want anyone to see me. What's going on around here? Why all the activity?"

"Master has simply told us to prepare some things. Provisions and the like, for a journey."

"A journey where?" I said.

He shook his head. "Master has not said."

I eyed him closely. "Victus, do you remember who you used to be?"

He flinched for an instant.

I added, "Because you were not always Victus. You were someone else entirely. And you were magical. Just like your *masters*."

He shook his head sharply, but I could see in his tightened features that there was . . . something.

"No. I am simply Victus."

I said, "Will you and others like you be going with your masters on this *journey*?"

He shook his head. "Only the masters. We will remain behind."

I nodded, thinking this over. "Victus, the prisoner who was in the Tower Room. Do you know where they took him?"

"I cannot say."

"Can't, or won't?"

"'Tis the same to me."

"I think not," I said sharply.

He flinched once more.

I wasn't sure why I seemed to be able to dent the enslavement effect that he had undergone, but I was glad I could.

I gripped his hand with mine. He instantly became invisible along with me. His skin was icy. But it suddenly began to warm under my touch.

"I think you could tell me if you really wanted to."

"I . . . I . . ."

"That person is my grandfather, Victus. He is a prisoner here. I want to help him. But to do that I need your help. You helped me once before. Will you do so again? Please? It's so very important. Is he underneath the castle?"

"You were very kind to me before, miss. You *thanked* me. I have never before heard those words here."

"That's because your masters are evil and they don't care about you. But I do. I want to free you, Victus. And all others like you. I hope you can see that."

As before, his lips began to tremble. A moment passed as innumerable emotions seemed to flit across his sightless features.

He said in a hoarse voice, "The person you require is not down below."

"Where, then?" I asked.

"He is in the Great Hall with our one true master."

My spirits collapsed. "What, the bloke in the big chair?"

Victus nodded.

"What's he doing in there?"

"I do not know. But I saw him there."

"Is he in chains?

Victus shook his head.

"Is he restrained in some way?"

Victus shook his head again.

"Thank you, Victus. You've been very helpful."

He bowed his head. At any other time the gesture might have appeared comical. But there was nothing funny about this place.

"I wish you luck, miss." He paused and then added, "Was I really magical?"

"You all were. And if I have anything to say about it, you'll be magical again."

I let go of him, turned and rushed toward the Great Hall with Harry Two right next to me.

We finally reached the grand doorway leading into the even grander room, even if it had, at its epicenter, such a foul thing.

*The one true master?*

The one true pillock!

I gingerly put a foot over the threshold, and my dog followed with two of his.

We slowly followed with the rest of ourselves.

I looked up and saw that the glass ceiling I had smashed through previously had been repaired.

The room was vast and empty.

Well, nearly so.

Up at the front I saw something. Something quite odd.

There was the throne. Seated it in was the awful creature I had seen before. I now knew it was the ancient Necro.

In his hand was a wand. It was the blackest thing I had ever seen. It reminded me of the darkness I associated with Orco, of the world of the dead.

The wand was pointed at someone.

As I drew closer, I could see that it was the pitiful person from the Tower Room.

I was taking another step forward when I saw that something was emanating from the wand and piercing the body of the other.

It was a light. But not a bright one, which was why I had not seen it until I drew closer.

It was as black as the wand and mostly hidden in the shadows of the room.

I pointed my wand at the leader of the Maladons and thought about what spell I would cast.

Should I kill him?

Could I summon the emotion necessary?

Should I merely knock him out?

What if it didn't work?

What if he turned upon me? Enslaved me? Put my magic in a bottle?

My mind was so jargoled that what I did was nothing.

Until I saw the poor faceless creature topple off the stool and fall to the floor when the other pointed his wand down and the black beam vanished.

Necro stood, flicked his wand once and vanished.

I rushed forward and reached the spot where the creature lay.

When I touched the skin it was cold and clammy.

The creature still had no face. I told myself that this had to be my grandfather, but how could I be sure? I heard sounds echoing all over the castle. I couldn't just stay here and ponder things. I had to make a decision.

Harry Two brushed past me and sniffed at the creature. Then he pushed his nuzzle against the cold hand, and I saw one finger twitch.

Harry Two stepped back and looked up at me as if to say, *There you go, mate, it's him.*

"Thanks, Harry Two," I murmured.

I had Destin around me, which meant my strength was greatly multiplied.

I lifted him up, and at my touch he became invisible.

"Grandfather," I whispered into his ear. "Are you okay? What did he do to you?"

I got no answer to my questions.

I rushed from the room with Harry Two at my heels.

The corridor outside was empty.

In my mind I assembled the floor plan for the castle and my method of escape.

We hurried along the long corridors until we reached the main gate.

Two Maladons were stationed there, obviously guarding the exit.

I slipped past them, ran farther on and then lifted into the air.

When I looked back down, the castle was as dark and silent as death.

Where had they all gone?

I had a sudden terrible thought. When I got back to Empyrean, would I find it destroyed? Delph, Petra, Pillsbury and Mrs. Jolly and all the others dead? Was that where the Maladons had gone?

I tapped my wand, incanted my spell, and the next moment I was standing in front of my ancestral home, which looked perfectly fine, I observed with a rush of relief.

Carrying my grandfather, I went inside with Harry Two right behind me.

I put my grandfather down and took out my wand, still ready for an attack if the Maladons actually were here. However, all was calm. I turned my ring back around and we became visible once more.

Pillsbury appeared in front of me, looking quite normal and unsurprised that a wretched, faceless creature was lying on his polished floor.

"Mistress Vega, can I be of assistance?" His visor pointed down at the creature.

"You can fetch Delph and Petra for me."

"Of course."

He vanished.

A few moments later I heard two pairs of feet hurtling down the stairs.

The next instant Delph and Petra, still in their night things, were standing in front of me.

"Where have you —" Delph stopped when he saw the creature on the floor.

Petra nearly screamed. "You . . . you went back and got him?"

I slowly nodded, perhaps realizing for the first time that that was actually what I *had* done.

"How did you manage it?" sputtered Delph.

I did not want to spend time answering questions. I had something else that needed doing.

I pointed my wand and said, "*Rejoinda* bottle of Virgil Alfadir Jane." I curled my hand toward me. This was now all so automatic that I really didn't have to think about it.

Next instant the large bottle came hurtling into the room, and I neatly caught it in my free hand. I had decided against taking it with me in case I was captured or killed.

I looked at Delph. "I have no idea how to get his magic back to him, but we need to figure it out. And fast. Necro did something to him. Maybe that book with the spell on how to take the magic has something about reversing it?"

He had turned to rush off and get the book when Harry Two did the most extraordinary thing. He leapt up, knocked the bottle out of my hand, and we all watched it fall right toward the crumpled figure on the floor.

We were frozen to the spot. I made no effort to even reach out and grab for it.

Right before it would have hit the creature, the stopper came off the bottle and the dust cascaded out, covering the body underneath it.

As we watched, goggle-eyed, the dust didn't simply land on the body and stay there. It was absorbed into the skin. It was as though sweat was reversing itself, and the thirsty body was greedily sucking up every last drop of it.

We all waited for what seemed like forever, but could have been only mere moments. Then a blinding flash of golden light seared across the room.

I shut my eyes and was sure the others had too.

When I opened them, there was no huddled mass on the floor.

Standing in front of me, nearly as tall as Delph, and robust in every way, was a man I had not seen since I was six years old.

My grandfather, Virgil Alfadir Jane, stood before us. And he seemed not to have aged a jot since I had last seen him.

My spirits soared. I wanted to leap into his arms.

"Grandfather, it's me, Vega!"

He looked at me. And in those eyes I saw many things: love and sadness chief among them. I could understand the former but not the latter. Not now. Not when we had been reunited at last. Not after all that had happened in between.

As I peered more closely, I could see that his image was wispy as well.

But that didn't matter to me. He was here. My grandfather and I had been reunited. All was right with my world once more.

He reached out his hand and took my fingers in his. They were not warm, but cold. Yet the look in his eyes was full of warmth.

And love.

He smiled at me.

"Oh, Vega, my very, very dear grandchild."

His words were like a wisp of smoke, when I remembered his voice to be a deeply powerful baritone with considerable range.

But I was trembling so badly when I heard his words that I didn't care how they sounded, only that they were being spoken. To me!

A single tear emerged from his right eye, fell out onto his cheek and slid like a waterfall in miniature down his long face.

"How I have longed to see you, Vega, over these many sessions."

His hand went to my chin and stroked it. I gripped his hand with both of mine, the tears spilling onto my face, and I made no effort to wipe them away.

This man had been gone from my life for so long. Yet looking up at him, feeling his hand upon my skin, it was as though we had just recently parted.

"I . . . I missed you so much," I stammered. "I've been trying to find you for so long. And now . . . now you're here. We're together."

Petra and Delph had taken a respectful step back when Virgil had risen. Their gazes toggled between the pair of us and the floor. I'm sure they were somewhat embarrassed witnessing such an intimate scene. But I wanted them to be here, to see this, to see that Virgil was with us. On our side. That he would now lead us to victory, even though that thought was secondary to me right now.

I hugged him tightly, pushing my face into his chest, breathing him in, squeezing him so hard that he couldn't possibly ever leave me again.

I felt him embrace me back with those strong arms that I remembered enveloping me when I was a child. When I was scared, he would comfort me. When I was joyful, he would rejoice with me. Every such memory came flooding back to me.

Then his grip suddenly weakened, and I felt him tremble.

"Grandfather?" I said, alarmed.

I felt his gentle embrace on my shoulders and he guided me away from him, so we could look at each other. "I always knew you were special, from the very light you were born," he said quietly. "You above all others. I knew it and felt it and I have not been disappointed in those beliefs." His face crinkled into a smile.

I felt my skin tingle as I smiled up at him. "Together, Grandfather, together we can manage this. We can defeat them. I know that we can do this. You're an Excalibur. And I'm, well, I can fight too. I think that —"

He held up a hand to quiet me.

What he said next made me forget everything else.

"But our time together will be very short, I'm afraid, my dear, dear Vega."

I froze. "What? No! I just found you. You can't leave me. You . . . can't!"

He paused for what seemed like an eternity as I stared up at him.

"I must. For you see, Vega, I am, unfortunately, already dead."

# Last Words

THERE ARE TIMES in everyone's life when loss strikes. When one's heart breaks.

And there are times when you truly feel as though you have no heart left, so shattered is it.

This was such a time for me.

I stared at my grandfather.

"You're . . . you're . . ." I could not say it. I could not say that word.

He stared at me, sadness now triumphing over the love. "He has killed me, Vega," my grandfather said simply.

"Necro," I said, my eyes brimming with fresh tears.

I glanced at Delph and Petra. They appeared to be cast in stone.

"He is a very powerful sorcerer," said my grandfather. "Who knows things that we never will. But we cannot dwell on that. We have things to discuss. And you must have questions. Even as a young you had more questions than every other Wug. So please, ask away, Vega."

Still unable to process that he was already dead, I said haltingly, "What . . . happened . . . after you left Wormwood?"

"I left to lead an uprising against those who had destroyed our ancestors."

Now I said what I had to say. "You . . . you left me behind in Wormwood."

I knew if he was dead that I should not say these things to him, but how could I not?

When he reached out his hand for me, I did something I never dreamed I would do, especially after all this time.

I stepped back from him.

"Vega!" said Delph in an admonishing tone.

My grandfather slowly withdrew his hand and sat down on the floor.

I looked around and noticed that Pillsbury and Mrs. Jolly had entered the hall and were staring at us.

I turned back to my grandfather. He was looking around the place.

Pillsbury took a step forward. "May I get you some refreshment, sir?"

Virgil glanced at me, and his eyes carried a twinkle. He turned to Pillsbury. "I have quite enough refreshment being with my granddaughter, thank you, upset though she may with me right now."

"Your granddaughter? Then you are a Jane, sir?"

"Virgil Jane. I wish we could have met under better circumstances, but there you are." He glanced around the room once more and said, "What is this place?"

"It's our ancestral home, Empyrean," I said. "But surely you know of it. You're an Excalibur. You know all."

"I know a great many things. But I do not know all, Vega. And I never knew about this place."

He looked at my pocket, where the end of my wand

276

was sticking out. He pointed to it. "Is that how you came to know of it?"

"Yes, it sort of pointed the way for me."

"And how came you by your wand?"

"Alice Jane Adronis, the last Jane to live here. It was the Elemental and then it became my wand. Astrea Prine trained me up in the Quag. Do you know her?"

"Alas, I do not, having not gone through the Quag myself." He eyed my finger. "I see that my ring made its way to you."

"It was at Quentin Herms's cottage. Thansius gave it to me before I fled Wormwood. Quentin also left me a map and a book."

"I know that he did. Before I left, I asked him to do so, when you were of a proper age."

I gaped. "You . . . you asked him?"

"Yes. Herms was my trusted friend. And quite magical as well. He ventured into the Quag as far as possible and mapped it and took notes of all he saw. At least I assumed he did. Those were my instructions."

"And my parents? I know you summoned them. I was there when it happened. I could have gone with them," I added, with a trace of bitterness.

"But I did *not* summon them, Vega."

I gaped again. "What! But if you didn't, how did they leave Wormwood?"

"I do not know. I had no idea they had left Wormwood. And I have not seen them here. I hope with all my heart that they are safe."

I took out the picture. "I think they're out fighting the Maladons too," I said proudly.

His face crinkled into a smile. "I am so pleased."

"How were you captured?" I said quickly.

"I have spent the sessions since I left Wormwood collecting information, making contacts where I can, and causing as much strife for the Maladons as possible. Because of my efforts I believe they have given the insurrection a name." He pointed to the wording on the picture.

"The Campions?" I said.

He nodded. "Of which your parents are apparently now members in good standing. I only wish I had been able to join them." He paused for a moment, as though gathering his thoughts. "Well, my efforts came with more and more risk. Finally, I found myself surrounded by fifty Maladons. And while I am, or rather was, extraordinarily powerful, the odds were a bit against me. I managed to kill a dozen of them before I was beaten."

"Was Endemen there?"

"Yes. Him and his hatted men. They are the most elite fighters of the Maladons. They and I have spent much time together since I was captured. They lavished considerable attention on me," he added drily. "I am sorry I will not be able to return the favor. They wanted information. Information necessary to get what they really wanted. Information that I would not give them."

"What information?" I asked.

"They wanted a way through the Quag. So they could finish the job."

This came from Delph.

Virgil glanced at him. "It's Daniel, isn't it? You're Duff Delphia's son?"

"Yes, sir."

Virgil pondered Delph for a bit before saying, "You're quite perceptive, Daniel. I remember you being the same way as a young."

Delph gulped and said, "Thanks."

Virgil next turned his attention to Petra.

"And I don't believe we have met."

Under his gaze, Petra looked like she had been hit by a lightning spear.

"I'm . . . I'm P-Petra , M-Mr. Jane. I l-lived in the —"

"In the Quag," Virgil finished for her. "Yes, I have heard of that being the case. The process was messy at the end. People were trapped between worlds, as it were. I'm very happy that you've survived and have joined this lot."

"Are my parents Excaliburs, like you?" I asked.

"No. But they are magical. And they know of things. Things that I shared with them."

"Which is why Morrigone cursed them into the Care," I said spitefully.

"I know not of that."

He studied me closely. "If I had the power to summon Wugs from afar, Vega, I never would have left you behind. Do not believe for one sliver that I would have." He paused. "You were only six sessions old when I left. You needed to discover things on your own. As I did. I knew you were special, Vega, but it was the only way to see if you had the heart as well."

"But they beat our ancestors in the war," I noted.

"Evil can triumph over good. But that has more to do with the failings of the good than the successes of the bad. Now," he said briskly, "I must convey to you what I know and what I have discovered."

We all of us drew closer to him, for his voice was definitely growing weaker.

"You've been to True and Greater True, then?"

I nodded.

"True is the place where they alter the minds of all who are nonmagic. Then they labor there with smiles on their faces until they die."

"We've seen how they do that," I said. "But can you explain Greater True? The young soldiers they have? And the arrogant people with the slaves as servants?"

I saw my grandfather's face turn to a furious scowl.

"That is the genius of it, Vega. The pure genius of the Maladons."

"What is?" I said breathlessly.

"The Maladons were very quick to see that there were relatively few of them, while there were a great many nonmagicals, or 'Ordinaries,' as they derisively refer to them. So what they decided to do was far more diabolical."

"They put blokes on the top and blokes on the bottom," said Delph.

We all turned to him, my face full of surprise.

"Yes, Daniel," replied Virgil. "That is precisely what they did."

Delph added, "And if some blokes have it better than others, with slaves and coin and all, they're content-like. They feel like their lives are good, so why would they want to change them. Eh?"

"Exactly," said Virgil, looking pleased.

I looked at Delph with even greater respect. "That was brilliant, Delph."

"Yeah, brilliant," echoed Petra.

Virgil said, "Mark this carefully. True and Greater True are the largest towns I have been able to locate, and I have searched high and wide. The rest of this world is made up of smaller establishments, scattered villages, small homesteads, where those who live there labor hard for little. Word of these train stations is slowly spread among them. Trains that will take them to a better life."

I shook my head. "We've been to Bimbleton Station. It was so awful."

"There is also a befuddlement incantation around the areas monitored by the Maladons. True, Greater True and the other towns of some size. No one unauthorized can ever find their way to any of those places."

"Which means folks have to take the bloody train," I said.

"The Maladons didn't stop there. No brainwashing plan is perfect. And of course people marry and have youngs and they grow up with certain independent thoughts in their heads. Thus, they also used a scheme to direct any natural anger or resentment that those in True or Greater True may have toward something other than each other, or worse yet, the Maladons, though their presence among even the elite Ordinaries, I have learned, is not generally known."

"How did they do that?" I asked.

"You mentioned the young soldiers with their uniforms and marching?"

I nodded.

"Well, they have a regular army as well, composed of males, the Elite Guard they're called. But the male youngs are compelled to be part of military training as well, from an early age, until they are ready to serve their time in the ranks."

"But *who* is their enemy?" Delph asked.

"When you don't want those you rule to revolt against you, you have to give them something else to fear, to hate. And everyone under the rule of the Maladons has been taught from a young age that there is a great enemy out there just waiting to invade them. They focus all of their hatred and attention on that imaginary foe, and thus they never realize that they have already been enslaved."

"But surely folks won't believe that rubbish if the enemy *never* attacks," interjected Petra.

That was a good point, I thought.

Virgil responded, "Oh, but they *do* attack. It's not the 'enemy' of course, because there is none. No, the Maladons accomplish that any number of ways. They take innocent folks and implicate them in attacks that they themselves have performed. Or they use their magic to perform attacks against the people by these 'enemies.' These attacks are then repelled by the military might, and everyone ends up feeling absolutely wonderful at such grand victories. They have even taken some of the enslaved whose magic has been robbed from them and portrayed them as 'others' who seek to overturn the freedom of the people. They are dealt with summarily.

You may not have seen this, but public executions are held in the center square of True."

"Public executions?" I said with a shudder.

"Of *innocent* victims," he pointed out. "And the crowd cheers!"

We all fell silent. This was a great deal to take in, and I noted with growing alarm that my grandfather was looking weaker by the moment.

I held up my gloved hand. "Underneath here is the mark that is on your hand. It was the Maladons' doing. It was burned into my flesh the instant I neared the end of the Quag. I keep the glove on it, otherwise the Maladons can track me."

He nodded, his features somber. "I found that to be the case too. I had no glove. But I managed a particularly complex spell that rendered any Maladon who saw my mark temporarily blind."

*That was rather smart,* I thought.

He pointed at the ring on my finger. *His* ring.

"Has this served you well?" he asked. "I assume you have discovered its true power?"

I nodded. "Without it we would all be dead. So yes, it has served us very well. How did you come by it?"

"I traveled back in time through the portal at Stacks. Eon gave me a choice: the past or future. I chose the past. The ring was given to me by an interesting fellow: Colin Sonnet."

We all gasped. I shot Petra a glance to find her staring wide-eyed at my grandfather.

"How did you come to meet him?" I asked.

"I don't know. When you go back in the past, there is not always rhyme or reason where you land. He owned a small shop with many interesting articles. And he had also penned several books on sorcery."

*I know of at least one,* I thought.

"But why did he give up the ring to you?" I asked, still glancing at Petra.

Virgil shrugged. "That was not clear to me then. He insisted that I take it."

"So he could see and hear you," I said.

Virgil looked at me with a bemused expression. "In contravention of what Eon said, yes. He could see and hear me. He seemed to think that a great war with the Maladons was nearing and, quite frankly, I don't think he wanted the ring to fall into their hands."

"What was he like?"

This came from Petra.

He looked at her expectantly.

She added nervously, "See, my surname is Sonnet. Colin was, was my ancestor, I guess."

"He was a good fellow. And solidly against the Maladons, though they had not yet adopted that name. Back then they were merely referred to as the worshippers of Necro."

"Solidly against the Maladons," repeated Petra as she stared first at Delph and then at me.

Virgil nodded. "He told me that the ring's origin was not incantation by sorcery, for there is none that will accomplish it as far as he knew. But rather the confluence of mystical powers coming together at just the right moment. Quite a phenomenon of serendipity, but magic is often that way."

A silence followed as I continued to gaze at Petra, who was now looking down at her bare feet.

I finally said, "Alice Adronis gave me the Elemental as she lay dying on the battlefield. It's now my wand because we were family. But I can make it the Elemental whenever I want."

I reached in my pocket and held it up.

"Transform it for me," he said quietly.

I willed the Elemental to its full, golden size.

My grandfather stared at it reverently.

"I never met Alice Adronis. But I have learned of her past from various sources, and it was a tortured one. Her father was hard and cruel and wanted only sons and never loved the daughter he had instead. He cast her out on her own one night and told her never to return. Between you and me, it seems that her father, even though a Jane, had more than a bit of the Maladon blood in him."

At these words I shot Petra a glance. She was staring defiantly at me.

I could read her thoughts in her features.

*So how does it feel to perhaps have a bit of Maladon blood in you too?*

I turned back to my grandfather. "What did she do?" I said breathlessly.

"She climbed to the highest peak in the land one night when a terrible storm raged. And on that peak was the tallest tree in the land. And she climbed to the very top of it, held out her hand as far as she could to the storm raging above and swore that if she was granted the wand she felt she deserved that she would always use it in defense of good, and to battle evil."

Petra gasped, "What happened?"

"A lightning spear shot down from the heavens and struck her right at the point of her finger. From that finger grew the Elemental. I don't know if you ever noticed that Alice only possessed four fingers on her right hand."

I shook my head. "She gave me her glove, which she said I had to wear in order to touch it. But Astrea Prine told me I needn't do so, and she was right."

"Then you are the true inheritor of the thing," pronounced Virgil. Next he groaned and clutched his head.

I knelt beside him. "Is there nothing that can be done? I have a stone that heals almost all injuries."

He looked up at me and managed a tortured smile. "Dear Vega. How I have thought about you all these many sessions. And to now be reunited for such a short period of time. It is hardly fair."

"It's *not* fair," I said, blinking back fresh tears.

"Such is life, I'm afraid." He drew a long breath. "The Maladons are everywhere. Of course at the castle, but also in True, Greater True and other places. They will look just like anyone else if they so desire. When they are at the castle they can revert to their natural form."

"I've seen them transform. They're hideous, foul things."

"What you see is the culmination of centuries of hate. It can make the most beautiful among us ugly and wretched." He paused. "I pity them, I do indeed."

I said incredulously, "You pity the Maladons? After all the evil they've done? After their leader has *killed* you?"

"Yes, Vega, I do. I suppose that is what separates us from them. We can feel compassion for others, whoever and whatever they might be. And regardless of what they might have done."

I noticed that his image had grown so pale that it was difficult to see him.

"'Tis very near the end," he said in a weak voice.

"Grandfather," I suddenly cried out. "I don't want you to leave me. I need you."

"All you need, Vega, my dear child, you already possess. And please know that above all else, you will carry my love for you wherever you go. For I have loved you with all my heart, dear, dear Vega, since the moment of your birth."

And with that he was gone.

# Farewell

I DID NOT COME out of my room for the next two days. When I finally did come downstairs with Harry Two by my side, Mrs. Jolly had made a scrumptious breakfast, which Pillsbury served despite my protests that I could serve myself.

I was halfway through my meal when Delph and then Petra made their appearances.

Each of them cast me furtive looks but seemed reluctant to add voices to these glances.

Finally, I said gloomily, "Well, it's just us now."

Delph laid aside his fork and looked at me. "But Virgil told us helpful things."

"He prepared us, best he could," said Petra. "And it was good to know that my ancestor helped him," she added, glancing nervously at me.

"Yes, it was," I said.

Then my thoughts ventured elsewhere.

If only I had managed to save my grandfather in the Tower. But I had failed. I had fled. And he had been finished off by the murderous Necro. He was dead because of my incompetence. How could I expect to lead others into a war when I couldn't even save one person?

Delph put a hand on my shoulder and said, "I'm really sorry, Vega Jane. Virgil was a great Wug."

I lowered my face because I didn't want either Delph or Petra to see my features.

I started when I felt the hand on my arm.

I looked up to see Petra staring at me.

I was surprised to see that there were tears in her eyes.

"I know what it's like to lose family, Vega," she said slowly. "And I know what it's like to . . . to not be able to save someone."

I thought of her family being slaughtered by creatures of the Quag. Losing her uncle to a lycan attack and being unable to save him. I thought of her guilt in losing Lackland, of not being fast enough to use her wand when she could have done.

But I was the leader. I couldn't fail. Yet if I knew I couldn't succeed? I had always thought that if I found my grandfather, he would lead and I could simply follow. That had always been in the back of my mind. Now that was not possible. Now it came down to me. The weight of this thought was crushing.

Before I could give voice to these revelations, Petra said, "And you can never save everyone, can you? But the thing is, if you don't try, then you'll save no one." She drew a quick breath and gave Delph a darting glance before turning her attention back to me. "I've seen what you can do, Vega. I've seen how many times you've saved us. From jabbits and the bloody Soul Takers and the like. I wouldn't be alive but for you, and neither would Delph. So if you're thinking you can't save blokes, well, you'd be wrong. Because you already have."

She fell quiet and removed her hand.

We all just sat there in silence, not looking at one another.

Finally, I rose and said, "If we're going to make a go of this, we need to make plans. We'll be surprised, no doubt, by what we'll be faced with, but we have to plan for that too. I don't want us ever to be so surprised again that all we can do is flee." I swallowed with difficulty. "And leave someone behind."

They both mutely nodded at this.

"Virgil told us a lot about this world. Some we knew and a great deal we didn't. The Maladons are well-organized and powerful sorcerers. We can't underestimate any of them."

"Vega Jane," began Delph. "Why do you think they picked now to . . . to kill Virgil?"

"I don't know, Delph. I suspect it had something to do with what was going on at the castle. There was a great deal of activity. And we need to find out what it was about."

"How do we do that?" asked Petra. "Go back there?"

I shook my head. "We've risked going back enough as it is. I think there might be a better way."

"What?" asked Delph.

"I think the answer to that lies in Greater True."

"Why?" asked Petra.

"Because that's where our army lies."

"Do you want to leave now?" asked Petra.

"In just a bit. I have a few things to do first."

As I marched up to my room, I had to admit that my "few things to do" was really just an excuse to gather myself.

I couldn't actually fathom that my grandfather was gone.

I couldn't see how I would ever find my parents.

And me being able to lead an "army" to defeat the

Maladons seemed totally barmy. I could imagine myself telling some git like Cletus Loon what I was expected to do and hearing him roar, "Barking, you are. Totally mad. Why, you're only a *female!*"

*Tosser.*

I opened the door to my room and then looked behind me.

Harry Two had not followed me up. I wondered what that was about.

I closed my door and sat on my bed. The room was fuggy. So was my head.

I lay back and stared at the ceiling.

It seemed like I had been running for my life ever since I stepped into the Quag, with no time to think things through.

Only, now I had to. I *had* to think.

I had set out from Wormwood — escaped really — to find the truth.

I had bloody well found it. Now I was supposed to change it all somehow. Make everything right. I had fought my way across the Quag, survived Endemen and his men.

For this?

Another challenge that looked positively beyond my ability?

It hardly seemed fair, and I was at sixes and sevens as to what to do.

My head was swimming. I closed my eyes and then reopened them.

And there she was.

Uma Cadmus was hovering right above me.

Her sad, sad eyes looked down upon me.

I sat up and gazed at her.

"My grandfather is dead," I said. "Virgil is dead."

She nodded slowly. Apparently, she knew this.

"I'm expected to defeat the Maladons, but I don't know how to do so. My grandfather told me a lot, but he didn't tell me how to do that."

Again, she nodded in a very knowing way. "He wouldn't have, would he?"

"Why not?"

"One can only defeat the Maladons by fighting them. And in fighting them one comes up with ways and methods and strategies to do so. One cannot sit back and contemplate how to manage it. One must be engaged in the war."

As she was speaking, she floated down from the ceiling to sit next to me.

I had to admit it was a bit disconcerting having, well, *regret* perched on my bed.

"Your father believed that Necro wanted peace," I said a bit crossly. "And instead he got a bloody war."

"My father was a good man who was fooled by a cleverer one," she said with proper spirit. I could imagine myself defending my father in the same way.

"Well, your father and my ancestor Alice Adronis and Astrea Prine were all great magical beings. My grandfather was an Excalibur. And they couldn't beat the Maladons. I hardly see how I have any chance of victory."

I watched as she stared off into the distance. There was so much hurt in her eyes that I seemed to feel it in my bones.

"You . . . you loved Jason very much, didn't you?"

She slowly turned to me. "As much as one could love another," she said simply.

"I haven't felt that for a male," I said.

"Are you certain about that?"

I looked at her in confusion. "What? Why wouldn't I be?"

"Because I have seen how you look at your friend Delph. And I see how he looks at you."

I felt the blood rush to my face and I had to turn away.

"We're just friends."

"Friendship often is and should be a precursor to love."

I glanced back at her. "You said you represent regret. Does that mean you regret loving Jason?"

"That is the only thing I do *not* regret."

Silence passed between us until I worked up the courage. Or the panic, I'm not sure which. Perhaps both those roads often lead to the same destination.

I looked at her with pleading eyes. "Uma, can you help me? Please? I . . . know I must do this, but I'm not yet sixteen years old and . . . and I'm terrified that I'm going to fail and let everyone down."

She reached out a hand and gripped mine.

This stunned me, for I had just assumed that she was not flesh and bone.

"Let me show you something," she said.

She rose and drifted out of the room. I hurried after her.

I followed her ghostlike form down this corridor and that, up that staircase and down that one. We finally reached a passageway that I'd had no idea was even there.

At the end was a simple wooden door.

She passed right through it, whereas I was forced to use the doorknob.

When I entered, Uma was hovering next to the far wall.

The room was not large, but it was brightly lit by torches that I was sure had just come to life at our entry.

There wasn't a stick of furniture in the room. In fact, there was only one item in the entire space: a small glass box hanging from the wall.

And in that box was a wand.

It was long and as golden in color as the Elemental when fully formed.

Even though no one was holding it, the thing seemed to pulsate with power.

"Whose wand is that?" I asked.

"My father's."

"That's Bastion Cadmus's wand?" I exclaimed.

"He was a tremendously powerful sorcerer. It was acknowledged by all that even Alice Adronis was second to him in ability."

"But how did his wand come to be here?"

"Alice recovered it and brought it here after he was killed."

"And if he was so powerful, how exactly did he die? On the battlefield?"

"No. He was betrayed."

"By whom?"

"Victoria, my mother."

I gaped. "Your mother? Then also his wife?"

She nodded.

"How did that happen?"

"She didn't do it voluntarily. I was already dead, and the war had commenced. She was placed under the *Subservio* spell and she gave the Maladons information about my father. When he would be home alone. She let them in and my father found himself surrounded by Maladons one night. There was no one to help him. He killed a dozen of them, but he had received a mortal wound. He died in the great hall of his beloved home."

"I'm so very sorry, Uma," I said.

"Necro did not want to face him on the battlefield. He knew my father would triumph. My father never wanted war. And he may have gone too far in trying to appease the Maladons. But he was a tremendous warrior, which is why they decided to get to him by trickery, using my poor mother."

"That's so awful, Uma."

"He was not simply my father, you know, but the father of *all* of our people. So when he died, much of the spirit went out of us," said Uma wistfully. "And the Maladons took full advantage of that. They fought even more fiercely. They could sense weakness. They smelled blood. Thus they did awful, terrible things. They desecrated the bodies of those they killed. They turned our kind against each other with their bloody incantations. It was all chaotic and, well, terrible."

I looked at the box as she traced her fingers over the glass. Though it could possibly have been my imagination, it seemed as though the wand sparked at her touch of the glass.

"I think that's why I remain here," she said. "To be some-where that was happy, that was safe. That was free of the Maladons!" she concluded fiercely.

"And your mother? What happened to Victoria?"

"She came out of the spell, realized what she had done . . . and killed herself."

I could think of nothing to say.

"Like mother, like daughter," said Uma gloomily.

"You thought the love of your life was dead," I said.

Delph's face shot through my mind.

*What would I do if something happened to Delph? If he were killed?*

She said, "Do you know what the most powerful thing in the world is?"

I shook my head.

She took my hand and pressed it against my chest.

"That is the most powerful thing there is, Vega. All magic, all grand sorcery, pales next to it."

I didn't get her meaning right away. Then, I did.

"You mean my heart?"

"And what it represents. It means desire, Vega. It means what you want more than anything else. But there are differ-ences in feelings. In their potency."

"How do you mean?" I asked.

"Some are fleeting, like fear and happiness. Others are more permanent. Like vanity or kindness. But in my brief life I found that there are only two that stand the test of time, that define who and what we are." She paused as I waited in great anticipation. "Love and hate."

"And so does that mean I will be soundly defeated as well?"

She again pressed my hand to my chest.

"The answer to that, Vega, lies right here."

And in the next instant, as was the case with my grandfather, she vanished.

I just sat there for what seemed a very long time.

I nearly jumped when I felt something touch my hand.

I looked down, and there was Harry Two. He had finally decided to follow me. I was a bit cross, but when I looked down into his beautiful, mismatched eyes so full of love, my annoyance slipped away.

Love was indeed very powerful.

And as I sat there thinking about that, a plan came together in my mind. I mean a real plan, with steps and a goal at the end. There were many reasons for me coming up with it. But the main one was something Uma had said.

I stood and took out my wand.

I guess it all came down to whether I believed in myself or not.

I went back to my room, packed my tuck, threw it over my shoulder and headed down the stairs with Harry Two marching right next to me.

My dog looked as resolute as ever I'd seen him.

I met the others in the foyer of Empyrean.

They looked as ready as I did.

That was good, because we would need to be perfect to pull this off.

Mrs. Jolly had prepared food for us. Delph put it in his tuck.

We stepped outside the front door tethered together.
We looked at one another.

"Well," I said. "This is it."

"Do you really think we can do it?" asked Petra.

"Let's bloody well go find out," I said.

# The Plan

A S SOON AS we were far enough away from Empyrean, I cast my *Pass-pusay* spell, and with the thought of the town in mind, we were instantly delivered to the center of True.

It was midday, so folks were bustling around. Motors zipped past, people chatted away as they walked, shops were open, doing a thriving business. I watched women scrubbing the cobbles and men soaping up storefront windows.

They all looked pleasant and happy and oblivious to the fact that an insidious race had stolen their very lives from them.

Perhaps because of that, they would never know a bit of unhappiness or true sorrow or maybe even pain.

Yet I thought that all of them, fully informed of the choice, would accept a real life of ups and downs over a manufactured one devoid of the whole spectrum of existence.

I very much desired to give them the chance.

Delph said, "I thought we were going to Greater True?"

"We are. But we need something from here first."

They followed me down the cobbles until we reached the place.

It had been our original hiding place on our first night in this new land.

The steeple rose up, and I could just catch a glimpse of the huge bell inside.

"Why are we going there?" asked Delph as he followed my gaze.

The door opened and a group of people came out, all well dressed and looking like they had just had a pious experience. One woman was carrying a baby draped all in white. The baby was screaming, while the mother was trying to calm it.

We did that with our newborns in Wormwood. Christened them at Steeples.

We slipped through the door before the wood thunked closed, and moved swiftly up the aisle.

The place was empty. The group that had left must have been the only one in the church.

The first night there we had headed upstairs. I didn't go that way. I had no interest in the upstairs.

There was a corridor down here. It was off to the right.

I went that way.

There was a wooden door partially open at the end of the corridor.

I peered through the crevice and saw a man sitting at a large desk writing something on a pad of paper.

It was the same man who had chased us when we'd left there before. The man wore the same stiff white collar. But all the rest of his clothes were starkly black.

*Too bloody ironic*, I thought.

He took off his spectacles and rubbed at his face as he

took a moment's respite from his writing, and then turned and opened a book.

What I saw sticking out of the open drawer of his desk confirmed my suspicions. He had seen us that night. And reported us. That's why the other bloke had followed us. He was a Maladon set here among the "Ordinaries." Just as my grandfather had warned me about.

Well, now it was my turn.

I raised my wand and said, *"Subservio."*

The jet of light hit him directly in the back, and he instantly stiffened.

I kicked the door open and moved into the room with the others trailing behind.

I reached across his still form and snatched the wand out of the desk drawer.

Through the spell books we had discovered at Empyrean, I had added a number of incantations to my quiver. I was prepared to use one of them now.

I might as well make certain.

I pointed my wand at the man, gave it a long sweep and said, *"Origante."*

The moment after my spell hit him, we all took a step back as the "person" transformed into the hideous Maladon that he was.

The face elongated. The hands became claws. The nose looked as sharp as a knife blade, the mouth cruel and hideously shaped. When he turned to us, his eyes were large red drops of blood.

Petra screamed, but I gripped her by the shoulder.

"Keep quiet. He's under my spell."

"What the Hel is that . . . that thing?" exclaimed Delph.

I had forgotten that they had never seen a true Maladon before.

"A Maladon in its original form," I replied. I glanced at Petra. She had a funny look on her face that took me a moment to interpret.

*She's worried that if I use the spell on her, she will turn into something like that.*

I looked back at our captive.

"What is your name?" I asked. "Your real Maladon name," I added.

When it opened its mouth to answer, I saw that, like the vile Orco's, its tongue was long and forked at the end. It was not surprising that these vile creatures shared that hideous physical characteristic.

The creature said, "My name is Krill."

Its voice was like a serpent's hiss and a banshee's shriek wedded at the vocal cords.

*Truly lovely.*

"And you work here to spy on the people living in True?"

"Yes."

"How do you report to those at Maladon Castle?"

He glanced at what I was holding.

"Wand wire."

"Wand wire?" This was a new term for me.

"We send messages using our wands. Like writing in the air. It leaves one wand and comes out through the wand of the intended recipient in the form of a thought in one's mind."

*That's actually truly clever,* I thought.

"Tell me the spell to accomplish that."

He did so, and I tucked that away in my memory. I glanced sharply at Petra. She nodded that she had done the same.

I turned back to Krill. "There are people who have had their magic taken from them. Do you know this?"

Krill nodded. "I do."

"And do you have information on these people? Where they are living and what they are called?"

That was why I was here. I thought if there was one place where such records would be kept, it would be here, a place of goodness and worship where all came together. Thus, it would make perfect sense that the Maladons would want to keep records of all their slaves in such a "holy" place. The very idea, though, made my skin crawl.

And the place was called Saint Necro's, after all. And his original followers had been called "worshippers."

Krill pointed to a large tome on a shelf above his desk.

"It is all there."

"Is that for only those in Greater True?"

"Greater True and Maladon Castle are the only places they are located. There are none in True."

"You're positive?"

He nodded. "Quite positive."

"Why is that, then?"

"These 'things' are rewards for the most elite among the Ordinaries. And they live in Greater True. And of course, a very few at Maladon Castle."

"Why only a very few at Maladon Castle? I'd have thought they would love to be waited on hand and foot by the enslaved."

"Because our masters do not like to be associated with filthy weaklings, regardless of how they are clothed." He spat on the floor.

I bristled at his foul words, but I did believe he spoke the truth. The Maladons *would* see us that way.

"Why do you keep these records at all?" Petra asked.

"We always keep records of *property*, however unsavory."

This statement made me want to curse him to dust.

Instead, I pointed my wand at the book, said the familiar spell and watched as it zoomed into my hand. I set it down, pointed my wand at it, said, *"Duplicado"* and an exact replica appeared in my free hand. I pocketed it and sent the original book zipping back onto the shelf.

I looked at Krill. "Do the Maladons know that there are intruders among them? Has Mr. Endemen spoken to you about it?"

Krill said, "Mr. Endemen does not speak to the likes of me. He uses intermediaries. But, yes, I have heard that there are those about what should not be here."

I pointed my wand at Krill and reversed my *Origante* spell. Then I said to him, "You will remember nothing of this, understood?"

He nodded. "Nothing."

"Turn around and go back to work."

He did so while I freed him from the *Subservio* spell and then used the *Pass-pusay* spell to take us from this unholy place.

Invisible and back out on the street, Delph and Petra were ecstatic.

"That was brilliant, Vega Jane," exclaimed Delph so loudly that I had to shush him.

I led them into an alley, took out the book and opened it to the first page.

I read down the page and said, "This is all we need to return the magic to those poor people. We have their names and where they live now."

"How many names on the list?" asked Petra.

I swiftly counted.

"Fifty-five. Fifty of them live in Greater True. The others are at Maladon Castle. One of them was the Victus we met."

"Blimey!" Delph said. "Fifty names. Where do we start?" he added in a hopeless tone.

I placed my thumb over the first name on the ledger.

"Amicus Arnold. He lives on Goldofin Street in Greater True."

"But what do we do when we get there?" asked Petra. "Like you said, we can't just free him without anyone knowing. And word will get out and everyone will be on guard."

"I've thought of a way around that," I said.

Next, I used the *Pass-pusay* spell to get us to Greater True.

We landed in the center of the place and looked around.

We had one obvious problem. We didn't know the streets of Greater True.

We wandered around for a bit until Delph exclaimed, "Look there."

We looked where he was pointing. It was a shop that sold maps!

We went to the shop door and I looked in through an open window.

I looked over the shelves as a bloke at the counter helped a customer.

A moment later I spotted the map I wanted. I waited until the bloke had turned his back and did my incantation. The map flew through the window and into my hand.

We hurried around to an alley and I opened the map. It took a few moments, but I located Goldofin Street. It was only three streets over from where we were presently.

Number Forty-Seven was the one we wanted.

We quickly walked there and looked at the solidly built brick house attached to its neighbors on either side. There was a bright red door that reminded me of blood. The place was impeccable, the windows sparkling clean with not even a smidgen of dirt on the stone pavement in front.

As we watched from across the street, the red door opened and we saw a blank-eyed man appear there with a rag and bottle of liquid in hand.

This was undoubtedly the unfortunate if elegantly attired Amicus Arnold.

*Elegantly attired!*

The truth about this suddenly occurred to me. It was a badge of humiliation. A cruel joke, for all the "elites" here knew that these people were slaves by their blank eyes. You could dress them up, but that didn't change the fact that they were owned by others. It was a heartless act.

And it fit the Maladons perfectly, because that's exactly what they were: cruel and heartless.

Arnold began to dutifully polish the brass knocker.

My blood began to boil because I knew he had had his magic and his life taken from him.

Well, I meant to give it back.

WE WAITED UNDER our cloak of invisibility until it turned dark and the streets emptied of both motors and people. Then we waited some more.

We quietly ate some of the provisions that Mrs. Jolly had so kindly given us.

We spoke only in low tones because I had no reason to believe there weren't spies throughout this horrible place.

Finally, when we heard a tower clock chime the lateness of the hour, I pulled a tiny bottle of dust from my pocket. On the label was the name Amicus Arnold. I used my wand to return the bottle to its full size. Then I looked at the others.

"Ready?" I said.

They nodded.

Petra had her wand out.

And Delph's hand hovered over the short-handled ax on his belt.

Harry Two's fangs were bared.

The red door opened with a spell cast and we were inside.

I assumed that the owners would sleep in the upstairs rooms.

That left the downstairs to their slave.

We passed through rooms that were lavishly furnished and past walls adorned with beautiful paintings. Our feet sank into thick rugs. Our eyes roamed over intricate wallpaper. As a former Finisher at Stacks, I had to marvel at the beauty I was seeing. But the foulness just underneath the surface quickly made all I was viewing remarkably ugly.

We found the sleeping chamber of Amicus Arnold. It was just off the kitchen in what appeared to be a broom cupboard. He was curled up on the floor snoring softly, his beautiful, spotless livery hanging on hooks on the back of the door.

I realized with a start that I had seen this bloke before. He was the one who had been trailing behind the couple and caught the item the woman had dropped. And gotten slapped for his troubles before I had blasted his "masters" with an *Engulifiado* spell.

Harry Two had shown me the best way to accomplish our task tonight.

I spun my ring around so that we became visible.

Then I uncorked the bottle, turned it upside down and let the dust sprinkle over the sleeping man.

It didn't take long for each particle to be soaked right into him.

A few seconds went by as Arnold glowed brightly.

Then he sat bolt upright, blinked and his gaze fell upon us.

And I truly meant that, because his eyes had come back. They were a lovely shade of green, as a matter of fact.

"What the —"

I held up my wand and said, "You're Amicus Arnold."

"I know I am." He looked around. "At least . . . at least now I do. It's all so muddy. How did I get here? And who are you lot?"

"My name is Vega Jane. This is Petra, Delph and my dog, Harry Two."

"What the blazes are you doing here?"

I conveyed an enormous amount of information as efficiently as I possibly could. When I mentioned what I had done to his masters, he smiled. "I wondered about that. But I guess I was under their . . . their spell thing. The thing is, I don't remember being . . . magical."

"But do you remember doing things that were inexplicable?"

He rubbed his jaw. "Well, come to think, yeah. I could talk to my cat. My mum thought I had a fever or something. And I could make a coin spin as long as I wanted it to."

"There you have it."

"So you're saying I was lured onto the train and my magic stolen and I was made a servant to the people who live here?"

"Yes." I held up the bottle with his name on it.

He slowly traced the letters of his name with his finger.

"Blimey," he said, tears creeping to the corners of his eyes. "And you came here to save me?"

"You and a great many others," said Delph.

I said, "But you must go on being enslaved. For now anyway. Until we send the signal that it's time to go."

"The signal that you told me about?"

"Yes."

"And you said we're going to fight the . . . the Maladons?"

"To the death, I expect."

His face fell and he shook his head sadly.

"I don't know how to fight. Not with magic."

I glanced at Petra and Delph before replying. "That's where we come in. We're going to train you. We're going to train all of you."

He glanced at my wand. "But I don't have one of those."

"You'll have a wand," I said.

Petra and Delph looked at me in surprise. I had not told them about *that* part.

Arnold's face crumpled and he said in dismay, "But, Vega, I don't know if I can pretend to be enslaved now. When I see their faces I might want to punch them or something. Then your plan will be ruined."

"You won't have to pretend."

I raised my wand.

"Do you trust me, Amicus?"

He slowly nodded. "Yes, I do, Vega. After what you've done for me, I surely do."

I performed the spell and he lapsed back to the floor and fell asleep.

There was one more obvious thing that needed doing. I knew no spell that could accomplish this directly, but I knew of one that might do so indirectly.

I touched my wand to his eyes and said, "*Eraisio.*" Held firmly in my mind was what I wanted to happen. A spell of necessity, as Silenus would say.

His eyes turned blank once more.

Having to return Arnold to slavery was not easy, not after just freeing him. But I had a plan and I had to stick to it. Or else we would all end up as slaves to the Maladons.

Or dead more likely.

We left Amicus Arnold and moved on to the next one.

That night we freed eight people in total, an equal number of men and women. Each was much like Amicus Arnold:

grateful, bewildered, uncertain and angry. But in the end they all swore to do what would be asked of them.

After that we retreated to the train station at Greater True. It was morning now but this place was not busy.

I had to remind myself that the reason was odious.

This town was for the *elites*, who, by definition, were far less numerous than the rabble.

As Petra and Delph fell asleep safely hidden behind our invisibility shield, I opened the book that I had duplicated back at the church in True. Using an ink stick, I ticked off the names of the people we had visited and freed.

Eight down.

Quite a few still to go.

I hoped we would survive to get to the last name.

And then, though it was hard to fathom considering what we'd already been through, the *real* danger would begin.

## One Death

THE NEXT NIGHT did not go nearly as smoothly.

We managed to successfully free a goodly number of people, including a bloke named Dennis O'Shaughnessy who wouldn't stop kissing me. He just about cried when I had to put him back under a spell until the time was right.

The next house after O'Shaughnessy's held an unexpected surprise.

The little girl with very dark skin whom I'd seen in the looking glass at Maladon Castle lay on her ragged bed in the bowels of a large house on Needles Court.

I gasped when I saw her. I had not known her name before. Now I did.

Miranda Weeks.

I returned her magical dust to her and she awoke. She stretched out her long thin limbs and then sat bolt upright. I explained what had happened to her. She took this all in, in a way that impressed me. She was surely mature beyond her years. Then I told her what I had seen at the castle. Her mother and her in the looking glasses.

I said, "We don't have another person with the surname Weeks on the list. Do you know what happened to your mother? I have her magical dust." I drew the bottle from my pocket. "I took it when I was at Maladon Castle."

She leaned back against the wall and brushed a tear from her eye. "Now that you cleared my mind, I remember." She paused, her face screwed up in pain. "I heard them talking, these . . . these Maladons." She paused again, and I could see her chin tremble. "They said me mum died. They said that happens." She fought back a sob. "They said it didn't happen often enough. And then they laughed."

We all stared down at her, unable to speak in the face of this atrocity until Petra sat next to her and held her. Miranda wept into Petra's shoulder as Petra whispered soothing things into her ear.

Miranda finally stopped weeping, and Petra let her go and stood next to me. I held Petra's gaze for a long moment. She was the most perplexing person I'd ever met.

I said, "Miranda, I promise you that if you trust me, we will avenge your mum, okay?"

She nodded. I cast my spell, crafted blank eyes and turned to leave.

"Petra, what did you say to her?"

She looked embarrassed. "I . . . I just told her that I was her friend. And that I would be there for her."

"Okay," I said quietly. "That was very nice."

We headed off, my mind still awhirl at the conundrum of Petra Sonnet.

In the fourth house we visited was a brown-skinned gent named Dedo Datt. I had seen a number of people back in True who looked like him. He was of medium height and skinny, with black hair swept back off his brow. He was, unlike the others, not asleep. He was sitting up in the corner of his little room next to the basement stairs.

He made no movement when I twisted round my ring and became visible. He said nothing when we sprinkled the dust over him. But when the magic was readily absorbed into him and his eyes were no longer blank, they filled with tears.

"I have waited so long," he said, rising and holding out his hand.

This stunned me.

"You were waiting?"

He nodded.

"So you remember what happened to you?"

"I remembered enough to know that I was not who I had become. But I was powerless to do anything about it."

"You're magical."

He nodded. "I knew that. I realized that was why I had been taken."

"The Maladons."

"Yes, the Maladons. What is your plan?" he asked.

"To beat them."

He smiled. "That is a very good plan."

As we left the house, I said to the others, "That shows the Maladons are not infallible." And then I smiled. That was a very good thing to know.

The next home was one of the largest we had yet seen. Indeed, so large was it that there were *two* people here who needed rescuing from their enslavement: Anna Dibble and Sara Bond.

Like so many of the others, we found them in the bowels

314

of the luxurious home wearing shabby nightdresses, their hair covered with ill-fitting bonnets.

We sprinkled the dust, and they slowly came around to their stolen pasts, as had the others. All that was fine enough.

Until I looked over to the doorway of the women's bleak sleeping quarters and came face-to-face with who I presumed was the owner of the opulent place. He was wearing silk pajamas and had on an expensive-looking robe with a tassel waistband.

And in one hand was a morta.

He pointed it at me and shouted, "What the bloody —"

He got no farther because Petra said firmly, *"Paralycto."*

He froze with the morta still pointed at me.

"Thanks, Petra." I studied him leisurely. "He's your master?" I asked the pair.

"Yes," they both said.

"Wrong. He *was* your master. He no longer is."

Sara and Anna looked at each other, and then tears slid down their faces.

"Is he the only one who lives here with you?" I asked.

"There's his wife, but you can't wake her, aye, even if you dropped every plate in the house," said Anna.

I walked around the frozen bloke and then pointed my wand at him once more.

*"Subservio."*

His features relaxed, and I said, *"Unparalycto."*

He slumped to the floor, his back against the wall, his eyes staring off.

"Your name?" I asked.

"Cyril Dudgett," he said in a lifeless tone.

"All right, Dudgett, you will remember nothing of this. When we're done, you will return to your bed as though you had never awoken, is that clear?"

He dumbly nodded, his puckered eyes puckering even more.

"You own this house?"

He nodded.

"Who are your masters?"

"I have none," he said sharply.

I smiled at this. The Maladons had done a very complete job making this fool believe his life was his own, though he was as much under their power as he was under mine right now.

"What do you do?" I asked.

"Do?" he said.

"In the way of work?"

"I am rich. I don't have to work."

"How very lucky you are," I said drily. "And the source of your wealth?"

His puckered eyes widened, as though he had never pondered such a question.

"My wealth is . . . my wealth. I have always had it."

"Quite fortunate."

"I am one of the chosen."

"Chosen by whom?" I asked.

Again, he faltered.

"I . . . I am one of the chosen," he said again. "Aren't I?" he added feebly.

"Blimey," said Sara. "He's off his noodle."

I turned to look at her. "His life is an empty one, not even his own. He lives in luxury and never questions anything. The perfect puppet."

I turned back to him. "Dudgett, do you know anything that would be useful to me?"

"Like what?"

"Anything of the Maladons."

"I do not know that term."

"Mr. Endemen, then?"

His mouth broadened to a smile. "A fine chap. A good man. He's always visiting us in Greater True. He always makes us feel . . . feel . . ."

"Feel so good about yourselves?" I finished for him.

"Exactly. So very good about ourselves."

"Because you're the chosen ones?" I thought of something and added, "Because you've earned the right to be . . . chosen?"

"Precisely. You've put your finger right on it. Yes. We've *earned* it."

"And how did you earn it?"

His smile collapsed along with his features. His mouth opened and closed but nothing came out.

"All right, Dudgett, we'll leave it at that. Before you go back to bed, I want you to tell Anna and Sara that you're sorry for what you've done."

Dudgett turned to them and said, "I'm sorry."

I looked at Anna and Sara. "I don't care if he didn't mean it. I thought you just might want to hear it."

I ordered him back upstairs and he dutifully went off.

I put Sara and Anna back to sleep and we set off for another house under cover of the invisibility ring.

"Those blokes don't know how good they have it," said Petra. "I mean they really don't know, do they?"

I said forcefully, "They've been fed a pack of lies and given stuff so they'll be nice little pets for the Maladons. Their minds have been taken over. Their lives are not their own. They're really slaves like the others, only they don't know it either. I wouldn't call that having it good." I stared over at her. "Would you?"

"I . . . I guess not. But they have food and a roof over their heads and nice clothes and servants. And plenty of money. And they don't have to work."

"Right, plenty of *stuff*," I replied. "The only thing missing from their lives . . . is a life."

We fell silent until Delph said, "I wonder how the Maladons chose the blokes? I mean did they create Greater True and fill it with people and make them better off than everybody else?"

"I think they might have, Delph."

"But what's the point to it all?" asked Petra.

Delph said, "Well, it's sort of what we was talking about, how they play one off against the other like. Like Virgil said. Create a pretend enemy so they have something to hate. Plus, considering that the folks from Greater True can travel to True, but those from True can't come here, I think it's a way to show those from True, and through them, all others living about in the country, that people can live better. That things can improve for folks. Those in True, brainwashed though they might be, can look at the rich from here and say, 'See, that could be me if I work hard and keep on the dutiful path. I can reach the promised land, so to speak.' It makes life seem fair somehow."

"I think you're exactly right, Delph," I said. "When my grandfather said the most bitterly awful place of all was one that Wugs didn't know was as wrong as wrong could be, he could have also been talking about this place."

We ventured to the next name on our list and did that one plus nine more.

The following night we did ten more. And the next night the same.

We had just returned to our hiding place in the bowels of the train station when we saw that the room we'd been using looked like it had been searched. We had left nothing here that was important, but it was still unnerving that someone had located this spot and gone through it.

"We'll have to move, I reckon," I said dully, for it was quite late and I was knackered, as we all were.

We packed up our few belongings and set off to find a new hiding place down there.

It was eerily quiet and so very dark that I was tempted to use my wand to provide illumination.

The second I did, a spell shot over our heads, barely missing us. It hit the wall instead and left a good-size, smoky hole.

I cried out and instinctively ducked.

The others tethered to me did the same.

Another spell shot out, lower this time. Had we remained standing, we would have been goners.

Flattened to the floor, I looked around to see where

the spells were coming from. But all I could see was darkness.

I lifted my wand and was about to utter an incantation when Delph gripped my hand and shook his head.

"Let me," he whispered.

He drew from his pocket a small ball. I recognized it at once as the same one that Astrea Prine had used to help train me on the *Rejoinda* spell. I'd had no idea that Delph had kept it.

I watched as Delph put the ball on the floor. He said to both me and Petra, "Keep your eyes peeled and get ready."

He gave the ball a little push and it rolled off. Once it was past the shield of invisibility, it hadn't gone more than a few inches when a bolt of light hit it, destroying it.

Petra and I pointed our wands at the source of the light and uttered our *Impacto* spells.

We heard a gasp and a crash.

We all leapt up and charged toward the sound.

Then out of the darkness we saw a figure.

It was a Bowler Hat.

He was lying under a pile of rubble. I supposed our spells had hit the wall, and the collapse of the stone had buried him under it.

I had supposed that he was unconscious or even dead.

As it turned out, he was neither. What he was, was dangerous still.

He exploded out of the rubble with a slash of his wand and a wordless incantation. Then he pointed his wand toward us and a light shot out. I knew he couldn't see us because of the invisibility shield, but the path of the spell was so broad that it caught us up in a whirlwind of sheer force and hurled us off our feet.

The impact with the wall I hit was so hard that I was momentarily stunned.

When I rose, the bloke was staring right at me. I mean he was seeing me!

What the Hel.

I looked to my left and right and saw Petra, Delph and Harry Two slowly regain their feet. The impact must have broken the magical tethers. I looked down at my ring. It had moved round my finger. Before I could move it back the Bowler Hat roared, "I've got you now!"

He cast another spell that I barely evaded.

Petra shot a spell at him but he effortlessly blocked it.

Delph pulled out his ax and hurled it.

The Bowler Hat laughed and said, "Oh, why that's a stunner."

He shot a spell right at Delph, and had I not blocked it, Delph would have been crushed. As it was, he was thrown heels over arse against the wall and slumped down, barely conscious.

Petra and I kept shooting spells and the Bowler Hat kept blocking them. He shot spells at us, and between the two of us we barely stayed alive. It was clear that he was by far the superior fighter, and had it been one on one, we would be dead.

He had backed us up against a wall. I felt the cold stone behind me with one hand while my other gripped my wand. I was frantically trying to think what to do. I had cast so many spells and blocked so many of his that I was completely exhausted.

But the Bowler Hat looked perfectly fresh and ready to battle on. They truly were elite fighters, as my grandfather had said.

He was actually sneering at us. "Well, luv, lucky for you that you're wanted alive, or I would have already killed you and your bloody mates."

When I was battling creatures in the Quag, it had not been nearly this tiring, but then I realized that most times a single spell had been sufficient for victory. I was reminded of Astrea Prine's warning that the Maladons would have no compunction about killing me. Looking into the vile face of our opponent right now, I could see why my kind had lost the war against his kind.

My wand was so heavy it felt like it weighed a thousand pounds. I glanced at Petra. Her chest was heaving and sweat poured down her face, as it did mine. Her wand hand was twitching uncontrollably.

Our foe, sensing our weakness, smiled and moved from side to side, seeming to build both power and momentum in his mind. I could see he was about to raise his wand and no doubt hurl some unbelievably powerful and tricky incantation at one of us. He could easily see that taking out one of us would be akin to defeating both of us. It was only together that Petra and I were able to hold him off.

*So*, I thought, *this is it. This is the end.* I could see no way around it. I didn't even have the strength to will my wand into the Elemental. I also feared to do that because if it somehow went awry I would be wandless and thus defenseless.

What I had not counted on was Harry Two.

He charged straight at the bloke, an easy target.

I screamed, "No, Harry Two!"

The Bowler Hat smiled nastily and leisurely took aim.

I raised my wand.

Yet the spell shot out of his wand so fast I had no time to block it.

"No!" I screamed again.

And then my mouth gaped.

The spell hit.

But Harry Two wasn't there.

The spell rebounded off the stone and blasted a hole in the ceiling.

I looked wildly around for my dog.

The fellow was looking madly around for him too.

Until Harry Two leapt out of the darkness and sank his fangs into the bloke's neck.

Then he knew right where my special beast was.

Green shot out of the neck wound, and the Maladon screamed in agony.

He twisted sideways and managed to knock Harry Two off with a glancing blow from a spell.

Harry Two hit the stone floor and rolled away.

I could see the venomous look in the Maladon's eyes as he located Harry Two and pointed his wand.

"*Rigamorte.*"

*I* said the spell, not him. And the killing incantation shot from my wand and hit the Maladon right in the chest.

He staggered back, looked at me with a disbelieving expression and slowly sank to the floor.

Dead.

I looked down at my shaky wand and then over at the dead man.

I didn't know how I had found the strength to do that. But I had. I could not allow Harry Two to die. There was nothing I wouldn't do to prevent that.

I felt something nudge my arm.

It was my dog. He looked perfectly fine.

And I wondered if he had done what he did to give me the motivation to finish off the Maladon. Putting himself in jeopardy to give me the emotional strength.

But how had he done what he did? He had vanished and reappeared behind the Maladon. I really wanted to know the answer, but it wasn't like I could ask him.

Yet in those bewitching mismatched eyes, I think I received all the answer I required.

He truly was more than a mere beast. In some ways he was as magical as I was. This was a thought that gave me shivers up and down my spine.

And they were *good* shivers!

I knelt down and hugged him, pushing my face into the wonderfully soft fur.

He had once more saved my life.

"Thank you," I murmured into his one remaining ear.

"Vega Jane?"

I looked up and saw that Delph had risen on shaky legs and was staring at me.

"We . . . we need to, um." He looked past me, an uncomfortable expression on his face.

"The body," interjected Petra. "We need to get rid of it."

I looked over at the dead Maladon and knew that she was right. If it was discovered, then for all I knew, every slave in Greater True would be rounded up and put to death. And our grand plan would be defeated before it had even been given a chance to succeed.

I rose and pondered the matter.

There was only one way that I could see.

While the others stayed behind, hidden in the station, I tethered the dead man to me, and, covered by the invisibility shield, I flew far out of Greater True, smack into the middle of the countryside.

I found a thicket of trees and landed in the middle of them.

It was so dark that I needed my wand to light the surroundings.

I found a patch of dirt near a mighty oak and used my wand to dig the grave.

I placed the Bowler Hat in it, unable to look at his face.

He was undeniably evil and would have killed us with absolute glee in his heart, I was certain. But still, I had ended his life.

And something in me, I was sure, had died alongside him.

As my grandfather had said, that was the true difference between us and the Maladons.

I magically covered him with dirt after breaking his wand in two and then smashing it to mere splinters with an *Impacto* spell. I sprinkled the remains of the wand over the country-side as I flew back to Greater True.

The words of Astrea Prine came back to me once more.

Could we really prevail against the Maladons, who were absolutely smashing at slaughtering their enemies?

I had killed, with ample justification, but I felt sick to my stomach.

I told myself that it would become easier over time.

But as I landed near the station, I knew in my heart that it would only become more difficult.

# A Well-Timed Piece of Advice

EMPYREAN.

The only place I had ever truly felt safe since leaving Wormwood.

But right now all I felt was frustrated.

We had freed all the slaves and then I had placed them back into a trance.

That had been the most difficult part of my plan. How do you free someone and then tell him they have to go on being a slave for a bit longer? I knew if it had been me I would have rebelled. But I also knew it was the only way to make this work. Otherwise, all would be lost. But still, I felt sick having to do it.

Now they were unconsciously waiting for the signal from me.

And I was desperately trying to make sure that signal could actually be sent.

I was sitting in the old chambers of my ancestor Jasper Jane, with virtually every book I could find in the place.

They were stacked haphazardly, some in towering piles. I had read them all, trying to make the idea in my head a reality.

But the problem was, I had thought of nothing that could absolutely do what needed doing. And there was no room for error.

I had a sudden inspiration, and took the parchment out of my cloak.

I summoned Silenus and he dutifully appeared moments later.

I explained everything to him, what I had done and what I needed to do.

He pondered all this for such a very long time that I seriously wondered if he had become totally frozen in the parchment.

Finally, he stirred. "The problem is you do not have the requisite knowledge to make this happen."

"But you once told me that magic was borne of necessity," I said sharply. "That if I needed a spell, I could create it. I was *counting* on that, Silenus."

"What I told you was perfectly true. But from what you've just said, you don't have in your mind the firm idea required to create the necessary spell. Are you certain that none exists currently to perform the task?"

I shook my head. "Not that I know."

"Then perhaps you should try to know more."

"What do you think I've been doing?" I pointed around at the stacks of books.

"Knowledge needn't always come from books," he noted.

Well, that was true enough, I thought. Astrea had been a font of knowledge. But she wasn't here. She was back in the Quag.

"I doubt that Pillsbury or Mrs. Jolly will know how to do the necessary spell work," I said in a depressed tone. "And there's no one else I can turn to."

Silenus looked around. "I sense certain *elements* here that one cannot see."

I thought about this. Well, there *was* Uma. But I could see her. Yet like Silenus said, she might not be the only *element* hereabouts.

"You think someone like that might be able to help me?"

Silenus said, "Well, when one has no other options?"

He disappeared from the page and I put the parchment away.

Sometimes, Silenus could really be an infuriating git!

Immensely frustrated, I headed back to my bedroom.

Along the way I heard voices.

I stopped at the door, which I knew was Delph's bedroom.

I put my ear to the wood.

There were two voices coming from within, and I recognized them both.

I knew I shouldn't, but I couldn't help myself.

*"Crystilado magnifica."*

On the other side of the wood I saw Delph and Petra sitting on his bed, talking.

They were very close to each other, their hands nearly touching.

I couldn't make out what they were saying, but I did hear my name mentioned twice.

Petra was smiling, but Delph looked unusually serious.

I released my spell and hurried down the hall to my room. Harry Two was asleep on the bed.

My mind awhirl with dark thoughts, I lay next to him, staring at the ceiling.

I finally concluded that what I had seen was innocent enough. It was not like they had been snogging. And I had been spending a lot of my time alone searching for what I needed. I had to confess: I had been ignoring Delph lately.

I sighed. I had been through this before. I was not going down this jealousy route again. I simply didn't have time for it.

I stared up at the ceiling and imagined the woman's face in my mind.

Sure enough, a few moments later, Uma appeared on the ceiling.

"Can I ask a favor?" I said.

My words stirred Harry Two. When he saw Uma he didn't react, but simply closed his eyes and went back to sleep.

Uma nodded.

I explained my dilemma. My needing more knowledge, anything that would allow me to accomplish the task I had set out.

"Come with me," she said.

I leapt up from the bed as she disappeared through the door.

She led me not up this time, but down.

I thought I had by now explored all facets of Empyrean, but I apparently had missed some things.

I thought we were in the very bowels of the place when suddenly a tiny door appeared that I had never noticed before.

Uma passed right through it. When I reached it, however, I found it would not open.

I used every spell I could think of to open the door, but none worked.

*Well,* I thought. *This is a bit of a pickle.*

I wondered if Uma would come back and tell me how to get in, but she didn't.

I rubbed my hand along the old wood of the door. It reminded me of the little door back at Stacks, through which I had passed to escape a pair of murderous jabbits.

Next, I used my wand to shine a light on the door.

I gasped.

The door handle I had gripped was made of metal. And it was cast in the shape of a tiny screaming Wugmort.

Just like back at Stacks.

Then I recalled that Stacks was really the former home of Bastion Cadmus. Which meant it was the former home of Uma Cadmus too.

But this wasn't Stacks. Stacks was back in Wormwood.

I stood there feeling like an idiot.

Was Uma on the other side of the door, wondering what had become of me?

I took a step back and pondered what to do.

It began as just a trickle of sensation down my spine.

But it was the commencement of inspiration, I well knew.

I looked over my shoulder. There was nothing there of course.

But there could be if I exercised one thing that I had long possessed in abundance.

*Imagination.*

A pair of foul jabbits had chased me all the way to the top of Stacks, or at least what I had thought was the top. That's when I had come upon a little door like this one. I never believed that such a puny thing could hold back a pair of enraged serpents. Still, I'd had no choice but to grip the tiny screaming Wug doorknob and flee inside.

In my mind, I re-created the fear, the total and complete horror that being chased by those jabbits through the darkened spaces of Stacks had instilled in me.

The awful slithers, the terrifying screams, which were their trademark cry right before they struck.

I put myself back outside that little room, so close to certain death. My lungs heaved; my heart pumped copious amounts of blood. I felt my skin tingling, my spirits plummeting and my hope near extinguished.

With all of that boiling inside of me, I reached out and gripped the screaming Wug.

The door opened and I was on the other side of it.

Uma was hovering right there. We were inches apart.

I thought I saw her smile.

"Good, Vega, very good."

She beckoned me onward, and I followed her down the revealed dark corridor.

We turned a corner, and the brightest lights assaulted me from all corners. Things were swirling to and fro, bits of what looked like tiny clouds whipping around like lightning spears.

"What is this place?" I asked Uma.

She didn't answer me, but she did put a finger to her lips and point toward a distant corner.

I crept toward this spot as Uma receded a bit.

Foot by foot, I drew closer to the blackness. And as I did so, I noticed the silhouette of a figure in the midst of the dark.

I edged right to the perimeter of this space and stopped.

At first the figure didn't move. And I wasn't sure what it was or whether it was capable of movement.

The next moment it turned.

And when I saw the face, all my breath left me.

My mind reeled back like a pitching sea to the great battlefield where I had seen her fighting valiantly, indeed saving my life, before being vanquished.

Alice Adronis was wearing the very armor in which she had perished.

My heart gave a jolt when I saw that the mortal wound to which she had succumbed remained bloody and gaping in the center of her chest.

When I had gone into the past courtesy of Eon back in Wormwood and seen Alice for the first time, I had thought that she and Morrigone looked quite a bit alike. I even told Morrigone that later. But now I could see quite clearly that it was Alice and I — despite our different hair colors — who looked very much alike.

Alice stared at me. We were roughly the same height; her auburn hair swirled around her broad, muscled shoulders.

There was movement in my hand, and I looked down in time to see my wand bending toward her. As it had at her grave, my wand, which formerly had been her Elemental until she had bequeathed it to me, bowed in respect toward her.

As Alice came fully out of the shadows, I saw that, like

Uma, she was not truly flesh and bone. How could she be, since she was long since dead?

Her cold eyes settled upon me, but she said nothing.

Slightly unnerved, I looked at Uma.

"What is this place?"

"'Tis a place of restless souls," said Uma. "For they need somewhere to go, and Empyrean is as good as any. We had such happy times here. And of course it was Alice's home. Naturally, she would return here."

I turned back to Alice. She was still watching me. Then her gaze dropped to the Elemental. She flicked her fingers and the Elemental sprang out of my hand and into hers. A moment later she apparently had willed it to its original state, six feet long and the color of lustrous gold.

She looked the Elemental up and down and as her hand stroked it, I saw a wistful smile emerge on her face.

After a few moments she turned back and held it out for me to take.

I tentatively reached out for it, but before it could make contact with my hand, the Elemental shrunk back to my wand and leapt into my hand, my fingers instinctively closing around it.

I was astonished by this, but when I looked into Alice's face, I could tell by her expression that I shouldn't have been.

"'Tis truly and properly yours now, Vega," she said quietly.

I looked down at the wand, and there was warmth that hadn't been present before.

And I felt strangely empowered.

I said, "Alice, I'm taking up the fight against the Maladons."

"I know."

"You're not by chance still alive somehow, are you?" I asked hopefully. "We could certainly use you."

She touched her chest at the site of the hole.

"'Tis not possible, Vega."

She looked me up and down. "You made it through the Quag."

"I did. Astrea Prine trained me as a sorceress."

"Astrea, ever vigilant. I'm surprised she let you pass."

"She knows what I came here to do. She agrees with it."

Alice slowly nodded. "Tell me your problem."

I explained about the slaves, and how I wanted to assemble them as an army to fight the Maladons.

Alice looked down at my wand. "All you need, you now have to accomplish that."

"But I don't know how! Not really. I just have vague ideas about how it could all work."

"Have the confidence of your convictions," said Alice.

"Can't you just tell me how to do it?" I asked, frustrated.

She pointed to the door through which I'd entered the room. "No one needed to tell you how to open that, did they? You figured it out all by yourself. By believing that you could do so."

I looked at the door and realized that it had been a test. A test of my wits, maybe? But I didn't see how that was going to help me now.

When I turned back, Alice was gone. When I looked around to ask Uma where she had gone, I realized that she had disappeared as well.

And then my eyes opened and I was lying on my bed, with a snoring Harry Two right next to me.

I sat up and looked wildly around.

Had any of that happened, or had I simply dreamed it?

I looked down at my hand. My wand was in it. And . . . it did feel different. The warmth was still there. The possibilities in my head were definitely still there.

I thought about what I wanted to do. And I thought about what Alice had told me. And in a tremendous flash of clarity, it all came together.

# The Inconceivable Incantation

FIVE MINUTES LATER I was staring at it. Bastion Cadmus's golden wand in the box.

I had reached up to lift the box off the wall when a surge of power hit me and knocked me heels over arse across the room.

Groaning, I slowly rose, rubbing my head, which had hit the stone.

*All right, we'll see about this.*

I took out my wand, pointed it at its golden counterpart and said with a backward sweep of my hand, "*Rejoinda*, Bastion Cadmus's wand."

Absolutely nothing happened.

I tried every spell that I thought might work.

Again, absolutely nothing happened. The little box remained on the wall.

Befuddled and irritated, I looked around the room for something, anything, that might aid me. But there was absolutely nothing there. I recalled the blank diary that had spoken to me when I was in the room full of battered and bloody weapons and Gunther Adronis's coffin. It said that if I did not want to pay the price, I could end my years in comfort and safety here at Empyrean.

"Oi," I said. "I don't intend to stay here and grow fat and old. I intend to leave and fight the Maladons and make things right. That's my decision. Now, you promised me aid if I did that. So I'm here and I'm asking for the wand in that box. May I have it? Or was all that a bunch of rubbish before?"

Before I had even finished, I felt something in my pocket. I withdrew it with my hand. It was the golden wand.

Just to be sure, I looked at the box. The wand was no longer there, because I indeed had it.

And along with it, I had a plan.

And because of that, we had a chance.

I ran back toward my room.

But then I halted.

I was in front of Delph's room again. And once more, I heard the voices coming from within.

Again, I shouldn't have done it. I realized that. But I did it anyway.

*"Crystilado magnifica."*

Instantly in front of me appeared Delph and Petra. They were still perched on the bed. They were even closer to each other. Her hand was on his shoulder. I saw the look on her face and realized I had probably had that same expression on my face when I was feeling especially affectionate toward Delph.

I felt my features harden, and there came such coldness in my heart that I didn't think I had ever felt before. It felt strange, terrifying.

Here I was using every bit of energy I had to come up with a plan to take the battle to the Maladons, and here Delph and Petra were, supposedly my friends, being all cozy with each other. I was their leader. They had told me over and over that I was to lead them. And this was how I was paid back? Did they think it was easy doing what I was doing? Did they think I could just come up with a brilliant plan whenever it was needed? Well, we would see about that.

I released my spell, pocketed my wand and knocked on the door.

"Hello, Delph?"

I heard movement from within as they no doubt scrambled off the bed.

Delph opened the door a few moments later, looking awkward.

"Delph, I have good news."

"What's that, Vega Jane?"

"We need to tell Petra too. Let's go get her."

"Um," began Delph. He wouldn't meet my eye.

"I'm right here," said Petra, who sauntered up next to Delph and gave me what I took to be a simpering smile that made my blood flame and hardened my decision to do what I was about to do. In reality, the look wasn't really simpering at all. But I couldn't see that at the moment.

"Absolutely cracking," I said. "Follow me."

I saw them glance uncertainly at each other before falling into step behind me.

We reached my room and entered.

Harry Two was on the bed, and he slowly lifted his head to peer at us.

"What's the plan, Vega Jane?" asked Delph.

I took a few minutes to tell them.

"Do you think it'll work?" asked Petra in what I, unfairly or not, interpreted as a condescending tone. Right now, nothing she said or did would strike me as anything other than negative.

"I have no idea. But do you have a better idea?" I added sharply.

She looked taken aback and shook her head.

"Now, there is another part to all of this, and you, Petra, are going to play an especially important role."

"What?" she said curiously.

"You will go to Greater True and take up a position near the center of town. You will be my eyes and ears, Petra. When I engage this spell, I have no real idea what's going to happen. But you can communicate with me via the wand wire incantation."

"But, Vega Jane, sending her there by herself, not knowing what's going to happen . . ." said Delph. "I don't think that's a good idea. Or fair to Petra."

I gazed up at him with what I hoped was an expression of utter surprise.

"Delph, we're a team. We all have roles to play. Petra is part of that team. I very much trust her to do this. Don't *you* trust her? Or do you think she's not up to it?"

His features collapsed as I neatly flipped his entire argument on its head.

"O'course I trust Pet." He hastily added, "Petra."

"Then I don't see the problem."

"I could go with her."

I shook my head. "You need to stay here and prepare for

the arrival," I said. "There's going to be a lot going on and we need to be ready."

"But —"

I talked right over him. "Petra will have the ring and her wand. I've gone to Greater True with just those two things and come back alive. I've gone to Maladon Castle alone with just those two things and returned in one piece. If I can do it, so can *Pet*."

I looked at Petra, slipped off my ring and handed it to her. "So, are you ready?"

She nodded dumbly, glanced at Delph and then quickly looked away.

"You'd better get ready to leave now. The preparations will take me a bit of time, but I want you in place. Send me a wire when you get there. Aim for near the train station and then work your way to the center when you've determined that the path is clear."

Delph blurted out, "But, Vega, if your plan causes things to go all wonky in Greater True, the Maladons might show up in full force. Petra might get trapped."

"She has her wand. And she can use the *Pass-pusay* spell to get back here if need be. It's no more dangerous than what I've done. And I don't remember you having a problem when it was *me* doing it."

"But . . ."

"But what, Delph?" I said, staring up at him.

His voice trailed off and he looked away, beaten.

I put out my hand to Petra. "Good luck."

She lightly shook it, turned and hurried off.

341

I looked at Delph. "You better take up your position outside by the front door," I said.

He nodded, gave me a furtive glance and then left.

My heart was beating so fast I thought I might faint.

The flint inside my heart started to break down a bit, and I told myself that what I'd done wasn't really that awful. We had come and gone before from Greater True without incident. She was invisible. She had her wand.

But Delph was right. I couldn't predict what would happen when I performed my spell. Petra might be caught in something that she couldn't get herself out of. She might be injured, captured.

Or killed.

As soon as I thought this, my head began to pound, and then I felt something wet on my forehead. I touched it.

It was blood.

For some reason, I looked down at my wand.

There was blood there too. As I watched, the blood from my head was being soaked up into my wand.

And then I remembered.

The blood oath! I had sworn allegiance to Petra and she to me. But by my actions I was breaking that oath. I didn't know what was going to happen to me. Was I going to oblivion?

I dropped to the floor, holding my head. Harry Two came over to me and licked at my hand. His tongue touched some of the blood and I felt a tingling sensation all over my body.

*Nothing is worth Petra being hurt by something you've planned,*

*Vega. It's wrong. If she loves Delph and he loves her, that's just the way it is. You're acting like a bloody Maladon. And you are not like them!*

I wiped the blood off, jumped up and ran to Petra's room. She was just coming out, her cloak on.

"Stop," I said.

"What?"

"I . . . I just figured out another way. You don't have to go to Greater True. You can stay here. It's okay."

"But you said —"

"Right, I know what I said, but it's okay, you don't have to go. Like Delph said, you might get trapped there. And . . . and that would not be good."

"If you're sure?"

"You and Delph can wait outside of Empyrean."

She looked at me oddly and then touched my forehead. "You're bleeding."

"It's nothing. Okay, well, I've got things to do, so . . ."

I turned and rushed off, leaving her staring after me.

In my room I sat on my haunches and laid the golden wand down directly in front of me.

I touched my forehead. The blood was gone. I looked at my wand. There was no blood there either. But if that hadn't happened? Would I have let Petra go? Possibly to her death? Did all the Janes actually have a bit of Maladon blood in them, as my grandfather had suggested after telling us the story of Alice's evil father?

I closed my eyes and then reopened them. I couldn't think about that now. I had to focus. There were many people counting on me.

Something that Uma had told me had given me this idea.

*He was not simply my father, but the father of all of our people.*

I was counting on that statement to be quite literal.

From my pocket I took the book with the names of all those enslaved by the Maladons. I set it in front of me, open to the pages listing them.

I tapped my wand against the pages and murmured, *"Accumuladis todos."*

When I looked at the pages, they had turned blank.

*Okay, so far, so good.*

I pointed my wand at Bastion's golden one.

Drawing another deep breath, I closed my eyes and cast my mind back so that I could recall the incantation exactly as the Maladon had told it to me.

Now it got tricky. Now I was in totally uncharted territory. But I supposed every spell had to be done for the first time by somebody.

The only thing was, I was planning to use an existing spell, but in a way that it had never been used, to do what I needed it to do. And it wasn't simply one spell. I was attempting to link three of them together and unleash them at the same time.

In my mind I formed a clear thought of what I wanted to have happen. It was actually multiple things occurring at precisely the same time.

I drew one more long breath. I was totally focused. I had never concentrated like this in my life. I hadn't even known I had the capacity to do it. But somehow, I had found it.

I had three images, neatly compartmentalized in my head.

The golden wand.

The names on the list.

And Greater True.

I touched the tip of my wand to the tip of the golden one.

Then I spoke the words tightly, curtly, firmly. Never had I possessed such confidence, such sheer willpower. It was like everything I had ever done to reach this spot, every strength that had shown itself in me on this long journey, every power developed from necessity, every obstacle overcome, every loss followed by a savage desire to triumph, had all been for this very moment.

*"Disassemblius, projecta . . ."*

I drew a breath.

*"Amplifius spectrumaca . . ."*

It was as though someone else was doing the talking and using me to channel the words.

But I held my focus, my absolute concentration.

*"Vamon recipitcus. Agante apertus."*

When I opened my eyes and looked down at the golden wand, it started to shake violently. But I kept my wand touching it.

A flash of light erupted from Bastion Cadmus's wand. It was blinding, and I could feel my eyes go wonky. The light covered the entire room, and I could hear Harry Two barking madly.

But I kept my focus.

Those three images: the wand, the names and the place.

Next moment the golden wand shattered into tiny pieces. These splinters of gold swirled upward as though caught in an overpowering funnel of air. Up, up to the ceiling they went.

*"Catapulus targerius."*

And then with a pop they vanished.

The light vanished as well.

And still my focus never wavered.

I was only halfway done.

New images replaced the old trio.

Faces, hands, eyes.

Words slipped from my mouth.

*"Erectica. Desimminus. Plutarium."*

I took another breath, kept the images clear in my head.

*"Emancipatico stelara."*

Eyes popped open in my mind. Faces became normal. Reason returned. Real pasts supplanted magically conjured ones.

Hands gripped hard objects across Greater True.

Still I pressed on. I had more to do.

I gripped my wand with both hands because it was starting to shake so violently that I wasn't sure I could control it with merely one.

I supposed I was at unprecedented levels of sorcery here. It didn't make me feel special. It made me fear failure. Because if I did fail, I had the terrible feeling that all these people were going to instantly die or forever remain in a limbo of my creation.

Now I had two images in mind: people and a place.

That place was not Greater True.

That place was right here.

Empyrean.

I was attempting to perform the *Pass-pusay* spell, only remotely, to move others. And not simply one.

I was going to bring fifty people here, to safety.

My wand was pitching and heaving like a ship on stormy seas.

Smoke started to emanate from its core.

The poor Elemental felt like it was going to burn up in my hands.

Yet still I held on.

*"Aggretata . . . Cumuladis . . . Elevata . . ."*

My wand was nearly out of control. It gave such a violent upheaval that it smacked me in the forehead. I felt blood trickle down my face.

I summoned all the energy I had left. This was the moment of truth. It was now or never, and while I was confident, part of me was also scared to death.

The normal spell, I knew intuitively, would not be enough. I had transported others with me using it, but not remotely and not fifty of them.

I screwed up my face, shut my eyes and —

*"Pass-pusay titanticus encapsulado principium todos."*

I paused, building my energy to the level I knew was necessary.

Now, Vega, now!

*"Domum nunc en pepertuum!"* I cried out.

A bolt of light issued from the tip of my wand and shot straight up and through the ceiling of my room, leaving a darkened mark there as residue.

As soon as the light vanished, I fell backward and passed out.

The next thing I remember was Harry Two licking me on the face.

I heard a commotion downstairs.

Then I heard Pillsbury shouting something.

I jumped up and raced out of the room and down the broad stairs, Harry Two barking at my heels.

The foyer of Empyrean was large, but it was now also crowded with figures.

Pillsbury and Mrs. Jolly were running around trying to restore order, although I daresay they were destined for failure, at least with respect to those who were unfamiliar with walking and talking suits of armor and brooms with appendages.

I raced into the foyer and shouted, "Everyone quiet down." When that didn't work sufficiently, I raised my wand to the ceiling, muttered an incantation and the resulting boom was so overwhelmingly loud that only quiet followed its release.

They all stood there staring back at me.

There was Cecilia Harkes, Anna Dibble, Sara Bond and Clive Pippen. Over near the door was Amicus Arnold, looking serenely pleased. Next to him was the chubby but buoyant-faced Artemis Dale. On his right was Miranda Weeks, looking confused but excited. Standing next to each other were Dennis O'Shaughnessy and Reginald Magnus, who looked so much like each other they could be brothers. And by a large vase of flowers, Dedo Datt stared around in silent wonder.

And on and on they went.

All fifty of them. They stared at me.

And I stared back at them, or at least at their hands.

I saw, with immense satisfaction, that a full-size golden wand was gripped in each.

My spell had worked.

I couldn't keep the enormous smile off my face.

Until I noticed something.

Or more to the point, I noticed the *absence* of something.

Even more to the point, the absence of *two people*.

I rushed over to Pillsbury.

"Where're Delph and Petra?"

"Oh, they left quite a while ago."

The blood iced over in my veins. "What?"

"Yes. They told me to be ready to receive what they termed 'guests' and then they left. Together."

I couldn't process what he was telling me. Where the Hel had they gone?

At the same instant I felt my wand tingle and shake slightly.

And in my head I heard:

*"Vega, help us! We're in Greater True."*

It was Petra. She was communicating with me by wand wire.

I barked to Pillsbury and Mrs. Jolly, "See that our guests have all the food and drink they require and then find rooms for them to rest. I'll be back as soon as I can."

"But —" began Pillsbury.

I shot forward and nearly collided with Alabetus Trumbull, who luckily leapt out of the way.

Charlotte Tokken and Pauline Paternas cried out after me, but I didn't really hear them. All I could hear was Petra's desperate plea.

I could not lose them. I just couldn't.

## A Close Call

M Y FIRST PROBLEM was that I could not become invisible without the ring, and Petra still had it. Thus, when I appeared on a street in Greater True, someone instantly saw me. Luckily, it was a doddering old man who continued to walk past as though someone materializing out of thin air happened all the time.

At least it was late at night, and I immediately withdrew into the shadows, attempting to regain my composure and my wits. This was hard to do because I was frantic to find Delph and Petra.

I peered around to see if anything unusual was happening in Greater True. I had just removed fifty of the servant class with one fell swoop. I was sure that the town would be up in arms about this. But then as I thought about it, I realized that might not be the case. It was very late at night, and most if not all of their former masters would still be sound asleep and unaware of what had transpired. The first they might learn of it was when they awoke and realized no one was there to serve them their morning tea.

But then again, I wasn't sure how my spell had manifested itself here. Had there been noise, incantation, lights? Had the former slaves been seen flying through the sky, if but for a moment? Had someone in one of the houses been up late, seen something suspicious and alerted the Maladons?

But why had Petra and Delph come here?

Suddenly in my head appeared another wand wire.

*"Train station. Same room. Hurry."*

I focused on the four walls of that room where we had slept while locating those whose magic had been stolen from them. I twice tapped my wand against my leg, muttered the spell and a moment later I was standing in the little room at the train station.

I looked frantically around for Delph and Petra, but they weren't there.

However, I wasn't alone.

Four Bowler Hats encircled me, their wands pointed directly at my chest.

I was so stunned I had no time to think, which was probably a good thing.

*"Embattlemento."*

Their four spells hit my shield, but my magic held. In fact, their spells rebounded off my conjured wall, causing them all to duck.

I used this opportunity to once more tap my leg twice and say the incantation.

I was instantly on the street outside the train station.

I was frantic now. Delph and Petra had obviously been captured by the Maladons. They must have used her wand to communicate with me.

I couldn't become invisible, which was a colossal setback. I wondered if they had taken my grandfather's ring from

Petra. But how would they have even been captured? They couldn't be seen behind its invisibility shield.

Next moment the four Maladons burst from the front of the train station and looked wildly around for me.

I scurried around a corner and then peeked back.

I performed my magnification spell and looked at them more closely.

I recognized two of them. My heart sank as four more joined them, appearing out of thin air, after no doubt having been summoned. I wondered if Endemen would make an appearance. Indeed, I was more than a little surprised that he wasn't right in the middle of all this.

Under the magnification spell, I searched the fingers of all of the Maladons for the ring. I didn't see it. I had been told that they had never learned how to make themselves invisible. They might not know the ring had such powers, or how to turn it around to engage the shield. But given time, they would probably discover its secret, or do so accidentally, as I had.

I looked nervously around, wondering how many more Maladons would appear to join the hunt for me. But my only goal was to find and save Petra and Delph.

Were they here? Had they already been taken to the castle? Were . . . were they already dead?

I looked down at my wand.

One wand against eight. But I had always been the underdog in every fight I'd ever had, including the Duelum back in Wormwood. And I had won them all.

Everyone said I was special somehow. Well, I guessed I was about to find out if that was really true.

When the Maladons had cast their spells, they had not used the *Rigamorte* curse, which my shield would not have stopped. They obviously didn't want to kill me. They wanted to capture me. And I was sure I knew why. They wanted to torture me to gain every bit of information they could.

Well, that worked both ways, didn't it?

And I instinctively realized that when you're outnumbered on the battlefield, you need to do one thing:

Divide and conquer.

I sent back-to-back spells sailing over their heads, each shooting off in a different direction. As soon as I'd done that, I used the pass-pusay spell to disappear and then reappear behind them. I saw them react to the spells and do what I'd hoped. They split up, four and four. Still not good odds for me, but better than they had been.

They charged off in different directions. I followed one of the groups down the street and watched them turn a corner and hurry after the lingering lights of one of the spells I had cast.

I hurried on and caught up to them, keeping just far enough back so they couldn't see me. I aimed my wand at the Bowler Hat bringing up the rear.

My *Subservio* spell hit him in the center of the back.

I whispered my instructions to him. He pointed his wand at the Bowler Hats in front of him and cast spells knocking them out. The fourth one turned in time to blast the one I had under control, and he crumpled in a heap.

I took aim at the remaining Bowler Hat, and my *Subservio* spell hit him full in the chest.

He went funny in the face and his wand hand dropped.

I hurried up to him, took his wand in my gloved hand and broke it in half. I did the same with the others' wands.

I pointed my wand at the last Bowler Hat and said, "What are you called?"

"Dullish," he said gruffly.

I said *"Origante,"* expecting his hideous actual Maladon self to be revealed, but he looked the same. I was bewildered by this. I had thought all of the Maladons would be the same underneath.

"Okay, where are my friends, Dullish?"

He looked at me quizzically. I realized I had to be more specific.

"The tall man and the young woman. Your lot used her wand to summon me here."

He nodded. "They are at the headquarters of the Elite Guard on the other side of Greater True."

"And they're alive?" I said sharply.

He nodded dumbly.

"Where is her wand?"

He shook his head. "I don't know."

"Well, then, who would know?"

He looked down at one of his fallen comrades. "He would."

I performed the spell to erase any memory of this encounter from him and then knocked the bloke out.

I pointed my wand at the man he'd indicated. *"Rejoinda,* Petra's wand."

It flew from his pocket and into my hand.

I thought for a moment and added, "And *Rejoinda* anything else of Petra's or Delph's or mine."

Nothing appeared.

I put the wand away in my cloak and turned just in time to ward off the first spell.

It bounced off my shield and exploded against the side of a building, leaving a gaping hole.

The other four Bowler Hats had appeared feet from me, no doubt having heard or somehow sensed the magical fight that had just occurred here.

Then the duel began in earnest.

I thought I had no chance. I well remembered the fight Petra and I had waged against a single Maladon. It had left us breathless, barely able to lift our wand arms, while our opponent appeared fresh and full of fight. We were lucky to have vanquished him.

But now, for some reason I could not fathom, my wand hand started to move in ways I had never envisioned, in ways I never thought myself capable of. I danced and parried, blocked spells, and sent off my own.

The longer I fought, the stronger and more confident I became.

*"Impacto. Embattlemento. Jagada. Paralycto. Embattlemento."*

I blasted one off his feet with an *Engulfiado* spell. Another fell to my *Impairio* incantation, and he started blindly firing off spells, sending his mates running and ducking.

The very air around us was boiling from all the magic cast.

I kept pounding away, saying spells and whipping my wand like it was a sword.

I charged forward, my gaze darting across the field of

battle, calculating all options, tactics and strategies, my mind going full bore, my concentration total.

They fell back, and I could see the panicked looks in their eyes. They had obviously not expected me to be able to hold my own against all of them.

But I wasn't done yet. And if I'd learned one thing with the Maladons, it was that you had to finish the fight.

I glanced down at their feet and decided I needed to end this sooner rather than later. I still had to find and rescue Delph and Petra.

I shot a spell at the cobbles under them. An enormous hole opened up, and they fell screaming down into this abyss, their wands sailing out of their hands from the suddenness of the descent. I sent *Impacto* spells raining down into the hole, one after another. The spells thundered into their flailing forms and knocked them out.

Then I flicked my wand across the hole and it sealed up.

Not wasting another moment, I leapt into the air and sailed across the darkened sky with grim purpose.

I had never been to the Elite Guard's bloody headquarters. But I had a very good idea of how I would find it.

And a minute later I saw that I was right.

The huge flag with the five-pointed star and the two burning eyes was waving in the wind atop a tall building on the western edge of the town proper. I could see several lights blazing from within. I went into a dive and landed next to the rear entrance.

Now I needed something. No, I needed *someone*. And I knew exactly how to get him.

I made the familiar pulling motion with my wand and I said, "*Rejoinda*, Dullish."

I had thought about performing this spell to get Delph and Petra back, but I had no idea how they were being imprisoned or if the spell was strong enough to break chains and doors. And I also figured whoever was watching over them would probably have time to stop them or even kill them if they started to soar away.

A few moments later I could see a black blob hurtling across the sky.

Dullish landed hard at my feet. I revived him after putting him back under the *Subservio* spell and then instructed him on what I wanted him to do.

I hid in the shadows as he approached the door.

He lifted his wand and the door opened, revealing a man in a black uniform.

He seemed surprised to see the Maladon.

I used my magnification spell to see inside the doorway and to the room beyond.

It was only the one guard.

"Dullish? We've got our pair here still. Did you get the one you were after?" the guard asked.

My spell shot straight over Dullish's shoulder and hit the bloke right in the face. He fell over backward.

I stepped inside and looked down at his prostrate form.

"No, actually he didn't, you prat."

I pushed Dullish ahead of me as I surveyed the set of stairs that led upward.

"Where are the other guards?" I asked Dullish.

"Most are asleep in the barracks." He pointed upward.

"And my friends?"

"In the room in the middle of the hall where the barracks are."

"How many guards watching them?"

"A dozen."

*Wonderful.*

I could imagine their mortas firing into my body until I looked like a mass of holes and not much else.

Then I had a thought. "Dullish, where do they keep their mortas?"

"Their what?"

"Their, um, weapons?"

He pointed to the left at a doorway I hadn't noticed before.

"Their guns are in there."

"Stay right here."

I used the *Ingressio* spell to open the door. Along the walls were racks and racks and shelves of *guns*.

I swept my wand across the room and said, *"Interfero todos."*

The sounds of something hardening could be heard around the room.

I closed the door behind me and once more went over to Dullish.

"Take me to my friends," I commanded.

We stealthily went up the stairs, turned right and passed a number of wooden doors. From within, I could hear the loud snores of sleeping men.

Dullish led me over to a large metal door. There was a small barred window in the middle of it.

I stepped past Dullish and peered cautiously inside.

With a sigh of relief, I saw Delph and Petra tied up in a corner. Delph's face was bruised and bloody and Petra was hunched over and grimacing in pain.

As Dullish had said, there were twelve uniformed men inside with them. And they all carried mortas, or guns, rather.

But I carried something too.

My wand.

And I wouldn't trade it for a thousand of their awful weapons.

I blasted open the door.

The guards all turned, as I knew they would, toward the door.

They lifted their guns to fire.

I already had my wand pointed.

*"Engulfiado."*

The torrent of water exploding from my wand tip hit them with the force of a lightning spear.

They were lifted off their feet and blasted backward against the wall, where they slammed into the stone and dropped to the floor, unconscious, their guns falling from their hands.

I leapt inside.

"Vega Jane!" exclaimed Delph.

"How did you find us?" asked Petra breathlessly.

"Not now," I shot back.

I quickly untied them and led them out of the room.

My spell had awoken the sleeping guards, as I knew it would.

We scrambled down the steps even as we heard doors slamming open.

We reached the main floor and hurtled across its width to the door leading to the outside.

I heard someone scream, "Get your guns and blast them to Hel!"

We were outside the building and running down the street when I heard someone yell, "Fire!"

I turned to look back and saw forty guards with guns pointed right at us.

"Look out!" screamed Petra.

"Don't worry," I said.

All forty guards pulled their triggers.

And all forty guns blew up in their hands, their barrels magically obstructed by yours truly.

"Wow," exclaimed Delph.

*Wow indeed*, I thought, a grin emerging on my face.

I tethered us together. And we shot upward, leveled out and zipped onward.

We weren't invisible, so I was concerned that a Maladon would see us and take up the chase. I just wanted to invoke the *Pass-pusay* spell and get back to Empyrean as quickly as possible.

I tapped my leg twice and said the incantation.

The next moment we were staring at the front of Empyrean.

Before we went inside I whirled, spitting mad, and barked, "Why the bloody Hel were you in Greater True? I *told* Petra she didn't have to go. Then I find out you *both* went! You could have been killed!"

Delph wilted under my fierce gaze, but Petra stepped up and said, "It was my fault, Vega. I thought you didn't want me to go because you thought I couldn't handle the job. I wanted to prove that I could. So I decided to go. But I told Delph."

"And I told her unless she let me go along, I'd tell you and she wouldn't be able to go a'tall."

I looked between them, fury and relief competing for control of my emotions. Finally, the latter won out, no doubt aided by the guilt I was still feeling for nearly sending Petra to her death.

I gave them each a hug.

I said, "Well, thank goodness you're all right. But what happened back there?"

"All Hel erupted, I guess, when you did whatever you did," said Delph. "I saw blokes soaring out of houses all over the bloody place, and then they just disappeared. Good thing it was so late at night and nobody was out and about to see it 'cept us."

"I did a mass spell for all the people on the list. They're here at Empyrean now."

"Eh, that's wonderful news," said Delph.

"But how did you get caught? You were invisible."

"*Were* being the right word for it," said Delph. "Your spell brought this huge wind across the town, like with the mighty Finn. Me and Pet got blown all over the bloody place. Landed in a heap against a wall all dazed-like."

Petra added, "And the ring got jostled. It never fit me proper. And it spun back around and there we were, visible. And before we could move a muscle, a bunch of Maladons were on us. They . . . they took the ring."

So my fear had been realized. The Maladons had the ring. "That wasn't all they took," said Delph. "Show her, Pet."

"No," Petra said fiercely.

"Show me what?" I said.

"Petra, show her. She's going to see at some point."

Slowly Petra held out her hand.

I felt sickened.

Not only was the ring gone, so was the finger on which she had worn it.

"Thanks for coming to save us, Vega," said Petra.

I reached into my pocket, took out her wand and handed it to her.

"How did you find it?" she asked, obviously thrilled to have it back.

"A bit of luck," I said dully.

"Thank you," she said. "You're a good friend, Vega. I know I can be quite the pain, but I know you're always looking out for me."

A pang of guilt hit me and I inwardly winced. Petra wouldn't be saying that if she had known of my original plan.

"I couldn't lose you. Either of you," I said. "We're in this together."

And that was truly how I felt.

"Tried to fight 'em off, but I couldn't," said Delph.

"I saw what you did to that Maladon that took my finger," said Petra. "Picked him up and threw him into a wall."

"I'm surprised they didn't kill you," I said.

Delph said, "They wanted to question us. And they knew about you, Vega Jane. They used Petra's wand to send you a message."

"I walked right into their trap."

"How'd you get away?" asked Petra.

"I fought my way out. There were eight Bowler Hats, but I managed to beat them."

"Blimey, eight of them!" said Delph, while Petra looked shocked. Delph added, "Eh, Vega Jane, you've been hit."

He pointed to my torn cloak and the blood soaking into it. I hadn't even noticed.

"It doesn't hurt much, Delph." I eyed Petra's bloody stump where her finger used to be. "In fact, it doesn't hurt at all."

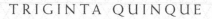

## A Motley Crew

I LED THE WAY inside Empyrean.

Pillsbury was waiting for us.

"Where is everyone?" I asked.

"They have been well fed and we have found rooms for all, Mistress Vega."

"That's good. I wasn't sure, as big as it is, whether Empyrean could hold fifty guests."

Pillsbury proclaimed proudly, "Empyrean is a place that will grow to the size necessary for those who require accommodation within its walls."

Pillsbury took his leave, and then I slapped my forehead as my gaze fell on Petra.

I raced to my room and came back down in a jiffy with the Adder Stone. I knew I couldn't regrow her finger, but I could deal with the pain and bleeding.

I waved it over her hand and thought especially good thoughts.

The wound stopped bleeding and healed over instantly, though the finger was still missing. I did the same with my wound.

I looked at Delph. I was sure he was thinking about his father's legs, which had been crushed in an accident back in

Wormwood. The Stone had dealt with the pain, but Duf Delphia now wore timber stumps. He gazed up at me with a weak smile.

"Dad," he said, confirming my thoughts.

"That's much better, Vega, thanks," said Petra.

Delph said, "We should get some sleep. We'll have a lot of work to do tomorrow."

We walked upstairs, and Delph bade us good night and went to his room.

I followed Petra to her door.

"So we have fifty people here who can do magic," she said. "Now what do we do with them?"

"We train them up," I replied promptly. "Just as Astrea Prine did me. And I did for you."

"I'm not sure I'll be much good at teaching blokes," she said worriedly.

"I taught you spells, Petra. You can do the same for them."

"Well, they will have to be mightily well trained up to take on the Maladons. Remember the one we took on."

I looked at her darkly. "I don't think I'll soon forget, since I killed him."

"That's not what I meant, Vega."

"Well, then?" I asked.

"We had a terrible time fighting one bloke. I was exhausted and I know you were too. And he seemed fresh and ready to keep fighting. And if Harry Two hadn't helped, I'm not sure either of us would be here."

"I don't disagree with that," I said. She was speaking the absolute truth. Harry Two had saved us both.

Then she looked at me, puzzled. "But you said you fought off *eight* Maladons to rescue us."

"That's right."

"So what happened to you between the one bloke and the eight?"

I looked down at my wand. I knew exactly what had happened. My wand was now truly and properly mine. None of it belonged to Alice Adronis anymore. It was as though her power and the entire line of my ancestors had been transferred to me. And now I recalled that that was exactly what Astrea had told us would occur back at her cottage.

Whatever the case, I was an infinitely more powerful sorceress. I just hoped I was powerful enough.

"I just got . . . better," I said.

She startled me by giving me a hug and then disappeared into her room, closing the door behind her.

I just stood there for a few moments as guilt once more ate away at me. How could I have even contemplated putting Petra intentionally in danger like that?

Was I more Maladon than I had accused her of being? I shuddered at this terrible thought.

When I returned to my room, Harry Two was waiting for me.

I patted his head.

When I looked down at him, the expression on his face was inscrutable. He wasn't smiling. His eyes weren't as animated as they usually were. Perhaps he was mad at me for leaving him behind.

As soon as my head touched the pillow, I fell fast asleep. But my sleep was troubled.

We had accomplished much. Rescuing fifty people from a lifetime of humiliating servitude was something to be proud of. But now it seemed that the task only became harder. These people had never wielded a wand before. They had never used magic in battle. And they would one day be pitted against the most murderous band of sorcerers in all of existence.

So truly, how many of them would survive the coming war? Or Delph, Petra or Harry Two?

Hel, would I survive it?

I restlessly turned over onto my side. Harry Two was right next to me, and I instinctively reached out and rubbed his fur.

This calmed me, but only a bit.

So was it better to be enslaved and alive?

Or free and dead?

The answer seemed to be obvious, only it wasn't.

It was always better to be free. That was clear enough.

But it was usually not better to be dead. That was also clear enough.

In my anxiety I sat up, climbed out of bed and started pacing.

When the sun rose I would be expected to commence shaping an army to go into battle.

Me, Vega Jane. I was not yet sixteen years old. I could feel a cold dread filling every inch of my being. But then I touched my wand and warmth flooded back into me. It was then that I realized I had accomplished a great many things I initially thought were impossible. So why not build an army? Why the bloody Hel not? I got back into bed. And this time I slept so soundly that I only awoke when I heard Pillsbury say into my ear, "Would Mistress Vega like some breakfast?"

I sat straight up and noted the light streaming in through the window. I yawned and stretched.

"I would indeed," I replied, feeling better rested and easier in my mind than I had since I'd left Wormwood.

"Very good, Mistress Vega."

"And the others?" I inquired.

"Taking their breakfast in the dining room. All in good spirits and curious as to what is to come! As we all are!" he added excitedly.

I washed up and changed my clothes. By the time I was done, my meal was there. I ate unhurriedly while Harry Two did the same next to me.

Finished, I picked up my wand and checked my appearance in the looking glass — giving myself a little inspirational wink.

I had a job to do and I meant to do it.

I strode purposefully into the Great Hall.

All fifty people that we had saved were there.

And so were Delph and Petra. They were surrounded by the others and I'm sure were being peppered with questions.

Yet all fell silent when they saw me walk in, and all eyes turned to me as though connected by magical tether.

I felt my face grow warm and my heart started pumping faster. Blimey! I wasn't used to all this attention. I stopped with Harry Two right next to me. My free hand went down to rub his ear while I surveyed the room as I supposed a general would his army.

Or, in my case, *her* army.

They all stood there looking back at me.

They were a mix of colors: very pale, white, brown, black and pleasing combinations thereof, roughly divided between males and females.

My gaze fell over first Delph and then Petra.

They each gave me encouraging smiles.

Before I could speak, something totally unexpected happened. Amicus Arnold, who was in the back of the room, began to clap. Another joined him. And then another. And soon the entire hall rang with the applause.

My face turned red and tears crept to my eyes, and it was only when I raised my wand that the tumultuous sounds ended.

"I welcome all of you to Empyrean, the home of my ancestors and of yours. Empyrean is safe from attack, but we must maintain constant vigilance to ensure that it remains so. It is a magical place with many facets, not all of which I have discovered." I pointed to my wand. "You each now have a wand. This will be the source of your magical powers. The Maladons made you what they call 'Ordinaries.' But I know each of you to be truly extraordinary. And now, along with my friends Delph Delphia and Petra Sonnet" — I indicated both with my wand — "without whom none of you would be standing here, we will begin the work of training each of you up so that you may realize the full source of your vast potential."

I paused here, both for breath and a bit of clarity.

"The training will not be easy or without risk. Injuries almost undoubtedly will occur. Mistakes will be made. Frustration will be rampant at times."

And didn't I know that better than most?

"But I promise you that if you work hard and with dedication, the sorcerer or sorceress you will become will be truly amazing." I paused to let this sink in and watched as each of them looked around the room at the others.

"Now, once you have been trained up, the most difficult task you will ever undertake will commence." I paused again here, because this truly was the entire crux of the matter.

"The Maladons enslaved you and have complete control of this world. They are a cruel, ruthless and evil lot. They are remarkably gifted at sorcery and employing that magic in the matter of combat. They vanquished many of our kind who were magically gifted in a long-ago war. I propose to take the fight to them once more. And this time, I intend that our side will win." I raised my wand. "Are you with me?"

As one, they all raised their wands.

And this time I decided not to stop the cheering. I decided to let it go on as long as they so desired. For it was indeed cheering to me as well.

Perhaps to me most of all.

## Simply, A Rose

THINGS WERE NOT going all that well really.

It was fine to make grand speeches and then to cheer them. It was quite another to actually train and mold an army of magical warriors from basically nothing.

We had taken over the Great Hall and used it for our training area.

I could now well understand Pillsbury's comment that Empyrean grew to accommodate its guests, for the Great Hall, large to begin with, had seemed to inflate and now easily held all of us and all the spells cast.

I had started out with a short lecture on the mind, body and spirit, sounding perhaps more like Astrea Prine than I had intended. I then had moved on to simple wand motions and the most mundane of spells. I well recalled how awkward I was while being instructed by Astrea. But compared to this lot, I was ten Excaliburs combined. In the back of my mind I could imagine all of them lying dead on the battlefield after having succumbed to the Maladons in record time.

We had divided the group into two equal components. Petra had taken on the job of training one group, while I headed up the other.

Delph also had a teaching role to play, and in a separate room he explained to small groups all about our history and the journey we had taken from Wormwood to here and everything in between. We had no idea what might be more important than something else, so we had made the decision just to tell them everything.

I ventured into the classroom from time to time and found that good questions were asked and lively discussions abounded.

Parchment and ink sticks had been provided by Pillsbury so that the students could write everything down and read and discuss it later.

Thirty days went by, and we finally saw some signs of improvement, but far fewer than I would have liked.

Someone knocked on my door late one night. When I opened it, there was Delph, looking uncertain and nervous.

"What is it?" I asked after he came in, and I sat on my bed rubbing Harry Two's ear.

"Miranda Weeks."

I sighed. "I know she's not very good, but —"

"She's the youngest of the lot," he interjected.

"I know that. And so it's going to take her longer than some of the others to get the hang of it."

"Not what I meant," he said.

I was growing annoyed at how cryptic he was being. "What, then?"

"I think she's too young to be trained up to fight. I mean I don't think it's right."

"Delph, we need everyone we can get. The Maladons have hundreds of fully trained sorcerers."

"Right, well, if it was your brother, John, would it be okay? And he's several years older than Miranda."

I had not anticipated this line of argument, and part of me was upset that Delph would bring up my brother to make his point. But then I thought about the boys in their uniforms marching along with their terrible flag. And they were older than Miranda too!

"So what do we do, then? Tell her she can't be trained up as a sorceress?"

"No, she *can* be. Who knows how many years this will take? But I don't think she should be allowed to fight until she's older."

"Okay, Delph, I'll talk to her."

He made no move to leave. "Is there something else?" I asked.

He drew a long breath and then plunged in. "You shouldn't go off by yourself no more without telling us, or letting us go with you," he said.

I stood. "What?"

"You going off to rescue Virgil or going to Greater True that time without a word. We were worried sick. 'Tain't right."

"Did Petra put you up to this?" I shot back.

He looked truly bewildered. "Pet? No."

"I wonder. But in any case, I don't recall your being my keeper, Delph. And so I'll go where I like when I bloody well like."

Delph's expression was not one of hurt, which I had expected. It was one of anger.

"Anything else?" I said imperiously, though I was feeling guilty at having treated him like this.

He turned and left without a word, slamming my door behind him.

I fell back on my bed and groaned.

We ate our meals in rotating groups, so as not to overwhelm poor Mrs. Jolly. Delph, Petra and I made a habit of eating at separate tables so that we could get to know those we would be fighting next to.

I found most of them eager, and full of both anger at what had been done to them and a thirst to strike back at their enslavers.

When the others had gone to bed, the three of us would sit up long into the night in the library to discuss matters. Delph never mentioned the confrontation in my room, but his attitude toward me was decidedly cooler. If Petra noticed, she said nothing.

In front of the flickering firelight six months into our training, Petra stretched out in front of the fire and looked up at Delph and me as we sat in comfy old leather chairs.

Delph was poring over parchment for his next class, while I was making flicking motions with my wand and thinking of additional spells that would be good to teach.

The silence was gratifying after a long training period with fifty people constantly barraging us with questions and seeking advice on mastering magic.

"Do you think this is going to work?" said Petra.

I stopped my wand movements, and Delph looked up from his heaps of parchment.

"What?" I asked, surprised.

Petra pulled her wand and aimed it the ceiling, where our fifty recruits were no doubt collapsed in exhausted sleep.

"Them!" she said pointedly. "At the pace we're going, we'll be dead and buried before they're ready to take on the bloody Maladons."

I glanced at Delph, who continued to stare at Petra.

"We're doing the best we can," said Delph sharply.

"I'm not disputing that," said Petra, now sitting up on her haunches. "But that doesn't change the fact that I'm not sure they'll *ever* be ready."

"They'll get there," I said hopefully. "It just takes time."

She glanced at me. "Really? Artemis Dale nearly severed his own foot because he employs the *Jagada* curse like he's wielding a bloody ax. And Charlotte Tokken keeps hurling her wand across the room with the simplest of motions."

"They're not used to any of this, Petra," I said defensively. "I had a great teacher in Astrea Prine, and it still took me a long time to get the hang of it. And besides that, we were forced to learn on the fly, fighting our way through the Quag, and once we left it we battled the Maladons. It was do or die. And the experience made us tougher and stronger. They haven't had the benefit of that. They've been slaves without one original thought in their heads for a long, long time."

"And maybe that's a fatal flaw in this whole thing," said Petra.

I sat up. "What do you mean by that?" I demanded.

Petra fixed a tight gaze on me. "I mean that what if their magic being taken from them originally means they can never be all that good at spells and such, even when their magic dust is returned to them? You have to admit, Vega, they are an incredibly clumsy bunch. We've been at this for a very long time, and not one of them can even consistently perform a *Rejoinda* spell. How long do you think it will take them to master the *Pass-pusay, Paralycto, Incartarata* and *Embattlemento* incantations? And do you really see any of them ever being able to perform the *Rigamorte* curse?"

I just sat there looking at her as awful, terrible thoughts flashed through my mind. The one I'd had before, of all of them lying dead on the battlefield while the victorious Maladons danced over their shattered bodies, made me shiver.

I composed myself and said, "I don't see what choice we have. We freed them. They're here. They're trying to learn. And we can't do this alone. We can't take on the Maladon empire by ourselves. We need help!" And then, full of anger and spite, I added, "Do you have a better idea?"

Petra sighed and lay back in the front of the fire once more. "No, I ruddy well don't."

"Maybe I do."

We all looked at Delph.

He put down the parchment and said, "You mentioned it yourself, Vega. Learning on the fly. Having to fight our way through the Quag. That made a difference. You can't learn everything in the classroom. You know that."

"What are you suggesting?" I snapped. "That we take them on a bloody field trip into the Quag?!" My response was more heated than was called for, but I did it because he had just referred to me simply as *Vega*. So he was still mad from the earlier argument about me going off on my own.

"No, not that."

"What, then?" barked Petra so sharply that Delph flinched.

"I'm suggesting that we take one or two of them with us

on occasion to True or Greater True. They can get a feel for what it's like out in the real world exercising magic. And if Maladons show up, well, then, they'll have to fight. And . . . stuff," he finished a bit lamely.

"Right, fight and bloody well *perish*," commented Petra.

But I thought Delph might have something there. "No, we could start off small like Delph suggested. Go into True with one or two of them and just look around. Let them see things. We'll do our best not to encounter Maladons, not until they're ready. But I think they need a lot more training up before we even think of doing such a thing."

Petra held up her hand with the missing finger. "Vega, you're forgetting that we no longer have the ring. If we go to those places, we go fully visible. And the Maladons know what we and their former slaves look like. They'll pounce immediately. "

My spirits plummeted. I had forgotten that. I was just so used to having the ring and the cover it provided.

However, I noted Delph's anxious face, regrouped and said, "Then we'll just have to disguise ourselves."

Petra did not look remotely convinced by this, but Delph said, "I bet this place has lots of clothes and stuff that we can use."

"I think it's a good idea," I said.

"Well, just for the record, I don't," said Petra.

"I'm going to bed," I said. I rose and quickly left before I said something I would long regret.

I did not sleep well.

Petra's words kept coming back to me.

But if this plan didn't work, if this "army" ended up not being able to fight, I had no alternative plan. The war would be lost before it was even fought.

ANOTHER THIRTY DAYS passed, and my spirits began to lift a bit when Sara Bond, a lanky female of thirty-three, performed a perfectly acceptable *Embattlemento* spell that actually blocked my incantation. I praised her, a comment that brought even more redness to her already rosy cheeks.

Tobias Holmes, on the other hand, was not progressing nearly as well. Tall and broad-shouldered and, I had seen for myself, a bit overconfident in his abilities, he could not seem to grasp the concept of pointing his wand at the actual target. Instead he vaguely waved it here and there, which meant that he ended up being a danger to himself and others around him.

I worked with him until he could at least aim straight.

I had spoken with Miranda Weeks after my conversation with Delph. She took my decision without argument, yet there was something in her look that made me think she was not okay with it. But I knew that Delph was right. She was simply too young. Besides, she had not a jot of confidence in her small bones. She held her wand as though it were a serpent about to bite her. She never looked at the target of her spells. She mumbled the words with no confidence and indeed seemed relieved when no magic was produced. She wouldn't have lasted a sliver in battle.

I stood in the corner watching her, and others like her, as my own confidence, bolstered a bit by Sara Bond's enhanced performance, now headed the other way. The truth was, there were far more Miranda Weekses among the fifty.

And several, like Louise Penny and Dom Sadan, didn't seem to want to fight at all. I guess I shouldn't have been surprised that among a group of fifty, I would get a great variety of blokes.

When I glanced over at Petra's group, I saw that the same held for her lot.

When I caught Petra's gaze, her thoughts were clear for me to see.

This was a growing cock-up of enormous proportions.

I quickly looked away.

At dinner that night there was one of us unaccounted for.

No one could find Miranda.

We searched high and low.

Until I stepped out into the rear grounds and heard the sobs.

I made my way down the garden path until I came to a bench nearly surrounded by large rose bushes.

Miranda was seated on the bench, her head in her hands while she wept.

Two marble statues were next to her, attempting to console her without a lick of success. The magical rake had a hankie poised on its handle, but she wouldn't look at it.

I told them I would deal with it and sent them off.

I performed a wand wire to Petra telling her that I had found Miranda and everything was fine. They were to continue on with their meal.

I sat next to her and waited until she stopped sobbing.

I was loath to break the silence. Sometimes it was better to let the person in distress speak first.

But when Miranda just sniffled without looking like she was actually going to say anything, I decided to plunge ahead.

"Things not going well?" I began.

She shook her head and then broke into more sobs.

I took out my wand and held it in front of me.

"Take out your wand, Miranda."

"What's the ruddy use, Vega? I'm simply all sixes and sevens with this . . . this magic stuff."

"You're just very young. Please, take it out."

Scowling, she drew her wand and held it in front of her. But she didn't look at it.

"Where do you come from?" I asked.

I had spoken with many of the others about their pasts, but had not done so with Miranda. It was probably because of her losing her mother. She no doubt thought about it all the time, and I didn't want to unduly add to this burden.

"Why?" she said stubbornly.

"I'd just like to know."

She rubbed her face and said slowly, "I was born in a little village called Drews. Me mum and me lived there. I couldn't tell you where it is now, but I remember it being pretty, with crumbling stone walls, a small creek running through it with a bridge over it. I caught a fish for dinner. Me . . . mum." She stopped, and her lip trembled. "Me mum was quite proud when I did that."

"I'm sure she was. Did you go to Bimbleton Station?"

She nodded. "Mum had heard of this train that you could take."

"I'm sure."

"So she brought us there. And then . . . then I remember me and Mum being put on the train."

She started to cry again, and I put my arm around her and just let her sob.

When she had recovered, I pointed to the mark on her hand. "They took you because of that mark. It shows you're magical."

"So why can't I do bleeding magic, then!" she exclaimed.

She looked at me with red, puffy eyes that contrasted sharply with her dark skin.

"Because magic is hard, and everyone comes to it in their own way. Some faster, some slower."

"I bet you came to it very fast. I bet you were doing spells when you were born."

"I performed my first spell when I was fifteen. Before that I had never done a lick of proper magic. I was incapable of it. And it took a very long time and a lot of hard work and many mistakes along the way for me to properly wield *this*." I held up my wand.

This confession of sorts clearly got her attention.

"Really?" she said, her eyes wide in wonder.

"How old are you, Miranda?"

"Ten, least I think."

"I'm nearly sixteen, and I can't tell you the number of cock-ups I had. The number of times I made a mess of things. But I picked myself back up and kept going. I've been watching you for a while now. Very closely."

"Why's that?" she said nervously. "You're . . . you're not thinking of sending me back to . . . to what I was? You already told me I couldn't fight the Maladons. So I'm no bloody use to you."

I gripped her shoulder. "I would never do that even if you could never properly perform a spell in your life. You are free now. And you're my friend. Friends don't hurt each other like that. You will remain free regardless of anything that happens here." I paused and said, "And I see a lot of you in me."

She shook her head hard. "Y-you're just saying that to make me feel better."

"I don't have the luxury of doing that, Miranda. I don't have time to make you feel better simply for the sake of making you feel better. Do you understand that?"

She fully straightened and looked directly at me. "Yes."

"When I first used my wand, I had no confidence. Not in it, and not in me. I wielded it like the thing and I were two separate bits of stuff."

She looked at her wand. "But aren't we?"

"No! That wand was created from the wand of Bastion Cadmus, the father of us all. It has a bit of him embedded in it. That bit is now your wand, which means it is also embedded in you. Your wand is you and you are your wand. You are truly inseparable. It will perform for you better and more powerfully than it will for anyone else."

"But it won't perform for me a'tall," she said miserably.

"That's because you have no confidence in yourself, meaning you have no confidence in your wand. It senses that. It *feels* that, Miranda; that's why it won't perform. Because you, as yet, don't trust it. And so it does not trust *you*."

She stared down at her wand again. This time, not like it was a serpent, but with a look of intrigue; with a look of one considering certain possibilities.

"You . . . you really think that's the problem?"

"Did you trust your mother?"

"What? O'course I did. She always took care of me. Always wanted the best for me." Tears leaked from her eyes, but she held my gaze, which impressed me.

"So does your wand. When you have it in hand, you will never be alone. It wants the absolute best for you, because it wants you to *survive*."

She gaped and looked down at her wand.

When she looked back up, I said, "Shall we go into dinner now, Miranda, or . . . ?"

I let my voice trail off and studied her, awaiting her response.

She stood, holding her wand loosely, as I had originally taught her. Then Miranda turned away from me, pointed her wand at a bush, her gaze set directly ahead, and then, while making the perfect pull-back motion, said, "*Rejoinda*, rose."

The flower was nipped off the bush and flew directly into her free hand.

She looked down at it for an instant before her gaze lifted to mine.

Both our mouths spread into wide grins, and then she hugged me.

"I did it!" And then she began to sob harder than ever. She was only ten, after all.

I hugged her back, the tears creeping down my cheeks.

"Yes, you did."

"I promise I'll make you proud of me, Vega."

"I know you will."

Blimey, it was like I'd just inherited a little sister.

But I had one thought firmly in mind.

*I hope you never have to cast a spell in battle. I hope it will be over long before you're old enough to fight.*

*And possibly die.*

# One Small Step

SIXTEEN!
I awoke with this thought. I turned sixteen sessions this morning. Or sixteen *years*. Delph, Petra and I routinely spoke this world's language now, otherwise our fifty pupils would not be able to understand us.

Delph and I had been gone from Wormwood for an entire year. It was hard to believe, but when I thought back to all that we had experienced, and survived, it felt like ten years had actually passed.

I dressed and headed down with Harry Two.

When I walked in to the dining room, Delph, Petra and all the others were there.

I made a plate of food and was carrying it over to a table with five of our pupils when I saw Delph waving at me to join him.

Mrs. Jolly and her kitchen staff swooped around, doing what kitchen staff do, and doing it very well.

When I sat next to Delph he grinned, leaned over and said, "Happy birthday, Vega Jane."

I looked down and saw in his hand a small wrapped package.

"Delph, you didn't have to get me anything."

I was actually surprised that he had remembered it was my birthday.

"Remember supper at the Starving Tove back in Wormwood?" he said. "It's been a year since then."

"I know, Delph. I was just thinking about that."

He looked at the package. "Go ahead and open it."

I did so and held up what was in it.

It was a finely wrought chain with a tiny disc at the end.

"It's to wear around your neck," he said.

I looked at the disc. On it was the image of the three hooks.

"Where did you get this?" I said, amazed.

"Didn't get it. I made it."

"How?"

"There's a little smithy in the back grounds here. Gus, he's one of them marble statues — a slep, um, horse — showed me. Got a little forge and metal and all the tools I needed."

"Delph, it's beautiful. Truly beautiful."

I put it around my neck. "Thank you so much."

He turned red but smiled broadly.

My features turned somber. "Delph, about heading off without telling you?"

"It's okay."

"No, it's not. You were right. I shouldn't have done it. And I shouldn't have spoken to you like that. So . . . so I just won't do that anymore, okay?"

He smiled warmly. "Thanks, Vega Jane."

He gave me a hug. When he sat back, he had a funny look on his face. It was as though he wanted to do something else.

"Delph? Are you okay?"

He nodded, rose and hurried off without finishing his meal, which was practically unheard of for Delph.

I sensed someone watching, and I glanced over to find Petra staring at me.

She slowly looked away.

The training had been going really well for a long time now. Artemis Dale had mastered the *Jagada* spell, and Charlotte Tokken hadn't lost control of her wand in two months.

Miranda Weeks had made enormous strides, wielding her wand with skill and confidence. But all of them had worked hard and shown true grit and determination. I knew it had not been easy because it had not been easy for me either.

TRAINING WAS GOING so well, in fact, that I sat with Delph and Petra that night with an idea.

"I want to take three of them to Greater True tonight."

They both looked startled at the abruptness of my suggestion.

"Why Greater True?" asked Delph.

"That's where we lost the invisibility ring."

Petra looked down at her missing finger.

I said quickly, "Petra, I have never blamed you for the loss of the ring. But I think we need to try to get it back."

"But how can you?" Petra asked. "You don't even know if it's in Greater True."

"You said the Maladons jumped you?"

"That's right."

"And one of the Maladons had your wand."

"Well, that makes sense if they were the ones that attacked us."

"But yet you ended up in the barracks of the Elite Guard and not in the custody of the Maladons."

Petra looked confused.

"How did they take the ring and your finger? By magic?"

"I . . . I . . . It happened so fast."

I glanced at Delph. "And you lifted one of them up and threw them against a wall. A Maladon with a wand? I know you managed that at Saint Necro's in True, but you were invisible then. You weren't invisible that night. You said the wind knocked you around and the invisibility shield was thrown off."

"That's . . . that's right," said Delph, looking puzzled.

I had been giving this some thought lately, and what they had initially told me now didn't make sense.

"Well, it was one of the blokes that attacked us," said Petra.

"So Maladons patrolling the streets en mass? And they just happened to be there when you became visible?"

"Well, yes. Right, Petra?"

He looked at her, but she didn't seem nearly as certain.

I asked, "What were they wearing? Suits and hats? Black cloaks with red hoods?"

"Cloaks," said Delph at the same time as Petra said, "Coats."

I gazed at each of them in turn. "Well, which was it?"

They glanced sheepishly at each other.

"I don't know," admitted Delph, and Petra shook her head

in agreement. "I was a bit wonky in the head from getting thrown by the wind."

She said, "Come to think of it, it might have been a knife that cut off my finger."

"Let me see it," I said.

She held it up and I studied the stump.

"This was not done by a spell," I said, wishing I had examined it more closely when it had first happened. "A spell would have been more precise, and it would have burned the skin. This is jagged and there is no burning. I think it was a knife."

Petra said, "They grabbed me and I couldn't really see what they were doing. And they didn't have to cut my finger to get the ring off. It was loose anyway; that's why we became visible when it got turned back round."

"They did it to cause you pain. I think members of the Elite Guard were the ones who attacked and captured you, not the Maladons. I wondered why you were taken to the barracks and not somewhere else, like the castle. When I used one of the Maladons to get into the barracks, the guard there said, 'We've got our pair here still.' And then he wanted to know if Dullish had managed to trap me. And when I searched the Maladons, I got your wand back but not the ring."

"So you think one of them Elite Guards might have it?" asked Delph.

"It's possible. He might have thought it was valuable and he could sell it. And regardless whether one of the guards or a Maladon has it, I want it back."

"Who do you want to take?" asked Petra.

"Amicus, Sara and Dennis."

Delph nodded. "Yep, they're three of the best."

"So it'll be the five of us?" said Petra.

I shook my head. "The *four* of us. You have to stay here. If anything happens to me, you need to carry on."

She looked at me as though the weight of the world had descended upon her shoulders.

"Me, carry on?"

"We took a blood oath, Petra. For me it was more than a way to stop our squabbling. It was also an unbreakable bond, so that if one of us falls, the other one will continue on. We can't count on both of us surviving."

She slowly nodded, and Delph said, "Then I'll go with you."

"No, Petra will need your assistance, Delph."

"Why don't I go with them, then, Vega?" offered Petra.

"You will at some point. But the first time, it has to be me, Petra. It just has to be."

Petra studied me, and I could tell by her expression that she knew I was right. I was the superior sorceress, especially now with my wand fully and completely my own.

I rose and went to tell the others so they could prepare. They were all excited *and* scared. Exactly what I had expected.

With their magic returned and their being trained up properly, all fifty of the formerly enslaved were now fully branded with the three hooks on their hands. That meant they could be traced by the Maladons once they left the protection of Empyrean. In response to this, I had performed an intricate spell that had produced fifty copies of the glove that Alice had given me. They would wear them whenever we left Empyrean. I was pretty confident they would work, but this night we would find out for certain.

When I went back to my room to get my cloak, Petra was waiting for me.

"Delph told me it was your birthday today."

"Yes, it is."

She looked at the necklace around my neck.

"Delph made that for you?"

I smiled. "He gave it to me as a present."

"Is that what you do on birthdays?"

My smile vanished even as my heart went out to her. Of course; why would she know about presents on birthdays?

"Yes," I said. "When is your birthday?"

She shook her head. "I'm not sure. I remember my mother telling me it was cold when I was born. And I know I'm seventeen because we would mark off the time when I was young. And I would cut a notch in a stick I kept for each one."

"Well, it's cold outside now, so maybe your birthday is coming up," I said.

She shrugged, but kept staring at the necklace.

I ended the awkward silence by saying, "I need to get ready."

"Happy birthday, Vega. And much luck on your journey. I'll . . . I'll see you when you get back. And I hope you find the ring."

"Thanks, Petra. I hope I do too."

She turned and left.

WE SILENTLY APPEARED at the rear of the train station in Greater True. We were wearing long coats and hats pulled low that covered most of our faces.

I knew that Dennis, Sara and Amicus knew this place better than I did, having lived here for so long.

We had gone over the plan several times before leaving Empyrean.

When I looked at them, I could tell they were ready. Their wands were held loosely in their gloved hands; their gazes were steady and calm.

I led them through the darkness toward the barracks of the Elite Guard.

Along the way I saw a paper tacked to a wooden post.

I used my wand to illuminate it so we could see what it said.

REWARD FOR ANY INFORMATION LEADING TO THE RETURN OF THE FOLLOWING INDIVIDUALS AND THE CAPTURE OF THEIR KIDNAPPERS

And there listed were fifty names.

Dennis, Sara and Amicus reacted when they saw their names there. I thought they might be frightened, but I was heartened to see that each of them looked, well, proud!

I took down the paper and balled it up. "So they turned this into a mass kidnapping instead of a mass breakout for freedom," I said. "And no doubt blamed it on the awful Campions."

As we continued on, I was hoping for something, and it turned out to happen.

"*Subservio.*"

The spell hit the uniformed bloke dead in the back.

Dennis and Amicus each grabbed an arm and dragged him into the dark recesses of an alley.

I looked at the blank-faced bloke for a moment. I didn't recognize him, which wasn't surprising. There were a lot of them, after all.

I held up the disc that Delph had made for me.

"Have you seen a ring with this mark on it?"

The man looked dully at the image and nodded.

"Where?" I demanded.

"The commander of the barracks has it. Major Nelson. He wears it on his hand. Spoils of war, he called it."

"Did he tell anyone else that he had it? Mr. Endemen or any of his blokes?"

The man shook his head. "No. He hides it from them when they appear."

"Because they'll take it?"

"They'll take his life."

This comment surprised me. It showed a deeper understanding of the Maladons than I would have given this gent credit for.

"You know that they are murderous?"

"I have seen them kill."

"Do you fear them?"

"We all fear them."

I glanced at the others, who were staring openmouthed at the man.

"Okay, where is Major Nelson now? At the barracks?"

He shook his head. "At home."

"The address?"

"One Hundred Greater True Court."

"That's right next to the general assembly building," noted Dennis. "Big brick building with a blue door. My mas — the ones who enslaved me lived only one avenue over."

I nodded.

I wiped the bloke's thoughts and sent him on his way, oblivious to what had just happened. We heard him whistling as he walked down the darkened street.

I looked at Dennis. "Lead the way."

We hurried through the darkness. I had to keep reminding myself that we were no longer invisible. When we heard steps approaching our way, I cast a befuddlement spell in front of us.

A moment later two soldiers appeared carrying guns. They passed right by us, the incantation having done what it was designed to do.

We kept going and reached the house five minutes later.

We looked up at the place from across the street. The building was imposing and totally dark.

"Okay," I said. "Everyone here knows that all you lot have disappeared. It's been a long time, granted, but they will still be on their guard. So if anything happens, we must act quickly and efficiently." I tapped Amicus on the shoulder. "You'll bring up the rear. Keep an eye out for anything that looks or sounds suspicious."

After he nodded I turned to Dennis. "You'll be on my left flank." I glanced at Sara. "And you on my right."

She nodded.

I lifted my wand to the ready position and they all did the same.

Their breaths were slightly elevated, as was mine. They had trained long and hard, but all within the safe confines of Empyrean. This was far different. This was the real thing, and there were blokes here who would want nothing more than to kill us.

Amicus looked determined, Sara keenly observant and Dennis a trifle nervous.

We entered through the back door. A simple incantation did the job.

The house was beautifully decorated and furnished but I didn't care a whit about that.

I just wanted my ring back. It was the only thing I had left of my grandfather's. Even if it couldn't turn me invisible, I would have wanted it back.

There was no one on the first three floors. That left the top floor.

I used my *Crystilado magnifica* spell to see inside the rooms until we came to the last one on the left.

The man was asleep in bed.

And on his finger was my ring.

*"Ingressio."*

The door swung open and we edged inside.

My gaze hit every corner of the room before it settled back on the bed where Major Nelson was fast asleep.

*"Rejoinda, ring."*

It flew off his finger and onto mine.

I instantly twisted it round.

When I looked at Sara, my heart sank.

She could obviously still see me.

*"Embattlemento,"* I cried out as the spell lights shot at us.

A dozen Maladons had appeared in the room and were firing spell after spell at us.

Dennis cried out as a spell ripped into his arm and blood shot out.

Using Destin, I soared above them all and fired spells downward.

"Triangulate," I cried out.

The three of them quickly formed a three-point perimeter stance, which I had taught them.

I continued to rain spells down on the Maladons, which meant they had to lift their wands and defend against me.

That gave my lot free rein to fire away.

Sara sent a wickedly curving *Jagada* curse at a Maladon. After slashing him, it bounced off and cut through another.

Amicus was a bloke on fire, sending *Impacto* spells that blasted a half dozen Maladons across the room.

One-armed Dennis ensnared two more Maladons and then knocked them out.

I finished off the rest with a brilliantly tricky spell that Astrea had shown me.

The first wave of the spell was a blinding wall of light. When they shot at it with their wands, they found out, too late, that the wall of light was actually a magical mirror that sent their spells hurtling right back at them.

When the last Maladon fell, I returned to the floor.

"Let's get out of here," I said. I was just about to magically tether them and cast my *Pass-pusay* incantation when he appeared inches from me.

"Looking for this?" sneered Endemen.

He held up my real ring.

"A useful *magical element*, wouldn't you say?"

There would have been a time when the mere sight of the bloke would have paralyzed me. That time had long since passed.

I lowered my wand and bowed my head.

"Acknowledging my superiority, Vega of Wormwood!"

I lifted my gaze to his. And right then I could tell the bloke knew he had made a mistake. But it was too late.

I knocked the sneer off his face, not with my wand.

But with my fist.

My gloved hand, powered both by Destin and all the loathing I held for this disgusting creature, hit him so hard that he was catapulted across the room and slammed into the wall with such force that he smashed right through it and into the next room.

I stared at the crumpled mess of a Maladon for one gloriously wonderful moment.

"*Rejoinda*, my *real* ring."

The ring shot off his hand and flew onto mine

I tethered us together, turned the ring around, said my incantation and we vanished.

This had been my absolute best birthday ever!

# The End of Me

ONCE WE GOT back to Empyrean, I used the Adder Stone to fix up Dennis's arm, a burn on Sara's face and a gash on Amicus's leg. I praised all three of them on their performance in battle.

At breakfast we all recounted the story of how we had gotten the ring back. When Sara got to the part about me blasting Endemen through a wall, the cheers rang out so loudly I didn't think they would ever stop echoing through my ears.

Having my grandfather's ring back buoyed my spirits wonderfully, and we continued our training. I threw more and more difficult tasks to my troops, confident that they were up to it.

As Astrea Prine had done with me, I used the *Golem Masquerado* spell to craft clay statues for us to use as targets. I know it was a bit cheeky of me, but I fashioned the statues so they all wore bowler hats!

As time passed, we moved on to ever more complex spells. And as I looked around the Great Hall, I saw lights zipping across and smashing into the statues, either exploding them or ripping them to pieces.

I noted with a certain satisfaction that the women seemed to be getting things faster than the men. And they were certainly more aggressive. And they gave no quarter to their opponents!

I was so proud!

No doubt emboldened by having fought Maladons for real, Sara Bond had become a spell machine, whipping her wand around and incanting like she had been doing it her whole life. And she had become one of the most popular among the fifty. For weeks after our adventure in Greater True, I could hear the others asking her to recount in exacting detail everything that had happened during the course of the battle.

Dennis and Amicus were inundated by these requests too, but I didn't mind. I wanted them to explain to the others exactly what it felt like to be in a fight for your very life. I knew that would be important later on.

Now that we had the invisibility ring back, Petra and I took turns shepherding groups of twos and threes to True, Greater True and even Bimbleton Station. We had several skirmishes with soldiers and Maladons but we always survived and came back intact. And the experiences were helping to mold my young army into quite the fighting machine.

And I grew to take a real interest in all of them, because I knew that at some point we would depend on one another to make it through the coming war alive. So while Dennis, Amicus and Sara were well on their way to becoming fine magical warriors, I needed all fifty to be at the same level.

Cecilia Harkes was a tall, lithe girl of nineteen. She had red hair, freckled cheeks and a quick but steady wand hand. We had rescued Cecilia from an elderly Greater True couple who thought nothing of making her sleep next to the coal bin, forcing her to eat her meals from a bowl served on the floor and slapping her across the face whenever they bloody well felt like it.

I gave her some finer pointers on the *Jagada* spell, showing her how to move and turn her hips together with the wand motion. As Astrea had shown me, it added to both the speed and potency of the incantation.

I watched her do it once more, and nodded approvingly as the clay statue became riddled with innumerable cuts and slashes.

"Nice job, Cecilia. Couldn't have done it better myself."

She swelled with pride as I moved on.

Across the hall, Petra was putting a group through the rigorous process of mastering the *Subservio* spell. I watched as Petra performed the incantation on Nicholas Bonham, a tall, sturdily built young man with handsome features, beautiful blue eyes and long blond hair. Nicholas stiffened and assumed a blank stare when the spell hit him.

Petra then made him jump and spin around.

And then she made him tell her that he loved her.

The rest of the group laughed, but I wondered about that last part.

Did Petra fancy the strapping lad?

I could only hope.

I had James Throckmorton, a small man who had been

enslaved the longest of the group, starting at age nine, perform the *Embattlemento* spell. I broke through it easily the first six times he tried, but the seventh time his shield held against my wand's blast.

His face sweaty and his chest heaving, he accepted my congratulations with a single nod before getting back to work.

I kept moving through the group, helping Alabetus Trumbull succeed in deploying the *Engulfiado* spell, which doused poor Pauline Paternas, a pugnacious woman of twenty.

As I helped her up and dried her off with a wave of my wand, I said, "Now it's *your* turn."

Which she took with a flicker of malice in her eyes. And her stream of water was far stronger than Trumbull's and sent him sailing headlong into the wall.

I had to work hard to hide my smile.

Aloysius Danbury struck Tobias Holmes blind with the *Impairio* spell but forgot how to reverse it, which I quickly fixed.

Charlotte Tokken straightened out a maze I had created in one corner of the hall by employing with confidence the *Confuso, recuso* incantation.

I shuddered when I recalled how that spell had saved our lives in the Quag as we were going through the First Circle.

Anna Dibble, a big-boned girl around my age with brown hair cut very short by her former masters, which gave her a face a severely intense look, trapped her sparring partner and former slave mate, Sara Bond, with the *Incartarata* incantation. As the white lights swirled around Sara, I recalled how that same prison had held a huge jabbit in Astrea Prine's cottage.

A jabbit that would have done me in, had I not been exceptionally fast with my wand!

I walked halfway up the stairs and looked back down, surveying my little army going about its training.

Over there Dennis O'Shaughnessy used the *Rejoinda* spell to take the wand of Miranda Weeks. She promptly turned the tables on him after she got her wand back and roped him neatly with an *Ensnario* incantation. In another corner a door was opened by Reginald Magnus using the *Ingressio* incantation. Another corner was brightened by the *Illumina* spell.

People rose with the *Elevata* spell and others fell with the *Descente* incantation.

A tree I had conjured in the middle of the hall had its trunk shrunk by the *Withero* spell.

I smiled. All in all it was a good day.

I wandered into the room where Delph was holding forth.

As usual, he was dressed in a suit with a vest and looked fetchingly handsome with his thick, long hair and tall, strong body. There were twenty students in the room and I noted, with a bit of apprehension, that all twelve of the young women sat there somehow managing to copiously write down every word Delph said while simultaneously gaping at him. I watched as several glanced at one another, patted their chests and giggled.

I closed the door to the room and walked away, shaking my head.

*Females.*

At dinner that night we all ate together. I usually liked to split the group up so as not to overburden the kitchen, but

Mrs. Jolly insisted that it was fine. And the meal was particularly splendid, with chicken and ham and vegetables from the garden and soft rolls that seemed to melt in my mouth. Then followed pudding, and soon we all sat there happy and drowsy.

We said our good nights and went our separate ways.

Petra caught up to me as I walked to my room.

"I think things are going rather well," she said. "Artemis Dale gets everything right after just a few attempts now. And Regina Samms nearly so. And Katie Watson's *Ensnario* spell is quite something. And Alex Prettyman's convulsing hex is nearly unbreakable."

"And Nicholas Bonham?" I said slyly. "He seems awfully good too."

Petra turned pink and looked away. "He's all right but he also needs a lot of work."

"And I'm sure you'll give him *all* the attention he needs," I said encouragingly.

I looked her over. Ever since coming here, it seemed to me that Petra had become even more lovely. She could now bathe regularly, wear clean clothes and wash her hair. And Mrs. Jolly's food had filled out her gaunt look. She was a beautiful woman, I had to admit. Nicholas Bonham would be fortunate to win her good graces.

"He tried to snog me the other night," she said, startling me.

"What did you do?"

"I hexed him."

"Really?"

She smiled. "But then I snogged him back."

I laughed. "Well, I'm sure he liked that."

"Delph wants to snog you."

My smile faded. "How do you know that?"

"He told me. That night I was in his room. We were talking about you. He really loves you, Vega. I've always known that. I guess I flirted with him sometimes just to make you mad. Anyway, he wanted my opinion about what he should do."

I thought back to that night when I had almost sent Petra to her death. They had been talking about me?

"And what did you tell him?"

"To follow his heart."

I shot her a curious glance. "So you're not . . . ?"

"I didn't say that, did I?" She paused, but only for a moment, before adding, "And I plan to follow *my* heart too!"

She said good night, spun on her heel and went off to her room, leaving me standing there.

*What else should I have expected from bloody Petra Sonnet?*

A moment later Delph came around the corner.

My face instantly felt warm and I said, innocently, "Hey, Delph, Petra and I were just talking about you."

"Really? What about?"

"Oh, nothing important. You've become a fine teacher."

"Right." He seemed distracted and I wondered why.

"What's up?" I asked.

"I'm glad you liked your present."

I touched the necklace. "I *love* it, Delph."

He edged a bit closer. "I wanted to give you *another* present on your birthday, but I wasn't . . . wasn't sure you'd like it."

"Delph, I'm sure I would love whatever you gave me."

He took another step forward.

And he kissed me. I mean he really snogged me.

And before I realized it, I was snogging him back. We stood there for about five minutes with our lips and bodies locked together. My heart felt like it might burst.

Then we heard a giggle.

And then someone cleared his throat.

We turned to find half a dozen people standing there watching us.

The two girls watching us looked like they might melt, though Cecilia Harkes did seem a bit disappointed.

The blokes, Amicus and Dennis among them, just looked embarrassed.

"Right," I said. "Well, good night, Delph."

We uncoiled from each other and I hurried into my room and closed the door.

I don't believe my face was wide enough to accommodate my smile.

Harry Two was already there.

But my dog wasn't asleep, though he usually was by now.

He was perched on my bed looking strange, I thought.

I sat next to him and rubbed his fur.

"You okay, Harry Two?" I said.

Usually when I said that he would lick my face. This time he didn't. He didn't move or even look at me.

Troubled by this, I undressed, washed my face and climbed into bed.

I lay there staring at the ceiling.

I could tell that time passed, and soon it was the darkest point before the rise of the sun and still I had not closed my eyes.

I might have been thinking about Delph the whole time. That kiss had confirmed much for me. And it made my heart leap for joy. But though I really wanted to dwell on that, I was thinking principally about Harry Two. He had not moved a muscle. He was still perched in the exact same spot, his body as rigid as marble.

I would occasionally lift my head and look at him, wishing that he would finally lie down and go to sleep. But he didn't. And I knew that nothing Harry Two did was without purpose. He was my early warning signal and always had been. He sensed things long before I did.

I finally crawled over next to my faithful companion and sat with my arm around him.

I worriedly scanned his face. His eyes were pointed straight at the door. His snout was clamped shut. He looked as serious as ever I'd seen him, even when death was staring us both in the face, in the shape of a garm or jabbit or Maladon.

Finally, I got dressed and was debating whether to go downstairs and prepare for the next day's lessons when I shot a look at Harry Two. It was clear that his senses had once again been faster than mine, for he had jumped down from the bed and was intently staring at the door to my room.

I rushed over to him.

"Harry Two, what is it?" I asked.

He never once looked at me. But his remaining ear had peaked.

And then he lunged and started to scratch at the door.

I flung it open and he raced out.

"Harry Two!"

He ran down the hall and then hurtled down the stairs.

I raced after him.

He reached the first floor, turned and bolted out of sight.

I caught sight of him as he galloped down a set of stairs.

I followed in time to see him turn and go down another set of rickety stairs.

Then my heart went into my throat because I knew where he was going.

Sure enough, he reached the little door with the screaming Wug on the doorknob. When I ran up next to him he looked at me and barked, as though to say, *Hurry up, will you?*

I used my wand to open the door. Harry Two raced in and I followed.

The sounds reached my ears as soon as I closed the door behind me.

It was someone sobbing.

The bits of light were swirling everywhere, as before, though there appeared to be more of them, and their flight more frenetic than it had been.

I rushed around looking for Uma Cadmus, or Alice Adronis, in her pierced armor and with her mortal wound. But they were not there.

So where were the sobs coming from?

Harry Two was not at a loss, though. He yipped and raced to a distant corner. I ran after him and found that the corner was actually a bend in the room that led to a much smaller room.

And in the very center of that room was a huddled figure.

I crept forward, unsure who or what it was. I doubted that any of the fifty people we had brought here would have found this place, or been able to access it. Was it one of the household staff? Was it another restless soul I had not met?

"Hello?" I said cautiously. "Excuse me? Hello? Are you all right?"

When the figure turned toward me, I didn't know how I kept from fainting, or my heart from stopping.

The ethereal image of *Morrigone* was facing me.

But I had left Morrigone behind in Wormwood.

So what the Hel —

My breath caught in my throat as my lungs seized up.

*Wormwood!*

We rushed over to her and I knelt down beside her.

I knew it was Morrigone, but it was a very changed Morrigone.

I had seen her in an image from Astrea Prine's cottage when I was in the Quag. Even then she had looked different from what I remembered. Always tall, queenly and flawless in all respects, she had looked older, withered, ill even.

The Morrigone I was looking at now was pale and frail, and the look in her eyes, even as recognition sparked there as her gaze fell full on my features, was one of abject horror undercut by a sense of complete despair.

I didn't know which terrified me more.

"Morrigone? It's me, Vega Jane."

But she knew who I was. I had seen that clearly in her features. At first she said nothing. But her hand reached out and gripped my arm. Or rather it tried to. It simply passed right through.

"Vega," she said in a near whisper.

"What happened?" I said. "How did you get here?"

"I am dead," she said in the same low voice, as though she barely had the strength to speak.

"Dead! But how?"

"They came."

*They? Who's they?* I wondered.

But then the images leapt back to my mind. There really could only be one *they*.

"The Maladons?" I said. "They came to Wormwood?"

She nodded.

"And killed you?"

She nodded again.

I could barely breathe. "And . . . and the rest of Wormwood?"

She said nothing. She simply shook her head.

"I . . . it can't be," I blurted out.

Now Morrigone's expression turned hard, cruel, loathing in every facet.

"I told you, Vega. I warned you what could happen. Well, now it *has* happened. Our deaths are upon *your* head."

Before I could say anything in response, she faded away to nothing.

I could only stare at the spot where she had been. My mind had gone blank.

When it was filled with thoughts a few moments later, they were all terrible ones indeed.

Wormwood? My home?

They had killed her. They had killed . . . everyone?

My mind went blank again. No, my mind went dead.

When it restarted, I slumped to the side and vomited up my dinner.

Next instant I jumped up and ran all the way to my room with Harry Two right behind. I was so out of control that I bounced into walls and crashed over furniture. It was a wonder the whole house wasn't awoken, but I reached my bedroom without anyone seeing me.

I put on my cloak, slipped Destin around my waist and put the harness around my shoulders. I snapped my fingers and Harry Two jumped into the harness as he had done so many times before.

We passed by first Delph's and then Petra's rooms. But this was something *I* had to do.

Alone.

We stepped outside of Empyrean and I tapped my leg twice with the destination firmly in mind as I said the spell.

A moment later Harry Two and I arrived at the spot where we had left the Quag so long ago.

It was dark and dreary.

When I walked over to the spot I raised my wand and said, *"Exposadus."*

There it was, the magical dome that had entombed both Wormwood and the Quag. And on it was the very slightest of impressions, like an exposed seam in a garment.

We had come out here.

I looked down at my ring. I had used it to open the dome, allowing us to escape.

*A useful magical element.*

Those were the words that Endemen had spoken to me in Major Nelson's bedroom. And I now I fully knew what he meant. I had used my ring to cut a seam in the dome to get out.

They had used my ring to get *in*.

When I was at the castle before and had seen all the pell-mell activity. That was when they must have found the spot where we came out. By making the seam we had exposed the location of the spell wall protecting both the Quag and Wormwood. It had been pristine and thus completely invisible. They had never been able to find it before. But with the seam marring the perfect surface of the dome they at least knew what they had to break through. But they hadn't been able to get in.

Until they got my ring.

My heart crumbled to bits.

I used my ring to pierce the wall. Then I tapped my wand against my leg and muttered *"Pass-pusay"* holding the image of the place of my birth singly in mind. I certainly knew it better than any other place.

The next moment my feet touched down on the High Street in the town square.

I had been gone from here it seemed like an eternity.

And it looked as though an eternity had passed.

The buildings were destroyed. The cobbles ruptured.

I walked numbly toward the Loons, where my brother, John, and I had lived after our parents had gone to the Care.

The building was a shell now, the doors and windows blown out.

I walked to the end where the majestic Council building had been located. I gaped, for there was only an enormous blackened hole in the dirt where it had once stood.

I wandered aimlessly around.

Steeples was burned, the pretty glass melted.

The hospital and the Care were similarly gutted.

I flew to Duf Delphia's cottage.

*Please, don't let it be. Don't let Duf be . . .*

As I drew close, I noted with horror that all of the beasts that Duf typically trained lay dead in the paddocks around the cottage, showing more bone than flesh.

I landed and crept up to the porch of the cottage. The door was gone, the windows simply gaping holes.

With a thrill of horror, I saw it.

A pair of wooden stumps leaned against the wall.

But Duf Delphia was not attached to them.

I backed away, with Harry Two still in the harness, and pushed off the ground.

I soared above and landed in front of my old family home, where I had gone to live after Morrigone had taken in John. Surprisingly, nothing was touched there. I walked in the door and looked around in wonder that they had not demolished this place, especially this place.

But then I saw the mark of the Maladons burned into the wall.

So they *had* been here.

I raised my wand and blasted their mark away.

I ran out and lifted off into the sky, and moments later landed at Stacks.

The towers were toppled, the massive gate caved in. When I walked inside I saw that everything had been destroyed.

When I reached my old worker station where I had been a Finisher, I saw that the brass nameplate with Vega Jane on it had been savagely defaced.

I pointed my wand at it, and wiped the marks away so that my name and my name alone was visible.

I went to Julius Domitar's little office. The furniture had been overturned, his precious ink bottles smashed to bits.

I headed up the stairs to the second floor and from there to the door with the screaming Wug as a doorknob. None of it was there. The door and the Wug doorknob were gone. The only thing there was a blank wall.

I left Stacks and flew next to my tree house.

It was still there with the boards intact against the trunk of the tree. One of them was still blackened from when the garm had attacked me here. I leapt to the top of the planks. Again, like my home, it was undisturbed, except for one thing.

Burned into the planks was the symbol of the Maladons. I took out my wand and uttered, *"Eraisio."* The mark vanished.

I lifted off, and Harry Two and I next arrived at Morrigone's home.

The beautiful gates were torn apart. The ornate door was blasted open.

All the fine things she had possessed, the case clocks, all the wonderful books, the china, the paintings, the lovely rugs, the splendid-looking glasses, they were all gone.

And my brother?

I ran up the stairs to where I knew his bedroom was.

I opened the door, terrified of what I might find.

And what I did find absolutely terrified me. But for a different reason.

The room had not been damaged at all. The horrible

pictures that I had once seen on the walls were gone, but everything else was like he had just walked out of the room.

I did not know what to make of it. I simply didn't.

I had saved my next destination for last.

My feet hit the dirt at the entrance to the Hallowed Ground, where Wugs buried their dead.

With a sense of foreboding, I walked through the gates.

And I found exactly what I thought I would find.

New graves were everywhere, with headstones and names etched on them.

The Loons were all lined up in a row.

Julius Domitar and Dis Fidus were buried side by side upon a little knoll.

Roman Picus, my old landlord and nemesis, rested at the end of one row, his garm-skin boots dumped on top of the pile of dirt covering his grave.

Tears spilled from my eyes when I saw Duf Delphia's plot.

And to the right was Herman Helvet, who owned the confectionery shop. And next to him were Jurik Krone and Non. And there was the foul Ran Digby, who Delph had beaten in the Duelum. And Ted Racksport, who had shot himself in the foot. And Darla Gunn, who had sold me my first set of nice clothes at Fancy Frocks.

Down near the end of another row was the grave of Ezekiel the Sermonizer, who presided at Steeples.

And on and on the graves went.

Until I located the last new one.

I stared at the name engraved there.

*Morrigone.*

And there was one more thing.

Every grave had been marked with the sign of the Maladons.

So everywhere I looked, those terrible eyes stared back at me.

But there was one grave missing.

My brother, John, was not there. I had searched everywhere for him, terrified that the next gravestone I would find would have his name etched on it.

But it was not here.

And I did not know what that meant.

As I walked along I realized that Morrigone's parting words to me when I had left Wormwood also made sense now.

I had originally thought she had been afraid that I would fail and perish in the Quag.

But the opposite had been true.

She had told me that she was afraid because she thought I would *succeed* and escape the Quag.

I looked around the graveyard.

And this . . . this was why she had been afraid.

Because what she had feared would happen, *had* happened.

And why had I never thought to come back here before now? To rescue my fellow Wugs? Well, it was too late for that now.

I hung my head so that my tears spilled onto Harry Two's fur.

I had never felt this miserable, this lost, in my entire life.

*Lost,* that was the exact right term.

For I had lost everything.

And worst of all, I was the reason all these Wugs lay dead. My fellow Wugmorts, wiped out. No more.

I was so numb that when Harry Two licked my face, I started back and refocused.

And then I heard it.

A sound off to my left.

My wand ready, I ran that way with Harry Two next to me. It was coming from behind a tree.

I reached the spot, and with my wand at the ready I charged around the tree, ready to strike.

I stopped dead.

"Tha-Thansius?"

How could I have missed noticing that he had no grave here?

Our mighty Wug leader looked as I had never seen him look before. His fine robes were filthy rags. His great chest and broad shoulders had fallen in. He wasn't much more than a skeleton.

He lay on the ground, a shovel next to him.

I knelt next to him and lifted his head with my hand. "Thansius. It's me, Vega Jane. Can you hear me?"

He looked a thousand sessions old, withered and gray. When he opened his eyes I saw, with horror, that his pupils were gone. They were simply white, like the slaves back in Greater True.

"V-Ve-Vega?"

"Yes, it's me. What . . . what happened?"

"D-de. All de-dead. E-except for me."

"But how did you survive?"

But even as I said it I thought I knew the truth. I looked at the shovel lying next to him.

He touched his sunken, bony chest as though in great pain.

I unbuttoned his torn and stained garment.

Underneath, burned into his skin, was the mark of the Maladons.

When my gaze fell upon it, my eyes filled with tears.

"Thansius, I am so sorry. I'm so very sorry."

Thansius had been so strong, so indomitable and so . . . noble; we all had looked up to him. Which was the only reason the Maladons had done this. To humiliate him. To show him as weak, inconsequential, not in their class!

Leaving him to dig the graves of his fellow Wugs.

"Thansius, do you have any idea what they did with my brother?"

"To-took him."

"Took him where?"

He gurgled a bit. I looked around and pointed my wand at a tree and mouthed the spell to draw water from it. I conjured a flask to catch it and then held it to Thansius's mouth.

"Here, drink this. I can help you. I'll take you with me. I'll nurse you back to health myself and everything will be just . . ."

I drew the flask back, for he had stiffened. And like Lackland Cyphers, he drew one last breath and then fell limp in my arms.

Thansius, mighty Thansius, who had stood for all that was good about Wormwood and Wugs in general, was dead.

I let go of him and rose.

With my wand I dug him a grave under a large, beautiful oak. I magically lay his body in it and covered it over with both dirt and a shield spell. I crafted the tombstone and placed it at the head of the mound of dirt.

On it I wand-wrote, HERE LIES THANSIUS, THE BEST AND MIGHTIEST WUG OF ALL.

Then I went to each of the tombstones and removed the mark of the Maladons. Finished, I kicked off and rose into the air. I flew over a place that no longer existed.

Except in my mind.

As I soared along, I cried. I sobbed. I called out to the sky the names of Wugs I had known all my life. I cursed the Maladons. Poor Harry Two howled in misery. I drew my wand, took aim and blasted a large rock to smithereens.

When I reached the Quag, I had no idea if a great storm would blow up to prevent my flying over. Part of me wanted that to happen.

Because I deserved to die too. For what I had done.

But nothing happened. It seemed that the magical force of the place was extinguished.

Should I try to find Astrea and her son, Archie? Had the Maladons found them already? I couldn't bear to find out.

I flew through the opening in the dome.

When my boots hit the dirt, I knew that I would never cry again, no matter what else happened.

I pointed my wand and a beam of black light heated the seam. And there was no longer a seam. Yet I kept my wand pointed and the light going for so long that I thought I might ignite the entire wall around the Quag.

But I wanted to use my magic to accomplish something.

Something permanent.

I moved the wand around, spelling out the words.

When I lowered my wand, my chest was heaving; my lungs felt scorched.

I looked down at Harry Two. He was looking at me in a way he never had.

He was looking at me in a way that told me my dog was seeing me differently than he ever had before.

And Harry Two's senses were spot on.

Because I was different. My trip back to Wormwood had been unlike anything I had ever imagined, even in the worst of my nightmares.

It had changed me.

I was not the Vega Jane of barely sixty slivers ago.

I turned away from the wall and kicked off.

We were sent soaring into the air.

I looked down. The words I had seared into the wall were plainly visible from here.

THIS TIME WE WILL TRIUMPH

I could feel every muscle in my body begin to harden as I turned and headed back to Empyrean.

But it wasn't simply my sinew growing stout.

It was also my heart that had turned to stone.

I was changed forever. I was the leader. And leaders could become close to no one.

I gripped my wand loosely as we flew along. I wanted to run into a Maladon. I wanted to run into an army of them.

Because I wanted to kill them all.

And as I flew back to the safe embrace of Empyrean, I swore to myself that I, Vega Jane, *would* destroy them all, even if it cost me my life.

# A Wugmort's Guide to Wormwood and Beyond

**adar** \ad-ər\
A beast of Wormwood often used as a messenger and trained to perform tasks by air. Although they appear clumsy on the ground, adars
are creatures of grace and beauty in the sky, owing greatly to their
magnificent height and wingspan. Most remarkably, adars can understand Wugmorts and can even be taught to speak.

**Adder Stone** \ædər-ston\
A stone known to possess healing powers, capable of erasing all traces
of a wound when held over the injury.

**alecto** \ə-'lek-tō\
A lethal creature in the Quag characterized by serpents for hair and
blood-dripping eyes. The hypnotizing sway of the serpents atop the
alecto's head can drive its prey to commit suicide.

**amaroc** \a-mə-räk\
A fierce and terrifying beast of the Quag, known to possess the ability
to kill in many ways. Amarocs have upper fangs as long as a Wug arm
and are rumored to shoot poison from their eyes. When captured, their
hides are used in the production of clothing and boots in Wormwood.

**attercop** \a-dər-käp\
A type of venomous spider indigenous to the Quag.

**Bimbleton Station** \'bim-bəl-tən ste-ʃən\
A ramshackle station where people wait to take a train to what they think will be a better life.

**Bowler Hats** \'bolər hæts\
The most elite fighters the Maladons have. They wear three-piece pinstripe suits and bowler hats, hence the name.

**Breath of a Dominici** \'breTH əv ə dä-mən-'ē-chē\
A long-stemmed flower with a fist-size bloodred bloom that gives off the odor of slep dung. The Breath of a Dominici grows only in viper nests.

**Campions** \'campions\
The insurrection focused on causing as much strife as possible for the Maladons.

**Care, the** \'ker\
A place where Wugs who are unwell and for whom the Mendens at hospital can do no more are sent to live.

**chontoo** \'chən-too\
A flying beast in the Quag comprised only of a head, the chontoo is said to wildly attack its prey in the hopes of using its body parts to replace the ones the chontoo does not have. Spawned over the centuries by the intermingling of different species, the chontoo is characterized by a foul face with demonic eyes and jagged fangs, and flames for hair. The chontoo is primarily found in the Mycanmoor.

**colossal** \kə-'lä-səl\
An ancient race of formidable warriors, of an origin largely unknown to the average Wugmort. The average colossal stands about sixty-five feet tall and weighs nearly seven thousand pounds.

**Council** \\'kaun-səl\\
The governing body of Wormwood. Council passes laws, regulations and edicts that all Wugmorts must obey.

**creta** \\'krē-də\\
An exceptionally large creature used in Wormwood to pull the plow of Tillers and transport sacks of flour at the Mill. The creta weighs well over one thousand pounds and is characterized by horns that cross over its face and hooves the size of plates.

**cucos** \\'koo-kōs\\
Small birdlike creatures that inhabit the Third Circle of the Quag. Brilliantly colored as if small bits of the rainbow are embedded in their feathers, the cucos are best known for glowing wings that can illuminate their surroundings.

**Dactyl** \\'dak-til\\
A Stacks worker whose job entails shaping metal with hammer and tongs.

**dopplegang** \\'dä-pəl-gaNG\\
A dangerous creature in the Quag, marked by hideous rows of blackened, sharp teeth, that morphs into whatever it sees. The power of the dopplegang lies in its ability to trick its unsuspecting victim into injuring or even killing itself, since striking the beast in its altered form is tantamount to striking oneself.

**dread** \\'dred\\
A black flying creature in the Fifth Circle created by Jasper Jane. About the size of a canine, dreads are characterized by their screeching cries and clawed wings that they use to cut their prey to pieces.

**Duelum** \\'dool-əm\\
A twice-a-session competition occurring outside of Wormwood proper that pits strong males between the ages of fifteen and twenty-four in matches against one another. Viewed by many Wugs as a rite of passage, Duelums can often be brutal.

**ekos** \\'ē-kōs\\
A small creature in the Quag exceptional for the mats of grass that grow on its arms, neck and face, and sprout from its head. The ekos have small, wrinkled faces and bulging red eyes.

**Empyrean** \\'ɛmp-ir-e-ɛn\\
The ancestral home of Vega Jane. Once the residence of Alice Adronis, it has remained safely under a spell that has rendered the grounds undetectable by Maladons over the years.

**Event** \\i-'vent\\
A mysterious occurrence in Wormwood that has no witnesses. Wugmorts presumed to suffer from an Event disappear entirely, body and clothing, from the village.

**Excalibur** \\ek-'skal-ə-bər\\
A rare type of sorcerer born with extraordinary magical powers already intact and a profound knowledge of Wug history embedded in his or her mind. It may take years for an Excalibur to become aware of his or her innate abilities.

**Finisher** \\'fi-nish-ər\\
A worker tasked with "finishing" all objects created at Stacks. Finishers must show creative ability at Learning, as the requirements for the job range from painting to kiln-firing items intended for the wealthiest Wugs of Wormwood.

**Finn, the** \\'fin\\
A magical element consisting of twine knotted in three places and looped around a tiny wooden peg. The untying of one knot brings a force of wind powerful enough to lift objects off the ground. Untying the second knot produces gale force winds, and undoing the third brings a wind of unimaginable strength with the ability to level everything in its path.

**firebird** \\'fi-yuhr-burd\\
A huge flying creature in the Quag known for its colorful plumage and sharp beak and claws. It's said that the firebird's feathers are so brilliant they can be used to provide light and warmth. A firebird can be a harbinger of tragedy.

**frek** \\'frek\\
A huge, fierce beast of the Quag characterized by an extensive snout and fangs inches longer than a Wug finger. The bite of a frek has been known to drive its victims mad.

**Furina** \\fuhr-'ē-nə\\
A Wug-like race indigenous to the Quag, made nearly extinct because of continuous attacks from beasts. The Furinas are descendants of a group of Wugs and Maladons who became trapped in the Quag while migrating from the great battlefields to the village of Wormwood.

**garm** \\'gärm\\
A large beast of the Quag, thirteen feet in length and nearly one thousand pounds in weight. The garm is a hideous creature, its chest permanently bloodied, its smell odious and its belly full of fire that can cremate its victim from several feet away. Wormwood lore maintains that the garm hunts the souls of the dead or guards the gates of Hel.

**gnome** \\nōm\

A creature of the Quag known for long, sharp claws that allow it to mine through hard rock. The gnomes are characterized by deathly pale and prunish faces and yellowish-black teeth.

**Greater True** \\gretər tru\

The land of the elites. Many of the people living here have slaves to serve them. The Maladons regularly patrol here as well.

**grubb** \\grəb\

A peaceful creature that lives primarily in tunnels beneath the Quag and can eat through rock faster than most any other species. Twice the size of a creta, the grubb is known for its strong, expandable hide; long slithery tongue; enormous jagged teeth; soft, slippery body; and eye color that differentiates males (blue) from females (yellow).

**High Street, the** \\hī 'strēt\

A cobblestone street in Wormwood proper lined with shops that sell things Wugmorts need, such as foodstuffs, clothing and healing herbs.

**hob** \\häb\

A creature in the Quag about half the height of an average Wug, characterized by its thick frame, small but powerful jaw, stout nose, long peaked ears, spindly fingers and large hairy feet. Hobs are typically amicable creatures that speak Wugish and make themselves of assistance in exchange for small gifts.

**hyperbore** \\hī-pər-bȯr\

A blue-skinned flying beast indigenous to the Quag characterized by a lean, muscled torso and lightly feathered head. More closely related to Wugs than any other creature, the hyperbore may serve as an ally or enemy and responds favorably to respect and kindness. Hyperbores set on their prey quickly, beating them to death with their compact wings and ripping them apart with their claws. The hyperbores live in nests high in trees.

**inficio** \in-'fish-ē-ō\
A large fiendish beast indigenous to the Quag that can expel poisonous smoke potent enough to kill any creature that breathes it. The inficio has two massive legs with clawed feet; a long, scaly torso with powerful webbed wings; a serpentlike neck and a small head with venomous eyes and razor-sharp fangs.

**jabbit** \'ja-bit\
A massive serpent with over two hundred and fifty heads growing out of the full length of its body. Although jabbits rarely leave the Quag, little can halt their attack once they are on the blood scent. Jabbits can easily overtake Wugs and have fangs in each head full of enough poison to drop a creta.

**Learning** \'lər-ning\
The institution youngs attend until the age of twelve sessions. It is at Learning that youngs gain skills necessary for work in Wormwood.

**light** \'līt\
The time of sunlight between one night and the next.

**Loons, the** \'loons\
A boardinghouse on the High Street.

**lycan** \'lī-kin\
A beast of the Quag covered in long, straight hair, whose bite turns its victims into its own kind. The tall, powerfully built lycan walks on two legs and wields its sharp fangs and claws to attack its prey.

**Maladon** \mal-ə-dän\
From the Wugish word for "terrible death," an ancient race whose highest calling is to inflict terrible death on others. A sessions-long war between the Maladons and Wugmorts forced the Wugs to found the village of Wormwood, around which they conjured the Quag for protection.

**Maladon Castle** \mal-ə-dän kæ-səl\
The headquarters of the Maladon race. It is here that Necro dwells, and also where the Maladons torture and enslave their enemies.

**maniack** \mā-nē-ak\
An evil spirit that can attach to a body and mind, driving a Wug irreversibly mad with every fear he or she has ever had.

**manticore** \man-tə-kȯr\
A swift, treacherous beast indigenous to the Quag with the head of a lion, the tail of a serpent and the body of a goat. Over twice the height of an average Wug and three times the width, the manticore's most formidable features are its abilities to read minds and breathe fire.

**Mill, the** \mil\
A place of work in Wormwood where flour and other grains are refined.

**morta** \mȯr-tə\
A long- or short-barreled metal projectile weapon.

**Noc** \näk\
The large, round, milky-white object in the heavens that shines at night.

**Ordinaries** \ȯrdənɛriz\
Those who do not possess magical abilities.

**Outlier** \aut-lī-ər\
A threatening two-legged creature that lives in the Quag and can pass as a Wugmort. Outliers are believed to be able to control the minds of Wugs and make them do their bidding.

**Quag, the** \'kwäg\
A forest that encircles Wormwood and is home to all manner of fierce creatures and Outliers. It is widely believed among Wugmorts that nothing exists beyond the Quag.

**remnant** \'rem-nənt\
A collection of memories from an assortment of Wugs; an embodied record of their remembrances.

**Saint Necros** \'sɔɪnt nɛ-kros\
The church in True where the people come to worship. It is named after Necro, the leader of the Maladons, who insists on being worshipped by all.

**Seer-See** \'sē-ir 'sē\
A prophetical instrument used by sorcerers to view other places. The Seer-See consists of sand thrown into a pewter cup of flaming liquid, the contents of which are then poured onto a table to display a moving picture of a distant location.

**session** \'se-shən\
A unit of time equal to three hundred and sixty-five lights.

**slep** \'slep\
A magnificent Wormwood creature characterized by its noble head, long tail, six legs and beautiful coat. It is said that sleps were once able to fly, and that the slight indentations noticeable on their withers now mark the spot from which their wings grew.

**sliver** \\'sli-vər\\
A small unit or brief period of time.


**Stacks** \\'staks\\
A large brick building in Wormwood where items for trade and con-sumption are produced.


**Steeples** \\'stē-pəls\\
A place the majority of Wugmorts go every seventh light to listen to a sermonizer.


*True* \\'tru\\
The first town that Vega and her friends encounter. It is seemingly filled with happy people, but has sinister secrets.


**unicorn** \\'yoo-nə-kȯrn\\
A noble and gentle beast characterized by a brilliantly white coat and mane of gold, with shiny black eyes and a regal horn the color of sil-ver. The soft horn of the unicorn is known to defeat all poisons, but can only be obtained by convincing the unicorn to surrender it freely or by killing the beast outright.


**Valhall** \\'val-hal\\
The prison of Wormwood, set in public in the center of the village.


**Victus** \\'vık-tus\\
The name given by the Maladons to those they enslave.


**wendigo** \\'wen-də-gō\\
A malevolent spirit that can possess whatever it devours. This ghastly, quasi-transparent creature lives throughout the Quag but is predomi-nant in the Mycanmoor. Signs that a wendigo is nearby are a vague

feeling of terror and a sense that the facts stored in your head are being replaced by residual memories of the prey the wendigo has devoured.

**whist** \\'wist\\
A large, domesticated hound of Wormwood known for its impressive speed.

**Wugmort** (*Wug* for short) \\'wəg-mort\\ (\\'wəg\\)
A citizen of Wormwood.

# Acknowledgments

In writing the third installment of the Vega Jane saga, I had a tremendous amount of support that made the story far better. To the folks listed on this page, Vega and I thank you!

To Rachel Griffiths, David Levithan, Mallory Kass, Julie Amitie, Charisse Meloto, Dick Robinson, Ellie Berger, Lori Benton, Dave Ascher, Elizabeth Parisi, Gabe Rumbaut, Evangelos Vasilakis, Rachel Gluckstern, Sue Flynn, Nikki Mutch and the whole sales team at Scholastic, for helping me send Vega and her friends headlong into yet another world.

To Venetia Gosling, Kat McKenna, Catherine Alport, Sarah Clarke, Rachel Vale, Alyx Price, Tracey Ridgewell, Lucy Pearse, Trisha Jackson, Jeremy Trevathan, Katie James, Lee Dibble, Sarah McLean, Charlotte Williams, Stacey Hamilton, Geoff Duffield, Leanne Williams, Stuart Dwyer, Anna Bond, Jonathan Atkins, Sara Lloyd and Alex Saunders at Pan Macmillan, for always being so wonderfully enthusiastic and supportive.

To Steven Maat and the entire Bruna team, for introducing Vega and Company to Holland.

To Aaron Priest, for two decades of great advice and counsel.

To Arleen Priest, Lucy Childs Baker, Lisa Erbach Vance, Frances Jalet-Miller, John Richmond, and Matt Belford for allowing me to focus on the books.

To Kristen White and Michelle Butler, for keeping Columbus Rose and me going strong.

# About the Author

David Baldacci is a global #1 bestselling author. His books are published in over forty-five languages and in more than eighty countries; over 110 million copies are in print. His works have been adapted for both feature film and television. He is also the cofounder, along with his wife, of the Wish You Well Foundation®, which supports literacy efforts across America. David and his family live in Virginia.